IN HIS BED

"Sine," Gamel whispered, "how was I to ken that ye were a virgin?"

She looked at him with faint curiosity. "And would ye have let me be if ye had kenned it?"

"Nay," he answered with quiet honesty as he eased the covers down her body.

"Then what matter? I am still in your bed through a bargain. I abide with you this night." Catriona said this even as she inwardly cursed the heat which flickered to life within her as he lightly trailed his fingers over her breasts.

"Not just this night, Sine Catriona. Ye are mine." Gamel bent his head to softly kiss the erect tip of each breast. "Ye are mine, Sine Catriona. Say it. Admit it," he ordered, framing her face with his hands.

She knew he was right. She was his. She knew that bond would hold no matter who or what came into their lives.

"Aye," she finally said. "Aye, I am yours . . ."

Books by Hannah Howell

Published by Zebra Books

SILVER FLAME

HANNAH HOWELL

ZEBRA BOOKS

Kensington Publishing Corp.

http://www.kensingtonbooks.com

ZEBRA BOOKS are published by

Kensington Publishing Corp.
850 Third Avenue
New York, NY 10022

All Kensington titles, imprints, and distributed lines are available at
special quantity discounts for bulk purchases for sales promotion,
premiums, fund-raising, educational, or institutional use.

Special book excerpts or customized printings can also be created
to fit specific needs. For details, write or phone the office of the
Kensington Special Sales Manager: Attn. Special Sales Department.
Kensington Publishing Corp., 850 Third Avenue, New York, NY
10022. Phone: 1-800-221-2647.

Zebra and the Z logo Reg. U.S. Pat. & TM Off.

ISBN-13: 978-1-4201-0107-2
ISBN-10: 1-4201-0107-2

First Avon Books Printing: September 1992
First Zebra Books Mass-Market Printing: May 2008
10 9 8 7 6 5 4 3 2

Printed in the United States of America

Prologue

Scotland, 1380

Silently, cautiously, Sine Catriona Brodie led her half brothers, Beldane and Barre, toward the beckoning light of a small fire. She knew it was dangerous to approach a stranger's camp, but she and the twins were hungry, cold, and afraid. The wood had been their hiding place for far too long, what sustenance they could find all too sparse for a young lass and growing three-year-olds. Sine Catriona could barely recall the last time they had slept with a fire to warm them, peacefully lost in their dreams. For them every shadow was an enemy.

But they could go no farther now. Driven by desperation, Sine Catriona studied the dark form of the man in front of the fire. His shoulder was to her, so she could see little—except that he was tall. Struggling to be brave, she left her brothers hidden in the shrubbery and stepped forward.

"We approach to request food and a place by your fire, kind sir," she said.

The man turned and stared at her. One of his dark,

long fingered hands rested on the hilt of a dagger but she did not immediately construe that as a threat. Whoever the man was he was handsome, gifted with all that was needed to make a woman swoon. Sine Catriona was young, barely twelve, but she knew that much. So too had she learned how much evil beauty could hide. However, he made no threatening move. Her hunger and that of her brothers persuaded her to take a gamble with him.

"Ye are welcome," he answered in a deep, rich voice. "I have little but I sense that 'tis more than ye have tasted in many a day."

"We are quite hungry, sir." She motioned to her brothers to move closer to the fire.

"Twins?" he asked.

The boys nodded shyly. As they sat and introduced all three of themselves by their first names only, the man handed them some bread and cheese.

"No family name?"

"'Twould be best if our family name wasnae given," Sine Catriona murmured.

"Child, while ye eat allow me to tell ye of myself. I am Farthing Magnus."

"Farthing?" She frowned. "'Tis an odd name, sir."

"My mother told me that a farthing was what it cost a mon to make me. My father was weel born. He tried to do weel by me, his bastard son, and trained me to the life of a warrior. 'Twasnae the life for me, I fear, and his legal family was unsettled by my presence. I thanked my father kindly for his generosity and left. Ye see before ye Farthing Magnus—conjurer and thief."

"A conjurer," she whispered, duly impressed.

"At your command, m'lady. And a thief."

"We are no strangers to that sin ourselves."

"One must needs survive—as long as 'tisnae from one poorer than oneself."

"Aye for ye could leave a mon with naught to eat and that could weel mean that thievery becomes murder."

"How old are ye, child?"

"I am twelve, and the lads are three."

"So verra young to be roaming this wood unprotected. Where are your parents?"

"My beloved father is wrapped in the cold clay, sir. My mother still lives, curse her eyes."

"Child, I believe ye have a tale to tell. 'Tis a long night that looms before us. I am but one mon, and one who swears that he would do ye no harm."

"Nay? Not even for gold in your pocket?"

"I admit freely that I am a thief and that my tongue isnae often burdened by the truth, but I do hold dear to a principle or two. I am *not* a mon to deal in blood money."

He did not flinch from her direct, probing look. A self-professed thief and liar could easily speak falsely with complete calm, yet Sine Catriona found that she trusted him. She also knew that, if he did prove traitorous, she and her brothers could not be caught and held by just one man.

In a quiet voice she told him of her mother, a woman twisted by greed and envy. She told him of the murders of her father and the twins' mother, by hired brigands in the wood and of the poisoning of her grandmother—all at the hand of Arabel Brodie and her lover, Malise Brodie, a kinsman her father had once trusted implicitly. Sine Catriona's father was barely dressed for burial when Arabel and Malise had wed. Sine Catriona spoke of the slow, painful realization that her own mother hated her, resented her youth and beauty, for Arabel's own loveliness was beginning to fade. Sine Catriona told Farthing of how she had taken the twins and fled into the night when she discovered that she and the boys were to be her mother's next victims. With their deaths, all the Brodie lands, fortune, and title would go to Arabel and Malise.

"So ye are left to wander in the woods amongst rogues, vagabonds, and wild beasts," Farthing said.

"Aye. I could think of naught but escape." Sine Catriona looked at the twins. "They are but wee bairns." She smiled at Farthing. "Howbeit, we cannae hide in the woods forever. We search for one who would aid us, one who doesnae cower in his boots and has the armed men we need. There has to be such a knight somewhere and I *will* find him. Howbeit, 'twill mean some wandering. I ken that weel enough."

"Aye, but I would guess that ye ken verra little of the wandering life."

"I will learn."

"That I dinnae doubt at all. 'Twould be best, howsomever, if ye had a teacher, a tutor."

"And would ye be that tutor?"

"There could be none better."

She bit her bottom lip, briefly revealing her fine white teeth. "I cannae wander too far afield for here is all that I must regain when the time is right."

"There is many a place where I might ply my trade along this strip of land separating the Lowlands from the Highlands."

"We are a danger to all who might aid us."

"I may not like the thought of living by my sword, but I weel ken how to wield it."

"The people we flee deal in poisons and daggers thrust from the shadows."

"And who kens the shadows better than a thief? And that is what I shall teach ye."

"Then we should like to wander with ye and, when I

regain all that is mine by birthright, I shall reward ye weel."

"I dinnae do this for reward." Farthing smiled faintly.

"I thought not." Sine Catriona frowned. "But then, what do ye do this for?"

"Mayhaps I am weary of being alone."

"Ye will teach us to conjure?"

"Ye shall be my assistants."

"And ye shall teach us to steal?"

"As none other can, may God forgive me."

"It sounds much better than cowering in the wood awaiting my mother's huntsmen."

He nodded at the twins. "Do ye think that they understand?"

She ruffled each boy's golden brown curls. "They understand what death is, Farthing Magnus."

"That is enough for now."

Chapter 1

Stirlingshire, Scotland, 1386

"I told ye it would be unwise to answer that wench's invitation," Sine Catriona Brodie complained, clinging to her seat as Farthing Magnus raced their cart down the road, away from a keep that held an amorous lady and a hotly jealous husband.

"So ye were in the right of it this time. How did ye ken it?"

"With every smile she sent ye ere ye crept off to her chambers, her husband's countenance grew blacker."

"I must remember to watch the husband as weel as the wife."

"Wisdom that is late in arriving is better than no wisdom at all."

Farthing laughed. "How verra wise."

"So I thought when I heard it. I dinnae believe they follow us."

Easing the furious gait of their horse, Farthing peered behind them. "Nay, it seems not, but we shall travel on. He could yet turn his fury our way. I should like to get to the fair still hale and whole."

"Doesnae it trouble ye that the lady may be beaten?" Sine Catriona straightened her cowl, hastily tucking a few stray silvery curls back beneath its folds.

"She was an adulteress." He grinned when she gave him a look of disgust.

"Did it ne'er occur to ye to save her from her sins by refusing what she offered?" she asked.

"Why should I go hungry when I ken that the meal will just be offered elsewhere?"

"Lecherous dog. Ye didnae even have time to tie all your points. Your chausses sag."

"At least I wasnae sent afleeing with my arse bared to the wind and moon."

"That day may yet arrive. Your ardor may yet send you to hell."

"As ye age, ye grow more pious," Farthing drawled.

"I hope to save your soul."

"My soul is past redemption, Catriona. I will ne'er see heaven, but I am resigned." He gave a heavy sigh.

She made a soft, derisive noise. "If ye are so resigned, why do ye still visit the priests to confess and attempt penance?"

"Drive the cart." He thrust the reins into her small, delicate hands. "I must rest," he murmured, and bent to fix his hose.

After tidying his clothes he slouched in his seat, tugged his hat over his face, and wrapped his cloak about himself. Maintaining the air of one nearly asleep, he eyed Sine Catriona from beneath his lowered hat brim. It was a neverending puzzle to him that he did not lust after her.

In the six years they had traveled together she had grown from a lovely girl to a breathtakingly beautiful young woman, ripe for love and marriage. She had a deep, low voice that brought the glint of desire into a man's eyes. Huge violet eyes dominated her small, oval face, and were encircled by raven lashes so thick and long that many suspected some artifice had been employed on them. Her figure was slender yet had all the curves any man could crave. The crowning glory to her beauty was her hair, its silver-white waves tumbling from her head to her knees. It always seemed a pity to him that she had to keep it hidden, tucked away for fear it would lead her treacherous mother to her. Everything about Sine Catriona was desirable. She exuded an innocent, subtle, and unpracticed sensuality that drew men to her like wasps to hot, sweet cider. Farthing could recognize all of that, yet felt no hint of passion for her.

The only answer to the puzzle was that she had become as close to him as his nearest kin. Despite the fact that he was just ten years her senior, at times he felt as if she was his child. He supposed some of that feeling arose because he had watched her make that almost magical change from child to woman.

Yet again he felt guilty that he had not, could not, help her regain what her murderous kin had stolen from her. He had not even been able to stop Arabel and Malise Brodie from declaring Sine Catriona and the twins dead. They had feigned an elaborate burial and taken hold of all the money, the lands, and the title. What was more, he felt troubled over how he had taught his charges to live—by theft and trickery. Yet, what choice had he? Those were the talents by which he made his own living.

What she needed was a warrior with a force of skilled, armed men at his command. She had said so while still a child and she had been right. She needed a knight who would not cower in his boots before the evil power of the Brodies, one with the coin, power, and force to battle them and win. She especially needed a knight with the wit to believe in the evil of the Brodies and avoid falling victim to their seductive ways. Farthing knew that, for all his cleverness and skill, he was not that man. Nor could he produce such a knight, though they had searched the border region for years, hoping to come upon the right man for the task. He sighed.

"I dinnae think your knight was at the keep we just fled," he said at last.

"Nay. How foolish I was all those years ago."

"Only six," he whispered.

She ignored the soft interruption. "I was foolish to think I but needed to find a strong knight, one who would help us simply because our cause is just. There appear to be few who have what I need."

"Mayhaps there are simply too many just causes and ye must wait your turn. Dinnae give up yet."

"Nay, I will continue to search. Howbeit, at times I begin to think I shall be old and bent ere I find him. Ah, but by then the twins will have become men and can fight to gain what is rightfully theirs."

"Aye, the three of us could easily carve up your enemy."

She laughed softly, then after a long silence asked, "Am I to drive all night with no one to talk to?"

"Ye talk and I shall grunt at all the appropriate moments."

"'Tis plain ye spent all your charm upon that wench we just fled, Farthing Magnus."

"I still possess charm aplenty. I merely need to rest. My charm isnae at its most glorious when I am weary."

"Farthing?" She looked his way but saw little, her dark companion well bundled up in his equally dark clothes. "Is it fun?"

"Is what fun?"

"Swiving."

"And where did ye come by that word, my sweet Catriona?"

"From you, my lusty conjurer."

"Ah, I must be more careful in my speech."

"Weel? Is it fun?"

"Aye, 'tis fun or I wouldnae risk so much to indulge myself. I ken nothing of how it fares for women, but to a mon, even the most fleeting and the lightest can be fun. I speak now of only the idle tussle, not the mating of true lovers."

"Love makes it better, does it?"

"Glorious, child. 'Tis love and passion beautifully entwined. 'Tis ferocity yet tenderness. 'Tis all emotion thrown together in the headiest of mixtures. 'Tisnae just what lurks between the legs that is involved, but the heart, the soul, and even the mind. There is naught to compare. 'Tis glory, 'tis paradise, 'tis the Land of Cockaigne, the sweet paradise upon earth."

"That is what I shall have," she vowed as she stared down the night-shadowed road.

"Aye," he agreed in a soft voice, "I do believe ye will. One such as ye can have no *less*."

Gamel Logan sat eating in the great hall of Duncoille keep, trying to avoid his stepmother's eyes. But she was too keen.

"Where are ye hieing to?" she asked him.

"A fair in Dunkennley but a day or so ride from here." Gamel kissed her smooth cheek.

"A fair? To wenching, ye mean," Edina muttered, and began to break her fast. She was a tiny, voluptuous woman beloved by everyone in the Logan clan.

Gamel just smiled. As he ate and conversed with his father and half brothers, he waited for his stepmother to

say what was on her mind. Since his burly father was unusually quiet, he suspected that what troubled Edina had
already been thoroughly discussed with her husband.
When Gamel finished his meal, he sensed Edina was
ready to speak. He wondered idly if she had thought to
save his digestion.

"Ye are eight and twenty now, Gamel." Edina frowned,
then nervously worried her full bottom lip with her
teeth. "Ye are a belted knight kenned far and wide for
possessing a handsome purse. Hasnae it come time for
ye to seek a bride?"

"I have been looking for years."

Before Edina could respond, the children's nurse bus-
tled into the great hall, explaining that the youngest
Logan had taken a tumble and Edina's presence was
needed. Gamel grinned as Edina grumbled with exasperation and left. He looked to his father to finish what
Edina had been struggling to tell him.

"Have ye sought out another possible bride then,
Father?" he asked.

William Logan grimaced slightly. "Aye. No promises
were made, just a meeting arranged. In a week's time
young Margot Delacrosse will arrive with her kin. They
will stay a while." He shrugged his massive shoulders.
"What will be, will be. Dinnae ye want a wife and children? But tell us so and we will leave ye be."

"I want a wife and a brood of children. I want what ye
have, Father," Gamel added in a quiet voice.

"I have been most fortunate."

Gamel ran a hand through his auburn hair. "'Tis hard
to put into words all that I seek in a woman. I want one
who can both enflame and comfort, one I can speak with
about anything—even of my fears. I can only keep saying
that I seek what ye have found."

Gamel shook his head before continuing. "Therein lies

my difficulty. I suspected that what ye and Edina share is rare, but I didnae ken just how rare. Search though I do, it continues to elude me."

"Mayhaps ye look too hard, son."

"Only God can say. Mayhaps I will settle for less one day." He stood up and smiled at his father. "For now I shall content myself with the pleasures of the flesh. A fair promises many a bonny, willing lass."

"Aye, and ye were blessed with your mother's fairness of face and her fine green eyes, so lasses will flock to ye. Go on, but be sure to return in time to meet the lass who journeys to visit with us."

"I will. No search is done until all stones are turned." He winked at his father. "I but pray the lass ye invited doesnae look as if she crawled out from beneath one."

Shaking his head, William chuckled. "I think not. Who goes to the fair with ye?"

"Sir Lesley."

"Ah, aye—your friend Lesley."

"Do ye tire of his company?"

"Nay. I like the lad. 'Tis just that he has been here for months. Should he not spend some time at his own family's keep?"

"He will, but not for a wee while yet. Lesley and his father havenae healed the breach between them."

"It will ne'er be healed if Lesley continues to hide here."

"I ken it and so does Lesley. He but needs time to prepare himself."

"I can understand that. Who else travels with ye?"

"My squire, Blane."

"No more?"

"I go to a fair, not a battle."

"Be careful nonetheless."

"May I go too, Father?" asked Ligulf, William's slim, fourteen-year-old son.

Raising his gaze to the ceiling, William sighed. "Go, and quickly, ere your mother changes my mind."

Laughing, Ligulf hurried away with Gamel, who wasted no time in preparing to leave. He knew his father suspected Edina might complain, although she would never try to stop Ligulf. Even she admitted to showing a perilous leniency with her children. His haste was in vain, however, for she stepped out of the keep just as they were about to ride out of the bailey. Gamel hid his grin as she handed them a small pack of what she considered to be necessities for any journey.

Edina looked at the slender Ligulf. "So, ye have decided to travel to the fair with Gamel."

"Aye, Mama. 'Twill be my first time."

"I ken it," she drawled as she turned and started back to where William stood. "Just be verra certain that she is clean and healthy."

"Mama!"

Gamel joined his companions in laughing heartily as they rode out of the bailey. Ligulf blushed furiously, color flooding his fair skin. The youth's blushes were only beginning to fade by the time Duncoille was out of sight.

"How did she ken it?" Ligulf asked Gamel, and combed his fingers through his dark blond hair.

"She has been through this before, this change from lad to mon. There was me, then two of our brothers."

"Aye." Ligulf finally laughed. "She is too clever by half."

When they reached the small glen where Gamel had chosen to camp for the night, there was little daylight left. The journey had been pleasant and uneventful, but the crude drover's trail they had used had left them all weary. Gamel was the first to crest the small wooded rise and see that their campsite had already been taken. He paused, his companions doing likewise, and tried to decide what step to take next. They were still fifteen miles or more from Dunkennley and he had no wish to cover the rest of the rough trail in the dark.

His gaze became fixed upon the maid below who was preparing a meal while two young boys wrestled playfully nearby. There was a sensual grace to her every movement, despite the mundane nature of her work. He had the strongest urge to hurry closer to see her face.

He was just about to give in to that urge when she and the boys were joined by a man on horseback. His mount careened into the small campsite and reared, tumbling him to the ground. Thinking only to help, Gamel started down the small rise. His companions hesitated only briefly before following him.

"Farthing!" cried Sine Catriona as she rushed to his side.

She was only faintly aware of the four armed men who galloped into camp and dismounted. Gripped by fear, she focused all of her attention on Farthing. She knelt and frantically searched for a wound or break upon his tall, lean frame. None of the uninvited company drew his sword or spoke a threat so she continued to ignore them.

"Farthing, speak to me," she demanded, her voice tense with concern. "I can find no injury. Can ye not answer me?"

Farthing hiccoughed.

Sine Catriona gaped at the prone man, then started to giggle. She was not sure whether it was from relief or a sense of the absurd. As the smirk on Farthing's flushed

face grew wider, her laughter increased. She fleetingly
noted that her laughter was echoed by the strangers who
had so recently joined them.

"Ye wretch!" she scolded. "Ye vile fool! I thought ye
were dead or broken asunder."

"Nay." Farthing struggled to sit up, hindered slightly
by his tangled black cloak. "I have been celebrating."

"S'truth? 'Tis a fact I ne'er would have guessed for
myself," she said with her hands on her hips.

Struggling to fix his obsidian gaze on the four men
behind her, he asked, "Who be they?"

"'Tis a fine time to be asking." She picked up his black
hat and handed it to one of the twins, Barre, to put away.
"I dinnae ken. If they were a danger to us, 'tis quite dead
we would be by now." She turned to look at the four
men. "If ye meant to offer help ye can see that your kindness was wasted." She frowned briefly at Farthing. "Howbeit, he may soon be in dire need of aid, for I begin to
think that doing him an injury would weel please me."

Gamel felt a constriction in his chest as he gazed into
her lovely, wide blue eyes. "We meant to offer a hand,"
he said, struggling to speak. "We had also planned to
camp here for the night."

"There is plenty of room."

"Thank ye, mistress. Allow me to present myself and
my companions. I am Sir Gamel and these are my
brother, Ligulf, my squire, Blane, and my good friend,
Sir Lesley."

Nodding her head, she replied, "Catriona, Beldane,
Barre, and Farthing Magnus. Ye are welcome to share
this place with us. There is food to spare. See to your
mounts while I see to this fool." She began to help Farthing to stand up.

By the time they were all settled around the fire Gamel
felt more composed. He could not, however, stop watching

her. She had the most beautiful blue eyes he had ever seen. Her voice sent his thoughts winging straight to the bed-chamber. The way she moved made his loins ache. He wanted her, faster and with more ferocity than he had ever wanted a woman before. He could not cease wondering if she was the one he had searched for so long and hard.

Then his heart clenched in his chest. She was already claimed by the man, Farthing, whose name she had so calmly linked with her own. She and her man had offered the hospitality of their fire and food. To make any attempt to satisfy his want would be an insult he could not inflict even if it took every ounce of willpower he could muster not to. He sat wondering what color her hair was, wishing she would shed that all-encompassing headdress.

Only once did he look at Farthing Magnus. That man sat struggling to regain some sobriety, yet watching him closely. The look in Farthing's black eyes told Gamel the man could read his desire and saw it as a threat.

Carefully pronouncing each word, Farthing told Sine Catriona, "I was celebrating."

"So ye have told us. Celebrating what?"

"A number of things. 'Tis hard to recall now."

She laughed softly. "Ye ken that ye have no head for drink."

"S'truth." Farthing ran a hand through his thick raven-black hair. "Howbeit, I couldnae let those dogs know it."

"Oh, aye, of course not. And of course they didnae see how cup-shotten ye were."

"I think they may have guessed." His fine mouth curving downward as he frowned, he added, "Could be why they offered to bind me atop my horse so I wouldnae tumble off."

As soon as everyone stopped laughing, Ligulf asked, "Do ye travel to the fair?"

"Aye," replied Sine Catriona. "This mon swaying before ye is Farthing Magnus, master conjurer. Howbeit, he will be unable to perform any of his craft tonight. 'Tis doubtful he could even relieve himself without fumbling," she muttered.

"That I can do, impertinent wench, and will do immediately—if the lads will but lead me to the bushes."

As Dane and Ree helped Farthing to his feet, Ree grumbled, "'Tis verra likely we shall have to fix his aim as weel."

Sine Catriona could not help but join in the laughter. But hers was short-lived, choked off when her eyes met Gamel's. She fought to break free of the man's gaze. There was such desire in his rich green eyes that it frightened her, especially when she felt something within her respond strongly and swiftly to it. She was intensely aware of every tall, lean inch of him. The moment Farthing returned to sprawl at her side, she huddled closer to him. She watched Sir Gamel's fine long-fingered hands clench tightly when Farthing threw his arm about her shoulders.

"Ye have two fine sons, sir," Gamel remarked.

"Ah." Farthing smiled at the twins. "Not my lads, although I often think of them as so. They are Catriona's half brothers."

"We are bastards, sir," Dane piped up. "So is Farthing."

Giving a small bow of his head, Gamel drawled, "There are many of us about."

Sine Catriona inwardly sighed, her heart sinking as disappointment set in. She had briefly wondered if he could be the knight she had been searching for. He looked strong, capable. However, as a bastard, he would not command a troop of men no matter what his position in his father's household, not if there were other legitimate sons. Bastards did not often have the strength or the power she needed so badly. If they had, Farthing could have helped her long ago, for his natural father was a wealthy and powerful laird.

A small part of her was glad of Gamel's lack of suitability. She feared what might flare between them if they were together for very long. Passion was a complication she simply could not afford.

"Your name is an odd one," Gamel said, looking inquisitively at Farthing.

"'Twas my mother's choice. She said it was what it cost my father to make me." Farthing smiled faintly at the shock the men could not fully conceal. "The sting of that eased many years ago." He yawned, then said, "To bed, my sweet Catriona. Ye as weel, lads. To your blankets," he ordered the twins, then looked at Gamel. "Ye, kind sirs, are most welcome to sit by the fire as long as ye wish. Ye willnae disturb us."

"Nay," Gamel replied. "We will bed down now as weel. We must rise at dawn. If we start out too late we will be forced to spend yet another night in the wood. I hope ye sleep with your sword at your side."

"Aye, I do," Farthing said. "These woods are rife with thieves who would cut your throat just to ease their theft of your purse."

It was not easy but Sine Catriona hid a smile. For a thief like Farthing to speak so disparagingly of thieves was a little amusing. However, she knew that Farthing's words were heartfelt. He had only scorn for those who could not or would not lighten a purse without hurting the owner. Farthing considered them the worst of all thieves.

She spread their blankets out close to the fire. One

brief, sharp glance from Farthing had told her that
tonight they would share a blanket. Farthing had obviously seen the look in Sir Gamel's eyes. Now he would let
the man know that she was not free for the taking. It was
the simplest of all their ploys. However, she had never
found so great a need to use it before.

That fire in the man's eyes called out to her. It was not
simply lust. Sir Gamel looked as if he thought she was
his, as if he thought she would and should understand.
What troubled her was that a large part of her saw nothing strange in that.

Keeping her back to the men, she took off her headdress, freeing her hair so that she could brush it out.
Sleeping in the coverchief would cause more suspicion
than the unusual color of her hair. Carefully she slipped
out of the short-sleeved brown dress she wore over her
linen chemise, then quickly got beneath the blanket. A
moment later Farthing, wearing only his hose and shirt,
crawled in beside her. She closed her eyes, struggling to
feel safe and calm as he tucked her up against him
spoon style.

"'Tis a bad night for me to be cup-shotten, though it
does begin to fade," he whispered.

"'Tis rare that ye overimbibe. Ye need no heady wines
to help ye enjoy life. Besides, how could ye ken that we
would have visitors?"

"And such visitors. The mon stares our way as if I am the
trespasser. 'Tis an odd look, more than lust, I see that
clearly enough. Dearling, dinnae flinch or act startled. I
am going to place my hand upon your breast."

"Why?" she asked even as she watched his rather beautiful dark hand cup her breast.

"'Tis a sign all men can read."

Daring a peek at Sir Gamel, she gasped softly. The
glance he sent their way was deadly. She had seen that

look before—in the eyes of jealous husbands. Turning sharply into Farthing's arms, she put her back toward the disturbing man. She wondered fleetingly if they had allowed a madman into their midst only to discover that she did not like the idea that those searing gazes might arise from lunacy.

"I swear, Farthing, he looks ready to run ye through."

"Aye, he does. Dinnae worry. He is far too polite to do so."

"This is a poor time for jests."

"Mayhaps. Settle here." He arranged her comfortably against his chest. "I am going to rest my hand upon your sweet tail now."

"Another sign?"

"Aye."

"Is it wise to goad him so?"

"He must be shown that there is naught for him here."

"S'truth, I dinnae understand this."

"I ken it, dearling. Go to sleep."

"Do ye have your sword at the ready?"

"Why, Catriona, I didnae realize ye felt that way about me."

She pinched him hard enough to make him grunt. "I speak of the one ye stick in men, knave."

"Ah, that sword. Aye, 'tis in reach. Sleep, lovely. Just pretend those green eyes of his arenae boring into your back."

"'Tis far easier said than done. I shall be checking closely for holes there in the morning," she muttered, but tried to relax, to welcome sleep's hold.

Gamel had been unable to tear his gaze from Catriona since the moment she had unbound her hair. He ached to wrap himself in the thick silvery waves that hung nearly to her knees. His need was so strong, so fierce, that he shook with it. All he could think of was that some madness had seized him.

When Farthing's dark hand had covered her high, full, linen-shrouded breast, Gamel had reached for his sword. The sight had seared his brain, twisted his innards, until he was near to bellowing like some enraged bull. When she had turned in Farthing's embrace it had helped little, then he had been forced to watch the man's hand tangle in her lush hair while his other hand slid down to cup her lovely derriere beneath the blanket. Their soft whispers threatened to drive him mad with envy. Gritting his teeth, he finally forced himself to turn his back on them only to meet Ligulf's concerned gaze.

"What troubles ye, Gamel?"

His soft laugh was shaky. "Simply that I burn to run a sword through that mon, a mon who does no more than bed down with his woman."

"She is fair," Ligulf murmured, frowning in obvious confusion.

"Aye, she is. Go to sleep. There is no understanding this lunacy." Gamel closed his eyes and fought to grasp the soothing oblivion of sleep.

Sine Catriona was confused when she suddenly found herself awake. It was not yet dawn and all appeared quiet. Without moving from Farthing's light hold, she looked around her. Her eyes widened when she caught sight of a stealthy movement in the shadows at the edge of camp. Struggling to maintain the air of one still asleep, she worked to covertly wake Farthing. With every muscle tensed, she found it difficult to feign the languid motions of one asleep.

"Thieves creep our way, Farthing," she whispered.

"Curse it. I had prayed for a quiet night," he muttered as he slid his hand toward his sword. "Turn on your side. When I give the cry, rush to the twins and have your dagger at the ready."

Still struggling to act like one asleep but restless, she turned again. Seeing the shadows edging toward them, she decided they must have bedded down in a large nest of cutthroats. The treacherous vagabonds had been unable to resist temptation.

Even though they were creeping up on a sleeping camp, the presence of five men should have deterred them. The thieves were either desperate or numerous enough to feel secure even if a battle developed. Neither circumstance boded well for her or her companions.

Unable to resist, she stared across the waning fire at Sir Gamel, only to find him staring at her. She carefully mouthed *Thieves*, praying that the ones creeping toward the camp did not see her. To her intense relief she did not have to repeat the risky gesture. Sir Gamel's subtle movements told her he had understood. Now there would be at least one other full grown man armed and ready.

"Now!" Farthing called, and she bolted.

She was nearly at the twins' sides as Farthing and Gamel leapt to their feet, their swords readied to greet the rush of the cutthroats. Their cries and those of their foes quickly roused the others. Sine Catriona was amazed at how speedily Sir Gamel's companions came alert and joined the battle.

"Up that tree," she ordered the two drowsy boys.

"But . . ." Dane began to protest while he helped Ree onto the lowest branch.

"Nay. Up the tree. Quickly."

The moment the twins were safely out of reach she took up a defensive stance at the base of the trunk, un-

sheathing her dagger and holding it at the ready. It was
not the best of weapons, but it would cause any attacker
to hesitate. She fought to keep herself alert for any
threat to herself or the twins, struggled against becoming too fascinated by the battle raging around her.

It was a fierce fight. The thieves had the advantage of
larger numbers, but she found some ease for her fears
in the display of skill shown by her allies. It far surpassed
that of the outlaws. Within moments she detected a def-
inite waning of enthusiasm amongst the band of rogues
as their ranks were ruthlessly culled.

Suddenly there loomed before her the biggest, hairi-
est man she had ever seen. He was so ugly, so filthy, that
he did not need the sword he held to look fearsome, nor
the leer that revealed his rotting teeth. Against such a
man her dagger was only a toy. Nevertheless, she held
her ground, wielding her weapon with every intention
of using it if she was forced to do so. She knew from the
look on his repulsive face that killing her was not, at the
moment, foremost in his mind.

He drew nearer, backing her up against the tree
trunk. Just as she tensed to make a desperate strike, the
twins dropped from the tree and landed on the man.
She watched in horror as, with a deafening bellow, he
flung the two small boys aside. They sprawled upon the
ground and did not rise in the brief moment she could
spare to look their way.

"Mine," he said as he reached for her.

Sine Catriona barely eluded his large grasp with a
move that held as much luck as skill. "Nay, swine. Never
yours."

"Aye, wench—mine."

Unnerved by the stalking giant, Sine Catriona threw
her dagger. Her usually excellent aim was off due to her
increasing fear. Instead of burying itself deep in his heart

as she had intended it to do, the dagger landed in the fleshy part of one massive upper arm. He gave out a thundering cry and lunged for her. She suspected her scream was just as loud when he grabbed her and tucked her beneath one thick arm.

The robbers had begun to retreat, leaving Gamel a moment in which to catch his breath. He immediately looked to see where Catriona had gone. Upon espying her difficulty, he raced toward her with little thought for strategy or his own safety.

"Put her down," Gamel demanded the moment he confronted the huge outlaw.

"She is my prize."

"Your friends have deserted you. Do ye mean to fight your way free—alone?"

The outlaw put his sword against the back of Sine Catriona's neck. "Cut me and she dies," he snapped.

Gamel froze, then covertly glanced toward his other men. Although they were now able to turn their attention to helping Catriona, they halted their advance. For an agonizingly long moment no one moved. Gamel was certain his heart and breath had both ceased. Even the twins, rousing from unconsciousness, lay still and wide-eyed. Gamel tried desperately to come up with some solution, but none was forthcoming.

Sine Catriona ceased her frantic struggles the instant the cold steel of the sword touched her vulnerable nape. On the morrow she would be eighteen. Even what the rank giant intended for her once he got her alone suddenly did not seem as horrible as death. Rape was vicious and degrading. She knew she would carry the scars all her life, but she *would* be alive. One misstep now and she lost all chance for a future. As she hung in his grasp like an empty sack, she fought to think of a way to save herself.

Finally, in sheer desperation, she balled one hand into a small fist and struck the outlaw in the groin with all her strength. The outlaw howled, dropped her, and clutched his abused privates, but he had no time to pamper his injury. Farthing launched an immediate and lethal attack which the rogue struggled to fend off. Sine Catriona cried out softly in surprise when Gamel scooped her up with one arm, yanking her out of danger.

"He is good," Gamel murmured, watching Farthing fight and holding Catriona close to his side. "He has been weel trained."

"Aye, by his natural father. Shouldnae ye aid him?" she asked.

Sir Lesley stepped up to them and shook his head. "To dart in now would do more ill than good, mistress. Too distracting." He nodded toward the pair so tightly locked in battle. "Blane and Ligulf flank the brute. They will move quickly if the battle veers the piker's way. 'Twill not, though. The outlaw has more strength than your mon but far less skill, and 'tis skill that will win out."

When Sine Catriona tried to move from Gamel's side his hold on her tightened, subtly but firmly, and she relented. Nevertheless, it set both her mind and insides awhirl to be held so near to his tall, lean body. She barely reached the pit of his arm. Her cheek was pressed against his smooth, hard chest, which had been left exposed by his unlaced shirt. A fine tremor began to ripple through her. She knew it was not in response to her near escape or the violence of the night. Such trauma was, sadly, no stranger to her. Her trembling was caused by the man who held her as if she belonged to him. More alarming was that she felt as if she did.

At last Farthing dealt the death stroke to his opponent.

The rogue's scream cut through the air. She turned her face into Gamel's smooth, tanned chest and felt him burrow his long fingers into her hair. It felt to her as if here was the haven she had sought for so long, in Gamel's arms. But the idea terrified her. She could not accept it. She could not do as other maids did and settle down with a man.

Farthing moved toward the pair, touching Sine's shoulder when he reached her side. "Are ye hurt, dearling?"

"Nay." The danger she had faced combined with her own overwrought emotions suddenly proved too much for her. "I am going to be ill." She broke free of Gamel's hold and raced toward the edge of camp.

"I will see to her," Gamel said, halting Farthing's move to follow. "Your boys need aid." He strode away before Farthing could protest.

As she struggled to get to her feet, Sine Catriona felt a slim, strong arm encircle her shoulders and a damp cloth gently move over her face. She was lifted into Gamel's arms, set a few feet away, then handed some wine with which to rinse her mouth. It was nice to be cared for, but embarrassing to be seen in this condition by the far-too-disturbing Sir Gamel. She was not sure why she should care, but she wished him to see her as a strong woman.

It was on the tip of her tongue to order him far away from her. However, she knew she would never speak the words. Disturbing though he was, she did not really want him to leave.

He was undeniably fascinating, with his light auburn hair, smooth, softly bronzed skin any woman would envy, and rich jewel-green eyes. His fine features seemed to have been molded by some skilled artisan, and he had somehow escaped the all-too-common scarring and broken facial bones of a warrior.

But it was the heat that glowed in his fine eyes that drew her most powerfully. That look stirred hitherto unknown emotions within her, igniting a responsive heat she was unable to control or, she feared, hide. She dared not think of what he would do if he could sense the feelings that raged within her.

Gamel made no attempt to disguise the desire that gripped him as he studied her. He suddenly knew for certain that this was how his father felt when he looked at Edina: stunned, almost fearful, yet filled with a near-violent need to possess her. A need coupled with a lurking eagerness to kill anyone who thwarted it. He was not surprised to see the unsteadiness of his hand as he reached out to brush the tangled hair from her small oval face. His entire body was trembling.

The disorder of her chemise left the upper swells of her full breasts exposed. One delicately slim shoulder was bared to view also. He could see that the light golden tone of her skin was not from the kiss of the sun, but wholly natural. He was unable to resist touching her, trailing his fingers over her skin. Gamel knew that the shadows and his own body blocked all signs of his impertinence from the others.

"Cease," she whispered in a raspy voice as he dipped his fingers beneath the edge of her chemise, yet she did not move away.

"All gold," he murmured. "Gold and silver. I ache for you."

"Dinnae say such things."

"I but speak the truth."

"Some truths should remain silent ones."

"What I feel must be spoken of."

"Ye must take your passions elsewhere. I am not free."

"One day ye shall be, or I will see that ye are, if but for one night only."

"If ye hurt Farthing, I will come to your bed only to cut your throat," she snapped, retreating from his touch and standing up, straightening her chemise as she did so. "Aye, cut it from ear to ear, my flame-haired lecher."

"I willnae kill the mon to possess you. Then I would be as low as the dogs we have just routed. Nay, I willnae shame myself or my family by stooping so low. But I *will* have ye. Come the chance to hold ye, even for but an hour, and I will seize it," he vowed as he stood up. "A fire such as this cannae be put out simply because another holds ye now. Ye ken what I speak of. The flame licks at your insides as weel."

"Nay," she cried, her voice holding more desperation than conviction, and she fled to Farthing's side.

As Gamel rejoined his brother, Ligulf whispered, "She belongs to Farthing Magnus."

"I ken it," muttered Gamel.

"Then ye must put her from your mind. I like the mon."

"So do I. Yet so do I hate him for his rightful claim to her. 'Tis a madness that has seized me. But fear not, I shallnae kill the mon over her. Nay, I willnae go that far. I fear, though, that murder is all I will halt at, that there is nothing else, however low or dishonorable, I willnae do to have her."

Chapter 2

"Farthing, ye rogue, it has been too long. I hoped this fair would draw ye back to Dunkennley."

"Business has been slow, has it?" Farthing laughed as he and the innkeeper, Ennis MacAdam, clapped each other on the back. "Do ye have rooms to spare for us?"

"Only one room. 'Tis for the best. With a fair comes many a lairdling, eager as any buck in season. Ye had best keep a close eye upon this wee, sweet lassie." MacAdam grinned at Sine Catriona. "The highborn think any lass who isnae chained down is theirs for the taking or buying."

"One room will be fine," answered Farthing.

"A fair such as this brings many a purse begging to be emptied," MacAdam commented.

"That is true enough," Farthing said, and winked.

Sine Catriona smiled, then shook her head as both men laughed heartily. MacAdam knew Farthing did not restrict himself to conjuring alone. He said nothing, however, for Farthing knew the way to avoid any outcry and left a share of the profits for the innkeeper. It was an amicable, often very profitable, arrangement.

"Lad," Ennis MacAdam called to the stable boy. "Come

and see to this horse." Putting an arm about Farthing's shoulders and urging the group inside, MacAdam continued. "Tell me how ye have fared this past sixmonth."

Since it was already late and she knew the morrow would be busy, Sine Catriona joined her brothers, who quickly sought their beds. She stirred only once when, much later in the night, Farthing slipped into their room. Although the smell of drink was faintly perceptible, she knew he was not drunk. She turned in the bed to look at him when he settled down on his pallet.

"He is here," Farthing murmured.

She knew immediately that he meant Sir Gamel. "Ye have seen him?"

"Aye, but he didnae espy me."

"Are ye certain of that?"

"Dearling, I can melt into the shadows, can I not? That is a skill of mine I thought ye had trust in."

"I do. Forgive me. Do he and his companions stay here at MacAdam's inn?"

"Aye, just down the hall. They hold the best rooms."

"Of course. Ah weel, there are wenches aplenty to catch his eye." She discovered that she loathed the idea of Sir Gamel enjoying another woman. "Master MacAdam's are said to be the best."

"'Tis true. Mayhaps he will take one on the morrow."

Both delighted and frightened by the news that Sir Gamel had bedded down alone, she nevertheless ventured, "A long ride can leave a mon verra weary, too weary for such idle pleasures."

"S'truth. It can. Go to sleep, loving. On the morrow ye must stay near my side."

"If ye believe it best."

"I do."

"All right. Good sleep, Farthing."

She turned away even as he mumbled a good-night.

That morning they had fled the camp before dawn, silently and swiftly. Despite their precautions, she was not surprised to learn that Gamel was near. She had known in her heart that he would follow. So too, she little doubted that he would find her at the fair no matter how well she lost herself in the milling, boisterous crowd. Closing her eyes, she prayed that Fate would keep them apart. Now was not the time for love or passion. Sine Catriona had a more important goal in mind.

The day was still new when Sine Catriona ventured into the already lively streets of town, her companions close at her side. Booths and carts pressed all around them. Jongleurs, jugglers, and acrobats wandered through the swiftly growing crowd. The air was filled with the cries of vendors selling their wares. She could hear the French and fine Scots tongue of the wellborn, the speech of the peasant, and even the tongue-knotting Gaelic of the Highlanders. The only part of the fair she avoided was where the bear- and badger-baiting was held. It was an entertainment that only made her ill. For a while she simply wandered with the others, surveying the wares offered for sale.

There were rugs, pottery, gourds, spoons, jewelry, prayer beads, pamphlets, and cloth. The variety of cloth left her breathless. The stalls held everything from the finest silks to the coarsest linen, and in every possible color. She wished she had the coin to buy herself just enough for one new dress.

The hawkers let no one pass unheralded. Everything from beautifully wrought bestiary books, with their real or fabled animals and moral allegories, to the simplest, roughest of blankets was called to the attention of all those who walked by. Knowing how hard the sellers' lot was, she sorely regretted not having the funds to buy something from each, at least one tiny thing.

"Catriona," Farthing said, drawing her attention his way, "I wish to attend the bear-baiting."

"So hie to it, Farthing. Why ask me? I have never told ye nay before."

"Weel, ye have expressed a distaste for them."

"Aye, but I still dinnae stop ye from attending."

"I dinnae wish to leave ye alone," he muttered.

"Oh." She glanced around but could see no sign of Sir Gamel or his companions. "I had forgotten about that problem. Weel, we have seen neither him nor his friends and I have the lads with me. If there is trouble, they can cause a row and run to fetch ye."

"That may be too late. One should watch to avoid trouble, not wait to call out when it has already arrived."

"The twins can run verra fast indeed. There is a large crowd here as weel. Just set us over there with a baked meat and some ale-bree," she said with an impish smile. "That should keep us content enough to wait for your return."

"A bribe," he grumbled even as he escorted them to a relatively clear area.

"Nonsense. Bribery would be if we asked for a sugar candy as well."

He was still chuckling when he left them after buying them each a meat pie, some of the hot ale flavored with spices, sugar, and toast, and a sugar candy too. Near the bench she and her half brothers occupied was a vendor of panaceas and indulgences. The vendor loudly claimed he had the cure for all that ailed the body and the spirit. With him was a puppeteer to draw the crowd. Sine Catriona enjoyed the puppeteer's antics as much as her young brothers did. She was soon engrossed in the show.

* * *

Gamel stopped so abruptly that Ligulf walked into him. He paid little heed to the younger man's angry query. His gaze, as well as most of his attention, was fixed upon Catriona. Suddenly the bear-baiting and the wagers to be won and lost were of no interest to him.

Ligulf groaned softly. "So ye have found her."

"Aye. Alone as weel."

"She has the lads with her."

"They shall prove no problem."

"Farthing must be near at hand."

"Not near enough."

"Can ye think of nothing to cure him of this madness?" Ligulf asked the husky Sir Lesley.

"Nay, not this sort," replied Sir Lesley as he rubbed a hand through his thick brown hair. "It seizes a mon by that which far too often leads him into folly—his loins. Come, or we willnae have time to lay our wagers."

"Place one for me, Lesley," Gamel ordered in an absent tone even as he started toward Catriona.

He could hear his brother still muttering as he deserted his companions. There was nothing he could say to ease Ligulf's concerns. The younger man was right to have them. Gamel heartily wished his own were stronger, at least strong enough to stop him from charging in where he did not belong.

But ye do belong, an inner voice whispered, and he grimaced. That was what drove him—a deep sense of rightness, the conviction that Catriona Magnus should and would belong to him. There had to be a way. He did not want to believe he had found all he had searched so hard for only to lose it. That was unacceptable.

* * *

"That mon comes our way," hissed Dane, putting a swift end to Sine Catriona's laughter. "Shall we fetch Farthing?"

"Nay," she murmured.

"But that is what he told us to do."

"Do it only if I fail to divert trouble. Leave Farthing to his sport for now."

She watched Gamel pause in his determined advance to buy three ticklers from a passing vendor. With a courtly bow, Gamel presented the sticks with the gaily colored ribbons tied on one end to her and her brothers. It was impossible not to smile at such a frivolous gift. However, she frowned when, uninvited, he sat next to her on the rough-hewn bench beneath the tree. The man was too impertinent for words.

"Thank ye, kind sir." She scowled when she realized there was no room for her to sidle away from him since her brothers were taking up the remainder of the bench.

"Ye dinnae look verra pleased with my wee gift."

"I am puzzled by the absence of your friends. Surely they were to join ye at this fair?"

"They have gone to the bear-baiting."

"And ye have no liking for the sport?"

"I spotted something I had far more liking for. Where is Master Magnus?"

"He is also at the bear-baiting. They will no doubt espy each other."

Gamel smiled slightly. "And then he will hie to your side, for he will ken where I have gone."

"Aye, he will." That knowledge eased her increasing nervousness only a little.

"Then I must hasten to make the best use of my fleeting time with ye."

"Nay, ye waste your time, sir. There is naught here for ye."

"There is heaven," he whispered, tracing the line of her cheek with his fingers.

"Mayhaps death," she said.

Her gaze shifted to her brothers, but they were paying her no heed. The lack of any immediate threat had caused their attention to quickly wander. They were now chasing each other about with the ticklers. She edged away from Gamel, making swift use of the new space upon the bench.

"Sir," she cried as he followed her retreat and suddenly caught her to him, curling one strong arm about her waist.

"Ye were about to go off the end, dearling." He held her close enough to feel the rapid rise and fall of her breasts against his chest.

She glanced around to ascertain that he spoke the truth, then mumbled, "I see that now so ye may release me."

"Nay, I think not."

"What do ye want from me?" she asked, her voice nearly a moan. "I am no gay lass whose favors may be gained by pretty words or a shiny coin. I cannae be won for I have already been claimed."

"A prize I mean to snatch from the one who holds it now."

"If that could be done 'tis a thing that requires more time than ye have. We stay here only briefly, as do ye, then we will travel far away. I can think of no way that is honorable for ye to achieve what ye seek."

"Then I will use a way that is dishonorable. All I willnae do is kill Farthing Magnus." He met her gaze and held it. "Though 'tis sore hard to resist when he sets his hands upon ye."

A soft gasp escaped her as, sheltered from view by their bodies, he slid his hand up her rib cage to cup her breast. She felt herself swell to his touch, her nipple tautening.

A tingling began there which cried out for soothing. She felt pinned in place by the heated look in his eyes, unable to tear herself from his touch or escape his gaze.

" 'Tis Farthing's right." It was a struggle for her to say the words.

"I will make it *my* right," he replied.

"Nay, leave me be. I dinnae want this." But she knew she was lying and feared it showed in her voice.

"Will ye tell me that my touch leaves ye cold?"

"Aye, cold and insulted."

"Then ye lie. 'Tis neither coldness nor insult that has the tip of your breast boring into my palm. 'Tis neither coldness nor insult that has it crying out to be taken between my lips and sipped upon. Aye, 'tis offering me its nectar."

His thick, husky voice and the words he spoke caused a melting warmth to seep through her body. She closed her eyes, but that only turned his words into visions. In her mind she could see his bright crowned head pressed against her breasts. A moan that contained as much helplessness as desire escaped her. She could not stop herself from succumbing to his touch.

It was not supposed to happen like this, she thought a little frantically. She had heard the minstrels sing of such things. A fierce passion such as this was supposed to be a man's province. Love was what a woman sought. This could not be love. That came slowly, often after marriage. She was being pulled into something she did not understand and it frightened her. However, even that fear did not give her the strength to break free.

She shuddered when he brushed his thumb over the hardened tip of her breast. "Nay," she whispered.

"Aye, ye burn as hot for me as I do for ye. Ye will be mine."

"I think not. She is mine."

Sine Catriona was both relieved and disappointed to hear Farthing's cold voice. She watched Gamel, worried that the violence she read in his face would be turned upon Farthing, who placed his hand upon her shoulder. When Gamel slowly stood up, he kept her hand clasped in his. He pressed a soft, warm kiss on her palm before releasing her. Only then did Gamel meet the look of cold fury on Farthing's face.

"For now," Gamel said, and strode away.

Staring at her hand, wondering why she had closed it as if to hold his kiss there, Sine Catriona sagged a little with relief and murmured, "He is verra arrogant."

"This is something he has a right to be arrogant about."

"I havenae encouraged him," she said, yet she knew, in part, that she was lying, for she had not discouraged him either.

"Nay, ye havenae. I ken that, my sweet. What burns inside of that knight needs no encouragement." Farthing sat down beside her and ran a hand through his thick raven hair. "Mayhaps we should flee this place—now."

"When we are in such need of money? He has said he willnae kill ye—" she began, knowing that Farthing was no coward but that he loathed bloodshed.

"Now, there is arrogance. Mayhaps *I* would kill *him* should we come to swordpoint."

She stared at Farthing. "I dinnae think I should like that either."

He put his arm about her shoulders to tug her closer. "Poor, confused Catriona. Ye ken so much more than most young lasses, yet ye ken so little. No matter. Ye are right; we do need money. So, we must stay here, and a curse upon the arrogant Sir Gamel."

By the end of the day Farthing was sorely tempted to do

more than idly curse Sir Gamel. He ached to run the man through. Gamel haunted their every step, sometimes covertly, sometimes openly. Farthing began to feel as hunted as he knew Catriona did. He could not make a move without finding Gamel's green stare fixed upon him.

"That cursed mon hounds me," he muttered as he joined Sine Catriona and her brothers for their evening meal.

"Yet he does nothing," she murmured.

"True, child. Even so, 'tis as if some adder sets at my side coiled to strike."

"I think Sir Gamel troubles ye far more than he does me. Yet that is odd. 'Tis a puzzle with no answer." She sighed, then shrugged.

"Life is full of those, dearling." He looked around, studying the crowd gathered at MacAdam's inn. "A good crowd and many a full purse at the ready. Prepared to lighten a few?"

"As ever."

"Good. Give these fools a while longer to cloud their senses with MacAdam's strong ale. Then I shall begin to entertain them. As I work, ye and my skilled lads will set about your business."

He smiled at his three companions, then forced his attention to his meal. It was not easy. Gamel sat a mere table away, watching them. Farthing tried to shake off a sense of foreboding.

Ligulf sighed and shook his head, only briefly distracting Gamel's attention from Sine Catriona and her family. "I think ye have looked nowhere else all day." An even mix of concern and irritation darkened his brown eyes as he studied his elder brother.

"No doubt ye are right." Gamel smiled faintly. "Master Magnus grows angrier by the moment."

"Gamel, she is *his*. They are a family. Cannae ye leave them be?"

"Nay. Dinnae ye think I would if I could? There is a heat in my blood that burns away all good sense." He glanced at a woman who was smiling at him and his companions. "Aye, and all desire for another woman."

"Weel, I can see no way to gain what ye desire. Farthing holds her, as he should, and she is no gay lass."

"Nay, that is true. Tell me," Gamel murmured, "what, besides conjuring, requires the skill of sleight of hand?" He watched his companions mull that question over.

Sir Lesley frowned, then finally asked, "Do ye think they are thieves?"

"I am *certain* they are thieves. Howbeit, I have yet to see exactly how she does it."

"She?"

"Aye, Ligulf—she. Master Magnus keeps all eyes fixed upon himself with his clever talk and deft conjuring, while she lightens the gawkers' purses. The twins are part of it as weel. 'Tis only the how of it that eludes me. When I have that, I will have her."

"How so?"

"I will threaten to cry them thieves unless she comes to me," Gamel replied.

"Gamel." Ligulf's voice was weakened with shock. "Ye ken the penalties for theft. Ye claim ye want her, yet ye would give her over to branding or worse because she denies ye?"

"Nay, I wouldnae truly cry her a thief, but they willnae ken that."

Ligulf frowned. "Somehow it doesnae seem right."

"'Tis not right, but then neither is thievery. Ligulf, this is the least damaging of all the plots I have thought of."

Gamel shook his head when Ligulf prepared to say more. "Nay, dinnae waste your breath. There is no way ye can talk me out of it. If I must, I will answer to my conscience later. Right now I heed another part of me." He looked at Ligulf and gave the lad a half smile. "And that calls to mind the fact that ye came afairing for a reason ye have done little about."

Sir Lesley hooted and Ligulf blushed.

"Aye, lad. I see more than a few likely prospects, like that one there who keeps smiling at you."

As the others teased Ligulf, Gamel quietly returned to watching Catriona. He knew that if he did not find a way to gain hold of her tonight, he could well lose all chance. Instinct told him the Magnuses would slip away at dawn again. Then he would have to search for her, which he could not do until he had returned to Duncoille for a while as he had promised his father. By then, the trail would have grown very cold indeed.

When Farthing took up a position that made him visible to everyone, Gamel had to admire the man's skill in drawing all attention to himself even before he started plying his tricks. However, Farthing was indeed a skilled conjurer. Most of those in the inn were easily tempted to watch the man perform, some vainly hoping to see the secret of it all. Even Gamel was tempted, but he kept his gaze on Catriona, his interest fixed upon the tricks she played.

Sine Catriona began to stroll through the crowd with a feigned idleness, her brothers shadowing her. She used the tavern maids to provide some excuse for her meandering, pausing to speak with each one. The crowd did not expect her to be interested in Farthing's chatter and tricks, for she had seen it all before. They soon ignored her as she weaved in and out amongst them. As soon as their attention was fixed upon Farthing plying his trade, she began to ply hers.

Skillfully, with only the faintest thrill of fear, she relieved each watcher of his purse. Swiftly, she extracted half the coin, sometimes less, and in but an instant smoothly returned the purse to its owner. Befuddled by drink as most of them were, they never guessed that a robbery had taken place. The few who suspected quickly doubted, for what thief did not steal all the money? Thieves took every hapenny and kept the purse as well. That belief was her shield, protecting her from any dangerous outcry. The twins stealthily pocketed her gains, then took turns hiding it away.

The only thing she found difficult this time was keeping her mind fully on what she was doing. Only with effort did she ignore one particular man among MacAdam's patrons. Gamel was still watching her. There was no doubt in her mind about that. Praying that his gaze was not upon her hands, she forced all thought of him from her mind. He was too great a distraction and the work she did required her full attention.

"I have her," Gamel cried in a soft, tense voice as he grasped Sir Lesley's thickly muscled arm. "Lesley, watch this. Curse their eyes, but they are good. Verra, verra good. Watch her pretty right hand, my friend. See? There. She now has the purse off of that fool, now she takes the coin and, there, she puts the purse back. Now, watch closely as her left hand feints toward young Dane. See it? The lad has just pocketed the spoils."

Sir Lesley scowled, then scratched his head. "Weel, aye, I sense that something goes on but, I confess, I cannae see all that ye do."

Ligulf frowned in confusion. "But why does she return the purse?"

"Ah, there is the true cleverness of their game. A mon doesnae cry thief if he still holds his purse and feels coins still weighting it. When the fool does count his coin, he will only be puzzled, not truly suspicious. Did I have three ales or four? he will ask himself. Mayhaps I came with less than I realized. These are the thoughts which will first come to his mind. And who would heed him if he did cry thief? The others would curse him for a cup-shotten fool. What thief leaves aught behind? People will tell the mon to count more carefully next time and cease making such a row."

"By the saints, that is clever, Gamel. But how will *ye* catch her then?"

Slowly rising from his seat, Gamel murmured, "I will catch her ere she can return her next purse." He began to stealthily make his way through the crowd toward Sine Catriona.

Smiling at the man who asked her how Farthing could thrust a dagger through his arm yet not bleed, Sine Catriona shook her head. "I cannae tell ye that, kind sir."

"Come, mistress, ye must ken your mon's secrets."

"Nay," she demurred, looking coy even as she deftly lifted his purse. "What woman kens all her mon's secrets?"

"Verra few, thank the good Lord." The man laughed.

She laughed too, expertly extracted a third of the man's worth and prepared to return his purse. Her blood ran cold when Gamel suddenly appeared, placing himself between her and her victim. He could not see the purse she held yet she knew at once that he was onto her game. That knowledge glowed in his fine eyes. She forcibly resisted the blind urge to bolt.

"Here now," Sine Catriona's victim muttered. "Best to beware, friend. 'Tis the conjurer's woman ye ogle."

"Will he turn me into a toad?" Gamel grinned at the man, who laughed heartily.

Sine Catriona was strongly inclined to stick a knife in both of them, but she fixed Gamel with a beseeching look instead. "Please, sir," she whispered.

"Come and share a drink with me, Mistress Catriona." He lightly trailed his fingers over her blanched cheek.

Suddenly she knew what price he would demand to keep his knowledge of her thievery to himself.

"Now," he commanded in a near whisper, taking her by her left arm. "Master MacAdam serves a very fine mead."

"Aye," agreed her victim. "He does and 'tis time for me to be refilled. Here," he muttered. "Where is my purse?"

With a skill she had learned early in the game, Sine Catriona bent and suddenly the purse was on the floor. "Ye but dropped it, sir." She picked it up and handed it back to him. "Mayhaps it was knocked loose when this mon nudged between us. Ye should make certain it is weel secured."

"Aye, good lass. I feared the pikers had come to Mac-Adam's at last."

"Nay, sir. He would ne'er allow it."

"Come," Gamel urged. "Your drink awaits ye. 'Tis in return for your, and Master Magnus's, gracious hospitality last eve."

Even as she obeyed his gentle but firm tug on her arm, she handed her spoils to Barre, who darted off to hide them. Although she was as careful as ever, Sir Gamel's gaze followed her fleeting movement, which strengthened her conviction that he knew everything. She briefly noted how Dane and Farthing watched as

Gamel led her to his table and sat down, tugging her to his side on the small bench. It was a seat made more for one than two. She prayed there would be no trouble.

"And such sweetness in your lovely face," Gamel murmured, giving her a look which said he mourned her lack of integrity.

"Thank ye, kind sir," she said, maintaining a false bravado in the face of his triumph. Then she tensed as she saw Farthing move toward them.

Having ended his trick and extracted himself from those who asked to see more of his art, Farthing strode to the table where Sine Catriona now sat. Gamel's expression held too much confidence for his liking. It was as if Gamel knew the game was won, and in his favor. Placing his hands palm down on the smooth table, Farthing leaned slightly toward Gamel.

"I hadnae thought ye were so slow of understanding, Sir Gamel. She is mine."

"She is a thief," Gamel retorted in a voice soft enough that no others heard the condemnation.

Glancing swiftly at Sine Catriona, Farthing watched her nod and felt himself go pale. Somehow Sir Gamel had seen what she was up to, and now intended to take full advantage of his discovery. Farthing experienced the cold, heavy realization that the man was right to think he had won the game. Gamel now held a weapon Farthing could not deflect.

"Would ye cry her a thief?" he asked, looking back at Gamel.

"I might." Gamel brushed Sine Catriona's still pale cheek with his knuckles.

"But ye might not." Farthing immediately guessed what bargain was about to be offered, and rage surged through his body.

"Nay, I might not." Gamel met Farthing's cold, black gaze.

"And what price do ye ask for this charity?"

"She abides with me this night."

"So ye willnae cry her a thief if she plays the whore for ye." Farthing saw a flash of regret, a touch of guilt, in the man's look, but knew it would be useless to try to play upon it.

"She abides with *me* this night," Gamel repeated.

"Nay, I think ye bluff, knight. Ye want her too badly to set her at such risk."

"Aye, I want her badly. There are those, however, who can want so badly they are willing to see what they are denied, denied to all. If they cannae have it, no mon shall. Are ye willing to test if I am such a mon?"

A fine tremor went through Farthing as he struggled to keep clear headed, fought the blinding fury building within him. He wanted to cut the man down on the spot. Sine Catriona's soft hand covering one of his tightly clenched ones brought his attention to her.

"Ye have ever taught me to weigh one choice against another." She held her hands out above the table, palms up, as if they were a set of scales. "Here is what Sir Gamel requests for his silence." She dropped her left hand down just a little. "Here is branding. Here is the gaol with the men who guard it. Here too is the chance they will wish the names of accomplices. Could I hold silent beneath their methods of inquiry? Here is the possible loss of my hand. Here is the possible loss of my life, mayhaps yours, mayhaps the twins'." She looked at her right hand, having lowered it with each possibility mentioned until it rested upon the table, then at her left, which still hovered several inches higher. "The choice is clear," she said, finally meeting Farthing's tortured gaze. "'Tis so clear that there really is no choice at all."

"I think I must kill this mon." Farthing's words came in harsh rasps. His hand went toward his dagger. But Sine Catriona reached across the table and stilled it.

"Please, Farthing. I willnae be the cause of bloodletting for the life of me. I beg you, leave it be."

He released a cry of rage and frustration, then straightened. He could see she intended to go through with it. There was nothing he could do to stop it without seriously endangering them all.

"I will be right outside the window. Just call and I will be there. I will break down the door, if need be." Then, with one sweep of his arm he sent the crockery on the table smashing to the floor and strode from the room.

Sine Catriona instinctively tried to follow him, but Gamel held her until she told her wide-eyed brothers, "Dane, Ree, go with Farthing. Stay with him."

For a while she kept her gaze fixed upon the door through which her family had left. When the mess of broken dishes that Farthing had made was cleared away and new drinks set out, she finally looked at Sir Gamel, noticing fleetingly that his three companions seemed less than comfortable with his actions. If Gamel felt the same unease, he was hiding it very well.

"Ye have hurt Farthing deeply," she told Gamel in a soft voice. "For that I may have to kill ye."

His eyes widening slightly, Gamel replied, "Methinks Farthing plans the same."

"Then ye had best seek absolution, for death is nigh. No mon can look two ways at once."

It annoyed her when he simply smiled, then draped his arm about her shoulders. She sipped her mead as she strove to remain calm. There was nothing she could do to change what had happened or to escape what would happen now. To tie herself up in emotional knots over it was foolish. That would only make what was to come all the harder to endure.

What she really feared was neither dishonor nor pain but enjoyment. He moved his hand up and down her arm, and occasionally stroked her neck. At times he rested his long, slim fingers on the increasingly fierce pulse in her throat. He roused such a heat in her she feared she would be scorched from the inside out.

In a desperate attempt to turn her thoughts from Gamel's nearness and from his effect upon her, she tried to concentrate on what was going on around her. Her gaze settled on the fair young Ligulf. He blushed in response to the overtures of a buxom brunette. It took her only a moment to know why he should feel so discomforted by what any other man would respond lustily to.

"Your brother's first time afairing?" she asked Gamel.

He slowly nodded, wondering if she meant what they all did when they spoke of afairing. He was not overly concerned with Ligulf's troubles at the moment. Hoping she could adjust to her situation, he was allowing her to finish her drink. Then he fully intended to drag her to his chambers, something he was painfully impatient to do. The night was going to be far too short.

"Then he doesnae want Mary," she said, waving another maid over. "She is too coarse and none too clean."

"Do you ken these women weel?" Gamel loathed the thought that she might have something in common with the tavern maids.

"We often stay here. Most of the women have been here a long time. Janet." She smiled at the raven-haired woman who stepped up to the table. "A lamb for the shearing."

Janet smiled slowly, her gaze settling on Ligulf even as she asked, "Where is Farthing?"

"In our room most like. Sir Gamel keeps me company for now."

Briefly Janet's gaze met Gamel's, her eyes widening slightly in a gesture of understanding. "I see."

"I thought ye would," Sine Catriona murmured. "I believe Mary lacks the touch needed here."

"Bah, she is a slattern. Here, Mary, MacAdam calls for ye."

Mary scowled but moved away from Ligulf. Gamel guessed that the woman dared not try to prove that Janet lied. He almost smiled as Janet quickly sat beside Ligulf, causing the departing Mary to curse.

After watching his brother and Janet for a moment, Gamel murmured, "It does go better."

Sine Catriona nodded. "Aye, Janet has a gentler manner. 'Twill cost him, though."

"We have the funds. After all, what can one throw cost?"

"One throw? Nay, sir. Time must be taken to shear the lamb weel. None takes such care as Janet. If your brother goes to her bed, he willnae be seen again until the morning."

"Careful indeed."

She shrugged. "Ye seek to make him a mon."

"And how is it that ye ken so much about such things?"

"I am no soft, gentlebred maid kept ignorant and secured in her boudoir until her wedding day."

"And yet methinks ye possess a certain innocence."

She hastily took a drink. Sir Gamel would all too soon know just how innocent she was. How she would explain that when she was supposed to be Farthing's wife she did not know. A little desperately she prayed Gamel might not notice that the woman Farthing Magnus claimed as his wife was a virgin.

"Hurry with your drink, Catriona," he murmured as he pressed a kiss to her neck.

"I drink as fast as I can." She winced at the telltale huskiness that had invaded her voice.

"Not fast enough." He moved his lips toward her ear. "God's teeth, I am sore pressed to take ye now— right here."

"There would be a fine sight for MacAdam's patrons."

"That other eyes would be able to look upon ye is all that holds me back. Drink."

"Ye willnae change your mind on this?" she asked, knowing it for a foolish question even as she spoke it.

"Nay. 'Tis not my mind that rules me now."

As she raised the gourd to her lips, he traced the shape of her ear with his tongue. Her drink nearly ended up on the floor. She trembled as desire gripped her so tightly she nearly cried out. The deep swallow of mead she took did nothing to dampen that raging fire. The moment she emptied her cup Gamel stood up, yanked her to her feet, and dragged her toward his quarters. She glanced only once at his companions. They still looked displeased, but no one moved to interfere.

Ligulf watched his brother leave and grumbled, "She has bewitched him."

Janet laughed softly. "Aye. She bewitches many. Her spell is all the stronger for she doesnae ken that she casts it."

"I cannae understand why he couldnae just leave her be."

Running her hand along his slim, strong arm, Janet murmured, "Come the morning, ye will." She laughed again. "Aye, and come the morning your brother will

be sorely confused, for Sine Catriona shall leave his
rooms as changed as ye will leave mine."

"Nay!"

"Nay ye or nay Catriona?"

"Nay Catriona," he muttered, blushing as he admitted
his own innocence, and Janet simply smiled.

Farthing stared up at Sir Gamel's chamber window.
He still ached to bury a dagger in the man—bury it
deeply. After raging over his helplessness for a time he
had sought peace in drink. That had failed him. His
blood ran too hot to be cooled, his mind too full to be
emptied.

The twins had finally fallen asleep, wearied from
watching him rail and storm, so he had left them in the
room. It had not been hard to discover where Sir
Gamel's window was. He stared at it, trying to think of
some way to help Sine Catriona, but all his plans were
rash, flawed. His hands were tied by the bitter knowledge
that Sine Catriona was right, there was no other choice.
He had trained her to be a thief and now she was paying
the price. His helplessness was heavily weighted with
guilt.

Although he knew he could not help or protect her
this time, he settled himself below Gamel's window. He
would spend the night right here. If but one cry of pain
or fear reached his ears, he would cut Sir Gamel's throat
and defy the consequences.

Chapter 3

"**U**ndress."

Sine Catriona tried not to flinch at the raspy order. She slowly turned to look at Gamel. He was leaning against the thick wooden door he had just shut and barred. Even as she met his gaze he moved to sit on the bed and remove his well-fitted boots. Her hard-won calm and resignation were not holding up very well at all.

"Catriona," he said, "I dare do it myself, though I dearly want to. I fear I shall tear your garments."

A tremor rippled through her at this further indication of his eagerness. Her hands were unsteady as she began to remove her cowl. With no brush at hand she had to use her fingers to comb out her hair. She tried not to look at how he watched her, nor consider how quickly he undressed.

Failing in her attempt to subdue her blushes, she took off her gown. Sitting on a stool, she removed her rough boots and worn hose. Standing up again, she reached beneath her chemise to tug off the braies Farthing had insisted she wear to further hinder any attacker. Just as she began to unlace her chemise, a naked Gamel moved

to stand in front of her. She tried to look anywhere but
at him as he pulled her into his arms.

He buried his hand in her hair, gently tugging her
head back and turning her face up to his. There was a
feverish quality to the short kisses he traced over her full
mouth. Sine Catriona's senses swam as she rested her
hands upon his smooth chest. He robbed her of all ability to think, infected her with his intense passion.

"I tremble like some untried lad," he said with a groan
as he picked her up and tumbled her onto the bed.

She was torn between excitement and embarrassment
when he hastily removed her chemise. The poor garment
barely escaped being torn. A deep color flooded her face
when he sat astride her to stare at her. When she tried to
cover her nudity with her hands, he grasped her wrists
and pinned them to the bed. Yet beneath her pained
modesty, she felt a hot pride in the delight he so plainly
found in her form.

Gamel's gaze moved over her slowly. As he had
thought, her skin was a pale golden hue all over. She was
slender, delicately built, yet had all the curves and sweet
tempting softness a man could want. Despite her lack of
height, her legs were long as well as taut and shapely. Releasing her wrists, he slid his hands down her sides to test
the smallness of her waist and the gentle swell of her hips.
He trailed one hand over her leg before lying down in
her arms.

Cupping her face in his hands, he brushed his mouth
over hers, murmuring, "Ye are far more beautiful than I
had envisioned."

A moan escaped her from low in her throat as he hungrily possessed her mouth with his. That sound tore at
his insides, feeding his already crippling desire for her.
When he stroked the inside of her mouth with his
tongue, savoring the sweetness there, she wrapped her

arms around him. That sign that her desire could match his left him shaking inside.

"Aye, Catriona, aye," he murmured as he cupped her breasts in his hands, edging his kisses toward that tempting fullness. "Touch me, even though it threatens to make me rush when I would go slow."

He felt her hands clench upon his back as he flicked his tongue over her hardened nipples and heard her murmur, "I am Sine."

"Sine?" Only briefly was he able to tear his gaze from how her lovely breasts swelled beneath his caresses.

"Sine Catriona. My full name is Sine Catriona. Ah, sweet heaven," she cried as he closed his mouth over the tip of one breast to draw upon it slowly, delighting in the taste of her.

Lifting his head, Gamel stared at the dampened nipple, only to bend and take another draw upon it before turning his attention to the other. "Sine Catriona," he murmured. "Farthing calls ye Catriona, so I will call ye Sine. God's teeth, but it must be a sin for a woman to taste so sweet."

Sine Catriona thought a little frantically that it must be a sin for anything to feel so good. She wondered if all trace of sanity had fled her. Instead of pushing him away or trying to talk him out of what he was doing, she held him close. She arched toward him as he continued to feast upon her breasts, stroking the rest of her body with his long, lightly callused hands. Even if she had wanted to, there was no way she could hide the intense pleasure he gave her.

The way he caressed her inner thighs seduced her into parting them for him. He trailed kisses toward her stomach as he slid his hand down to the silver curls at its base. A shudder went through her at his intimate touch. She held him more tightly when he groaned and pressed his face against her abdomen, his breath coming in harsh gasps.

"Pardee! Ah, Sine, ye are already hot with welcome. The mere feel of your warmth and I am near spent. I cannae wait any longer," he muttered, his voice hoarse and unsteady as he made ready to possess her.

He covered her mouth with his even as he joined their bodies with one swift stroke. His kiss stifled her cry of pain as she felt him tear through her innocence. When he yanked his mouth from hers, his trembling body tense and still, she met his look of shocked disbelief.

"Ye were a virgin," he whispered in a rough voice. "How can this be?"

What pain he had inflicted swiftly faded and she shifted her body in a silent plea for what his stillness denied her. She needed to say something, so she quickly lied, "Farthing suffered a grievous wound years ago."

"So, he cannae and willnae ever taste what I have tonight."

The deep satisfaction in his voice annoyed her. That irritation briefly flickered through the passion she was unable to control. He did not know she was lying. In a way he was savoring the mutilation another man had suffered.

"Nay, but that doesnae change the fact that I am *his*."

"Mine, Sine Catriona," he muttered as he began to move and all her senses delighted in it. "Mine."

Passion chased all thought of argument from her mind. She clung to him, a soft cry escaping her as she wrapped her limbs around his lean, strong body. The fleeting thought that she was far too wantonly vocal in her pleasure did nothing to halt her cries. His name was often on her lips as his movements grew more frantic, the kisses he pressed to her throat and face more fevered.

He slid his arm beneath her hips, holding her close as his body bucked with release. Her name was an exultant cry upon his lips. At nearly the same moment she tumbled into desire's final, blinding grip. She held him as tightly as she could as it took full hold of her. Long after he lay sprawled in her arms, she still squirmed with the pleasurable effects of it all.

They lay together, spent, for a long time. But gradually sanity returned to her, and with it came shame. She closed her eyes and averted her face when he cleansed them both of the remnants of her innocence. The loss of her purity did not trouble her as much as her enjoyment of that theft did. When Gamel returned to bed, she tried to avoid his touch, but he would not allow it. He tugged her into his arms with a gentle but inescapable firmness. She ruefully admitted to herself that she liked being there.

"Sine," he whispered, "how was I to ken that ye were a virgin?"

She looked at him with faint curiosity. "And would ye have let me be if ye had kenned it?"

"Nay," he answered with quiet honesty as he eased the covers down her body.

"Then what matter?" She inwardly cursed the heat which flickered to life within her as he lightly trailed his fingers over her breasts. "I am still in your bed through a bargain."

"The bargain was necessary to remove ye from Farthing's bed."

"That makes it justifiable? But I am here. I abide with you this night."

"Not just this night, Sine Catriona. Ye are mine."

Something in his tone thrilled her, but she denied it. She did not even allow herself to think on whether she wanted to be his or not, or if he meant as leman or wife.

None of that mattered, nor could it be allowed to matter. When she had fled from her father's murderers, she had vowed revenge as well as retrieval of all that had been stolen from her and the twins. Nothing could interfere with that, not even a beautiful auburn-haired man who set her blood to boil with but a touch.

Gamel bent his head to softly kiss the erect tip of each breast. "Ye are mine, Sine Catriona. Say it. Admit it," he ordered, framing her face with his hands.

She watched his head against her breasts, then met his jewel-bright gaze. Behind that commanding tone lurked a hint of desperation.

Though it puzzled her, she knew he was right. She was his. To admit that did not mean she vowed to stay with him. It simply acknowledged the bond that existed between them. She knew that bond would hold no matter who or what came into their lives.

"Aye," she finally said. "Aye, I am yours."

Beneath her hands she felt a fine tremor pass through his body as he kissed her. The matter of possession was clearly important to him. She wondered how much or how little emotion was behind that need. A man's desire to possess could be such a shallow thing, no more than a point of pride. Sine wondered why the possibility that his was should make her so sad.

She also felt a bit guilty. He now believed she had promised to stay with him. It was going to be an agony to walk away from him when dawn lightened the sky, but she would walk away. All she could hope for was that he was either too proud or too busy to hunt her down.

He made love to her again. The fierce need still flared between them. Sine sensed that he maintained some control of his passion. She had none at all as she clung to him, singing out her pleasure.

* * *

"Why do ye stay with Farthing?" Gamel asked a while later. "He cannae be all a mon should be with ye."

"Love isnae based upon what dangles between a mon's legs."

Gamel's hand clenched on the tankard of wine he shared with her. "Ye dinnae love him."

She moved slightly from where she sat curled up at his side. "Aye, I do."

"Nay, ye cannae, not when ye say ye are mine. Not when ye feel as ye do."

"How do ye ken what I feel or dinnae feel? I dinnae ken it myself. Ye have given me no chance to think."

Encircling her neck with his arm, he gave her a deep, fierce kiss. "That. That is what ye feel for me."

"Fire. Passion beyond reason. Fear."

"Fear?" He jerked away from her. "Nay. Dinnae say ye fear me."

"And why not? I was a virgin, untried in all the ways of loving. Suddenly there comes a mon who but looks at me and sets my innards afire, fills me with emotions I ken little of and understand less. Aye, I fear ye, as any maid would. Ye have thrust me into womanhood without wooing or preparation."

"No matter how ye arrived within my bed, I would have been unable to grant ye either." He took a deep drink of wine, set the tankard aside, then pulled her into his arms. "I have ne'er ached so badly, ne'er wanted so fiercely. Wooing was beyond me. I believe I barely avoided rape."

"Now there is consolation."

"Sine, this isnae something to fear. 'Tis something to revel in. I have kenned my share of women, mayhaps more than my share, but never have I tasted such as this."

"The Land of Cockaigne."

"What?"

"Farthing claims such as this is the Land of Cockaigne, paradise upon earth." She could see that mention of Farthing did not please Gamel at all.

"How long have ye been with him?"

"Six years."

"Ye were but a child when ye joined him. What? Ten, eleven?"

"Just twelve. A child who needed someone to care for her and her brothers."

"And ye call it caring when he teaches ye to steal?"

"Aye—taught us to steal with skill. Theft and conjuring were his only skills and he shared them with us."

"He has a fine talent with a sword."

"Aye, so? He should sell that, should he? How would he keep us if he became some lordling's hired sword? Such work is also hard, rewards not often forthcoming even when weel earned. The risks are verra high. He cares for me and the twins. He protects us. We had no one and he took us in. I willnae question his life, for he shared it with us willingly, kindly. I love that mon. Aye, ye may growl, glare, and curse all ye like if it makes ye feel better," she added when he did just that. "Howbeit, none of that will change the fact."

"Then love him, curse your beautiful eyes." He pushed her onto her back. "Love him, but it will never change the fact that ye are mine. Mine, Sine."

"Yours."

She whispered the word as she stood by the bed a few hours later, watching him sleep. Each ache in her body

brought forth a heated memory. It was hard to leave the
shelter of his arms, harder still to dress in the faint light
of a swiftly approaching dawn. She knew that, in his
mind, her actions would put the lie to all she had said.
That realization brought her close to weeping. It hurt to
think that what memories he held of her would be
tainted by her departure.

With skillful stealth she slipped out of the room.
There was one thing she had to do before she left the
inn. Cautiously, she made her way to Janet's tiny alcove.
It was easy enough to slip inside. She mused wryly that
she could have slipped right into the bed Janet and
Ligulf shared except that Ligulf was awake. By instinct,
he grabbed for his sword, then gaped when he recognized her. She watched his surprise quickly alter to concern.

"Does something ail Gamel?"

"Nay." She moved to the side of the bed, smiling
faintly at Janet, who began to wake up. "He still sleeps."

"Then why are ye here?"

"I hope to fend off his first unkind thoughts when he
finds me gone. I wish to keep such bitter conclusions
from settling in his mind, although in truth, he deserves
little consideration from me." She held out a medallion
of finely wrought silver. "Will ye give this to him, please?"

"Where did ye get something like this?" he asked as he
accepted it.

"'Tisnae stolen. 'Tis a trinket from my past. My past is
what rules me now. I must find it and restore it."

"I dinnae understand ye."

"There are wrongs I must set right, grievous wrongs.
Things stolen that I must regain, murders—aye, murders—
I must and will avenge. My heritage has been stained with
blood and treachery. I intend to wipe that stain away. I
vowed to do all this for myself and for my half brothers six

long years ago. For six years I have clung to my vow. I cannae, willnae, allow myself to be swayed from it. Not for your brother. Nay, not even for Farthing if he asked it of me."

"Gamel asked ye to stay with him?"

The shock in the youth's voice stung a little. "He expects it, but I just told ye why I cannae."

"Why didnae ye just tell him yourself?"

Faint color seeped into her cheeks. "I would have had to wake him."

Janet laughed softly. "And then there would have been no leaving."

Sine grimaced. "Just so."

Ligulf eyed Sine curiously. "Are ye certain Farthing still waits for ye? Mayhaps he left."

"Nay, Master Ligulf, he would never leave me. Farthing spent the night beneath your brother's window." She managed to smile at his surprise. "I must go now or all my stealth will be for naught."

"Wait but a moment. I am confused. Are ye saying ye would leave your husband for Gamel?"

"I would leave Farthing for him, but I wouldnae forsake my vow."

"Nay, ye are wed. Gamel would never bring an adulteress into our home," he muttered. "Ye must have misheard him."

"He said, 'Not just this night, Sine Catriona. Ye are mine,' and he pressed me to admit it. Howbeit, he went no further than that. He offered me no honorable situation, no choice of becoming his wife or his leman. Nevertheless, 'tis certain he doesnae mean for me to leave."

"Nay, 'tis certain."

"Be sure to tell him all I have said *as* I have said it."

"I will, but he will still ken that ye have climbed back into Farthing Magnus's bed."

Again she smiled, unable to hide her amusement. "Oh, nay, nay. He will never think that." She grew serious again. "Tell him that when my vow is fulfilled I will return, although I dinnae expect him to wait for me. Not only am I unsure of what he meant by my being *his*, but my work could take months, years. It already has.

"Tell him he was right. It pleases me little to say so, to admit I am his. He has been extremely arrogant and most unkind to Farthing. Howbeit, I fear I am his. No matter what time or events transpire, no matter what people come between us. I feel not only ravished this dawn, but also branded and bonded."

"Yet ye leave."

"I told ye—I must. 'Tisnae easy. 'Twill be impossible if he wakes. So give him my medallion and tell him it is all I may leave behind."

"Good luck, Catriona."

"Thank ye, Janet." She gave the confused Ligulf a parting smile and slipped out of the room.

Farthing left the shadows beneath Gamel's window as soon as he saw Sine Catriona approach. Without a word he held out his arms, and pulled her close when she stepped into them. He could see that she was unharmed, but he knew she was now changed. He also sensed that she was deeply troubled. Guilt gnawed at him. He had brought her to this impasse but could now only stand by helpless and sympathetic.

"Do ye give up your quest now?" he asked.

She shook her head. "Nay, I cannae. 'Tis not only for me, is it? 'Tis for the twins as weel. Aye, and 'tis to ease the souls of my murdered father and their murdered mother."

"Then we best flee from here—now. The twins are

already in the cart. 'Tis wise to be as far away as we can be ere that knight rouses," he said as he released her and started toward their conveyance.

Hurrying along at his side, she asked, "Do ye think he will give chase?"

"Aye, if he has no commitment to draw him elsewhere for now."

"We could never outrun him, Farthing."

"Nay, but there are only four of them. They dinnae ken where we head. That leaves them with a dozen or more routes to choose from. That gives us an admirable advantage."

It was not until she, Farthing, and the still-sleeping twins were all well on their way down an obscure, little traveled route that Farthing touched upon the matter of Gamel again. "Ye considered staying with him."

"Aye." She sighed. "He didnae make clear what he intended for me but, aye, I thought on it. 'Twas difficult beyond words to leave him this morning."

"Ah, poor Catriona. To find the one who lights the flame, only to have to leave him behind?" He shook his head.

"Ye dinnae appear surprised. Ye could see how it would be?"

"Aye."

"Then what was the cause of all your fury?"

"It had many causes. The mon gave ye no choice. We didnae, and still dinnae, ken who he is. He meant to dishonor ye. So too did I sense that ye would find yourself as torn as ye are now. I sorely wished to save ye from that. Then again, he is a bastard, said so himself. Ye are legitimate and highborn."

"That matters little. 'Twas verra clear to see that he is learned, trained, and not poor."

"Verra clear. Are ye sure he couldnae be the knight ye seek to aid ye?"

"Sadly, aye, verra sure. As he told us, he is a bastard. They dinnae command armies."

"Rarely. They are mercenaries usually. They arenae liege lords who could demand service. A shame. He was an admirable swordsmon." He eyed her closely. "Catriona?"

"Aye?"

"The Land of Cockaigne?"

She smiled, although it was an expression heavily weighted by sadness. "Oh, aye. Aye. Innocent though I was, with naught to compare it to, I think there can never be any to excel. At least I have tasted that."

"Remember it, dearling. 'Twill ease the loss. Recall that ye have tasted what few of us have or ever shall have."

"I think it will come to ye someday."

"Mayhaps, but I think I will have to leave it behind as ye have. In truth, I have e'er been careful to guard my heart and not try to win some lass's affections, for I possess nothing to give the giver."

"Bah, ye have yourself, Farthing Magnus. 'Tis no small prize." She glanced behind them. "Do ye think he follows?"

Farthing shrugged. "Whether he does now or later, we best hope we can evade him."

As each hour passed and there was no sign of Gamel's pursuit, Farthing could see Sine Catriona relaxing. But she looked sadly torn between relief and hurt. Farthing tried to get her to share his conviction that only a prior commitment or an inability to find their trail would keep Gamel away from her. The look in her eyes told him that he failed, that she began to fear that brief moment with

Gamel had been no more than passion for him, no more than a brief flirtation.

They were nearly twenty miles away from Dunkennley, a long tedious day's journey, when they began to search for a campsite. They met up with others who clearly had the same plan. Farthing scowled as they slowly approached the group of people just ahead of them. Few clearings existed along the somewhat obscure route he had chosen. The caravan they now neared had taken one of the best and driest. Suddenly, he recognized the people and slowed up instead of passing them by.

"Weel, may I be roasted in hell's stinking fires."

"No doubt ye will be," drawled Sine Catriona. "Howbeit, why make mention of it now?"

The grin that curved Farthing's mouth was one of both relief and amusement. Sine Catriona had been very quiet, withdrawn, and sad. Her tart remark was very like the ones she had tossed his way before Sir Gamel had intruded in their lives. He grew less concerned that she suffered beyond repair.

"I think, sweet shrew, I recognize the people resting so comfortably in the spot I chose for us."

"Aye? What impudence to steal your chosen place," she murmured. "Who are they then?"

Before Farthing could reply, a tall, slender man moved forward. Farthing could tell by the wide-eyed look on Sine Catriona's face that her question had been answered. The man's face was illuminated with happiness as he hurried over to them.

"Farthing, m'lad! 'Tis truly ye?"

"'Tis indeed me, Father." Farthing leapt from the cart and was immediately clasped in Lord Magnusson's arms.

Gripping Farthing by the shoulders, Lord Magnusson stepped back a pace to look him over. "I have been searching long and hard for ye, son. God's beard, but ye are as elusive as a shadow."

"Searching for me? Why? I keep ye weel informed as to how I fare."

"Aye, ye do. What ye dinnae tell me is exactly *where* ye fare. I have a great need for ye now, a great need."

"How so?"

"Ah, son, the plague settled over us a few years back. My wife and both my children were taken." He nodded when Farthing clasped his shoulder in a silent gesture of sympathy. "Many another was lost as weel. Most of my other kin. Your cousin, wee Margot, who sleeps in the cart o'er there, is about all that is left. Ye are my heir now, Farthing."

"Your heir? Nay, I am a bastard. Ye cannae make a bastard legal, can ye?"

"'Tisnae done too often, but 'tis done nonetheless. Ye have been named my heir these three years, and with the king's approval. Ye will gain the barony, lands, and what meager fortune I may leave behind. There will be no quarrel o'er it even if there is anyone left with a remote claim. The king owed me. Aye, and ye. This is how he repays us both—by approving my choice. Dinnae fret. I have it all written out and afixed with the king's seal."

"This news will take time to swallow fully. Catriona, ye can set the wagon over there."

"A fair maid," murmured Lord Magnusson when she was out of hearing. "When did ye marry her?"

"We arenae wed," Farthing replied somewhat absently.

Lord Magnusson was unable to hide his relief. Farthing puzzled over that. Sine Catriona was not a woman any man would think a poor choice for a bride.

"She is your leman then. I see."

Farthing suddenly understood that his father thought Sine Catriona was some lowborn lass, and his smile was cynical as be said, "Nay, not my leman either. I begin to suspect my change in fortune brings curses along with blessings. Nay, Catriona isnae my lover at all. She is my friend, my assistant. I love her, but not as ye think. She has been with me for six years, she and her young twin brothers. The boys are sleeping soundly in the cart now."

"For six years ye have ridden with such beauty at your side yet ne'er touched the lass?"

"I swear to God I never have, even though, as she so often tells me, I can be a lecherous dog." He smiled briefly when his father laughed. "What feelings I have for her are as a brother for a sister. Even if that were not true, ye would have naught to fear. The lass is better born than I, and legitimate, though her birthright's been stolen from her. Howbeit, I can only tell the tale if she gives me leave to do so. 'Tis hers to tell."

Farthing and Lord Magnusson joined Sine Catriona by the fire and shared a meal. When they were through, the older man asked her to relate her life's story. It was only natural that he should wonder about her. She felt no qualms about telling him everything. They all sat far away from Lord Magnusson's men-at-arms and the cart where Margot and her maid slept so that none could overhear and she quickly gave Farthing permission to tell all.

As Farthing began to speak she studied Lord Magnusson. The likeness between father and son was truly startling. No one regarding the pair would question from whose loins Farthing had sprung. Seeing Lord Magnusson confirmed an opinion she had long held. Farthing's looks would age well. Lord Magnusson still held all that was needed to catch a maid's eye.

"They stepped out of the wood one night, six years ago," Farthing said. "Hungry and dirty they were, seeking warmth and a bit of food. When I gave it to them she told me what had driven three such young children into the wood."

"And he told me what a rogue he was," Sine Catriona said.

After sending her a brief admonishing glance he continued. "She told me her father and the twins' mother were dead. Ah, and her grandmother. All dead by the hand of her mother, Arabel Brodie, and the woman's husband, Malise—a cousin who took everything her murdered father had left behind—land, title, money, and wife. This cursed pair sought to place Sine Catriona and her brothers in the cold clay as weel."

"Her own mother would allow such a thing?"

Sine Catriona briefly took over the tale-telling to explain how she had slowly realized that her mother felt nothing but hate for her. Arabel Brodie resented her daughter's youth and that resentment had grown with the passing years. Then Sine had discovered that Arabel planned to rid herself of Sine and the twins. She had taken the twins and fled into the woods.

"With our deaths, she and Malise truly would hold all."

She carefully watched Lord Magnusson as she nibbled at the remains of her meal. Although she did not think the man would cry them liars or fools, she was relieved to see anger harden his features. It was an incredible tale. She would understand if the man had some doubts, but it was clear he did not.

"But would no one have questioned where ye went?"

"Malise told everyone that we had been ailing and died. He even held a burial. I pray that the three shrouded forms he entombed were sheep, but he and Arabel had already killed three innocent people so . . ." She shrugged.

"The murdering bastard," Lord Magnusson hissed.

"Ah, so ye have met my stepfather," Sine murmured.

Smiling with honest enjoyment, he drawled, "Such a tart tongue. Aye, I have met Malise Brodie. He is a beast who parades himself as a mon. I could see the rot beneath his smile and fine manners, although I fear others could not. And his wife . . ." He choked to a halt, eyeing Sine a little warily.

"Please, dinnae think that you must restrain your tongue for my sake. I have disowned my mother."

"Have ye now? I thought it was the privilege of the parent to disown the child."

"I have decided to do it the other way around. In truth, m'lord, I may have slid from her body, but she is no mother of mine and never has been. She doesnae possess any maternal feelings at all. Nay, not even the natural softening any woman holds toward a child, any child. She plotted my death and that of my half brothers. She murdered our father. I will make her pay for that. Nay, she isnae my mother, despite what the law might say. I am but my father's child."

"Such strong feelings." Lord Magnusson shook his head. "I believe ye, yet 'tisnae easy. A mother wishing to murder her own child?"

"She hates me and has done so from the start. From the moment of my birth I was put completely into the care of my father and grandmother. They sheltered me from most of my mother's venom while they were alive. Carrying me within her womb marked my mother. Not much, but she bears each tiny mark as if it was some battle wound. She believes that I steal her beauty, as if I am some sorceress who sucks it away. 'Tis hard to explain."

"Aye, but I can see it clear enough. She ages and ye are young. There is no real sense to all she might blame ye for, but *she* believes each charge. So, do ye mean to regain what has been stolen from ye and your brothers?"

"I do. For now I search for a mon who holds the soldiers and arms to aid me in my fight."

"Farthing now has both," Lord Magnusson said in a soft voice, then grinned at her surprise—a reaction echoed by Farthing.

"By the saints, so I do," Farthing muttered, looking completely stunned by the realization.

"And will ye help me?" she asked him, sure that he would, but needing to offer him the choice.

"Of course, if my father permits." He looked at his father. "After all, I am but the heir, not the master. And, God willing, I shallnae be for many years yet."

"Fight away," Lord Magnusson commanded with a smile. "The cause is a good one. S'truth, there are many about who would like to see that devious pair sent straight to hell. I fear it must wait just a wee bit longer though. My journey isnae merely for pleasure."

Sine Catriona shrugged. "I have waited six years already. Patience is something I have in abundance."

"At times," Farthing murmured. Ignoring her scowl, he turned to his father. "Where do ye travel to?"

"To Duncoille. 'Tis but a half day's journey from here."

"Oh? And what is the purpose of this trip, Father?"

"To try and get my niece, Margot Delacrosse, a husband. I doubt that ye would recall the child from when ye lived with me, but that doesnae matter for ye will meet the lass tomorrow. She sleeps now, exhausted by the travel."

"No match was made for her?"

"Aye, there was one, son, but the plague took the mon. A pity, for they were in love. Her dowry is small, but the mon I hope to wed her to is a bastard son. He may not have much of a choice, despite his rumored wealth and fair face. His father has many another legitimate son."

"The lass isnae fair?" Sine asked.

"I see naught wrong with the child, but what is thought to be beauty is ever changing, Catriona, my lass. There are more brides than suitable grooms, so a poor, modestly bonny lass could be left aside. I will travel the length and breadth of the country ere I will allow that. She is a good girl, but more than that, she is all that remains of my wife's family. It was dying out even before the plague struck."

"Who do ye hope to match her with?"

"The bastard son of the fierce Red Logan himself. Now there is a clan to be allied with. Aye, I will be weel pleased to wed Margot to a Logan."

Chapter 4

"Something ails the lad, William."

William Logan smiled at his petite wife as she paced the solar. "A mon can have his moods."

"True, but this is no mere mood. It has lasted since his return from the fair. Cannae ye speak with him? Our visitors are due at any time."

Dropping a kiss upon her forehead, he started out of the room. "I will speak to Gamel, but I make no promises. He has never been reticent, yet has spoken naught of what troubles him now. He may not wish to share it."

He found his son in the great hall of Duncoille, sprawled on a seat beneath one of the large windows. In Gamel's hand dangled some sort of medallion which held his full attention. William realized that his wife had been right to urge him to talk to Gamel. The young man was in too dark and somber a mood to welcome the Delacrosse lass as he should. In the temper Gamel was in the coming meeting with his prospective bride could not possibly go well.

"Gamel?" William was struck by the desolation he saw in his son's glance. "What besets ye?"

Returning his gaze to the medallion, Gamel stared at

all he had left of Sine Catriona. It was all he might ever
have aside from memories. How could he answer his
father? The pain he had felt three days ago when he had
awakened to find her gone still knotted his insides. He
struggled to understand her reasons, but her desertion
was all he could think on.

"What besets me?" he repeated in a soft, sad voice.
"The loss of all I have searched for."

"Are ye certain ye truly held it?"

"Aye, but I had no time, no time at all. Only one night.
In the dawn she slipped away from me."

"Why? Didnae she feel the same?"

"She said she was mine but that she had made a vow
years ago. That vow has yet to be fulfilled. She talked of
some crime which needed to be avenged, things stolen
which needed to be recovered. 'Tis an odd tale."

"I have both the time and the patience to hear it, son."

"My part in it isnae one to be proud of. I didnae act
with much sense or even honor."

"Ah, weel, there are a few things I did in my early years
with Edina that I have little pride in." He sat down next
to Gamel. "When that madness grabs a mon, he sometimes doesnae ken what he does." He grimaced. "Or says
or thinks."

"Madness is the only word for it." Gamel shook his
head as he recalled how he had acted. "God's beard, I
stalked her from the moment I set eyes on her, even
though she was claimed as wife by another mon—
a good mon."

"That is something ye had best not tell your mother."

A faint smile curved Gamel's lips despite his black
mood. Edina was a sweet, loving woman, but she did possess a temper. The crime of adultery was one thing that
could rouse it, for she was a moral woman with a deep
belief in the sanctity of marriage.

"Fear not, Father. 'Twas but a hoax. She wasnae even the mon's leman."

"Why should they lie?"

"In the hope of turning aside the men who desired her."

"Ah, so she is fair then?"

"By God, is she fair. Small, delicate, possessing the complexion of a dark-haired woman but with thick, pale silver hair. It flows to her knees. And her eyes." He shook his head. "Huge eyes the shade of violets."

"Fair indeed. Are ye certain she was neither wife nor leman to the mon?"

"Aye. A wench at the inn told Ligulf that they werenae wed or lovers, that 'twas only a ploy. She kenned them weel. Also, the lass was a virgin. Master Magnus was wounded ere he could enjoy the beauty who stays so faithfully at his side. The wound is such that he never will either."

Gamel winced. "When she told me that, I could only be glad of it. I regret that now. The mon is a conjurer and lightens a few purses, but he is a good mon nevertheless. Truly. I sensed that even as I wished to spit his heart upon my sword for touching Sine Catriona, for having that right. I fear my jealousy isnae eased much now that I ken the truth of their relationship."

"If she stays so faithfully at his side, how did ye come to hold her?"

Gamel told what he had done, and was not at all surprised to see his father frown. "At least I can say that I didnae rape the lass. The heat that burned within me ran as hot in her. Yet she left me. Why? I cannae understand it."

"She didnae explain it, didnae give ye any reason at all?"

"Nay. Weel, she didnae speak to me of it. She went to Ligulf, slipping from my bed ere dawn had lightened the sky. She told him her reasons. She said, 'There are wrongs I must set right. Things stolen that I must regain. Murders I must avenge. My heritage has been stained with blood and treachery. I intend to wipe that stain away.' She said she had vowed to do so six years ago, vowed it for herself and her brothers. She would allow nothing and no one to turn her from it. Not me. Not even her Master Magnus."

"Words worthy of some gallant knight. 'Tis strange to hear them spoken by a conjurer's woman."

"So I thought. And what of this?" He held out the medallion for his father to inspect. "She swore it wasnae stolen. I, and Ligulf, feel she spoke the truth. Yet, how did she get it? No conjurer's woman would own such a fine thing."

"Nay. 'Tis a mystery. Strange, the design seems familiar. It touches some memory, but I cannae grasp it."

"In her I thought I had found all I had sought. Yet, here I sit, alone, left with naught but memories and mysteries."

"Ye mean to search for her?"

"Aye, I do. I am sorry. That girl coming today . . ."

"Dinnae trouble yourself over that. A meeting was arranged, that is all. No promises were made. Howbeit, I will ask ye to think long and hard on this woman ye mean to find. Ye ken little about her. She may be no more than what she appears—a thief and a conjurer's companion. She could be suffering from some delusion, believing she is something she isnae and never could be.

"'Tis true that ye are a bastard, but all your kin openly acknowledge ye. A fine marriage could be made for ye. Ye have gained much honor and wealth fighting for the king and in mercenary service in France. There are also the lands I have given ye. The lass who comes today is but one of many ye could choose from."

"Tell me, Father, if ye were I, if we spoke of Edina, could ye turn your back on what ye might have with her?"

William sighed, then grimaced. "Nay, but I didnae wish ye to act without even a thought upon the other choices ye have."

"And I see no other choices," Gamel murmured as he slipped the medallion back around his neck. "The search may not be as difficult as I fear. Each sixmonth they return to that inn, to that town. I dinnae think they would expect me to be there after so long a time, but I will be."

"Weel, I wish ye luck." After a moment of silence William murmured, "Our guests will be here soon. I ken that there is no chance of a match now, but the game must be played out. We must greet them and entertain them."

"Of course." Gamel stood up. "I will hasten to don my finest clothes. Although I shallnae be ready to greet them the moment they arrive, I swear that ye shall find no other fault in my hospitality."

"Dinnae worry. Our guests will wish to remove the dust of their journey first so there is no need to concern yourself about insulting them. Ye may escort your mother down to the hall for me," he added, smiling faintly.

"My pleasure." Gamel glanced toward the doors of the great hall. "It sounds as if your horde of offspring are heading this way."

"Ah, so they are. I must play nursemaid for a while."

"And I shall flee up to my chambers and swiftly, ere I am also put to that use." Gamel hastened from the hall, pausing to return the effusive greetings of his half siblings as they hurried toward their father.

In his chambers a hot bath awaited him. Gamel wasted no time in making use of it. As he sat enjoying the soothing heat of the water, he stroked the medallion that hung about his neck and swore he would find Sine Catriona. She had eluded him for only a little while. She had not, could not, escape him completely.

As Farthing drove their cart to the bailey of Duncoille, Sine Catriona murmured, " 'Tis a fine, strong keep."

Lord Magnusson, riding his mount alongside their cart, nodded. "One of the strongest in all of Stirlingshire. 'Tis the keep of a mon who kens weel the ways of battle, offensive as weel as defensive. I had the honor of fighting alongside the mon many a time in our younger days. Lord Logan was a mercenary until he wed, gaining land as weel as a wife many men envy him for. That should have been enough but, men being the prideful fools that they are, he felt she needed a titled husband." He grinned when Sine Catriona giggled. "So, he went out and gained his own title through the enviable skill of his sword. Sadly, he also gained many a new scar and lost a few toes, as weel as the sight in one eye. The injuries keep him from fighting anymore, but I believe he is little troubled by that. From what I have seen, he is more than content to stay here at Duncoille with his wife and bairns."

"Here comes your host," drawled Farthing. "And with his brood in tow."

There ensued a confused round of greetings and introductions. Sine Catriona struggled to follow them. As she met her host, Lord William Logan, she barely noticed his battle scars or fearsome looks. It was his fine eyes and gentle smile that held her attention. She felt badly when Margot quaked before the man. The girl's reaction clearly bothered him. She was unsettled a bit herself, however. His rich voice, auburn hair and grin reminded her strongly of Gamel. She was glad to escape to

her chambers for a little while before the memories of
her lover became too overwhelming.

She was not surprised to find that no bath had been
readied for her. She and Farthing had not been expected. She assured the fretting maid that she was well
pleased with the full bowl of heated water she had been
given. A thorough washing freshened Sine Catriona and
restored her composure. After a last check of her appearance she sought the great hall, only to find Farthing
already there, the children gathered around him. He sat
on a bench facing away from the main table, showing the
fascinated children how he could make coins appear
and disappear.

"Holding them enthralled with your meager talents?"
she jibed as she sat by his side, then smiled her thanks at
the page who hastily served her a tankard of mead.

"Meager, is it, wench? And ye can do so much better,
can ye?" he challenged.

"I would ne'er shame ye so before such a large crowd,"
she demurred, fighting a smile.

"Oh ho." William Logan laughed. "The apprentice
challenges the teacher."

"Such ungratefulness is often her way, I fear," Farthing
replied with an excess of drama.

Lord Magnusson laughed. "They often go at each
other so, William." For a moment he watched his son
and Sine Catriona make coins disappear, only to retrieve
them from ever more unusual spots upon one of the giggling children. "The lass is good, nearly as good as Farthing," he murmured. "He told me she was, but I now
see that 'twas not just polite flattery."

"Ye have but just met your son's woman?"

"Aye, William, except that she isnae his woman. I see that
ye share the same surprise that I felt when he told me."

"She is verra fair to look upon."

"Verra, but he met her ere she was a woman grown. It takes only a moment of watching them to see the truth. They are bound to each other, but not as lovers. They are like close kin."

William studied the pair very carefully before nodding. "That must have eased your mind some, since he is now your heir."

"Aye, it did, yet had it been any other way, I could have accepted it. He is now my only child. I thank God more times than I can count for sparing him. The lass is comely and clever. Matters could have been smoothed out. That he might have wed some common wench seemed a pitiful concern when I thought on all I could have lost had he too been taken by the plague. God was verra kind to you during that black time."

"He was. That curse drew near, but its fatal touch ne'er reached us."

"Mayhaps that Devil's concoction was afeared of such a clean place," Lord Magnusson drawled, smiling faintly.

"I ken that ye jest, m'friend, but many of us begin to wonder on just that. Even the lowest of our people work toward that cleanliness, for my wife keeps a watch on all around us. She ne'er raises a hand against any of them, but they struggle to please her. What vermin slip into Duncoille live a verra short life. Rats, lice, fleas—they all breed in dirt. Mayhaps that's the same ground which breeds that Devil's curse. The lack of such dirt is all that makes us different from many another keep. We suffer few other ailments as weel."

"'Tis something to consider. 'Twould explain how the plague can creep into even the most weel-guarded fortress. I sealed myself and mine away, let none in from the time word of it first reached us, yet it still came." He smiled toward his son. "I believe Farthing but outran the death that crept over this land. Since he left my keep years ago, he has settled nowhere."

"Howbeit, he will settle with ye now?"

"Aye, I hope so. And soon I may have Margot settled. . . ."

"She is a fair lass and pleasant-spoken."

"There is a hesitation in your voice, William."

William grimaced faintly. "I wish I could have sent word, but there was not time for it. 'Twas but hours ago that I discovered that the match we had hoped for can never be. The lass . . ."

"Will suffer no great sorrow over it." Lord Magnusson sighed. "She came here just to please me. May I ask what objection your son has to the match?"

"Well, he had none until he returned from a fair. 'Twas held in Dunkennley, a town but a few days' ride from here. When he returned I noticed a darkness in him, a melancholy, but I didnae press for a reason until this morning. His mood wasnae the right one to greet guests with and I had hoped to lighten it."

"Ah, but ye couldnae," Lord Magnusson murmured. "'Twas a sickness of the heart."

"Exactly so. He has seen what a blessing God granted me in Edina and sought the same for himself."

"As any mon with good sense would do."

"Thank ye. He believes he has found that for himself, but the girl slipped away from him."

"And he didnae give chase?"

"He had promised me that he would return to meet ye and Margot. I believe he hoped it would prove to be naught but a strong lusting, a heat in his loins that had robbed him of all sense for a wee while. He now sees that that isnae the way of it."

"Weel, then he should be on his way after her."

"Mayhaps, yet I feel it can do him little harm to

hold back for a bit. It has been only a few days since he first beheld this lass. Time could weel ease her grip upon him."

"Verra true. I hope it does—for his sake. A sickness of the heart is a curse. The young feel it all the more keenly than we older folk. The years have slowly taught us to accept the will of God and the fates. The young cannae always see when 'tis time to bow to them."

Gamel strode into his stepmother's bedchamber, smiling as he watched her check her appearance in a mirror. "Ye look lovely, Mother. No more needs to be done."

"The first meeting is always the hardest for me. Once that ordeal is over, I no longer feel such a need for perfection. That will be all, Mary, thank ye." As the maid left, Edina turned her full attention to Gamel. Her welcoming smile faltered as she studied him very closely.

After enduring her intent study for a moment, Gamel jested, "Have I grown a new eye?"

Her chuckle was brief and faint. "I had thought that your melancholy had eased, but I now see that your smiles float on the surface of darker things."

"I willnae carry my gloom before your guests."

"That isnae what troubles me. I have ne'er seen ye suffer so dark a humor. Does our attempt to find ye a bride displease ye so?"

"It pleased me weel enough before I went afairing. Now I have no interest in it."

"Ye have found the one ye want?"

"Aye, I have, but she slipped away from me. Now I must hunt her down. I will start as soon as our guests have left. I dinnae believe she will be so verra hard to find."

"Did ye speak to your father about this?"

"I told him all of it. I am certain he will tell ye when ye

seek your bed tonight, so there is little need to repeat the whole tale." He grinned when she blushed faintly.

"When ye smile like that, ye look so much like William," she murmured, then shook her head. "I dinnae understand how the woman could walk away from you."

"Thank ye. She did it verra softly whilst I slept." He grimaced. "I acted like some madmon when I woke up alone in my bed."

"She shared your bed? But ye were gone only a few nights."

"I tricked her into my bed, but I swear to you no force was needed to gain my prize. Her blood ran as hot as mine. The fever that gripped me was a shared one. Ah, and now ye may set aside the thought I can see forming in your mind, Mother. She was a virgin. S'truth, that was a gift I hadnae expected." He shook his head. "Yet, still she left me. Even though she said she was mine, mine no matter what might come between us."

"*But* she didnae say that she would stay, did she?"

Gamel stared at Edina blankly for a moment, then muttered, "Weel, mayhaps not in words . . ."

"Ah. A silent vow? That is no vow at all. Tell me, did ye ask her to stay with ye? No need to reply, I can see by the look upon your face that ye didnae. Mayhaps if ye had she would have told ye that she couldnae stay and why. Then ye wouldnae be so troubled with questions about her leaving. And did ye tell her what future ye had planned?"

"Weel, nay, I didnae, but . . ." he began a little weakly.

"Then how was she to ken it? She was left to wonder why ye wished her to stay and what for. Did ye mean her to be your leman or your wife or simply an amusement for a wee while? These are the questions she would have asked herself.

"A woman cannae read a mon's mind. And when a

mon can find pleasure in any woman's body, why should she *not* wonder? Such things must be spoken aloud, Gamel. A woman kens that at such moments her heart cannae be trusted."

"And does my father speak all his thoughts aloud?" Gamel snapped, annoyed by the indisputable wisdom of all Edina said.

"Not always but, do remember, he and I have been together for many years. There are times when he doesnae need to speak. I ken him so weel that words are unnecessary. I am also his wife *and* he has told me that he loves me. These are important things that must be said. 'Tis such knowledge that gives a woman the strength and freedom to follow her heart."

"I thought I had time. What flamed between us was so verra strong."

"As it was between William and me from the moment we set eyes upon each other. Yet, we doubted each other at the start. Now, when ye find your lass again, ye *must* let her ken exactly what future ye plan for her, what ye mean to be to her. Believe me, things will flow more smoothly if ye do."

"Ye dinnae ask me about her birth or her dowry."

"From the moment ye claimed she was the one ye have searched for, I kenned that it would be useless to speak about such things. Ye dinnae need me to remind ye what ye can gain or lose by marriage. If she is what your heart craves then I shall find no fault with her, even if she is a tavern whore's bastard who owns no more than what she wears upon her back."

"Thank ye for that, Mother. Howbeit, ye may be at ease concerning her blood, or so I believe." He showed Edina the medallion he wore. "She left me this, claiming it was rightfully hers. No lowborn tavern wench would own such a thing. These are the baubles of the weelborn."

"True." Edina frowned as she studied the medallion's design closely. "Strange, it seems familiar to me."

"Do ye recognize the crest then?"

"I think I do, but I cannae put a name to it."

"Yet, it troubles you."

"Aye, I fear so, although I cannae say just why. This may sound foolish to ye, 'tis but a feeling I have. . . ."

"'Tis only a fool who would ignore *your* feelings. They have proved right far too often."

"Weel, this crest makes me feel, not afraid, but worried. Anxious. Mayhaps I ken of some dark tale attached to it, but I cannae recall it just now. The family which bears that crest may weel have a troubled history."

"She did speak of murder and theft, of wrongs she needed to set right." He shook his head. "She spoke just like a mon set upon some quest for vengeance."

"A woman can feel so, Gamel. Women can feel hate as deeply as any mon. They can want blood for blood. They simply lack the strength to act upon their feelings and often have to turn to men to see their need for vengeance sated."

"She didnae turn to me."

"I shouldnae take that so to heart. Mayhaps she didnae ken that ye had the means to aid her."

"Ah, true. I did tell her verra little about myself. I thought I had time for that later."

"Weel, there is yet another thing ye must set right when ye find her."

"And I *will* find her."

"Aye, I think ye will." Edina frowned, then began to smile as the sound of running feet approached her door. "I believe one of my children has slipped free of

William's rein. In truth, mayhaps he let it happen to remind me I am somewhat late."

Even as she spoke, little Lilith burst into the room, her young face alight with excitement. Gamel smothered a laugh as the five-year-old stood impatiently while Edina gently lectured her on the lapse in proper conduct for a lady. Lilith was rarely concerned with such matters.

"I am verra sorry, Mama, but I *needed* to hurry," Lilith said.

"Ye have news of such great importance, do ye?" Edina smiled at her daughter.

"Oh, aye. We have a guest ye *must* come to see."

"I was just leaving to go to the hall."

"Oh, Mama, there is a mon down there who does tricks."

"Tricks, loving? What sort of tricks?"

"He can . . . he can make coins disappear then come back. He even made one come right out of my ear. And he does clever things with cards too. Ye *must* come and see."

"Has Lord Magnusson brought a conjurer with him to entertain us then?"

Lilith vigorously shook her head. "The mon is his son, Mama, but he can still do tricks."

"Are ye sure, dearling? 'Tis strange that a laird's son would do tricks like some conjurer."

"But he does, Mama. He does. And he looks *just* like his papa."

Gamel suddenly recalled Lord Magnusson's looks and fought the hope growing inside of him. He still felt compelled to ask, "Is the mon tall, slender, and dark?"

"Aye, Gamel. Just like that. And, oh Mama, he has such bonny hands." Lilith looked at her own childish and somewhat plump hands. "They are so long and . . . graceful."

"Is he alone?" pressed Gamel.

"He is with his papa."

It was difficult not to shout at the child, but Gamel suppressed the urge. He had learned long ago that the only way to gain information from a child was with patience. Little Lilith could not possibly realize how important the matter was to him.

"I ken that, dearling. What I meant was—is there someone with him besides his papa? Mayhaps a woman and two young lads?" He tensed as he awaited her reply.

Lilith frowned severely for a moment. "Aye. They are with him. She can do tricks too. The lads can too, but not as many. Oh, Mama, ye will want to see the lads. They look alike, just the same, more than Colin and Cospatrick."

"Ah, so they are twins as weel then?" Edina asked.

"Aye, that is it. Twins. 'Tis hard to see which is which." Lilith shrugged. "Their sister kens."

Crouching before his tiny half sister, Gamel took her small hands in his and asked in a tense voice, "Do ye ken what their names are?"

"I think so. The lady is called Catriona." She scowled a moment, then brightened. "The lads are named Dane and Ree."

"And the mon, Lilith? What is the mon's name?"

"'Tis a funny name," she mumbled.

"Farthing? Is his name Farthing?"

"Aye, that is it. Although, I call him Master Magnusson as I should," she added with a glance toward Edina for a nod of approval, which was quickly given. "The lady has verra pretty eyes, Gamel."

"Violets. They are like violets," he whispered in a hoarse voice as he slowly stood up.

Lilith nodded. "Big, big violets. And she has skin like gold. She is so bonny. Mayhaps she is a princess."

"One can never ken, child," Edina murmured absently.

Edina watched her stepson a little nervously. Gamel had gone very pale, but there was a glitter to his eyes which, after so many years of marriage to a passionate man, she recognized all too well. The mere thought that the girl might be near at hand had sent desire racing through his veins. It had gripped him with such strength he almost smelled of it. Edina was not sure that intensity was safe. There was no knowing how a man in such a state would act.

"It has to be her," Gamel muttered. "It has to be."

"Now, Gamel," she urged even as he started out of the room, "it would appear so, but ye should move warily. If it *is* her, ye dinnae wish to afright her, do ye?"

"If 'tis her, I shall chain her to the bed," he growled as he picked up speed. "This time she shallnae creep away from me at dawn's light. By all that is sacred, she shall *not*." He began to race down the hallway toward the stairs.

"Oh, sweet Mary, here is trouble." Edina sighed as she started after him.

"Mama," cried Lilith as she hurried to keep pace with her mother. "Ye said that lasses must *not* run and ye are running verra fast."

"Running is the only way I can catch up with Gamel, dearling," she answered as she lifted her skirts a little and began to run faster. "And I think it is verra important that I do that now. More important than behaving like a lady."

Totally unconcerned about the attention he was drawing to himself and the fact that his stepmother was hot on his heels, Gamel raced toward the great hall. He was stunned yet alive with emotion. While he dared not believe that fate would be so kind as to place Sine Catriona beneath his very own roof, all Lilith had told him indicated that that was exactly what had happened. It was almost frightening. He realized that he was reluctant to go and see for himself, afraid to discover that fate was playing a cruel jest on him. It was not just the running that had his heart beating at an alarming rate.

A small voice in his head told him that he was acting like some madman, that this was no way to behave when there were guests at Duncoille. Every other part of him, however, told him to hurry. He could not fully shake the fear that, if he did not rush, the one he hoped to find in the hall would vanish as she had before. A long search for Sine Catriona was something he had begun to resign himself to.

"Gamel! Gamel, will ye slow down?"

Edina's voice was not all that caused Gamel's steps to falter near the doorway of the great hall. He had entered battles with far surer steps than those with which he was entering the hall. He had faced the possibility of death with far more calm than he was facing the chance of seeing one tiny female. That realization gave him the strength to enter the hall with surer and slower steps.

"Ah, I see," drawled a recognizable male voice. "Ye mean to show the children the way to wipe their chins."

"Farthing, I shall demonstrate true skill despite your raillery."

That sweet, husky voice caused Gamel to come to an abrupt halt only two steps inside the great hall. "Sine."

"Gamel," Edina whispered as she reached his side. "Step slowly."

He barely heard his stepmother's words of caution. His full attention was upon the group in the hall. There was no mistaking Farthing or the twins, but his interest rested upon them only briefly. His gaze was fixed upon the owner of that seductive voice. She stood amongst his half siblings, but it took a moment to believe what he was seeing.

As though starved for the sight of her, he simply stood and stared. He stared until he felt belief grip him, until he was certain it was really her. Her every movement brought memories that heated his blood. The sound of her voice caused his need for her to swiftly rise. He ignored his father's look of concern and shook off his stepmother's light grip upon his arm. This time Sine Catriona would not escape.

Chapter 5

"Sine."

Sine Catriona froze, her hands clenching tightly on the linen cloth she had been using to do a trick for the children. She did not really need to see the look upon Farthing's or the twins' faces. She knew exactly who stood only feet away. The voice was hoarse and soft, but it was one she would never forget. Slowly, she turned to see the very last person she had expected to meet striding purposefully toward her.

"Gamel," she whispered as he halted before her.

She did not move as he reached for her. With visibly unsteady hands he tore her headdress from her head. The faint look of lingering disbelief upon his face vanished as her hair cascaded free of its bonds. She gave a soft cry of surprise when he grasped her by the shoulders and gave her a shake. If the look upon his face was any indication, the man was suffering a tumult of emotions.

"This time, Sine Catriona, ye willnae slip away at dawn."

Before she could respond, Gamel was abruptly torn from her. Farthing stood between them. Her shock was quickly pushed aside by fear. The anger that had seized Farthing back at the inn had returned in full. With the threat that had tied his hands before now gone, she doubted even consideration for her feelings would deter him. Farthing had suffered a deep injury that had cut at his pride and manhood. He clearly felt a strong need to avenge that wound.

When Farthing drew his sword on Gamel, Lord Magnusson cried, "Nay! We are guests, Farthing. Ye cannae draw a sword upon the mon's son beneath his verra own roof."

"Then we shall draw swords outside," hissed Gamel as he resheathed his own sword, which he had drawn the moment Farthing had come between him and Sine.

Racing to her stunned husband's side, Edina urged, "Do something, William."

"I am not sure there is verra much I can do, sweeting."

"Methinks the lass is about to try," murmured Lord Magnusson.

William nodded. "If anyone can stop this, Thomas, 'tis her."

Sine heard their soft words and prayed they were right as she hastily plotted her next move. After signaling to her brothers, who nodded in understanding, she put herself between Gamel and Farthing. They reminded her very strongly of bristling dogs. It was difficult not to think of herself as some bone—or worse, some bitch in heat—that they were snarling over.

"Move aside, Sine Catriona," commanded Farthing. "Ye willnae stop this."

"What is done is done," she said in a vain attempt to soothe him. "There is naught which can be gained by a battle now."

"There is much to gain. He stole from both of us."

Gamel met and held Farthing's glare. "And I feel the need to be rid of his constant interference."

Inwardly, Sine cursed their intransigence. "I demand that ye cease this fighting at once."

"Ye have no say in this," snapped Farthing.

At the same time, Gamel growled, "This isnae your battle, Sine."

They both pushed her out of their way. Sine quickly glanced at her brothers, who nodded, relieved that they had accomplished their task as she had accomplished her own. She made no further attempt to stop the men. She watched calmly as they strode out of the great hall. Unlike the rest of the people who raced after the quarreling pair, she followed at a slightly more leisurely pace, her young brothers flanking her. She briefly paused behind the worried parents of Gamel and Farthing.

"William." Edina clutched her husband's arm. "She didnae stop them so now ye must do so."

"Dearling, as I said, there is little that can be done. Ye dinnae ken the full tale."

"Are ye saying that there is a good reason for them to want to cut away at each other?"

"A verra good reason. Gamel served Farthing a deep shame and Gamel is jealous."

Sine Catriona was not sure that latter conclusion was right, but she said nothing as she slipped around the group just in time to see Gamel and Farthing again reach for their swords. She could not help but smile as they clutched then gaped at their empty scabbards. Then their expressions slowly changed. She was not surprised when they looked her way, bringing everyone else's confused gazes to her as well.

"Looking for these?" she queried with false innocence as the twins held up the swords they had stolen when the men were still squabbling back inside the great hall. A ripple of surprise and amusement went through the crowd gathering in the bailey.

"Ye took my sword," Gamel mumbled in utter disbelief.

"So sharp of wit," she mocked.

Gamel glared at those onlookers who could not fully restrain a laugh, then fixed his fury upon Sine. "Hand it back to me, woman."

Being called "woman" in that particular tone of voice did little to soothe Sine's rising temper. "Nay, this 'woman' will not. Nor will this 'woman' return these." She held up the daggers she had neatly stolen from them while caught between them in the great hall.

"God's beard." William choked out the words as he struggled not to laugh. "The lass has disarmed them."

"Aye, she has, husband," murmured Edina. "Howbeit, they now look ready to fight with her."

That was an observation Sine heartily agreed with. It was an effort for her not to retreat from the glares Farthing and Gamel were directing her way. She found little comfort in the knowledge that, for the moment, the adversaries were united. Telling herself not to be such a coward, she straightened her shoulders and glared right back at them.

"Now ye cannae fight each other." She could see that few people really believed that.

"Can we not?" Farthing delivered a sound punch to Gamel's jaw.

Grimacing with distaste, Sine watched Gamel quickly retaliate with a strong blow to Farthing's stomach, and the fight began in earnest. Farthing doubled up, but even as he gasped for breath, he lunged at Gamel's legs. In an instant both men lay sprawled in the dirt. Gamel managed to extricate himself from beneath Farthing, but by the time he got to his feet, Farthing was also up and swinging at him. The bailey echoed with the sounds of fists striking flesh, and the grunts of the men pummeling each other. It was not long before Gamel and Farthing were smeared with blood and dust. Sine shook her head over the foolishness of men.

Her disgust deepened when she saw how the majority of the spectators who had gathered in the bailey were thoroughly enjoying the fight. Even Lord Magnusson and Lord Logan loudly joined in the riotous calls of encouragement. She looked around, but she could find only one observer who appeared to share her disgust. Sine quickly moved to Lady Logan's side. She touched the woman's sleeve and prayed that she would find a sympathetic and helpful ally.

"Ye are Lady Logan?" she asked.

Edina tore her gaze from the fight to look closely at the girl who had stirred such a fever in Gamel. She could not decide which was more startling—the girl's silver-white hair or her huge violet eyes. Inwardly, Edina suddenly grinned as she thought a little whimsically that Gamel and Sine would make a very colorful couple.

It took a moment, but Edina forced herself to be serious again, to try to look beyond the girl's beauty. None of her inner senses, which had proven correct so often in the past, raised a warning. Edina could find nothing about Sine to trouble her. The girl met her intent gaze without wavering, those violet eyes clear and honest.

"Aye, I am Lady Logan."

"I humbly beg your pardon for all of this trouble, m'lady."

"Bah, 'tisnae your doing, child. 'Tis but the foolishness of men. Howbeit, I do heartily thank ye for disarming the young hotheads."

"It was naught, m'lady. In truth, I could wish that I hadnae been so clever." She frowned at the men wrestling in the dirt. "A quick thrust with a sword would be far cleaner than this."

Edina laughed softly and nodded. "There will be many bruises and much moaning." She shook her head as she watched Farthing and Gamel. "This willnae cease until they are both senseless."

"Oh, weel, I had thought about how to stop it before that happens."

"I would like to do that too, but I cannae see how it can be done."

"I think it can be, m'lady. 'Tis a trick my father used to part dogs. It can work as weel with men, I think."

"Then let us try it. What do we need?"

"Two buckets of water. Cold water if possible. The colder the better."

Giggling faintly as she realized what was to be done, Edina took Sine by the arm and they hurried to find what they would need. In a few moments, full buckets in hand, they took up positions on either side of Farthing and Gamel. Edina grimaced as she saw how Farthing tried to pin Gamel to the ground.

"Cease this fighting at once," she ordered.

After a moment, Sine shook her head. "They willnae listen to us, m'lady. Best be careful of your skirts."

Sine and Lady Edina took great care not to soak each other. They held their buckets out as far as they could and arched their bodies away. Sine decided that they probably looked somewhat comical themselves as they emptied the buckets of icy water over the wrestling men. Sine took a hasty step back when Farthing and Gamel cursed viciously and abruptly parted. She noticed that Lady Edina had done the same. It was hard not to step back even farther when, still sputtering and dashing water from their faces, both men glared at her and Lady Edina. Some of the people who had been watching the fight grumbled a complaint, but one glance from Lord William silenced them all.

"Why have ye put an end to this fight?" demanded Gamel.

"Aye," snapped Farthing. "Why? I was winning."

"Winning?" Gamel yelled as he staggered to his feet, slipping a little on the now muddy ground.

Farthing stood up as well, meeting and matching Gamel's furious stare. "Aye—winning."

Edina swung her bucket toward both young men, lightly winging each. "Hush. Enough of this squabbling. 'Tis over. I declare ye both winners."

"There cannae he two winners," grumbled Gamel, rubbing his ribs as he became more aware of his many aches and pains.

Wiping a hand over his bleeding split lip, Farthing narrowly eyed Gamel. "As a guest here, I suppose 'twould be best to agree to that and thus placate my host's stung vanity."

"Stung vanity, is it?" Gamel hissed.

"I said—enough of this." Edina gave each of them a cross look. "If being declared both winners doesnae suit ye, then I shall declare ye both losers. There is no need to beat each other senseless to prove it."

"They are weel matched," murmured William as he reached his wife's side.

"Aye, lads," added Lord Magnusson, joining them. "'Twas a good fight."

"Lads?" Farthing twitched his bruised lips in a half smile. "I am seven and twenty, Father."

"No need to tell me that. I ken your age as weel as I ken my own. For each year ye gain, so gain I. I am thinking, howbeit, that ye will be a lad to me e'en after ye give me grandchildren."

"Aye," agreed William, laughing softly. "And long after that."

Gamel frowned, wondering why Lord Magnusson spoke of grandchildren. He then decided that the man had not yet been informed of Farthing's injury. It was understandable that Farthing would hesitate to tell his father that he was no longer virile. He quickly turned his full attention to Sine. Grabbing her by the arm, he tugged her to his side, ignoring her scowl.

"Speaking on the begetting of grandchildren," he said, "ye must find me a priest, Father."

"A priest?" squeaked Sine, gaping at him.

"Aye—a priest."

Farthing grabbed her by her other arm and yanked her to his side before she could respond. "Yet again ye try to lay claim to what isnae yours."

"She isnae yours and never has been." Gamel yanked her back toward him. "That was proven."

Sine yanked free with a sharp cry of annoyance and swung her heavy bucket at both men, her anger increasing when they ducked and completely avoided it. She knew it was dangerous to swing such a weighty thing at the men, but she had a strong urge to injure them, if only in some small, insignificant, but highly uncomfortable way. "Cease all of this pulling at me. Ye will split me asunder and then there truly will be need of a priest."

"There is need of one now," bellowed Gamel as he neatly wrenched her bucket from her grasp, tossed it away, then tugged her back to his side.

When Farthing reached for her again, she pulled out the daggers she had stolen from them. "I said to cease or I shall bury your own steel in your flesh. What need do ye have for a priest?" she demanded of Gamel.

"To wed us."

Even though she had half suspected that would be his

answer, Sine was still shocked. A large part of her thrilled to the idea of being married to Gamel. It eased all of her fears that he saw his feeling for her as no more than a passing lust, fed and forgotten. Nevertheless, she had to fight that weakness, and the urge to cry out an immediate aye. Her deep-seated need to fulfill her old vow had to come first. She needed to be free to seek retribution and revenge, to vanquish the fear she had carried for so many years.

"I am not free to wed." She discovered that it hurt to say those words and she struggled against the inclination to take them right back.

"Nay? Ye arenae wed to this rogue." Gamel spared a brief glare toward Farthing before scowling at Sine. "That was a lie. Janet told Ligulf all about it."

"She is still mine," Farthing yelled.

"She was never yours nor any mon's." Gamel indicated Ligulf, Blane, and Lesley with a curt wave of his hand. "There stand three men to vouchsafe my claim that no mon had kenned Sine before me."

A bright blush flooded Sine's cheeks at this deeply personal revelation, which caused her to be the center of a great deal of interest. She hissed, "Three is quite enough. Ye need not make it hundreds by telling all who are gathered here. And it matters not. I am still not free to wed."

"And why not? Ye are not his wife, his lover, or his kin. Unless ye are his serf, ye are free. And I will call ye a liar if ye try to tell me he holds ye as chattel. Ye are free and we shall be married."

Infuriated by his arrogance, she snapped, "Ye ken nothing, absolutely nothing, about me."

"I care nothing about the past or even your blood-line."

He sounded so sincere that she was taken aback for a

moment but quickly recovered. "Nay? Heed this—my mother is a whore, a base intriguer and a murderess."

"Then we are weel matched, for so was mine."

Although shocked, she was also curious, but she knew that now was not the time to satisfy that curiosity. "I am a thief."

"Do a penance then. Once ye are my wife ye will have no need to provide for yourself in such a manner." He grabbed her by the shoulders and gave her a little shake. "And I willnae hear ye speak of that again," he ordered.

His intransigence as well as his commanding air angered her. "I begin to think that your head is made of hollowed wood, for my words enter in one ear and flee straight out of the other," she snapped. "Would ye force me to wed ye?"

"Aye, if need be."

"Weel, there is a strange wooing."

"Ye give a mon no time for courtship."

Before she could continue the argument, a soldier hurried up to Lord Logan, briefly drawing everyone's attention. "My laird, a page stands at our gates," he announced. "He comes to request a night's shelter for his master's party."

"And who is his master?" Lord William asked.

"Sir Malise Brodie, baron of Dorchabeinn. The party is but an hour's journey away, mayhaps less."

Beneath his hands, which still rested lightly upon Sine's shoulders, Gamel felt her shudder. "What is wrong?"

Farthing moved to grasp the soldier by the arm and demanded in a hoarse voice, "Who did ye say approaches?"

"Sir Malise Brodie, baron of Dorchabeinn," the man replied while warily eyeing Farthing.

Without another word, Farthing snatched his sword

from Barre. Gamel was forced to release his hold upon
Sine when Dane thrust his sword toward him. He could
almost smell the tension and fear that had seized the
group, though he could not fathom the cause.

"Get to the cart," Farthing ordered the twins even as
he reached for Sine.

Gamel quickly tugged Sine to his side and demanded,
"Where do ye hie to now?"

Lord Magnusson spoke up quickly. "Son, the cart
cannae be readied so swiftly. They are too close already."

"Then they must hide inside of it until it can be readied. Let her go," Farthing commanded Gamel.

"Nay, she stays here."

The very thought of facing her enemies when she
was so unprepared freed Sine from the shock that had
held her silent and motionless. "Nay," she cried as she
yanked free of Gamel's hold. "Not now."

Edina placed her hand upon Gamel's arm when he
moved toward Sine again. "'Tis clear that ye have no
wish to meet with these people. Ye shall risk doing just
that if ye try to flee now, even as they enter. They draw
nigh as we speak. Why are ye so reluctant to face the
Brodies?"

"'Tis true—we cannae meet them, but there is no time
for me to explain it all now," Sine answered. "I swear to
ye on my father's grave, 'tis no mere matter of dislike.
'Tis life and death, m'lady. Can they be refused entry?"

"Not without good reason, and as ye say, there is no
time left for ye to give me one. Ligulf, take the lass and
her brothers to my chambers. They will be verra safe
there," Edina assured a frowning Farthing. "'Tis the
one room no guest would dare to enter unless asked to
do so."

"I will have the reason for this," Lord Logan finally said.

"Aye, m'lord," Sine agreed as she moved to follow

Ligulf and her brothers. "I will tell ye all ye might wish to ken about it as soon as the Brodies have left."

William ordered that no one in the household speak of the presence of Sine and her brothers. Farthing was not sure he shared the big man's confidence that his command would be obeyed or that it would be relayed to all within Duncoille before the Brodies arrived. However, he knew he had little choice in the matter. As soon as William ordered his man to tell the waiting page that his master was welcome, he turned his attention to Farthing. Farthing tensed, not sure of what might happen next.

"Ye cannae say anything about this now?" demanded William.

"Nay—truly. 'Twould take more time than we have," replied Farthing. "Neither do I dare to speak upon it when the Brodies lurk within these walls. Sine didnae lie when she claimed that it was a matter of life and death, m'lord. I swear to ye, she has committed no crime against these people. Ye arenae sheltering her from their justice. That is all I dare say right now."

"'Twill suffice. I have met this baron but once. 'Twas enough. It troubles me not at all to hide someone from him. He willnae discover your friends."

"Thank ye, m'lord." Farthing suddenly caught sight of the medallion Gamel wore. "Hide that or all shall be lost," he ordered in a hoarse voice.

"Do ye think me incapable of protecting my own?" Gamel muttered even as he quickly tucked it beneath the neck of his jupon. "Is this why ye demand that we hide everything and everyone?"

"When all is revealed, ye will understand why hiding is the only way to act at this time." Farthing suddenly smiled faintly. "Once her fear has eased, 'twill sorely trouble wee Sine Catriona to be hiding away."

* * *

Immediately upon entering the large, well-appointed chambers of Lord and Lady Logan, Sine rushed to see if she could observe the arrival of the Brodies. Though disappointed that she could not see into the front bailey, she told herself it was for the best. If she was peering out of some window, there was always the chance that the Brodies could catch sight of her.

"What do ye search for?" asked Ligulf, who followed her as she went from window to window in the chambers. "None can gain entry to these rooms through the windows. Ye must ken that."

She smiled at the youth. "Aye, I ken it. 'Tis not possible attack points for which I search, but some place from which to view the Brodies as they arrive. And to do so safely."

"Come." Ligulf gently took her by the arm. "The nursery lies behind these doors. From that room ye will be able to view most all that occurs in the bailey." He grabbed a cloth from a table as he passed it and handed it to her. "If ye cover your hair ye will appear naught but a curious maid if any chance to look up."

"Ah, good. I was worried about being seen."

"That hair cannae be too common."

"Nay, 'tis not. I myself ken of but one other who has hair like this," she murmured as she finished wrapping the cloth about her head and edged up to the window, the twins close behind her.

Her heart began to beat at a furious pace. However, she was not sure of the emotion which prompted the response. Fear lurked within her, but so did myriad other emotions. It had been six long years since she had set eyes upon the ones she sought vengeance against. While the fear that had driven her to flee her home was forever with her, she now found that she resented the need to hide. She wanted to face her foes, to accuse them, to make them suffer for their many crimes. It was a desire she fought to subdue, for she knew the time was not yet right.

"Why do ye refuse to wed Gamel?" Ligulf asked as he stood beside her.

Not shifting her gaze from the gates of Duncoille, she answered Ligulf's soft inquiry. "If I wed him then I am bound to him. For now I must be free of all bonds."

"But there would also be strength in such a union. That is needed in any battle."

"One swordsmon, no matter how strong and skilled, isnae enough."

Before Ligulf was able to correct her erroneous impression by telling her that if Gamel joined her fight he would not do so alone, the Brodies entered Duncoille. He frowned when she grew alarmingly pale. Her eyes grew bright with an emotion he could not read clearly. A hundred questions crowded his mind, but he struggled for patience. He would wait to hear the tale just as the others had to do.

Edina was hurrying to clean Gamel's cuts before the Brodies arrived. "I wish courtesy didnae demand that we welcome these people," Edina mumbled as she smoothed a dampened cloth over his brow.

"Ye dinnae like them, m'lady?" Farthing asked, quickly wiping the dirt from his own face.

She gave him a faint smile. "I have 'feelings' about people. Some folk may decry them as naught but foolishness, yet they havenae failed me yet. Not once."

"Or failed us," added Gamel.

"And ye have feelings about the Brodies?" Farthing pressed.

"Aye. The baron caused my blood to chill. A darkness rests within that mon. I could read it in his eyes. His smooth words, pretty manners, and fine clothes could-nae hide it from me. I am not one who is easily deceived by such things. I met him just once. I am little pleased to have to meet him again."

Farthing nodded. "Have ye met his wife as weel then?"

"Nay. We met the mon whilst we were at court. She did attend with him, but we never had the chance to see her. William and I were leaving just as they arrived. She was resting, I suppose. Still, I couldnae help but pity the woman who is bound to such a mon."

"Dinnae," Farthing said in a cold, flat voice. "Those two are weel matched."

"Ye ken who they are?" Gamel demanded.

"Aye, Sir Gamel, though I have never met them. Beware of them even though they are guests for but one night. Honor is nothing to them. They deal in treachery and death. Even as they smile and feast at your table, they will slip a dagger between your ribs without hesita-tion if they think they can gain from the act. Each one of their party, mon or woman, should be seen as a spy."

"'Tis clear that a nest of vipers is about to slither into my home," Edina drawled.

"Aye, that says it aright, m'lady."

"Dinnae frown so, Master Magnusson," Lady Logan replied. "I dinnae scorn your words. In truth, they but confirm what I feel. Howbeit, there is no turning them away at this time. We can only watch them closely and be wary."

Edina sent him a reassuring smile. "Your friends will be secure where they are. When the time comes to seek our beds, they will be moved through a little kenned passage into a pair of secret rooms. I would place them there right now but the rooms are dark and verra small, more like prison cells. They were made for hiding, not for comfort. Gamel can slip away later and move the lass and her brothers." She ignored Farthing's dark scowl, an expression repeated by Gamel when she added, "Ye will share Gamel's chambers during the night."

Gamel glanced at her. "Dinnae ye fear that we might kill each other before the morning dawns?"

"Nay, my son. I believe that your sense of hospitality will prevail over your petty quarrel."

"Petty quarrel?" he snapped. "'Tis no petty quarrel. He means to hold from me that which is mine."

"Catriona isnae yours," insisted Farthing.

"Cease, will ye?" Edina ordered in exasperation. "Our guests are entering now through the gates. If ye werenae so occupied with glowering at each other, ye would see that. Your actions could easily draw their curiosity. That would be verra unwise."

After one last fulminating glare at Farthing, Gamel gritted his teeth against any further argument. He was not sure what lay behind Sine's fear of the Brodies, but her fear was enough to win his caution. She felt that the Brodies were a threat to her. For now, he would accept that as fact and offer what protection he could.

He knew his impatience would be the hardest feeling to quell, harder than curiosity or his urge to argue with Farthing. Sine was within reach, but he was forced to wait at a distance. He could not fully dispel the fear that Sine would somehow manage to slip away from him again. It was going to require a real effort not to stand guard over her constantly to insure that she would still be within his reach after the Brodies left.

Even so, as he stood watching the unwelcome guests arrive, he had to fight the urge to join Sine in his stepmother's chambers. His body ached with need for Sine. He had never experienced such a fever for a woman. Although he had been seeking just that for a long time, he was not sure he liked it. He could not help but wonder if the benefits could ever outweigh the travails of such a condition. Shaking away those thoughts, he forced his attention to the Brodies.

"They adorn themselves as if they are royalty," muttered Farthing.

Gamel nodded, grimacing with distaste and seeing that expression briefly reflected in Edina's face. "They are weighted down with jewels and fine silks whilst their vassals shiver in rags."

"Aye. The vassals have the pinched, hungry look of the abused. 'Tis the men-at-arms who worry me," Farthing said.

"Mercenaries. The worst of their breed. Not the sort my father was in his youth."

"Nay, these men hold allegiance only to coin. They are loyal only as long as they are paid or no better offer comes along."

"And while they maintain that tenuous loyalty, there is no act too dishonorable for them to perform. There could be trouble in the soldiers' quarters tonight, mayhaps even a death or two."

"Ye cannae house them apart from your own men?"

"Nay," Gamel replied. "I wish we could. There isnae the room, and such an act of inhospitality could raise questions we dinnae want to answer just yet. That the baron hires such men tells me a lot about him."

"And all of it bad," murmured Farthing. "These men were hired for reasons other than to fill the ranks of an army. Trust me in this—the baron is as low in character as his hirelings."

Frowning, Gamel closely studied the man who was

now approaching his father. Lord Malise Brodie was lean and not ill-favored. The richness of his attire and the profusion of jewels upon his person were nearly blinding. However, they failed to fully hide the sly look in the man's eyes.

Accustomed over the years to Edina's feelings about people, Gamel had begun the careful study of people's faces and mannerisms. Although some called it fancy, he had soon discerned certain features and actions which could tell him nearly as much about the person's character as Edina's feelings told her. His method so often brought results close to hers that he could not totally discard it.

Lord Brodie was a handsome man and his smile was courteous, yet Gamel distrusted it. It had the air of a well-practiced gesture. The man's eyes were heavy-lidded, his gaze shielded from view. Gamel was certain that, beneath those lowered eyelids, Lord Brodie was surveying Duncoille and its people, their strengths and especially their weaknesses. The way the man moved, his every gesture and smile, also told Gamel that here was a man to watch and watch very closely. Sine Catriona's deep fear had alerted him to the dangers, but as he continued to study Lord Brodie, he admitted to himself that he might initially have been fooled by the man otherwise.

"I thank ye for your kindness, Sir William." Sir Malise's voice was smooth, almost like a purr. "Ye as weel, dear Lady Edina. Bandits abound in the area these days. I feared for my dear wife's safety if we tried to continue on towards Stirling with the night drawing near."

"Aye," murmured William. "Travel grows more treacherous every day."

"True, and the road to Stirling is weel watched by thieves, for they ken that those of better birth and circumstance must travel it to attend the king's court at Stirling Castle. I have often cursed the lack of some other route from our keep to the king. Howbeit, in a fine, sturdy keep such as this one we shall feel most secure."

"I hope so, Sir Malise—ye and your lady wife."

"Have ye met my lady wife?"

"Nay," Edina replied. "The opportunity has ever passed us by."

"Ah, then allow me to introduce her." He took the hand of the woman who moved to stand next to him. "My wife—Lady Arabel Brodie."

When Gamel finally turned his full attention to the baron's wife, he grew deaf to the introductions and murmured courtesies. He responded out of habit, not thought. He struggled to dispel the image before him. Nothing altered what he saw.

He saw huge violet eyes that were achingly familiar to him. From beneath an ornate, rich headdress a few strands of silver-white hair showed themselves. There was a distressing familiarity to the deep husky tones of Lady Brodie's voice even though her words were tainted with a cool insincerity as she expressed delight in meeting them.

There were some subtle differences. Gamel struggled to fix upon those in the hope of shaking away the conclusion that was taking shape in his mind. Her nose was sharper than Sine's. There was a hardness in the lovely eyes and that full mouth despite the brief come-hither look she cast his way, a look which told him that she held a hunger which, if satisfied, might give those eyes a passing softness. The subtle differences between Sine Catriona and Arabel grew a little clearer the longer he stared, but he could not dispel his conclusion.

A quick glance toward his parents and friends told him that he was not alone in his shock. They hid it well enough, but one as knowledgeable of them as he was could still read it in their faces and movements. Lord Magnusson studied the tips of his boots, a clear ploy to hide his expression until he could control it.

It was in Farthing's black eyes that Gamel found his final confirmation. When he briefly met the man's gaze, he saw no sign of shock, no surprise, no confusion. There was, however, a flash of warning—a warning to be silent. Farthing wanted him to give no sign of the fact that he found himself face-to-face with a woman whose looks nearly matched Sine's. Gamel could no longer argue away his own conclusion—Lady Arabel Brodie was Sine's mother.

Chapter 6

"Life or death?" Lord Logan asked as he and Farthing entered the great hall. The guests had refreshed themselves and were now assembling for dinner.

Farthing calmly met Lord Logan's gaze as he answered the hushed question. "Aye. I swear it upon my immortal soul, m'lord." He glanced toward one of the Brodie retinue who lurked close by them.

"Aye," muttered William, briefly glaring at the man Farthing had noticed. "I am spied upon in my own hall, a sore abuse of my hospitality. Daylight cannae come too soon for my liking." He glanced toward Lady Brodie as he led Farthing to the head table. "And that wench eyes ye verra hungrily, m'lad."

"And ye, m'lord. Best beware or your lady wife might become jealous," he teased.

William grinned. "Do ye think so?" He shared a soft chuckle with Farthing before growing serious again. "Lady Brodie eyes most everything in hose whilst her husband leers at all in petticoats. I think this shall be a verra long meal."

* * *

Gamel tried to keep his thoughts focused on eating his meal, but the undercurrents at the table were too strong to ignore. As Lady Brodie ogled his father, Edina grew more and more furious, a fact indicated by how coldly polite she became. Gamel knew that Edina trusted her husband, yet to have a guest try to seduce him at their own table was far more than even the sweet Edina could bear.

When Lady Brodie, clearly frustrated by a lack of response from William, turned her sweetly seductive attentions his way, Gamel was stunned. He had accustomed himself to her close resemblance to Sine, but each hint of the woman's unsavory character lessened that resemblance in his mind. Nevertheless, the indications that Lady Brodie had a whore's appetite unsettled him. She sat at her husband's side yet made it clear that she would grant most any man in the great hall her favors if they cared to approach her. Worse, she did it so subtly, using her beauty, voice, innate sensuality to excite a man, that it was dismayingly easy to feel drawn to the woman. It was far too easy to forget that this lovely, gracious woman was the same one who made Sine Catriona go white with fear.

He began to wonder what could possibly make a child fear her own mother as Sine feared Lady Brodie. For all Gamel disliked and mistrusted the woman who had borne him, he had never feared her. His mother had tried to end his life before it had truly begun, but once she had given him over to William she had ceased to be a threat to him. What trouble his mother had caused had been for Edina and William. It was difficult for Gamel to believe that a mother, any mother, could be a real threat to her own child. Yet he could not doubt Sine's fear.

"Ye are verra fortunate, Lady Logan," Lady Arabel murmured. "Ye have so many healthy children."

"God has been verra good to us," replied Edina. "That hasnae been your fate?"

"Nay. Malise and I have yet to be blessed with a child, although we have been married for nearly seven years."

"Ye must not let that discourage you."

"Ah, but that isnae my only sorrow, I fear. The only fruit of my body, begot in my first marriage, withered and died. 'Twas a girl child. Alas, poor Sine Catriona was too delicate, too weak, to resist a fever. It robbed her of life at the tender age of twelve."

Delicate Sine certainly was, mused Gamel, but definitely not weak. If he had not already met Sine Catriona, however, he knew he would have accepted Lady Brodie's tragic tale without question. Such losses occurred with heartbreaking frequency. Lady Brodie's voice held all the appropriate sorrow. Gamel could see how easily he would have been compelled to sympathize if he did not know that Sine was very much alive.

"The line may weel be doomed," continued Lady Arabel. "Even my late husband's bastard sons died that year."

As Edina murmured all the appropriate words of condolence and hope, Gamel glanced down the table to Farthing. That man gave no sign of a reaction to Lady Arabel's words. Even so, Gamel was certain that the three people who hid in his parents' chambers were the very ones Lady Arabel claimed were long dead. He began to wonder exactly what trouble he might have plunged himself in the middle of. The problems besetting Sine could well be very complicated and dangerous. Life or death, Farthing had said. Gamel grew more convinced with each passing moment that Farthing had spoken the absolute truth.

* * *

Farthing studied the pair who had forced Sine Catriona, Dane, and Ree to flee for their lives. He had never doubted Sine's tale, and proof of it had been easily available over the years. The Brodies' common response to resistance or opposition was murder or betrayal. However, he now wondered if even Sine knew how treacherous the pair was. Over the years, he had not always told her the worst things he had heard about them in the hope of sparing her some pain. He began to doubt that Sine was fully aware of how much she would need to stop them. Only death would halt the plotting of the Brodies. Farthing was certain of it.

He was also determined not to let Sine Catriona and the twins get too close to the Brodies. It had often astounded him that so many people got caught in the Brodies' net. Now, however, he could see why. They were good at deceiving folk—clever and beautifully subtle. If he had not known the truth, he would easily have believed their appearance of amiability and candor. It was his knowledge that made him look more deeply and remain so wary. Sine Catriona could well have the wit to see the danger no matter what Lord and Lady Brodie said or did, but Farthing doubted that the twins would. The boys would be especially vulnerable to the wily woman.

The glances Lady Brodie sent his way mildly amused Farthing. Her husband revealed no hint of jealousy when Farthing responded to those looks with a welcoming smile. Lord Brodie clearly allowed his wife the freedom to satisfy her lusts as she pleased, a freedom he also allowed himself. Farthing continued to respond to Lady Arabel's subtle invitation. Since he was the only one at the table who did so, he soon had her undivided attention. Lady Arabel was plainly more than eager for an adulterous tumble.

For a brief moment Farthing wondered if he should encourage the woman—but only briefly. There was always the chance that he could gather some valuable information as he satisfied the needs of his body. It was a combination too tempting to refuse. By the time the meal was over and Farthing found himself maneuvered into a private corner by his father, he had already decided.

Lord Magnusson frowned with a mixture of disapproval and puzzlement. "Why are ye answering that slut's invitation?"

"Why not?" Farthing asked.

"Ye mean to say that ye would bed down with that adder?"

"Aye, but that doesnae mean it must bite me."

"Can ye be so sure of that?"

"Worry not, Father. 'Tis more than lust which guides me."

"I had already guessed that. Howbeit, even the most noble of reasons may not be much protection against that woman's poison. Do ye think that ye can fool her, that ye can gain any useful information from one as sly as she?"

"She isnae the only one who can be sly. I may gain nothing of value, but I cannae let this chance elude me. Dinnae worry so. I ken verra weel see what danger I court."

"For now I shall trust in your judgment." Lord Magnusson frowned toward Margot, who was talking to one of Malise's men, a fellow named Martin. "I wish I could feel some trust in young Margot's."

"She seems taken with that young mon."

"He is one of Malise's closest aides and a kinsmon—

a cousin, I believe. I learned that the last time we were all at court. He spies for Malise, even chooses the mon's next victims."

Farthing watched the couple for a moment. "Me thinks Malise should take greater care in choosing his right hand."

"What do ye mean?"

"The looks Martin casts Malise's way arenae those of a dedicated aide or loving cousin. They are bitter looks, twisted with cynicism. Martin little likes his cousin. Howbeit, that is no recommendation. Where is the mon ye mean to try and match her with?"

Lord Magnusson grimaced. "I meant to try and wed her with Sir Gamel."

"Ah, I see. All hope for that match is gone, is it?" Farthing asked, although he was already sure of the answer.

"Ye ken verra weel that it is. I have told Margot so already. Methinks she was relieved by the news. Sir Gamel is, weel, too much mon for the lass—too fierce in his feelings. She is a sweet, shy maid. A wee bit timid. She needs a quieter mate. Mayhaps that is why she moves toward that mon who always stays within the shadows," he muttered.

William arrived in time to hear Lord Magnusson's last statement. "He stands there for good reason," he said. "He is Lord Brodie's minion, his spy. He is never too far away from the mon."

Thomas Magnusson nodded, frowning deeply. "Aye, I ken it. I should take Margot out of his reach."

"Why, Father?" Farthing shrugged. "What harm can there be in a mild flirtation?"

"Margot isnac one practiced in the ways of subterfuge. She may not guard her tongue as closely as she ought to."

"I wondered on that," murmured William. "So I have

set young Ligulf near the couple to guard it for her. Let the lass have her fun, Thomas. Ligulf has a verra keen ear. If she even begins to let slip the wrong word, he will catch it." He looked at Farthing. "Our lady guest is calling to ye with her eyes again—and with most all of the rest of her."

"Aye, I see her glances. Ah, weel, duty calls," Farthing said with theatrical reluctance.

"Does he ken what he is stepping into?" William asked Thomas as Farthing wandered away.

"I believe he does. He is skilled at such play and, when the need arises, can be verra sly. Methinks he plans to try and gain some information. If such can be gained, then Farthing is the one to accomplish it. Better he than me." Thomas glanced around, saw how neatly Brodie's men were placed around the hall, and muttered, "It will be good when we are able to speak freely again."

The time for people to seek their beds was drawing near when Gamel finally managed to gain a moment alone with his father. "Ye may tell Farthing that he has the full privacy of my bedchambers for the night. I shall bed down elsewhere."

"With your brothers?"

"Aye, with my brothers," mumbled Gamel, hurrying away as Lord Magnusson approached.

Seeing how William was frowning at Gamel's retreating back, Thomas asked, "Something wrong?"

"Gamel says he will bed down with his brothers."

"Ah, and ye doubt the truth of his claim."

"Completely. Oh, he may weel spend part of the night with them so as not to be a liar. Howbeit, as soon as all is quiet, he will seek out Sine." William laughed softly. "And I have just recalled exactly how he can reach her.

The hideaway we have set Sine and her brothers in has another entrance. 'Tis so little used that I had forgotten it. But Gamel has remembered it. I would wager most anything that he means to make use of it."

"Do ye plan to move the lass out of his reach or even speak with her?"

"Nay. I dinnae plan to get caught up in the midst of all of that. Gamel willnae hurt the lass."

"I ne'er thought he would. Still, they seem, weel, contentious at the moment."

"Aye. Verra contentious. Mayhaps some time alone together will put a stop to some of that. 'Tis a strong heat he suffers from. Aye, and jealousy, even though he kens weel that she has ne'er been with another mon. I can almost pity the lad, but I ken what treasure can lie at the end of such trials and agonies."

"And I can pity that poor wee lassie," added Edina as she stepped up beside her husband. "She must suffer from such idiocy. Mayhaps I should have a word with her, or him, or even the both of them."

"Nay, loving." William draped his arm about her shoulders and kissed her cheek. "Best to stay weel clear of it."

"Mayhaps. For now." She looked at Lord Magnusson. "And do ye mean to stay weel clear of your son's doings?"

"Ah. Ye refer to his acceptance of Lady Brodie's lusty invitation."

"Aye. Dinnae ye think it may be a foolish move? I mean no insult but—"

Lord Magnusson held up his hand in a gesture to halt her unnecessary apology. "I understand. It could be foolish. But the young are often led more by the heat in their blood than the wit in their heads. Howbeit, something could also be gained."

"Aye," agreed William. "Farthing may get some information that could prove verra useful. Now, what has ye looking so puzzled?" he asked his wife.

"How can Farthing take up Lady Brodie's invitation at all?" asked Edina.

"As readily as any other mon."

"Nay, husband. Recall what Gamel has told us about Farthing's wound." She clapped a hand over her mouth and stared at Lord Magnusson in some dismay.

"Oh." William also eyed Thomas warily. "That wound."

"What?" Thomas frowned at both of them. "Was Farthing recently wounded?"

"Weel, I dinnae ken exactly when it happened, not for certain." William hesitated. "I dinnae wish to be the bearer of any sad tidings."

"Tell me—please."

"Gamel told us," replied Edina, "that Farthing had suffered an injury which rendered him unable to enjoy a woman." She frowned a little when, after gaping at her for a moment, Thomas began to laugh.

"'Tis a lie, of course," Thomas managed to say between hearty chuckles. "Farthing's only trouble in enjoying the lasses, m'lady, has been to answer such invitations as Lady Brodie's too often and too quickly." His laughter deepened briefly when William started to grin.

Her hands on her slim hips, Edina scowled at the two men. "So, 'tis a lie. I can see that now. Howbeit, I fail to see what is so funny about it and why such a lie should have been told in the first place."

"Dearling," William answered, "what better way to explain why one is a maid when one is supposed to be a wife. I shouldnae like to be that wee lass when our Gamel discovers that she has lied." He started to chuckle again when Edina began to giggle.

"Nor when Farthing hears of the slander," added Lord

Magnusson, and he joined the Logans in their hearty laughter.

Farthing smiled crookedly as the door to his bed-chamber was softly eased open. There was no mistaking the lush female form that was briefly silhouetted in the threshold before the door was shut behind her. Nevertheless, he feigned surprise. Acting as if he feared some assassin was approaching him, Farthing grasped hold of his sword and aimed it at the intruder.

"My good knight," murmured Lady Brodie in a husky voice. "That isnae the weapon I came here to see unsheathed."

"Ah, then come closer, m'lady. Ye shall find that other sword equally ready to prove its worth."

"Ye prompt me into committing a sinful indiscretion." She stepped closer to the bed.

There was some hesitation to her step, a hint of reluctance and indecision. Farthing knew it was a trick to make him think that his virility could overpower her modesty and morals. He felt the tickle of male pride and almost laughed. The woman was truly a master at her trade.

"Your good name will be safe in my hands, m'lady." He reached out to take her hand in his and tugged her closer. "None shall e'er hear of this transgression from me and I shall do my utmost to make ye free of all regret."

"I ken that ye will, my bonnie knight. 'Tis why I risk my immortal soul to be with ye."

As she slipped into bed beside him, Farthing set his sword aside but kept it within reach. He would use Lady Brodie to sate his lusts but would never ease his guard in her presence. It would please him greatly, however, if he could get her to ease her guard, if only for a moment—just long enough to gain some useful information.

As he pulled the woman into his arms, Farthing thought briefly on Gamel and Sine. He hoped Gamel was not after Sine, but decided he could not allow himself to worry about that now. Before turning his thoughts completely to carnal matters, Farthing decided that Sine could take care of herself tonight. She was, after all, neither helpless nor unwilling.

Sine abruptly woke up, fear choking her, when a hand covered her mouth. Before she could struggle, she was neatly gagged and bound in her blanket. She felt herself being lifted up and tossed over a broad shoulder. But then her fear swiftly changed to anger. Her enemies had not discovered her after all. It was Gamel who was snatching her from her warm, safe bed. When he released her, she intended to make him very sorry indeed for his dark-of-the-night chicanery.

"Are ye certain this is a wise thing to do, Gamel?" asked Blane as he took Sine's place on her cot.

"Nay, but I shall do it all the same." Gamel ignored his burly squire's snort of amusement.

"'Tis not love words she is spitting behind that gag."

Gamel grinned and patted Sine's backside. "I ken it, and she will no doubt sear my ears with angry words and curses when I remove that gag. It matters not. 'Tis all she can do, for she must hide from her enemies. She will be trapped where I set her until the Brodies have ridden out of Duncoille. I doubt that knowledge will do verra much to sweeten her temper." Gamel smiled a little crookedly.

"It might be wise to be sure she is unarmed before ye release her," Blane drawled.

Laughing softly, Gamel crept from the hidden chamber and stealthily made his way to the western tower of Duncoille, keeping to the hidden passages and shadowed, little-used halls. Although it was reckless of him to steal Sine from her shelter, he did not completely forget that a threat to her life lurked within Duncoille. He watched for that threat every step of the way, and breathed a small sigh of relief when, still unseen, he finally reached the top chambers of the western tower and bolted the door behind him.

Cautiously, Gamel set Sine down and released her from the blanket. The angry gestures with which she pushed the tousled hair from her face and the fury of her glare made Gamel hesitate briefly before removing her gag. It was going to take a lot of sweet words and clever talking to soothe her. As he looked at her standing there in her thin shift, her lovely hair tangled around her slim shoulders, Gamel felt little inclined to do either.

"'Tis clear that ye have gone completely mad." Sine spat out the words between gritted teeth.

"That is a possibility." Gamel tugged her into his arms, ignoring the tension that stiffened her slim frame. "The fever ye set raging through my blood could easily burn all reason away." Despite the way she hunched her shoulders he managed to nibble her ear.

Sine struggled not to let Gamel's nearness soften her anger but that was proving a fruitless effort. She shuddered and clutched the front of his jupon as he lightly traced the shape of her ear with his tongue. What little resistance she tried to cling to was swiftly banished when he slid his hands beneath the hem of her thin chemise and gently cupped her backside. She met his kiss with a heat that matched his.

In her mind Sine could hear him speaking of marriage. Those words soothed all of her concerns about being just some object of a strong but fleeting lust. Her passion responded to that memory, pushing aside her annoyance over his behavior. Desire also pushed aside the fear that had gnawed at her since the Brodies had driven within the gates of Duncoille. Sine much preferred the blinding heat of desire that Gamel could stir within her to the chill of fear or the bite of anger, however temporary her release from those emotions might prove to be.

With those thoughts in mind she made no attempt to halt his removal of her chemise. She burrowed her fingers deep into his thick bright hair as he kissed a path to her breasts. Sine closed her eyes as she reveled in the rich sensations his heated caresses brought her, the sweet aching fullness caused by his gentle suckling. She murmured a soft protest when Gamel withdrew his skilled attentions to her breasts and brought them lower, to her abdomen. Before she could express her faint disappointment or find a way to subtly urge his warm mouth back to her breasts, he kissed the silken tangle of curls at the very base of her torso.

She cried out in a mixture of protest and stunned delight, clenching her fingers in his hair. What little clear-headedness she had left faded when he slowly stroked her with his tongue. Sine sank beneath the strength of her own passion as it raged through her. As she grew weak-kneed, Gamel grasped her by the legs to hold her steady for his intimate caresses. When Sine felt her desire reach its height, she cried out his name but he did not heed her. She nearly collapsed as her release shuddered through her. Yet still he did not halt his stirring attentions and soon her passions were renewed.

Suddenly, Gamel picked her up in his arms and set her down on the soft bed. Sine lay there trembling with hunger for him as he shed his clothes. The only clear thought in her head was that he was glorious, beautiful in his nakedness. When he knelt between her legs and crouched over her, she frowned slightly over his hesitation to do what they both ached for. She wrapped her legs about his waist and tried to press his loins against hers, but he held himself firmly away yet tantalizingly close.

"Gamel?"

"Do ye want me, Sine?"

"Would I be lying here like this for some other reason?" She scowled at him when he had the audacity to grin.

"Say it," he demanded. "I want to hear ye say that ye want me."

"I want ye. There. Pleased?"

"Aye." He grinned at her again. "Wee shrew."

Before she could protest that slur, he slowly joined their bodies. Sine quickly forgot everything but the feel of them as one, their unified drive toward pleasure's heights. As another release swept over her, she clung to Gamel, delighting in the way he echoed her cries, joining in her ecstasy.

Afterward, as they lay entwined upon the bed recovering from the fierceness of their lovemaking, Sine recalled exactly how she had arrived in the tower room. That thought pushed away the last of her pleasure. Muttering a curse, she punched Gamel, and was about to do it again even as he moved away, rubbing his arm.

"Ah, so my lovemaking didnae soothe your sense of outrage," he murmured, eyeing her warily.

"It but caused me to forget it for a moment."

"A moment?"

She ignored that muttered interruption. "What right have ye got to drag me here and there as ye will?" Sitting up, she yanked one of the linen sheets around her body to hide her nakedness. "And what of the danger ye could have placed me in? I wasnae cowering in that hiding place for the joy of it."

"I made verra sure that no one saw us."

"Ah, I see. Weel then, ye can put me back."

"Nay."

"Nay? Ye arenae my lord and master. Do ye mean to hold me prisoner then?"

"Nay, I mean to make ye my wife."

"I cannae marry now."

Gamel reached out and grasped her by the shoulders, giving her one brief shake. "Why?"

Sine pushed his hands away and frowned at him, unsettled by his intensity. "I told your brother the why of it. He must have repeated my message, for I can see that ye are wearing my medallion." She discovered that she was dangerously touched by that gesture, even found herself wondering what it might say about his feelings for her.

"That message said little. I ken something about a vow ye say ye must fulfill, but nothing of the cause of the vow."

"And ye dinnae wish to wait until it is all explained on the morrow."

"Nay." He rose from the bed, walked to a small table, and poured himself a goblet of wine. "Do ye wish to have a drink?"

"Aye." She began to scowl as he brought her a goblet of wine and sat down beside her on the bed. "Ye *planned* to bring me here. Ye had this room readied for us."

He nodded as he drank. "I mean to hold ye close this time. Ye willnae creep away from me at dawn again."

"Oh, aye, I am certain to try that. I could always beg a ride from the Brodies," she muttered, then took a long drink, annoyed that he plotted to thwart any escape on her part even though she had not planned one.

"Lady Arabel Brodie is your mother."

She sighed and eyed him with an even mixture of resignation and irritation. He would not give up, rather would badger her until she told him everything. The man was not only arrogant, but also annoyingly stubborn. She wondered why she felt so drawn to him.

"Aye—by blood. There is no other bond between us. She cut all of them when she murdered my father and the mother of the twins. Aye, and then when she turned her deadly glance our way."

"Are ye certain of that? Wrong as those murders were, they could have been the result of jealousy. The twins are much younger than ye are, which means that your father broke his wedding vows to your mother."

"Only after she had broken hers many times over. She refused him after I was born—refused him her bed and any further children. I was so young that it was a verra long time before I understood it all. The twins are so much younger than me because my father clung to his vows for many years despite his wife's infidelity and ruthlessness. The love he had once felt for her made him even blinder to her faults than the other men she has entrapped and betrayed. Then he met Lady Seaton, the mother of the twins. She was a sweet loving woman, a widow. Father turned to her for some warmth, and away from his own wife's cold cruelty. The boys carry his name even though some laws would name them bastards. 'Tis good that Scotland isnae as harsh to bastards as England is rumored to be."

Shaking her head as she set her now empty goblet upon the floor and straightened, she continued, "Jealousy may weel have been behind my mother's actions. Arabel holds tight to most all that she considers hers. She didnae want Papa but probably hated sharing him, hated to know that he was happy despite her. Mostly it was greed. Arabel and Malise had found that they shared a great deal—immorality, for one thing. They wanted the

Brodie land, power, and money, but Papa was in their way. I can only surmise that they killed Lady Seaton and Papa's mother to silence any accusations they might have made against them. Then they plotted to remove me and my brothers, for we also stood in their way."

"Six murders? So many must have brought some attention their way. Questions must have been asked."

"So ye would like to believe. Some questions may weel have been raised, but not enough. Death is so common and these murderers are so verra clever. Those nearest to us feared Malise or believed all of his smooth lies. Arabel is an even better liar than Malise. She could convince some men that the sun was black and the sky green." She shrugged. "Lies or threats—both worked to silence the curious. Malise and Arabel work in poisons, daggers thrust out of the shadows, accidents. My grandmother was an old woman. No one is verra suspicious when the old die."

"But she didnae die of old age?"

"Nay. 'Twas poison. Grandmere told me as much herself as she lay upon her deathbed. All those about us thought that she was beyond the power of speech and so left me alone with her. She begged me to warn Papa, but I was too late. Arabel hated Grandmere, ye see, and as the poor old woman lay dying, Arabel taunted her with the tale of her only child's impending death. Papa was to be killed by thieves as he rushed from the king's court at Stirling to be at his dying mother's side. His mistress was to be slain too, and Grandmere dearly loved Lady Seaton."

"But ye were too late to warn them?" Gamel took one of her small, tightly clenched hands in his.

"Aye." She shuddered as the memory of her mad, fruitless ride north on the road to Stirling came back to her. "I arrived at the spot only in time to mourn the dead. 'Twas not far from here, in truth, about five miles from here towards Dunkennley. Papa, Lady Seaton, and three men-at-arms were slain. They were shot by arrows, given no chance to fight for their lives. As I cowered in the wood bordering the road, I recognized one of the men who helped to strip the bodies, thus making the tale of pikers seem true. I returned to Dorchabeinn, and lied. Quite weel I thought. I claimed I had tried to meet Papa but had become hopelessly lost. Since I was only a child of ten at that time, I felt that they would believe such a tale. Still, Malise and Arabel suspected that I now kenned too much."

Gamel set his goblet down beside hers, edged up beside her, and put his arm about her shoulders. "Yet they hesitated to kill the twins, who were now alone and helpless."

"Not completely defenseless. When their father was murdered, they were with their Seaton kin, but Arabel soon convinced those poor fools to let the boys come to her. After all, they were now the heirs to a great deal of Papa's property and the Seatons were poor and aging. They were easily convinced that the twins needed to be at Dorchabeinn, where they could learn the ways of knights. Few others thought it odd either. A laird's son should reside at his father's keep, be he legitimate or nay.

"I thought we would be left alone, allowed to live in peace for a wee while. We were so verra young. Arabel and Malise could enjoy all that was ours for many a year. Surely, to kill us too quickly would only serve to harden what few suspicions there were." Sine leaned against Gamel's shoulder and slipped her arm around his waist, needing his closeness as she recalled her fear. "Then I heard the pair of them planning how to be rid of us with the least possible suspicion raised."

When she fell silent, Gamel waited a moment before pressing, "How did they plan to do it?"

She shrugged. "They had several choices—poison, an accident. They even pondered exposing us to every fever and ill in the area until we fell sick and died. I took the twins and went to one of our neighbors, but the mon was either too afraid of Arabel and Malise or he thought me mad. In any case, he took us back. Oh, I neglected to say that Arabel was married to Malise by this time. She had wed Malise within weeks of Papa's burial."

"No one questioned the swiftness of that wedding?"

"Some, but they had all kenned that Papa had a mistress and that Arabel had not been faithful either, so they soon lost interest in the matter. Unhappy unions are sadly common."

"And so then ye ran."

"Aye, into the wood. Arabel and Malise no longer suspected that I had guessed their game, they were certain of it. I crept about my own home like some lowly thief, listening at every door. Did ye meet a mon called Martin Robertson tonight?" she asked abruptly, frowning up at Gamel.

He nodded. "He is Malise's cousin, one of the mon's closest minions."

She nodded and rested her cheek against his chest. "I ken that he saw what I was doing, yet he ne'er told them about it. Nor did he try to stop me. 'Tis true that he ne'er helped me either, but I think he isnae as much Malise's minion as Malise might believe. The mon took a great risk in saying and doing naught. In truth, he risked his verra life. There must be some good in him, for he let us escape, I am certain of it. I have wondered if he might be a weakness within the enemy camp, but I have never gained what would be needed to make use of the mon if he is."

"I could look into that possibility. Ye havenae answered—when did ye finally run away?"

"When I discovered that Arabel and Malise had made plans to send me and the twins to a family who had been stricken with some illness, mayhaps even the plague. I could tell that their attempts to kill us were about to begin in earnest, that they had discovered a way to do it without raising an outcry. Children sicken and die every day, dinnae they?

"I could hesitate no longer. I kenned the family that we were to be taken to. They were strong and not given to sickness, yet they were dying—one after another, a new death nearly every day. I felt sure that the twins would succumb to whatever was killing that family so I grabbed the lads by the hands and slipped away into the night."

"And met up with Farthing," Gamel muttered, frowning down at her.

Glancing up at him briefly, Sine decided not to placate him. "Aye—and Farthing kept us weel hidden and alive."

"By making ye become thieves and putting ye in constant danger of a different kind. Why didnae he turn to his father for help? There appears to be an affection between them."

"Aye, there is. Yet, there was some trouble there. Lady Magnusson was a good woman, but she couldnae fully stop herself from worrying over the bond between her husband and his bastard son. Her mother's heart caused her to fear that something might be taken away from her own children. Then there came the time to choose a wife for her son. There was some difficulty in keeping the maids from flirting with Farthing and the other son began to suffer the pangs of jealousy." She shrugged. "Before things grew too troubled, Farthing set out on his own."

Gamel wondered if that was when Farthing had suffered the wound which had stolen his virility, but he decided not to ask. He could understand the strife Sine spoke about. It had not taken him long to realize that Edina was the exception among stepmothers in the way she loved him and brought her own children up to accept him as their brother and not "the bastard." Although he felt sure Lord Magnusson would have helped in any way he was able, Gamel could easily understand Farthing's reluctance to ask the man.

"But now Farthing can help me," Sine continued.

"*I* can help ye." Gamel gently grasped her chin, turned her face up toward his, and gave her a deep, fierce kiss. "Farthing can attend our wedding," he murmured as he brushed light kisses over her upturned face.

"How kind of ye, except that I havenae said that I will marry ye."

He muttered a curse, turned, and pressed her down onto her back. "There is no reason for ye to hold back."

"There is my vow. There is the fact that people are hunting me, people who mean to kill me. 'Tis not the time to speak of marriage. And," she added when he continued to mutter oaths against her throat, "cursing willnae change my mind."

"I will find a way to change it." He tugged the sheet down to her waist and cupped her breast in his hand, sliding his thumb back and forth over the tip until it hardened.

Her voice grew soft and husky. "Cannae ye just leave it be for now?"

"Is it because I am a bastard? Ye *are* better born than I am." After staring at the erect tips of her breasts for a moment, he began to lathe them with his tongue, liking the feel of her fingers burrowing into his hair.

"Dinnae be such a fool," she replied in a breathy voice as she pressed his head closer to her and he began to gently suckle.

"'Tis a reasonable question."

"I dinnae want any more questions. I answered so verra many and must answer many more on the morrow."

"Nay, I will tell my parents all that ye have just told me.

Then ye may join us and answer what few questions remain. The least I can do is save ye one more repetition of that painful story. Would ye want me to do that?"

"Aye, that would be a help."

"Then it shall be done. And what else do ye *not* want, Sine Catriona?"

"I dinnae want to feel fear. I dinnae want to worry any more. I want to forget everything, if only for a wee while."

Turning on his side, Gamel yanked the sheet completely away. For a moment he studied her, savoring her beauty and marveling at the way looking at her could so quickly and fiercely stir his desire. He put his hand upon her taut stomach, then slid it down to the silvery curls at its base. After watching himself lightly, intimately caress her, he met her heavy-lidded gaze. She desired him—as fiercely as he did her. It was a beginning. For now he would have to be satisfied with that.

"And does this steal your fear away?"

"Aye." She gave a shaky laugh. "It steals all thought from my mind, curse ye."

"Cursing will not stop me," he drawled, and smiled when she responded with a soft, husky laugh.

"I have yet to find the way or the strength to stop ye."

"Good."

"Good for ye—aye."

"And for ye, since I shall keep those fears and worries from troubling ye."

"At least in the night."

"Aye. In the night—every night," he murmured as he bent his head to kiss her.

Chapter 7

"**S**o, there is all that I ken about Sine's problems."
Gamel sprawled in a heavy oak chair and closely
watched his father's face. He, Farthing, and their parents
had all gathered in the elder Logans' solar and had just
spent an hour or more discussing Sine's troubles. The dust
of the departing Brodies had barely cleared the Duncoille
bailey when Gamel had done as he had promised Sine,
and begun telling them all her story. At times he had not
had answers for the pointed questions his father asked. It
had been left to Farthing to reply, with Gamel resenting
the man's superior knowledge of Sine. Now, he tensely
awaited his father's decision about aiding Sine Catriona in
her fight.

"'Tis a dangerous request the lass wants granted. Aye,
she has right on her side, but the ones she must fight
have deadly guile and the will to use it," Lord William
muttered after several moments of quiet thought.

Gamel sat forward a little, dreading his father's reply
even as he asked, "Do we join that fight?"

"Do ye wish to?"

"Aye."

"We havenae a large force—twenty weel-trained

men-at-arms at most. Beyond that we must look to our
farmers and shepherds to join us."

"Lord Magnusson has some men and he is willing to
help." Gamel glanced briefly at Farthing's father, who
nodded. "That would near double our fighting force."

"Only if Thomas leaves his own keep and lands completely unprotected." William smiled faintly when Gamel
flushed and cursed softly. "I havenae said nay yet."

"Ye havenae said aye either."

"Son, ye ask that we step into a quagmire of murder,
deceit, and treachery. I ken these Brodies from court
and have heard naught but ill of them from those who
have the wit to see behind their beauty and clever wiles.
To take up a sword against those who have no honor,
who wouldst cut your throat as ye sleep, is a course of
action one must consider carefully. We could bring a
great deal of trouble down upon our heads and not gain
anything for it. I also have the lives of my men to consider, men who have been with me for years."

"I understand. How much time do ye need to make
your decision?" Gamel could not think of another way to
argue his position. His cause was just, and his father
knew it.

"I have already decided." William ignored his petite
wife when she pinched him for dithering at Gamel's ex-
pense. "We will fight for the lass."

Gamel slumped a little with relief. "It could be a long
and bloody fight," he felt compelled to add.

"We ken that all too weel," Edina answered from
where she sat at Lord William's side, his large callused
hand clasping hers. "Your father and I are in agreement,
though. I confess that I dread what might come. But
'twould be far worse to turn our backs on the lass. She
has been cruelly wronged and she needs help."

"I thank ye, as I am sure Sine will," Gamel said, then stood up. "Shall I bring her to ye now?"

Lord William nodded. "Aye, fetch the lass. She should be part of this now."

"Did ye learn anything of importance from Lady Arabel?" demanded Lord Magnusson of Farthing the moment Gamel was gone.

Farthing looked at his father, vaguely wondering why he had waited to ask until Gamel had left the room to fetch Sine.

"Why not wait until Gamel and Sine have returned before we talk about what little I gleaned from her mother?" Farthing asked.

"Do ye not think that the lass may feel a wee bit ill at ease if she kens that ye have bedded her mother?" Lord Magnusson spoke quietly and watched his son closely as Farthing considered his words.

"Ah, aye, she might. Howbeit, Gamel wouldnae care. Why not wait until he can hear what I have to say?"

"He could accidentally tell Sine where such information was gathered. I truly believe 'twould be kinder if she didnae learn of your tryst with her mother."

"Mayhaps. It doesnae really matter. There isnae a lot to tell."

"Your seductive powers werenae strong enough to make the lady speak freely, hmmmm?"

Farthing decided to ignore his father's sarcasm. "Lady Arabel told me only one thing that is of any importance— the names of some of her many amours. The woman has bedded some verra powerful people, from lowly sheriffs to some of the king's own council. Mayhaps even more important is how much she kens about each and every one of them. 'Tis knowledge they wouldnae wish spread about too widely."

"Which means that she can force them to act on her

behalf," muttered Lord William, briefly clenching his big hands on the back of the heavy oak chair in which his wife sat.

"Aye," agreed Farthing. "We shall have to be verra careful or we could find more than the Brodies and their pack of curs facing us."

Lord William nodded. "Ye had best give us what names ye can so that we willnae be deceived or surprised. We may even be able to turn her allies to our side, for all ken that I can be trusted with their secrets." He held up his hand to silence Farthing even as the younger man began to speak. "Later. I hear Gamel returning."

Edina moved to hug Sine the moment Gamel brought her into the solar. "Oh, my poor wee lass."

Sine tensed slightly in the woman's embrace, then felt a little ashamed of herself. This was no Arabel. There was no dagger hidden in this woman's hand. When she met Edina's gaze, Sine saw only understanding there and she was able to relax.

"We intend to do all we can to help, be it covertly or in open battle. My husband has agreed to it," Edina continued. "Although I hope it doesnae come to fighting."

"I hope it can be bloodless as weel," Sine murmured.

It was difficult to hide her confusion. Gamel was a bastard, yet clearly the Logans meant to put all of their strength behind him. Sine saw Edina smile as the woman stepped back a little.

"Ye arenae the first one to puzzle o'er the ways of this family, m'dear," Edina said quietly as she took Sine by the hand and led her to a seat. "Gamel is our son. 'Tis all there is to say."

Still pondering over that, Sine sat down on a large comfortable bench. Gamel immediately took a seat on her right. She had to struggle to restrain her blush as memories of the heated lovemaking they had indulged in for most of the night rushed to the forefront of her mind. When Farthing quickly sat down on her left, she looked at him in order to deter her errant thoughts. The way he and Gamel eyed each other made her sigh. This constant bristling between the two men could quickly grow very irritating. Edina's next words told Sine that she felt much the same way.

"And ye two young gentlemen can just smooth those ruffled feathers down."

"Ruffled feathers?" muttered Gamel indignantly.

Edina continued as if he had not spoken. "Now is the time to be united. We must help Sine and the twins."

"Weel, my father and I have already offered all that we have," Farthing said in a stiff voice.

Lord Magnusson, who stood behind Farthing, gently rapped his son on the head with his knuckles. "The more the better and weel ye ken it. What we must discuss now is how best to combine our forces to make the wisest use of each other's strengths. Ye two can quibble over the lass when the matter is all settled."

"'Tis more than a quibble," grumbled Farthing.

Sine almost giggled but forced it back. Farthing looked a lot like one of the twins when he was reprimanded— just a little bit sulky. Then she frowned and looked around the room, realizing that her brothers were not in attendance.

"Where are Dane and Ree?" she asked.

Farthing replied, "Weel, since they are but nine and can add little to any plan I thought it just as weel to leave them out of it."

"Aye, child," added Edina. "They are happily at play with my youngest boys. Howbeit, if ye feel otherwise, we could fetch them."

"Nay. Let them play. 'Tis rare that they have other

children to play with. As ye say, Farthing, they can be of little help, so why burden them? And I deeply appreciate all of your help," she added. "Yet, 'tis a dangerous game ye will enter, so I shall understand any reluctance ye may feel. I cannae ask—"

"Ye dinnae need to ask," said Lord William. "If naught else, many another would appreciate seeing that pair brought to justice. It took me some time but I finally recalled that I fought side by side with your father once. That was the reason the medallion ye gave to Gamel was so familiar to me. That and the shock I first felt when I saw the same medallion around Malise Brodie's neck. Your father stood at my back in one battle and I was sorry to ken that he had died before I could repay that debt."

"I am certain that he kenned ye would have if the chance had ever arisen," Sine replied.

"Aye, but now repayment can be made in a different way. There is one thing I must ask ye."

"And that is?" she pressed when he fell silent, frowning at her.

"Ye do realize that to gain back all that is yours and the twins', to avenge your father's death, could weel mean that your mother must die—either by our hands or those of the law."

"Aye, I ken it."

"Weel, then, we can start by having ye tell us all that ye can about the Brodie keep—Dorchabeinn." Lord William moved toward a table where a quill and paper were already laid out, then waved at the others to join him.

"I fear I dinnae recall verra much, m'lord," Sine warned as she walked over to the table, Gamel on her right and Farthing to her left.

"Tell us what little ye do ken, lass," Lord William advised. "'Twill be a start, a base of knowledge we can build upon."

She nodded and slowly began to tell them of Dorchabeinn, plunging deep into her memory for every elusive detail. Each question asked of her revealed how dim and inexact her memories were. And as she spoke, it was difficult to subdue the sudden fear that she had begun a battle she was ill prepared to fight.

Sine stood on the high sturdy outer walls of Duncoille staring blindly out over the fields that surrounded the keep. Most of the morning had been spent planning how to deal with the Brodies, yet she had taken little part in it all. They had prodded her for information about Dorchabeinn, as well as about Malise and Arabel, but that was about all she had contributed to the plot. Her vow was now being fulfilled, but she was having very little to do with it.

Her thoughts also kept straying to what Lord William had said—that once begun, the attempt to retrieve her property and avenge her father's death could well mean her mother had to die. Sine had believed that she had already accepted that fact, yet now she felt very unsure. Malise had killed her father and grandmother and fully intended to kill her and the twins—and all with her mother's approval and aid. It did not make sense to feel hesitant. For some reason, now that she was nearing her goal she was lacking the strong sense of righteousness she had carried with her for so long.

She sensed Gamel's presence even before he reached her side. That also left her confused. She had barely known the man a week, yet he had become a complex, integral part of her life. It was hard not to resent that a little, especially when he did it so effortlessly. As he

tucked a stray lock of her hair back beneath her headdress, she eyed him with something less than welcome.

"I thought your temper would be sweeter now that ye
have the aid ye have sought for so long," he murmured.

"It should be." She leaned her arms on the top of the
rampart. "Mayhaps there is just something I have missed
in the planning and the slight confusion leaves me irritable," she mumbled.

Leaning his back against the thick wall, Gamel crossed
his arms over his chest and studied her. He suspected
that what she had just said was a lie. Something was troubling her, but he was going to have to nudge her quite
persistently before he found out what it was. And then
he hoped he had the answers he needed to solve the
problem.

"Sir Lesley is traveling with the Brodies. He claimed he
needed to go to court and begged the privilege of ac-
companying them for added safety. He could prove a
most valuable spy."

"Or get himself murdered."

Gamel ignored that sulky response. "Father has sent
word to the king."

Sine nodded. "Aye. I saw the messenger leave."

"The messenger will tell Robert the Second what is hap-
pening here and Father has no doubt but that the king
will give his full approval to the actions we plan to take.
And good wishes for our success. 'Tis true that the king
rarely interferes in such interclan squabbles, but Father
decided it could only be to our advantage to make the
king aware of the trouble and our part in it. Father says
that Robert has long been suspicious of the Brodies. The
king has often grumbled about them to Father. They gain
too much influence and wealth. Too many deaths have
followed their rise to power. Suspicions abound but no

proof has ever come to light. The king will appreciate someone finding that proof."

"If proof can be found."

"It will be. Those two have far too much to hide. They cannae cover all their tracks. Father and Lord Magnusson will send word to everyone they know, asking them what they ken or even suspect. They will also send word to all they ken who have had dealings with Malise and your mother."

"I ken it. And they will offer protection and the promise of full confidentiality to any and all who fear that murderous pair and what might happen if they tell the truth."

"Exactly. He has even said that he will take on the protection and care of their wives and children if 'tis needed. So, I have little doubt that some will come forward. They will be glad of a chance to shake free of the Brodies' hold. I also have little doubt that ye ken each and every step we have planned thus far, so what troubles you?"

Sine grimaced, then looked directly at Gamel. "What do *I* do?"

"Ah, I see. Ye feel pushed aside, nudged out of your own plans for vengeance, do ye?"

When he reached out and tugged her into his arms she tensed briefly, then relaxed against him with a sigh. She really did like being held by him. It was probably foolish to keep fighting him. Nevertheless, she suspected that she would continue to do so to some extent, if only because he pressed her so hard, so consistently, that she could barely think straight.

"Aye. I fear I might. Ungrateful wretch that I am. I have all the help I have sought for so very long yet I seem to resent the fullness in which it is given to me."

"'Tis best the way it is, Sine. For many reasons. The

Brodies will soon ken that someone is probing too deeply into their affairs. They will look around to try and discover who is being so dangerously curious. 'Tis best if ye and the twins arenae too readily visible. Aye, we are protecting ye now, but the moment the Brodies discover that ye are here that protection will need to be increased tenfold. The longer we can delay carving up our strength in that manner the better." He idly rubbed his hand up and down her slim back.

It was all true, far too true and sensible to argue with. She felt that touch of resentment she had been suffering begin to ease. After all, she had sought help for much the same reasons. To do it all by herself would have been to expose herself and the twins to the murderous plots of the Brodies.

"Did ye think ye but needed to gather an army, ride to Dorchabeinn, and just toss them out?" he asked.

"Nay." She smiled faintly, for she had envisioned just such a course of events many times. "S'truth, I did ponder such a swift, impressive end to it all now and again, but, nay, I always kenned that it could ne'er be so simple." She frowned. "Ye said 'many reasons' for keeping me excluded from helping with your plans, but ye really only gave me one, mayhaps two."

"Two. Searching out proof and protecting ye and the lads."

"Gamel." She leaned back a little to look up at him. "Ye said 'many' reasons."

He slid his hands down her back to cup her backside. "Would ye care to forget your worries and fears for a wee while?"

Sine gave him as stern a look as she could manage as she tugged his hands away from her. "Gamel."

He sighed, then replied, "There is the fact that this

will end with your mother's death. I cannae see any other way."

"Neither can I." She pressed her cheek against his chest and slipped her arms about his trim waist.

"I wish to keep ye as far away from that as is possible. I want to keep your hands as clean of it as I can."

"I have set the hounds on her trail. I am already in great part responsible for whatever happens."

"'Tis not the same. Ye now only work to end the threat against your own life and the twins'. That is far different from actually taking part in her death, weel deserved though it may be. Nevertheless, she *is* your mother."

"That doesnae stop me from seeing the evil in her. The blood tie didnae stop ye from seeing how wrong your mother was, did it?"

"Nay, but my mother wasnae quite the villain yours is."

She frowned at him. "Ye said she was the same."

"Aye, she was in many ways. She had a whore's morals, she was utterly heartless and sometimes cruel, and she had no love for me. Nay, she did her best to kill me whilst I was still in her womb, and even once when I was but newly born. The nuns at the convent where she had taken refuge stopped her from smothering me."

Sine tightened her grip on him as sympathy flooded her heart. "'Tis a grievous knowledge for a child to bear."

"Aye. It can still pinch. My father's wife, Edina, eased the sting of it years ago with her kindness and her mothering. My birth mother was later confined to that convent for life. Her family could no longer abide her lecherousness, and they were deeply shamed by the way she had tried to hurt my father and Edina. I rarely see or hear from her."

"And I have had little to do with my mother. We share that curse."

"True, but do we share the ability to see the dangers our mothers can pose for us?"

"I ken verra weel that Arabel is a threat to me."

"Aye, but, as I have said, she *is* your mother, and at some point in this deadly game that must, and will, make ye hesitate."

"It already has," she whispered.

"I am glad that ye have already seen it. Can ye also see how dangerous that hesitation could prove to be?"

"Aye—easily. *She* will have no reluctance."

"Nay, and, if I judge her correctly, she will take swift advantage of yours. Ye have one weakness already."

"Oh, and what might that be?" She frowned up at him, not sure whether she should feel insulted or not.

He touched a kiss to the tip of her nose. "Ye care about those around ye. But one look and it can be seen that ye love those two lads as if they were your own."

Nodding, she cuddled up to him again, recognizing all too well the weakness he spoke of. "Aye, and there is Farthing."

She almost smiled when he muttered a curse, a now familiar response to any mention of the man. There just might be some truth to Lord William's assertion that Gamel was jealous. It was highly contrary of her to like the thought when she was refusing to marry him, but she did. They were, after all, lovers, and it was pleasant to see that hint of possessiveness in him. She would not cater to it, however. Farthing was her family. Gamel would simply have to get over his animosity.

"And, of course, ye do like me some," he drawled.

"Do I? Hmm. I cannae recall deciding on that just yet. Must think on it for a while."

A squeak of surprise and alarm escaped her when he suddenly grasped her around the waist and set her on top of the wall. She clutched his arms and closed her eyes, fighting the compelling urge to look down. Even the firm clasp of his strong hands on her waist did not make her feel completely safe.

"Gamel, set me back down."

"I thought ye might be able to think more clearly up there."

"I cannae think at all save to contemplate how far it is to the ground."

"Ho," bellowed a strong male voice from below. "Is that our fiery-haired brother up there trying to toss some poor lassie off the walls?"

"Did the poor lassie fail to scent your pristine sheets?" yelled another male voice.

Sine found herself quickly set back on her feet. She leaned against the wall to calm herself and listened to Gamel exchange railleries with the two Logans below. Here was just more proof of how completely a part of the family Gamel was. When he finally took her by the hand, she expected to be led back to the great hall to meet his brothers. But Gamel did not immediately move, so she glanced at him, only to find him scowling down at her.

"I am not sure I should let them meet ye," he grumbled.

"And why is that?" She fought a sense of insult, often too quickly stirred, waiting for some clear reason for his hesitation.

"My brothers, Norman and Nigel, are closer to your age than I, being but nineteen and twenty. They also have a great deal of charm and an eye for the lasses."

"I have yet to meet a mon who doesnae." She started on her way, lightly tugging him along with her. "What puzzles me is why ye should think me so wooden-headed as to be easy prey for a flirtatious eye and a pretty word." She could not resist adding, "Ye certainly offered me neither."

"Weel, I did have a flirtatious eye."

"Flirtatious? Hah! 'Twas lustful. And there were no pretty words—only threats."

He made no reply to that, only said, "'Twould help a poor besotted fool feel more sure of himself if his lady would give him some sense that she is bound to him."

"Have I not said that I am yours?"

"A word or two before a priest would nicely convince me."

"Weel, ye shall have to learn to be satisfied with my word alone for now."

Gamel grumbled a curse but said no more. He simply quickened his step until he was towing her along behind him. Sine supposed it would not hurt to soothe some of the insecurity he was beginning to reveal, yet she hesitated. He had asked her to be his wife, but there was little said of what he felt in his heart. When she considered how he had thrust himself into her life, she decided it was a bit unfair of him to press for words of love from her yet offer none of his own.

After stumbling into the great hall behind him, she was summarily dragged into a brief round of introductions to the newly arrived Logans. That was followed by a boisterous family greeting for Norman and Nigel. Sine found herself seated at Gamel's side, listening as her story was told yet again, questions asked and plans reviewed. Norman and Nigel were quick to vow to join the fight, assuring her and their hesitant father that the man they were squires for would wholeheartedly agree.

She studied Norman and Nigel closely but as covertly as possible. They were certainly fine-looking young men. They probably did not need pretty words to catch a maid's heart. The eldest of the pair could be considered the fairest, although she saw no fault in either of them. Norman had golden hair and rich blue eyes. Younger by little more than a year, Nigel had reddish-blond hair and golden brown eyes. Both were tall young men, but with his stronger build, Nigel was more like his father. She suspected the two set many a maid's heart beating faster. Even though she knew some of their sweet flattery was spouted as much to irritate Gamel as to compliment her, she found that she heartily enjoyed it. She also enjoyed seeing that neither young man shared Gamel's animosity toward Farthing. That there would not be a united front of Logans against Farthing could be only for the good.

"Are we to stay here then?" Ree asked as Sine tucked him in bed later that night.

She sat down on the edge of the bed the twins shared, which had been placed in the far corner of the room that Gamel's youngest brothers occupied. "That is the plan for now," she answered with a nod.

"And these people are going to help us get Dorchabeinn back?"

"Aye. They *and* Farthing's father."

"I hope no one will be hurt," Dane murmured.

"I pray for that as weel, loving," Sine answered in a soft voice.

"Why do Farthing and Gamel hate each other?"

"They dinnae hate each other. In truth, I think they could be the best, most loyal of friends. They must settle the anger between them, however. That will take some time. Mayhaps, as they work together to help us the breach will be mended. Now, to sleep ye two. The others will be wandering in soon."

After kissing each boy's cheek, she sought out the chamber that had been assigned to her. A hot bath awaited her and she took quick advantage of it. The comforts of Duncoille were all too easy to grow accustomed to, she mused, as she enjoyed her bath.

Once the tub was removed she sat down on a thick sheepskin rug before a small but comfortably warm fire to brush out her hair. A soft rap at her door startled her. As she called out her permission to enter she decided it was probably not Gamel. He would just walk in. Lady Edina entered the room and softly shut the door behind her.

"Ah, dinnae get up," Edina told Sine, who began to rise. "I have come to meddle." Edina sat down next to the younger woman. "Here," she said as she took the brush from Sine's hand, then edged behind her and gently began to brush her hair. "'Tis always easier to have someone else do it when 'tis as long and thick as yours."

"Thank ye, m'lady."

"Ye must call me Edina, although I have hopes that ye shall soon call me Mother."

"M'lady," Sine began a little awkwardly, for she was not sure how she could explain herself. "I . . ."

"I ken it—ye have refused to marry our Gamel. That vow ye made holds ye back, or so he says. I mean to speak on that, although my husband strongly feels that I would be wiser to just stand back. My compromise was to swear that I would simply speak what is on my mind, then leave ye be. I shallnae press ye on the matter."

"Gamel does," Sine sighed, for while that was the full, honest truth, she feared that she might sound impertinent.

"Aye, and kenning our Gamel, I feel certain that he shall continue to do so. I would speak to him about that, but it would do no good. Worse, I could easily press him to make some promise that he would surely break."

"I should not wish that," Sine murmured, wondering how everything had gotten so very complicated.

"Nay, I have guessed that much. Ye have our laddie sadly befuddled, m'dear."

"I did naught to bring it about."

Edina gently patted Sine's cheek. "I ken it. All here ken it. M'dear, ye have lain with our Gamel. Is it truly the vow that is all that holds ye back from taking him as a husband?"

Sine opened her mouth to say aye then slowly closed it. She was no longer certain. It suddenly looked so much more complicated than that. Her mind was crowded with muddled thoughts, and the reasons for her hesitation were so tangled up that it was suddenly impossible to sort one from another.

Gamel had her cornered and was not giving her any chance to think. He just continued to press for what he wanted. There was also the passion that flared between them. It both drew her to him and frightened her. That passion was so strong, so overwhelming, that she often felt it had to be wrong, even dangerous. Gamel used it to keep her close by his side and that worried her. A part of her was afraid that her own emotions could be used to enslave her. The mere thought of that chilled her. Then there was Farthing. Would Gamel finally force her to choose between him and Farthing? Would Gamel ever accept Farthing and what he meant to her? And there was the fear that she tried so hard to ignore, the deep, ever-present fear that she might carry within her the same evil that infected her mother. Sine knew she could not tell Edina any of that, however, and struggled to set aside her confusion and answer the woman.

"I dinnae ken if 'tis only my vow which makes me refuse Gamel," she muttered and briefly massaged her temples. "He pushed his way into my life, tricked me into his bed, and I havenae had a moment to think clearly since that night at the inn."

"And ye willnae for quite a while yet." Edina took hold of one of Sine's hands.

"Then what am I to do?"

"I think that ye must solve each problem as it comes to you."

"I have no time to solve my problem with Gamel. I must fight my enemies."

"Ye need little time to solve matters with our Gamel—only as long as it takes to kneel before the priest."

"Ye want me to marry him? What would that solve? I have just told ye how pitifully confused I am."

"Oh, aye, and how weel I can understand that. Aye, verra weel indeed. My marriage to William was an arranged one. We had to sort through many troubles before we found our happiness."

"Weel, I have no marriage arranged for me. Gamel tries to drag me before the altar."

Edina patted Sine's hand in a vain attempt to ease the girl's increasing agitation. "Think for a moment, child. Ye are *not* free; ye have merely eluded the confines all other weelborn lasses suffer. Ye are an unwed lass. That means that ye are the chattel of your kinsmen."

"Nay," Sine whispered, though she knew in her heart that Edina only spoke the truth. "My kinsmen are murderers."

"That is only suspected. There is no proof of it yet. It will take time for us to fully expose their villainy. Until we can do that, the laws that make ye the chattel of your kinsmen cannae be ignored."

"But my kinsmen cannae reach me, so what does it matter? The law can do them no good at all."

"One can ne'er be certain of that, child. We intend to hide ye weel and protect ye. Howbeit, Lord and Lady Brodie are verra skilled at the game they play. They are good at finding out all manner of secrets and keeping the whispers of their own crimes and sins from becoming bold accusations. They also have some verra powerful friends, mayhaps more than we realize. The law gives them a weapon in that it makes ye their chattel to do with as they please. If they ever discover that ye are alive and that they have such a weapon, they will surely wield it."

"Aye, they will. Weel then, I must leave here."

"And spend another six years running from every shadow? Ye have the chance to fulfill your vow now. Dinnae run from that. Stand and fight. There is one way to elude the threat we have just spoken of—marry Gamel."

"How can that help me?" Sine began to feel so completely cornered that it nearly restricted her ability to breathe.

"If ye werenae so distraught, I believe ye would have the wit to see the answer for yourself. All lasses begin life as the chattel of their kinsmen, but then they become women and are married."

"And become the chattel of their husbands," Sine added in a flat voice. "How can ye be certain that such a ploy would halt the Brodies? The marriage wouldnae be one which they had arranged and sanctioned. Arabel and Malise could rightfully claim that they still held the rule over me."

"They could claim it but 'twould take time to try and snatch ye from your husband. A marriage performed by a priest isnae something anyone takes lightly even if it is one which the parents havenae condoned. It would also be enough to give Gamel, and us, the right to fight for ye without risking outlawry."

"Is there any chance of that?" Sine began to fear that she was pulling her champions into far more trouble than she

had any right to do. "Gamel said that the king doesnae trust
or like Arabel and Malise."

"That might not matter. The law is clear. We would
be holding what was rightfully Arabel's and Malise's."

Sine rubbed her temples again as she tried to think.
She did not know where to turn. In all the years she had
waited and plotted her revenge, she had never realized
how complicated it could become. It had always seemed
a simple matter of right against wrong. However, she had
no real proof, only her word that the Brodies had actually done any wrong, and until she could get some, she
and her allies would have to tread very warily.

Edina slowly stood up and briefly rested her hand
upon Sine's head. "Think about all I have said, child.
There is no need to make any decisions tonight."

"Aye, I shall think about it, Lady Edina. Howbeit, I
cannae help but think that ye have set before me a verra
poor reason to get married."

"There have been worse reasons. And I believe that ye
would find a great many others in your own heart if ye
were but given the time to look. Sadly, I dinnae believe
ye will have that time until your enemies are defeated."

"And so I must make decisions that could alter my
entire life without even having the full knowledge of
what I need or want. It seems a verra poor way of doing
things."

"It need not alter your whole life," Edina said in a
quiet voice.

"What do ye mean? Marriage sanctified by the Church
is forever."

"'Tis what they would have us think, but that isnae
completely true. Ye could cry coercion; ye are far higher
born and wealthier than Gamel and it would be a marriage that wasnae condoned by any of your kinsmen or
guardians. If ye think hard enough, I am certain ye can

think of even more reasons why ye could petition the Church and have the marriage declared invalid."

"Mayhaps, but it doesnae seem the sort of thing ye should be telling me."

"I have great sympathy for your verra difficult situation. Also, as a mother, I seek only Gamel's happiness. Ye could easily make his life a pain-ridden hell if ye decided that ye didnae want him, and I would do most anything to save him from that." She bent and gave Sine a light kiss upon the cheek before walking toward the door. "'Twould be far better for him to suffer the clean, complete loss of his wife than to spend his years trying to win your love when ye cannae give it to him." She opened the door and looked back at Sine. "And, for now, 'tis better for ye—aye, for all of us—if ye become a wife. Think on it, child, and try to think without letting your emotions lead ye."

Edina had barely finished shutting the door behind her when she saw Gamel striding toward her. She took a few steps in his direction and halted him a foot from Sine's chamber door. It was hard not to smile at his expression of annoyance, which he could not hide, but she quickly pushed aside her amusement. Gamel was not going to like what she had to say. Edina could only hope that he retained the wit to see the good sense of her plan.

"Ye have been talking with Sine?" Gamel asked, and briefly stared at Sine's chamber door before fixing his gaze upon his stepmother.

"Aye, and I am pleased to be able to have a word with you ere ye join her. 'Tis about the marriage ye are demanding of her."

"Ye said ye had no qualms about it."

"And I meant it. Although I cannae approve of the way ye are pressing the lass."

"I wish to tie her to me as securely as I can. I dinnae want her to slip away again."

"Gamel, marriage willnae stop her if she truly wishes to leave. Howbeit, that isnae what I want to speak about. I have been trying to convince her to marry ye. Dinnae look so pleased. My arguments werenae about your worth as a husband, or lack of it."

"Then what could ye say to make her consider accepting my proposal?"

As Edina related what she had told Sine, Gamel began to frown. He did not like it. He wanted a great deal more from Sine than to be used as a shield to deflect her kinsmen's claims upon her. When Edina began to tell him that he must promise Sine that he would not fight any annulment after her enemies were beaten, he swore.

"Nay! I willnae let her go. I have said so often enough."

"Ye cannae hold the lass captive and force her to feel as ye do," snapped Edina. She sighed and took Gamel's clenched hand in hers. "Try to think clearly for a moment, will ye? 'Twill take us some time to defeat her enemies. Ye can use that time to win her heart. Howbeit, if the lass wishes to be free in the end, ye must let her go or ye will both suffer, and I think ye ken that verra weel. *And*, if ye dinnae offer her that chance, she may weel still refuse to wed ye. Dinnae make her feel so tightly chained that she will never heed your wooing."

Gamel nodded, silently acknowledging the wisdom of Edina's advice. He prayed that he could find the strength to follow it. After kissing his stepmother's cheek, he went straight to Sine's chambers. As he shut the door behind him, he met Sine's gaze and inwardly sighed at the wariness he read there.

"Edina has been talking with ye," he murmured as he walked over to Sine and knelt before her.

"Aye, but I havenae had much time to consider her advice."

"'Tis verra good advice."

"Did she tell ye what she said to me?"

"Aye. Ye need that protection, Sine, and I think ye realize it. Aye, and *we* would be the stronger for it as weel. Ye may have many a fine argument against wedding me, and many a good reason, but ye cannae deny the wisdom of Edina's words. If ye wed me, then ye can fight any claim your kinsmen try to make upon ye."

"I *can* see the wisdom of it. In truth, it really doesnae require a great deal of consideration."

He lightly grasped her shoulders. "Was that an aye then? We will be married?"

"Aye, whene'er ye wish it."

"On the morrow. There is no need to hesitate."

The pleasure she read in his expression was very soothing, but she fought its allure. "Did Edina tell ye about the promise I must ask of ye?"

"Aye. That I let ye end the marriage when the battle is o'er."

"And will ye promise to allow me to seek an annulment if that is what I wish?"

Finding it impossible to say the words, Gamel just nodded. The way Sine visibly relaxed and allowed him to pull her into his arms stung a little. As he tipped her face up to his, Gamel swore that he would make her want to stay with him, that by the time her enemies were defeated an annulment would be the very last thing Sine would want.

Chapter 8

"**M**arried? Ye mean to marry that mon?"

Sine stared at Farthing in surprise. It took her a moment to realize what he was saying. Her ears still rang from the sound of her chamber door slamming against the smooth stone wall when Farthing had made his abrupt entrance. She was not sure why Farthing was so upset. Custom demanded marriage to restore her honor, which Gamel had stolen when he had taken her innocence. It was not the reason she was marrying Gamel, but when she had agreed to the wedding last night she had briefly thought that it would be the one reason Farthing would approve of.

"Aye, I am to be wed to Gamel within the hour." As she continued to brush out her hair, she kept a wary eye on Farthing, who shut the door behind him with a little less force than he had used to open it. He began to pace her room.

"Why, lass? Why?"

"Mayhaps because I was a virgin of good birth when he coerced me into his bed?"

"Aye, he owes ye the protection of his name, but he has already offered that and ye refused him." Farthing stopped by the stool she sat on, put his hands on his trim hips, and frowned down at her. "What has happened to change your mind? Did he finally seduce ye into agreeing to marry him?"

She began to understand why Farthing was so troubled. He was afraid she was being forced to do something she did not wish to do.

"Nay," she said, "although he might weel have succeeded in doing just that before too long. There are times when that mon could tell me that the moon is green and I would believe him. Howbeit, that blindness eventually fades away and my senses return. Of course, if he seduced me right *at* the altar, then I might say aye ere I kenned what I was doing."

"Sine Catriona," Farthing snapped, "cease that nonsense. Playing the light-witted lass willnae work with me. I ken ye far too weel. Why are ye marrying that mon?"

"I dinnae think ye will like the truth any better than ye liked the nonsense. Lady Edina reminded me that as an unwed lass I am the chattel of Arabel and Malise."

Farthing stared at her for a moment, then viciously cursed. "Of course ye are. Aye, and that black-hearted wench holds sway o'er enough people in high places to make that a real threat."

"How do ye ken who Arabel holds sway over?"

As Farthing abruptly recalled where he had learned of Arabel's far-reaching grip, he murmured, "We have been watching that murderous pair and trying to learn all about them for six long years, sweeting. Now, what does Arabel's having the legal right to ye have to do with ye suddenly deciding to wed Gamel?"

"Weel, once wed to the mon, I shall be *his* chattel and not Arabel's and Malise's."

"Ah, I see. But it might not be enough. Neither of them would have approved the marriage."

"True. Howbeit, they willnae find it so easy to demand my return if a husband stands in the way, a mon bound to me by the holy sanction of a priest and the law of the Church."

"Aye," Farthing agreed slowly. "The men Arabel would seek out to aid her in asserting her right to hold ye would undoubtedly be reluctant allies, for their allegiance was not given willingly, but threatened out of them. So, they would be quick to call a husband an impediment. They could answer her call yet rightfully say that the law prevents them from acting."

He walked over to her bed, leaned against one of the ornately carved posts which supported the canopy, and folded his arms across his chest. "Howbeit, ye will be binding yourself to Gamel Logan for life just to escape what could easily prove to be a verra temporary threat."

"The marriage need not be for life."

"Dearling, he hasnae offered ye handfasting, which can last for but a year and a day. He takes ye to stand before a priest. Vows spoken before one of those holy men are vows chiseled in stone."

Sine put down her brush and turned on the stool so that she faced Farthing squarely. "It appears that that isnae the complete truth. Lady Edina listed several reasons my marriage to Gamel need not be so verra final. For one thing, Gamel is a bastard and I am weelborn. Unkind though it is, that could weel be reason enough for a petition for an annulment to be granted. She also mentioned coercion and the fact that I am far wealthier than he is."

"Fair enough. It could work. But would Gamel agree to such a thing?"

"He already has. I wouldnae consent to the marriage, even though it would be for my own protection, unless he swore that I could end it when my enemies were defeated."

"I wager that agreement was hard wrung."

"It was given reluctantly—aye."

"And do ye believe that he will hold to that promise?"

"Aye." She frowned. "Ye dinnae think that he is a mon of his word?" Sine found that she felt insulted over the implied slur upon Gamel.

"Oh, aye. I believe the fool is an honorable fellow, but he is also a mon of fierce passion. He may weel intend to keep his word, may be sorely shamed if he doesnae, but there is ever the chance that his passions could overrule his honor in this matter. They did at the inn."

"Mayhaps, although there are few men who would see it so. He but tricked a lass into his bed. The fact that his actions that night still trouble him only proves that he has a deep sense of honor. Nay, whatever he may feel, he will hold to his promise. In truth, this passion he suffers could weel wane by the time we beat the Brodies, and Gamel would be fair pleased to be free of me." Sine discovered that that thought was a painful one and inwardly shook her head over her own vagaries—she had insisted that Gamel leave her a chance to be free and then felt hurt that he might well let her take it.

"I believe he will do his utmost to try and make ye stay," Farthing said, disrupting her musings.

Sine shrugged. "Would that be so bad, Farthing? I mean, if Gamel makes me want to be his wife, then there would be no reason to end the marriage."

"True, if he actually makes ye want him and doesnae simply keep ye so confused that ye dinnae ken what ye want." He walked over to her, took her by the hands, and tugged her to her feet. "There is another way to play this game."

"Aye? What is it?"

"Marry me." He gently enfolded her in his arms. "Ye would have the husband ye need yet not have to suffer the demands we both ken Gamel will put on ye."

For a moment Sine just stared at Farthing. He was right. It all looked so simple, the perfect solution to her problems, but then she saw the flaw. It would not put an end to Gamel's demands, in fact it would only increase them. Farthing was already a thorn in Gamel's side. If she married Farthing, she dreaded to think of the turmoil that would result. She could even lose Gamel's support in her fight and she desperately needed it. Farthing and his father did not have the power the Logans had to turn the Brodies' reluctant allies against them. That was perhaps a very selfish reason to turn aside Farthing's offer, but it was one she had to consider.

She was about to refuse Farthing's generous proposal when she heard the sound of the door latch being lifted. Even as she turned her head to see who was entering her chamber, the door was suddenly thrust open so violently that it slammed against the wall again. Gamel stood in the doorway, his hands clenched into fists at his sides. He wore an expression of cold fury as he glared at Farthing. Sine expected Gamel to immediately lunge for Farthing but, to her surprise, he made no such move. She wondered if Gamel was finally trying to control his animosity toward her friend.

"Might one ask what ye are doing?" Gamel's voice was low and hoarse, anger giving it a slight tremor.

"One might," drawled Farthing. "Then again, one might have the courtesy and the wit to see that 'tis none of his concern."

Gamel took a step toward Farthing and Sine quickly moved to put herself between the two men. She tried frantically to think of something to say that might distract them. Forcing a smile to her lips, she held out the skirts of her rich blue gown, a gift from Lady Edina.

"Is this not the bonniest gown ye have e'er seen?" she asked.

Sine sighed when both Farthing and Gamel looked at her as if she had suddenly changed into some strange creature. It *had* been a foolish thing to say. She consoled herself with the fact that, idiotic or not, the statement had diverted their attention on her.

"Aye, verra bonnie," murmured Gamel.

"Oh, curse the gown," snapped Sine. "I just wish the pair of ye to cease snarling at each other like feral dogs."

"Then mayhaps ye can explain what he is doing here in your bedchamber," demanded Gamel as he strode over to Sine and tugged her away from Farthing.

"And why shouldnae he be here? What is wrong with it?" Sine glanced toward Farthing and saw him calmly leaning against the bedpost watching her and Gamel as if they were some fascinating entertainment.

"Ye shouldnae allow strange men into your bedchamber," answered Gamel.

"Strange men? Farthing? I have just spent six years of my life sharing sleeping quarters with the mon."

Gamel did not appreciate being reminded of that fact and glared all the harder at Farthing, who smiled back with an irritating sweetness. "The two of ye were looking verra friendly."

"We were discussing my marriage."

"He needed to hold ye in his arms to do that?"

"It seemed an appropriate position, considering that he was asking me to marry *him*."

The moment the words were out of her mouth Sine knew it had been the wrong thing to say, at least while both men were still in the same room. Again, she quickly placed herself between them. It annoyed her when Farthing continued to act the calm observer, leaving her to tend to Gamel all on her own.

"Ye willnae marry him," Gamel snapped, raising his clenched fists in Farthing's direction.

"Nay, I willnae. And this foolishness is but one good reason why."

"Foolishness? I find him in your bedchamber, holding ye in his arms, and because I question the rightness of that ye call it foolishness?"

"Aye, for that is exactly what it is. The problem of ending Arabel's claim on me would be solved just as neatly if I were to wed Farthing as it will be when I marry ye. Howbeit, whilst Farthing's feathers willnae be much ruffled o'er who I choose to wed, yours would be in a frenzy. And, hard as it may sound, I shall wed ye because I havenae the time or the strength to deal with an angry lover now, and I certainly cannae afford to lose the aid ye could lend me." She wondered why Gamel suddenly looked so affronted. As distasteful as it was, she spoke only the bald truth and they both knew it.

"I believe I shall go and prepare for your wedding," Farthing murmured. He slipped around Gamel and Sine to walk toward the door. "Gamel," he called, pausing in the open doorway, "why do ye call our Catriona by her first name—Sine?"

"Because *ye* dinnae," grumbled Gamel, too agitated to care if he sounded foolish.

"Ah, of course." As Farthing stepped out of the room and shut the door behind him, he said, "I shall meet ye in the chapel within the hour, Sine." The closing of the door cut off the sound of his soft chuckle.

"Ye shouldnae have told him that." Sine grimaced when Gamel swore and slapped the bedpost. "He will pinch ye about it now."

"He would have figured it out for himself soon

enough." Gamel turned to face her. "So, ye considered marrying Farthing instead of me?" He crossed his arms over his chest and watched her with a stern expression.

"Aye, I considered it. In many ways it would have been a more perfect solution to my problem. Farthing would have been a shield against the claims of my kinsmen, yet he would make no husbandly demands upon me. I dinnae think I am wrong in believing that whilst ye act as my shield, ye *will* make demands."

He took her hand in his and slowly drew her closer to him. "Aye, I will expect ye to act the wife in all ways, even if ye plan to make the bonds last only for a wee while. And, if ye did choose Farthing, I would still seek your bed."

"And that would create a verra difficult situation."

"Aye. I think I would be driven to kill him."

His voice was so cold that Sine shivered slightly. "I believe ye and Farthing hold an equal strength and skill, thus ye would probably kill each other. Which is why I shall marry ye, not him. I may not understand what causes this constant bristling dislike between the two of ye, but I see it clearly enough."

"Then mayhaps ye will try harder to keep the mon at a distance."

"I think not. We may not share a blood kinship, but Farthing is my kinsmon."

"Fine. I have heard enough about that cursed Farthing for the day." Gamel briefly wondered if his voice sounded as sulky to Sine as it did to him. "Ye do look most lovely," he said abruptly, his voice soft and low. "This gown flatters your eyes, although they need no such enhancement. Ye should always be so weel adorned. I would be willing to make myself a pauper for the pleasure of keeping ye prettily gowned."

Although she blushed a little with pleasure at his

words, she also suffered a twinge of nervousness. Such soft words were the sort a man used to woo a woman. But Gamel already had her body and did not need to flatter her into his bed. There could be only one reason Gamel played the sweet-tongued courtier. He had already stirred her desire and claimed her body—now he sought her heart, her soul, perhaps even her mind.

For a brief moment Sine wondered if she had grown too wary, was too quick to suspect his every word and action. Then she recalled Farthing saying that Gamel might try to make her wish to remain his wife. She had responded by asking what did it matter, but it *did* matter. It mattered a great deal. She was still afraid that she was carrying Arabel's bad seed, a seed that might grow into the evil that now tainted Arabel. Sine feared that she might one day turn on those she loved, and those who loved her. And worse, she thought with an inner shudder, she could pass that taint on to her children.

She was using a sponge to try and prevent any pregnancy but the fear was still there. The only sure way to prevent childbirth was abstinence and she did not have the strength to turn from the pleasure she shared with Gamel. She knew that if she did have a child, she would have to hide it from Gamel. She could not bear to see his hate when he discovered she had tainted his child with the evil carried in her blood.

That possibility meant that love was not for her, marriage was not for her, and a family was not for her. Gamel was trying to win her love and she had to fight that. She strongly suspected that she already loved the man, but she would do her best to deny it—to herself and most certainly to Gamel. She realized that she was condemning herself to a bleak and loveless future. It was enough to make her weep.

Gamel cupped her face in his hands and asked, "Why does my flattery make ye look so forlorn?"

Those soft words yanked Sine from her dark thoughts and she struggled to compose a plausible lie as she met his concerned and somewhat confused gaze. "Nay, 'tisnae your words. Any lass would find such kind words pleasing to hear. I cannae explain what ails me. Your words but made me think on all that lies ahead of us. Aye, and mayhaps a wee bit about all that has been stolen from me. Not just the gowns I might have had, for they are but fancies, but my home, family, food, and even a soft bed. I thought on how my father should be here to see me grown and adorned so prettily for my wedding." Sine discovered that, although those were not the things she had just been thinking, they were all true; such things did sadden her and were often in her mind.

"Nothing can bring your father back, but the rest shall soon be restored to ye." Gamel began to brush soft, warm kisses over her face. "I swear it."

He was just touching his mouth to hers when there was a sharp rap at the door. Sine could not resist a grin when Gamel swore and abruptly released her, then strode to the door. It was flattering to have such a man become so annoyed when denied her kiss. She tried to look more serious when Gamel opened the door to admit Lady Edina.

"Ye shouldnae be here," Edina scolded Gamel as she entered and went straight to Sine's side. "I am verra certain that ye can find something to busy yourself with until Sine is brought down to the chapel."

"I am breaking some unwritten law, am I?" Gamel asked, smiling faintly.

"Aye, ye are. Now away with ye." Edina made a shooing motion with her hand. "In fact, ye can tell everyone that the bride will be on her way in but a few moments."

"Keep a firm grip upon her, Mother. She has a disturbing habit of slinking away."

"Slinking?" Sine cried in protest, but Gamel was gone before she could say any more. She turned to Edina. "Surely he cannae think that I would slip away now? If naught else—where would I go?"

"I wouldnae give his words another thought, child. In truth, I think it does a mon good to suffer the pangs of uncertainty from time to time. They surely make us suffer from them."

Sine laughed but quickly grew serious again. "I suppose we may as weel go to the chapel."

"Ye have a moment or two, lass." Edina moved to a table beneath the narrow, shuttered window and poured Sine and herself some wine, then handed Sine a goblet. "Down it all, child. 'Twill soothe your nerves." Edina raised her own goblet in an unspoken toast, then took a long drink before adding, "Ye may feel no need of wine now, but ye will be glad of it with each step ye take that brings ye closer to the altar."

Twenty minutes later, Sine was able to see the wisdom of Edina's words. As she stepped into the chapel—a small, elegant chamber crowded with the people of Duncoille—she wished she had drunk another goblet of the heady wine. Even recalling Gamel's promise to let her end their marriage when and if she chose to did not ease the increasing tightness in her stomach. There was a small voice within her head which kept whispering that she would never be free, that the words the priest was about to speak over her and Gamel were merely the verbal affirmation of bonds which were already there. The strong possibility that the small voice was right was what truly enhanced her fears.

Farthing stepped over to her and she grasped his arm but found no real comfort in his silent support.

Gamel stood down by the altar, watching and waiting for her. He looked splendid in his rich green tunic and hose, the gold embroidery on the sleeves and hem of his snug jupon glinting in the candlelight. He was a man whom any maid would hunger for and in but a few moments the priest would declare him her husband. She was not sure she would have the strength to ever give him up.

"Sine Catriona?" Farthing lightly tugged on the draped sleeves of her gown to draw her attention to him. "We had best start on our way toward the altar or your lover will think that I am holding ye back."

The way Lady Edina kept frowning at her even as she hurried to take her seat next to William made Sine aware that her hesitation was beginning to stir the curiosity of the guests. "Aye, ye are right, Farthing." She looped her arm through his. "I but suffered a brief fit of timidity."

"Timidity or doubt?" he asked as he began their slow march toward the altar.

"'Tis quite acceptable for a bride to feel both upon her wedding day." She espied Margot in the crowd and frowned slightly, for the girl was looking very sad. "Farthing? Are ye certain that your young cousin doesnae mind my marrying Gamel?"

"Quite certain. Why do ye ask about her now?"

"Weel, I am ashamed to admit that I havenae taken much time to talk to her. She was brought here to meet and, most probably, wed Gamel. Yet, only as I prepare to wed Gamel do I think on how she may feel about it. She sits to the right of us, next to your father, and looks as if she is about to weep."

"Ah, so she does. The foolish lass pines for Martin Robertson. Although their acquaintance was verra short, she took a strong liking to the Brodies' spy. I saw it clearly, for I kept a close watch on them until I grew confident that Margot could be trusted to keep our secrets. She will overcome the madness."

"Mayhaps ye shouldnae discard the matter so lightly and quickly. Martin may weel suffer from a like attraction, and he isnae as black of heart as those he serves."

"Yet he continues to serve them."

"Once caught in the Brodies' net, ye serve them faithfully or ye die. 'Twould take a great deal for Martin to turn against them, for he kens verra weel how they deal with those they no longer trust."

"And ye feel that the wee Margot may be the spur to force Martin to try and break free? That the love of a good, sweet lass may make the mon try and redeem himself?"

"Ye dinnae need to sneer so," scolded Sine. "It has happened before. Not everything the minstrels trill about is an impossibility."

"Aye, ye are right. I will keep a close eye upon the lass. There may come some chance to reach that minion of the Brodies through her. And here stands your glowering courtier. 'Tis your last chance to flee, dearling."

"I begin to think that there is no place left to flee to," she whispered, and stepped away from a frowning Farthing to take hold of Gamel's extended hand.

As she knelt beside Gamel before the aging priest, Sine suppressed an urge to bolt. She repeated her vows and listened to Gamel repeat his. There was a quiet strength and determination in Gamel's voice as he spoke. That same force and a defiant touch of possessiveness could be felt in the way he held her hand. It was not a painful grip, but it was decisively firm and unrelenting.

Only once did she glance at his face. He was staring at her as she spoke. In his beautiful eyes was the glint of challenge. He was making a vow to himself even as he exchanged the marriage vows with her. Gamel was planning to make the marriage permanent.

Sine knew she had not been foolish in fearing the step she was taking. He would not make her retreat an easy one. It was not truly his strength she feared, but her own weakness. Somehow, despite whatever ploys he tried, she would have to retain the will to leave him, to walk away from something she desperately wanted.

Guilt became her overriding emotion when the ceremony was done and she and Gamel made their way back to the great hall of Duncoille. The congratulations of Gamel's people were heartfelt. It was evident that the promise of freedom Gamel had made to her was known to only a few. Sine felt like the worst of deceivers.

As Sine took her place beside Gamel at the head table she was briefly distracted by the feast spread out before them. There was suckling pig, chestnut-stuffed pheasant, rabbit pie, and mutton. There was even fresh venison still turning on a spit in the huge fireplace. Bowls heaped with onions, carrots, and turnips were on every table. Sweet and savory pies filled the air with their mouth-watering scents. Such plenty was a clear sign of wealth. Only those well blessed with coin could produce such a hearty meal, especially on such short notice.

Gamel touched her arm and held her gaze as he sipped wine from a heavy pewter goblet. When he extended it to her she was forced to sip from the same place upon the goblet's rim that he had. It was nearly impossible to break the grip of his intent stare. He touched a kiss to her mouth and the people in the great hall all cheered while she inwardly trembled. Gamel was definitely going to be a force to be reckoned with.

The celebratory feast soon became an ordeal. Sine tried to act as if she was perfectly content, but she knew that she was failing to deceive Gamel. His glances her way grew more frequent and piercing as the elaborate meal was consumed. She was heartily relieved when Lady Edina and Margot escorted her to the chambers she would share with Gamel. She was sure that she would face a confrontation with Gamel once they were alone, but she was pleased to be able to discard the false smiles and joviality.

"Lass?" Edina began to unlace the sleeves where they were attached to the armholes of Sine's gown. "Has this made ye verra unhappy then?"

"Nay, and I am sorry if I have left everyone thinking it has."

"Not everyone, child. 'Tis just that I am fully aware of all that brought this marriage about and watched ye more closely than others. There is something that troubles ye. Do ye wish to speak on it?"

"'Tis naught. I but feel a wee bit sorry for myself." Sine helped to hold her hair out of the way as Margot began to unlace the bodice of her wedding gown. "'Twasnae the wedding I had always dreamed about. There are too many shadows, too many troubles and threats. I also felt as if I was the lowest of deceivers."

"No one needs to ken the whole truth. Ye havenae deceived yourself or Gamel. 'Tis all that matters."

"Aye. Ye are right. 'Tis our concern and no one else's." Sine stepped out of her gown and watched how Margot lingered over the dress as she put it away in the clothes chest, a soft melancholy expression on her oval face. "Margot, I have been callous and inconsiderate not to speak up ere now. Howbeit, I pray that ye havenae stepped aside simply because ye were too shy or too kind to speak out."

"Nay." Margot shook her head as she finished setting the gown in the chest and stood up. "I dinnae doubt Gamel's worth as a husband or as a mon, but he wasnae the match for me. I but pitied myself, which is an ill thing to do. I have poor luck in the men my heart softens for. One succumbed to the plague and the other—" She quickly shut her mouth and nervously eyed Sine and Edina.

"And the other is the hireling of my enemies," Sine finished, smiling gently when Margot flushed.

"I willnae aid him in the fight against ye. I swear it. I ken what he is and the danger he can be to ye and the twins. I am not quite as naive as some people think."

"I believe ye. Howbeit, it couldnae hurt to try, in some small way, to aid him in freeing himself ere he is beyond saving."

"How could I do that?"

"There would be no real danger in an exchange of letters, would there, Lady Edina?"

"Nay, none at all." Edina helped Sine shed the last of her clothes and slip into a delicate, thin nightdress of linen and lace. "If ye speak of naught of any importance concerning Sine and her brothers or of our plans to defeat the Brodies, then it can do us no harm. It might even help us in a small way. Ye might turn his loyalties our way. Just keep in mind with each word ye put to paper that Martin Robertson is a Brodie mon. Eventually the Brodies will ken that Sine and her brothers are here and ye shall have to be e'en more wary."

"Aye, m'lady. Martin will ne'er trick me into helping those murderers. I may not be able to stop my heart from choosing blindly, but it hasnae stolen my wits. I may weep o'er his grave but, if he continues to choose to stand with the Brodies, I willnae betray any of ye to keep him alive. Aye, and he will have to do a great deal ere I will believe that he has changed sides. Are we done here then?"

"Quite done," answered Sine.

Lady Edina nodded. "Go and tell Gamel that he may come to Sine now." As soon as Margot was gone Lady Edina turned to Sine and asked, "Do ye think it is worth the risk? Can we gain anything from Margot's writing love letters to Martin Robertson?"

"Mayhaps not, but I dinnae think we shall lose anything either. I believe that Martin isnae as black of heart as those he serves. Margot could easily touch that softer side of him."

"The Brodies may forbid it."

"At first they will find it amusing, but once they ken that I am here, they will encourage it. They will hope to gain some information from Martin and Margot, something to use against us."

"And ye dinnae think that they will get that from Margot?"

"Nay. Margot may not be devious or sly, she may not have what is needed to trick any secrets out of Martin, but she *can* keep our secrets. Ligulf kept a close watch upon the pair whilst the Brodies were here and he told me that Margot was verra good at guarding her tongue. Farthing said the same and I have great faith in his judgment on such matters. She will tell that mon nothing. I feel certain of it."

"Aye, so do I." Lady Edina kissed Sine's cheek and started out of the room. "I will understand if ye end this marriage when ye are free of all of these dangers, but I do hope that ye will decide to remain Gamel's wife."

"I thank ye for that, Lady Edina."

Once Lady Edina was gone, Sine made herself comfortable on the large canopied bed. She already wished that she could remain a part of the Logan family. It was all she could have hoped for if her father and Lady Seaton had not been so cruelly murdered. She sighed and tried to banish such longings from her mind and heart. Such delights were not for her, Lady Arabel Brodie's daughter.

Gamel stepped into the room but moments after his mother had left. Sine inwardly grimaced as she watched him walk to the bed, shed his robe, and climb in beside her. He looked far too serious for an eager bridegroom. She was certain that he was going to question her on her odd mood and she dreaded having to tell more lies. In an attempt to divert his attention she turned toward him, slipped her arms about his neck, and proceeded to kiss him, savoring the taste of his fine mouth and the tickle of her awakening desire.

"I am glad we were spared the bedding ceremony," she murmured, caressing a narrow path down his chest with her hand and watching his beautiful eyes turn a darker shade of green as his passion stirred to life.

"As ye recall, I let on that I had already bedded ye that day Farthing and I fought in the bailey. So none saw the need for it, and Mother agreed."

"I dinnae think there are many at Duncoille who would oppose Lady Edina."

"True, but 'tisnae out of fear. She is too often right." He shuddered faintly and closed his eyes when she curled her long fingers around his erection and slowly stroked him. "Does this mean that your melancholia has passed?" he asked.

"'Twas but a brief sadness as I thought too much upon my own troubles and losses." She nibbled his ear and traced its shape with her tongue. "I am sorry if my mood spoiled the feasting in any way."

"Nay. Few noticed." With slightly unsteady hands he unlaced her nightdress, then abruptly yanked it off her and tossed it aside. "I but wondered if ye had some new doubts."

"Everyone has some doubts at such a time."

"I had none."

"I have come to realize that ye are a verra odd mon."

Sine trembled and softly murmured her delight when he cupped her breast in his hand and lathed the tip to hardness with his tongue. She tangled the fingers of her free hand in his thick hair to hold him in place. He licked, nibbled, and suckled until she was squirming with eagerness for him. When he moved to cover her with his body, she embraced him with her legs in a gesture of invitation and welcome. She gave a soft, low moan as he eased their bodies together. He grew still and she opened her eyes to look at him, only to find him watching her with an intensity that briefly dimmed her desire.

"When ye leave me, Sine Catriona, ye will leave this behind as weel. Can ye will yourself to forget this pleasure? Can ye stop yourself from hungering for it?"

He withdrew, then returned with a measured slowness that infected her with an intense mixture of delight and frustration. "Nay, Gamel," she whispered in an unsteady voice. "Dinnae turn this against me. 'Twould be so verra cruel."

Gamel muttered a curse, kissed her, and rested his forehead against hers. "Aye, so it would be. But, by God's bones, ye drive me to it, woman. Forgive me. I willnae do it again."

She believed him and her passion returned in its full glory, racing hot and free through her body. "Aye, I forgive ye, although I dinnae think a wee bit of atonement would be amiss." She shifted her body against his in a way that told him clearly what sort of atonement she wanted.

"'Twill be the sweetest penance I have e'er served," he murmured, and kissed her.

Sine held him close as he began to move and she started

to make the swift descent into blind passion. In her head the voices of common sense and self-preservation cried out in protest, urging her to hold back and not give so freely. Each time she and Gamel made love she lost another piece of her heart and became more enthralled, thus increasing the pain she would suffer when she had to leave him. She ignored the warnings of her inner self, pushed them aside by concentrating on the pleasure she was enjoying. Her time with Gamel was limited and she intended to savor each precious moment to its fullest.

Chapter 9

"That mon has shadowed our steps for o'er a week," snapped Arabel as she agitatedly paced the cramped, dark chambers she and Malise shared in Stirling Castle. "I dinnae trust him."

Idly eating grapes, Malise watched her from where he lounged on their bed. "Ye dinnae trust anyone."

"Which is why I am still alive." She stopped by the edge of their plain, rope-strung bed, put her hands on her hips and frowned at her husband. "'Tis the wit to ken when to grow suspicious that has gained us all we now hold. Sir Lesley had no real reason to join us on this visit to Stirling, yet he did. Why is he here?"

"'Tis not to bed down with ye, my dear wife. I think that is what truly troubles ye about the mon. He chose to bed your handmaiden Margaret instead of you."

"'Tis irritating that he would select plain, wee Margaret when he could have enjoyed my favors. The stupid wench will pay for that insult. Howbeit, that isnae why I suspect him. There doesnae appear to be any purpose for his presence here. He but lurks around the castle, around us. Why? Why should he be interested?"

"Mayhaps we have done some harm to one of his kinsmen."

Arabel shook her head. "Nay. I thought on that and found out all I could about his family. None of the names were familiar to me. There must be some other reason."

Malise turned on his side to watch her more closely. "What other reason could there be? Margaret?"

"I am certain that that pathetic coupling didnae begin until after we had left Duncoille."

"Someone at Duncoille seeks to learn more about us then."

"I considered that possibility as weel. There was nothing. We have had little to do with the Logans or the Magnussons."

"Ah, aye, the Magnussons. Mayhaps Farthing Magnusson seeks to discover more than your bedding skills."

"Nay. If he wished to ken more, he would have seen to the matter himself, not sent some fair young lad like Sir Lesley. There is something afoot, but it eludes me. I dinnae like that. And I dinnae like being spied on, and I am certain that is what young Lesley is about."

"Then kill him." Malise flopped onto his back again and returned to idly savoring the fruit in a basket at his side. "Have Martin see to the matter."

"I am starting to have doubts about your cousin Martin. He begins to hesitate, to argue and question, although not too vehemently yet. His reluctance is still mostly silent, but 'tis there. In truth, I begin to think that it has always been there. I have often wondered if he could have done more to stop Sine Catriona and those little bastards from fleeing."

"'Tis too late to ken the truth of that. If ye dinnae trust Martin to do as ye want, then how is it to be done?"

"I shall see to the matter myself. And, when her lover

is gone, I will tend to that wench Margaret as weel. If she
has told that young knight anything of importance, I will
soon learn of it. And ye might do weel to consider what
must be done about your cousin. Even if ye think he
might still prove useful, it may weel be time to cease
making him privy to all we say and do."

Martin tensed when he saw Arabel. Although he was
weary and eager to seek his bed, he stopped. He pressed
himself deeper into the shadows of the hallway as he
watched her slink along the badly lit corridor, then halt
before one of the chamber doors. His eyes widened a
little when he realized it was the door to Sir Lesley's
chambers. Arabel crept into the room and Martin felt a
shiver of dread. Only ill could come of Arabel's acting so
clandestinely so late at night.

It was several minutes before Arabel came back out of
the room. She looked around carefully before hurrying
away. Martin cursed and silently debated the wisdom of
spying on Arabel and her activities. It did not really surprise him that the woman was engaged in some plot he
knew nothing about. He had sensed Arabel's growing
suspicions of him and that did worry him. When Arabel
lost trust in someone, that person ended up dead. His
place within the Brodie entourage was becoming an extremely precarious one and he knew it would only grow
worse. It was increasingly difficult to hide his revulsion
at the things Malise and Arabel did and his guilt over his
part in it all.

Just as he decided he would go and have a look inside
Sir Lesley's chambers to see if he could discern what
Arabel might have done, Martin heard someone else approaching. He cursed softly when Margaret came into
view. The maid scratched at Sir Lesley's door and, when

there was no reply, she giggled softly and slipped inside the room anyway. Martin grimaced, for now he had two choices—take his chances and talk to Margaret, or continue to stand and watch.

Several moments later his decision was made for him when Sir Lesley appeared. Martin shrugged and, as soon as Sir Lesley entered his chamber, started to leave. A muffled bellow of shock and anger from the room brought Martin running back toward that door instead of strolling on to his own cramped alcove. He flung open the door and gaped for a moment before hastily controlling his expression.

Sir Lesley was crouching over Margaret's sprawled form. The young woman lay on the floor near the bed. Her face was twisted into a grimace of pain. Martin saw the goblet on the floor by the girl's side, a small puddle of wine now staining the floor. Sir Lesley ceased trying to revive Margaret and turned to glare at Martin, his hand moving to his sword. Martin took a hasty step backward in reaction to the fury in the man's gray eyes.

"'Tis no surprise to see ye here," snarled Sir Lesley as he rose to his feet. "Carrion e'er trails close to the wolf."

"Ye cannae think I had aught to do with this. I but came in answer to your shouting."

"And how is it that ye were near enough to hear me? Could it be that ye were fleeing from your dark crime, saw me, and now try to hide your guilt with this show of concern?"

"Nay, I have been your faithful shadow for days. Aye, I have been watching ye ere ye joined us outside Duncoille." Martin felt as surprised at his own honesty as Sir Lesley looked upon hearing it, but he knew that it was the only tack to take, the only one he wanted to take. "Margaret is dead?" he asked, then briefly regretted the question, for Sir Lesley grew angry again.

"Aye. Ye and your soulless masters have taken her life."

"I had naught to do with this." Martin quickly shut the door and, ignoring the furious Sir Lesley, walked over to Margaret. He sighed and shook his head in a gesture of honest sorrow when he saw her wide and sightless eyes. "There was no need for this," he muttered, and picked up the goblet at her side. "Poison." He walked to the small table on the far side of the room where there was a black leather jug of wine and a second goblet. After sniffing the jug, dipping his finger into the wine, and very gingerly licking his finger, he cursed. "'Tis a strong dose and not one of the gentler poisons either."

"But why kill poor Margaret?" Lesley asked, shaking his head. "She was a good lass. What wrong could she have possibly done?"

"It wouldnae have had to have been a verra big wrong. Howbeit, I still say that there was no need for this." He looked at Sir Lesley. "Methinks this death-sweetened wine was meant for ye. 'Tis ye she wanted to kill."

"She? Ye ken who did this?"

Martin gave the younger man a crooked smile. "I ken that ye would be wise to leave this place and hie back behind the thick walls of Duncoille. I will help ye with Margaret."

"There is no need. I can tell the guards myself."

"Nay. Ye will tell no one."

"I have naught to hide."

"True. I doubt anyone would think ye were guilty. Howbeit, she was murdered in your bedchamber. Ye will no doubt become tied here as they try to find the murderer. Ye cannae afford to linger here, Sir Lesley. 'Tis no longer safe, and the danger which is sniffing at your door isnae one ye can fend off with your sword or a gallant heart. We will put Margaret back in her own bed. Ye can help me get her back to her chamber door and I will place her in her cot."

"The other maids will see you. They will ask questions."

"They are wise enough to ken when to shut their mouths. Margaret will be found dead in her own bed and every maid in the room will swear it happened whilst they slept."

"Ye act so sure of that, as if it has already been tested and proven true."

"It has. Lady Arabel begins to find it difficult to get a maid." Martin knelt next to Margaret's body, smoothed her features as best he could, and hefted the maid onto his shoulders. "Ye can be my guard, Sir Lesley." When Sir Lesley did not answer, simply looked at Margaret with an expression of sadness on his craggy face, Martin murmured, "'Twould be best if we werenae caught with the poor lass."

Sir Lesley nodded, moved to open his door, and looked up and down the hallway. "'Tis clear." As soon as Martin passed through the doorway, Sir Lesley shut the door after them and followed Martin through the dimly lit hall. "Why are ye doing this?"

"My hands arenae as bloodied as ye might think. I do what I must to survive, but I try verra hard not to extract too high a price for my own life. I dinnae ken why ye are spying upon the Brodies and I truly dinnae care. 'Tis certainly not something ye should die for and that is what ye will do if ye linger any longer at Stirling. Flee here tomorrow, Sir Lesley."

"Why wait? Should I not leave now?"

"'Tis treacherous to ride at night and ye would raise too many questions with such a swift flight. Nay, leaving early on the morrow would be the wisest thing to do. Take your leave calmly and openly, but take it. Whate'er your game is, it has been discovered. Ye have lost the wager. Dinnae lose your life as weel."

"And do ye think that ye shall be safe?"

Martin stopped before the door of the handmaidens' cramped quarters and smiled faintly. "Safe? I have ne'er been safe, Sir Lesley. I but stay alive. Go and do the same. All I ask is that ye take a letter to the fair Margot for me. I will slip it to ye ere ye leave. God's speed, Sir Lesley."

"I owe ye my life."

"Aye, ye do. I may yet have need of such a debt," Martin whispered, and silently entered the maids' quarters.

"Margaret is dead," announced Arabel as she strode into her chamber and slammed the door behind her.

Malise abruptly sat up in bed, blinking sleepily. He shook his head slightly, then rudely kicked awake the woman sprawled at his side. "Get out of here, wench. My dear wife has returned."

Arabel crossed her arms over her chest and lightly tapped her foot on the floor as she waited to speak to Malise. She coolly watched Malise's bedmate stumble to her feet and haphazardly tug on her clothing. As soon as the woman was gone Arabel looked at her husband, who had plumped up the pillows behind his back and was sipping from a goblet of wine.

"She wasnae one of your better choices," she drawled, nodding toward the departing maidservant as she walked over and sat at the foot of the bed.

"The rogue ye chose for your evening's entertainment looked a wee bit long in the tooth."

"'Tis the selection at Stirlirg. 'Tis verra thin."

"Aye. Now, what is this about Margaret?"

"She is dead."

"Ye questioned her with a wee bit too much vigor, did ye?"

"Nay. I ne'er got the chance to question the slattern. She was found dead this morning in her own dirty little cot. Sir Lesley left for Duncoille soon after sunrise. It appears that Margaret drank the wine I had so carefully prepared for her lover. She must have slipped into his chamber ere he returned to it."

"If she drank the wine, then how did she get back to her own bed? Would she not have died exactly where she stood?"

"Aye, but she was found in her own bed. She must have been put there in the dead of night."

"It seems a verra devious act for the noble Sir Lesley. Are ye certain he did it?"

"Nay. Those foolish sluts who shared Margaret's chamber claim to have seen naught. They woke to discover her dead. I dare not question them too harshly. They arenae all my maids, and they are quick to seek the protection of their mistresses. To press the matter would gain me little or nothing, yet it could easily turn suspicion my way. Too many people would find my sudden concern o'er a mere handmaiden verra suspicious indeed. In truth, all that matters is that I didnae succeed in permanently ridding ourselves of the overly curious Sir Lesley. I sent some men after the fool, but I dinnae believe that will help."

"But ye *have* rid yourself of Sir Lesley. He has left Stirling."

"But not *permanently*. And why was he here at all? Why was he watching us? What information is he taking back to Duncoille and what do the Logans want with it? There are too many questions, Malise. Far, far too many."

"'Tis time we did a wee bit of spying ourselves."

Arabel nodded. "More than a wee bit. There is

something else I have discovered. Lord Angus MacGregor, Sir Patrick Douglas, and Lord Robert Fergueson have all received messages from Lord William Logan. Lord Angus makes plans to go to Duncoille and the other two have answered the messages—extensively and without hesitation. I had no success in intercepting those messages either. They sent out their best and most loyal men whilst I am cursed with incompetent fools. Something troubles me about all this, for these arenae men the Logans have had aught to do with 'til now. Why the interest now? We need answers."

"Should we send along a spy of our own? There may be a way to slip one of our own in amongst the Logans."

"There may be, but I believe we shall do a bit ourselves first."

"Ourselves?"

"Aye—ourselves. We shall leave here for Dorchabeinn in a few days and must pass by Duncoille. We will stop in one of the nearer villages for a few days and see if we can discover anything."

Malise shrugged. "If ye believe 'tis worth the trouble. I am not so sure I do. I dinnae believe the Logans have aught to hide."

"My dear husband, *everyone* has *something* to hide. I am certain that, if we are careful and look close enough, we shall discover that even the gallant Logans have their secrets."

"I begin to feel like a prisoner," Sine grumbled as she rested her arms on the top of the parapets and stared out over the fields surrounding Duncoille. "Our wedding was a fortnight ago and since then I havenae stepped beyond these walls once."

Gamel smiled faintly as he leaned against the wall

next to her and offered her a small bouquet of heather blossoms. "'Tis just that ye have spent so much of your life in that cart, roaming from place to place, sleeping beneath the stars. If ye hadnae been forced from your home, ye would have grown to womanhood behind walls much akin to these."

"Aye, but I would have been able to step beyond them now and again." Sine murmured her pleasure as she inhaled the sweet scent of the bouquet, touched by the courtly gesture even though she knew she ought to resist its allure.

"True, for it would have been safe." He reached out and ran his hand over her thick braid. "'Tis not safe now. Not for ye. Not for the twins." He slid his hand beneath her braid and moved his fingers up and down her slim back in a soothing caress.

"I ken it. It makes it no easier though. Howbeit, I try and comfort myself with the knowledge that we inch closer to victory each day."

"I believe we move at a faster pace than that. Lord Angus MacGregor is most eager to come here and speak with my father. They fought many a battle together when they were younger. He has already sent us a great deal of information through his squire, a mon he trusts with his life. Also, a Sir Patrick Douglas and one Lord Robert Fergueson have responded to my father's inquiries in some detail. And Farthing returned but a few hours ago from visiting a sheriff and a knight or two in Perth who proved most helpful. They told Farthing of how the Brodies worked their wiles in Perth until nearly every mon of consequence became an unwilling ally."

"None of it is the clear indisputable proof of the Brodies' crimes that we seek though."

"Nay, but with my father promising aid and protection, the number of men—and women—willing to speak up against the Brodies grows day by day. They but fear that they might expose themselves to the censure of their peers or worse. Father has refused the aid of one or two, for they wouldnae say why they had helped the Brodies or why they turned on them now."

"None of them are innocents."

"Nay, but some of them have allowed the Brodies to make a small sin appear a bigger one, to use the guilt their victim suffers to wield power o'er them. What takes shape is a tangled mass of lies, fear, guilt, and blackmail. All were used by the Brodies to help hide their own crimes, of which there are many. We may not have real, hard proof but we begin to gain a veritable army of people ready to speak out against Arabel and Malise. The moment they are told that others have begun to speak out, the truth spills forth, as if each one welcomes the chance to confess."

"And mayhaps free themselves from my mother and her husband."

"Aye, there is that. Some grow weary of being beneath the thumbs of the Brodies. Some fear that they may yet be dragged into some verra dark crime and not just the petty sins and favors so far demanded of them."

Sine turned sideways to face Gamel more directly. "Ye have been verra careful not to tell me what crimes Arabel and Malise are guilty of. Do ye think to spare me, to protect me from kenning the whole truth?"

Gamel winced. "Mayhaps. 'Tisnae pretty."

"I ne'er thought that it would be pretty. Arabel is a woman who sought to kill her own child and did murder her husband. I dinnae think ye could tell me anything that could pain me more than that. And, considering how all of this must end, it may weel be kinder to let me ken just how sinful she is. If I am to be the one to cause her death, 'twould be best if I ken how richly she deserves it."

He put his arm around her shoulders and tugged her closer. "I dinnae intend to let ye stain your bonnie hands with your mother's blood."

"I have sought vengeance for six long years. I have begun this battle. I am already a partner in her death." She knew she could not let herself forget the fact, for although ignoring it now could ease her mind, she would pay dearly for that peace later. "So, tell me, what have ye discovered?"

"A veritable knot of deceits, of grasping for power and riches. And murder. The Brodies put a swift end to anyone who gets in their way. 'Twould take the rest of the day to tell ye all we have learned thus far. But if all we have been told is true, then the ones who found an association with the Brodies to be fatal number about thirty."

"Sweet Jesu," Sine whispered, horror shuddering through her body. "So many."

"Since people are quick to blame all wrong on ones they fear, there are undoubtedly some people included in that tally who shouldnae be there."

"And ones who arenae but should be simply because their deaths were unmourned or cleverly contrived. And what have they gained from such bloodletting?"

"Riches and power. The king doesnae trust them yet must court them. They hold such strength and wealth that he cannae afford to ignore them. He could weel have need of the army they can raise, or the strength of their allies, or even some of the coin they could gather. Nay, nor does he dare anger them without sound justification. A Scottish king ne'er sits too securely on his throne. He must tread warily. Robert wouldnae wish to make the Brodies too angry, for they could weel prove to have the strength to turn on him and win."

"And sound justification to resist them will be verra hard to obtain."

"Aye, for the Brodies are sly. Their enemies die so conveniently yet the Brodies cloak themselves in innocence. All ken who did the murder yet none can prove it. 'Tis only seen that the Brodies benefit from the death."

"How can people let it continue?"

"Well, let us consider poor Lord Angus MacGregor. He is a pious mon and deeply in love with his wife. The vows they spoke before a priest would have been enough for such a mon. Howbeit, in a gesture of gallantry he swore to his wife, on his honor and his sword, that he would be ever faithful."

"And Arabel made him break that promise."

"Oh, aye. He went to the king's court and she was there. He spoke to us of being bewitched. He lingered at court to be near to her and followed her when she returned to Dorchabeinn. He lied to his wife again and again to explain away his long absences. Arabel drew him deeper and deeper into what he calls a well of depravity—he alludes to a taste for cruelty on Arabel's part. His guilt is compounded in his mind because it was his wife who, all unknowingly, pulled him free of that mire. She sent a message to him. She had been taken to bed with the birthing of their third child, but it wasnae an easy birth and she wished him to be with her."

"Was everything all right?"

"Aye." Gamel kissed Sine's forehead. "Angus claims 'twas as if he was slapped awake. He left the Brodies' almost immediately and sped back to his wife's side. He was greeted with a healthy son and a weary but healing wife. It wasnae long before he learned that his guilt and shame werenae the only penance he would have to pay. The Brodies kenned his weakness, that he didnae want his wife to learn of his sins. Angus hasnae been drawn into any true crime, but he was coerced into aiding them at court and keeping his mouth shut when he learned of any wrong done by them."

"If he now aids us, then the past indiscretions he seeks to hide will become known."

"Aye. He kens it. He plans to tell his wife ere he comes here. 'Tis why he sent his squire along first."

"In truth, I dinnae think she will be verra surprised."

"Do ye think she already kens?"

"She must have sensed some change in the mon. He speaks of guilt and shame. Such strong emotions cannae be hidden weel, especially not from a loved one. I but pray that she is the forgiving sort. 'Twould be verra sad if Arabel's machinations destroy what seems to have begun as a great love." She turned to look back out over the fields, then frowned. "A rider approaches, Gamel."

Gamel also turned to look and, after watching the rider for a moment, said, "'Tis Lesley. He returns much sooner than I had expected him to."

"At least he returns alive." Sine was relieved to see Sir Lesley, for she had not liked the thought of Gamel's dearest friend being in danger, especially when that danger came from her kinsmen.

"Aye." He took her by the hand. "We had best go and hear what he has to say."

Sine grew increasingly tense as she and Gamel made their way toward the great hall. Once there, they had to wait while Sir Lesley went to his chambers to tidy himself and the others gathered. Farthing, Margot, and Lord Magnusson were the first to hurry in, followed by Lord William, Ligulf, Nigel, Norman, and Lady Edina. They had all barely been seated at the lord's table and served some mead when a refreshed Sir Lesley strode into the hall. Sine dreaded the man's news and, as Sir Lesley joined them, she took several deep sips of her drink in a vain attempt to steady herself.

As Sir Lesley told his story, Sine discovered that her sense of dread had been warranted. She grieved for the young maid who had been murdered, yet was guiltily pleased that Sir Lesley had not sipped Arabel's deadly wine. It also annoyed her that, yet again, even though Arabel's guilt was obvious, only Martin had seen the woman enter Sir Lesley's chambers. And Martin would never accuse either Brodie.

"Ye say that Martin aided ye?" she asked Sir Lesley.

"Aye. I was prepared to go to the king himself, or at least his guardsmen. Martin convinced me to act as if naught had happened and leave Stirling as soon as possible. As I rode here I feared I had been talked into acting cowardly."

"Nay—wisely," said Gamel. "Who kens what sort of tangle may have ensued? The Brodies are verra clever. They could even have turned suspicion your way. They would certainly have done their utmost to try again to murder you. Ye were alone in the midst of the enemy. 'Twas best to retreat."

"So Martin Robertson said. I wasnae sure whether I should trust him."

"In that circumstance ye could," said Sine, then faintly grimaced. "Martin was able to do what was right, without putting himself in danger. I wouldnae trust him if there was any risk to him involved, however. Martin's law is to protect his own back above all else. That was evident to me even as a child. Aye, and my father once said as much himself. I have mixed feelings about the mon. He isnae free of the sins and crimes of the Brodies. Nay, he has a great deal he must atone for. Mayhaps not so much that he needs to pay with his life though. I believe there is some good in the mon and I can even pity him his place in life. It cannae be easy for him. And he cannae be happy."

Sir Lesley shook his head. "Nay, not easy at all. I asked him if he thought he would be safe and he said that he has ne'er been safe—he but stays alive. Aye, one can feel some pity for him. He did ask one favor of me—to give this missive to Mistress Margot." He took a letter from a pocket in his jupon and handed it to Margot, who sat across the table from him. While she read the letter under the watchful eyes of her companions, Sir Lesley continued. "I fear I wasnae the best of spies. Martin kenned that I played some game and I feel certain that he began watching me from the moment I asked to journey to Stirling with them."

"I am sure he did," agreed Sine. "Watching is what Martin does best. The Brodies are suspicious of anyone they have no hold on. In truth, I doubt they trust even those they do rule. They would have had Martin begin to watch ye from the moment ye rode away from here."

"So he probably told them whom I talked with. What we talked about, and even when we met."

Sine shrugged. "Mayhaps. Mayhaps not. Martin ne'er warned them that I had learned of their plans for me and the twins. If he had, I ne'er would have gotten free. Ye just cannae be sure what Martin Robertson will do."

"He may weel be looking to break free of the Brodies." Sir Lesley glanced toward Margot before continuing. "I acknowledged that I now owed the mon my life. He said that he may yet have need of such a debt."

Gamel frowned and slowly rubbed his chin. "'Twould be verra helpful to gain such an ally, but I dinnae think we should raise our hopes too high. Aye, and if he does come to our side, we should accept his aid verra cautiously."

Lord Magnusson turned to Margot when she sighed

and carefully refolded her letter. "Did he say aught that we should be told about?"

"Verra little," Margot replied. "He is as careful with his words as ye warned me to be. 'Tis little more than sweet words and talk about his unworthiness. He does begin with a prayer that Sir Lesley arrived safely."

"Did ye have any trouble on your journey here?" Lord William asked Sir Lesley.

"Nay, not truly," he replied. "I am certain that I was pursued, but I was able to elude all trouble. I caught a glimpse or two of a small knot of men at my back, but I kept weel ahead of them. They soon turned away."

"There is only one other thing that may be of interest," Margot said. "Martin tells me that he may have a chance to call upon me in a week's time. The Brodies must be planning to leave Stirling and return to Dorchabeinn soon." She frowned. "He hopes to see me, yet in the verra next sentence says that it might be best if I returned to my own home ere he arrives. That could but mean that he believes I would err in accepting his courtesies."

"Aye." Lord Magnusson frowned. "It could also be a warning, as strong a one as he dares to give. The mon may sense trouble brewing and wishes ye to be weel away from it. He should have been a wee bit less subtle though."

Gamel smiled faintly at Lord Magnusson's cross words, then quickly grew serious again. "We shall take both meanings into account. The Brodies surely ken that Sir Lesley was spying upon them and they will want to ken the why of that. They could also intend to spy upon us now. We shall be prepared."

Although Sine was not sure how one could prepare for such a thing, she said nothing. In a week the game of spying, of messengers sent and received, could come to an abrupt end. In a week Arabel could discover that she had not rid herself of the daughter she loathed. The thought of that terrified Sine. At that point there would truly be no turning back.

While Gamel washed up and prepared for bed he kept a close but covert watch upon Sine. Since they had met with Sir Lesley in the great hall she had been unusually quiet. Now she was sprawled on her back in their bed, staring up at the canopy. Gamel knew she was troubled, but he was not sure what he could do about it.

He silently cursed as he shed the last of his clothing and climbed into bed beside her. They had reached an unspoken truce since their wedding. He did not speak of the future and neither did she. Whether their marriage would last or end with the defeat of the Brodies they simply did not discuss. The only things they faced with any openness were their passion for each other and their united fight against the Brodies. Gamel did not think he had ever felt so frustrated or uncertain. Even now he was not sure if he should ask her what was troubling her or hold his tongue and hope that her mood would pass. As he tugged her into his arms, he decided that ignoring her silent, somber air was beyond him.

"Sine, I ken that ye are troubled," he murmured, brushing a kiss over her forehead as he combed his fingers through her hair. "It sometimes helps to share your woes."

"I ken it." She idly smoothed her hand over his broad chest. "The game will soon grow more serious. Arabel will soon ken that the twins and I are still alive. The thought of that terrifies me."

Gamel tightened his hold on her. "Ye willnae have to face her alone. Ye have many allies and we *shall* win this battle."

"But at how high a cost?" she whispered.

"'Tis far past time that those two were made to pay for their crimes. Come, we arenae untried lads. We have fought a battle or two. Ye need not be so afraid."

"The woman within me kens that and kens that too much fear can be dangerous at such a time. Howbeit, the wee lass who saw her father murdered still lingers within me too, the one who heard her own death planned and fled into the night. That wee lass is cowering with fear. I find that it isnae easy to cease running and hiding and suddenly stand to face my enemies." She glanced up to catch him watching her with concern. "Dinnae worry o'er me. I will soon calm that wee lass. 'Twas but worrisome to discover that I am not as ready to fight as I had thought I was." She grimaced. "Nor as brave."

"'Twas certainly no coward who, at the meager age of twelve, took her wee brothers in hand and fled. Lady Arabel's the one who should be all atremble."

Sine laughed and slipped her arms about his neck. "Struck with terror o'er having to face such a fierce warrior?"

"Aye." He brushed a kiss over her full, inviting mouth. "Although 'tisnae your fierceness as a warrior which holds my greatest interest at the moment." He trailed slow, stroking kisses over her throat.

She smiled and rubbed her body against his, her smile widening when he groaned softly. "Ye prefer my ferocity to reveal itself somewhere other than on the battlefield?"

"Here would be pleasing." He gently pushed her onto her back and eased his body on top of hers. "Dinnae give in to your fears, sweeting," he whispered, his tone abruptly becoming soft and solemn. "Fight them with all the strength ye can. Aye, with all the strength I ken ye have within this slim, fine body. Those fears are a weakness

Arabel Brodie would quickly scent and use against you. Fight them."

"I will," she vowed as she cupped his face in her hands and tugged his mouth down to hers.

She prayed that she would be able to keep that vow. Sine knew that her mother would indeed use those fears to weaken and defeat her. Even worse, Sine knew that Arabel would try to use those fears to hurt anyone she cared about.

Chapter 10

"Ah—freedom." Sine held her arms out wide and grinned up at the sky. "Its taste is as heady as the finest wine."

She grasped the reins of her mount and nudged the sleek mare to a swifter pace, then laughed. All six men riding with her quickly brought their mounts in line with hers. Their protectiveness was both amusing and mildly irritating. She was free of the safe but confining walls of Duncoille, but not free of her self-appointed guardians.

It had taken her three full days to convince Gamel that she would go mad if he did not allow her outside the walls of Duncoille. Gamel had agreed, very reluctantly, to take her to a market day at a small village called Kilbeg just north of his family's lands. Farthing had joined them, partly to help protect her and partly to annoy Gamel. Sir Lesley, Ligulf, Nigel, and Norman rode along as well, swords at the ready to fend off any trouble. It was an impressive entourage.

Sine felt a little bit guilty but was willing to endure that for the pleasure of being, more or less, free for a few hours. She did wonder, however, how long it would take Gamel to realize that her claims of needing more materials for her needlework were false. Not only were there ample supplies at Duncoille, but she was a verra poor needlewoman. She did it as seldom as possible, her skills restricting her to mending. After taking a deep breath of the clean, crisp forest air, she decided it was worth the deceit and whatever penalty she might have to pay in return. She glanced at Gamel, who rode on her right, saw his deep frown, and wondered if he had already guessed her ruse.

"Is something wrong?" she asked Gamel.

"Besides the fact that we are presenting ourselves as an easy target for attack?"

"Aye—besides that." When Gamel gave her a mildly disgusted look, Sine smiled sweetly.

"Ye keep speaking of freedom as if we have kept ye locked and chained in some dark, damp cell for months." Gamel inwardly cursed, afraid that he sounded foolish, yet unable to completely subdue a sense of hurt and insult over her delight in being away from Duncoille.

A light flush of embarrassment, mixed with a hint of shame, rushed into Sine's face. She had been thoughtless. Not once had she considered how her remarks might sound to others. Gamel was rightfully proud of Duncoille and her calling it a prison had to pinch at that pride.

"There is naught wrong with Duncoille, Gamel," she said quietly. "'Tis a keep few can equal. I find it both comfortable and pleasing. 'Tisnae Duncoille I rage against but the ones who hold me besieged within its walls. I dinnae resent the walls, only that the Brodies force me to cower behind them. I am sorry for the insult. I ne'er intended to deliver ye one. I was thoughtless."

"Nay." Gamel grimaced faintly. "I was too quick to find offense." He smiled at her. "I do understand what ye feel.

A few years ago I was fighting in France and was caught within a castle besieged by the English. I owed my life to the fact that the castle was strong, easily defended, and weel supplied. It was a rich, fine place that any king would envy. Howbeit, when the siege ended and the gates were finally opened, I was one of the first to flee the place e'en though we had won the battle."

"Aye, he wouldnae e'en allow us to savor the celebration of our victory," drawled Sir Lesley.

That remark prompted a round of companionable bickering between Gamel and Sir Lesley. Sine relaxed and concentrated on simply enjoying a beautiful day and the sense of peaceful happiness it brought. When the small village came into view, with a crowd of people milling amongst its thatch-roofed cottages, Sine felt as excited as if she were riding into Edinburgh. She wryly decided that she was not suited to a cloistered life if, after a short and necessary confinement, she could be so pleased by a tiny village's market day. The narrow streets were littered with every sort of farm animal. Men dragged reluctant goats along. Chickens darted amongst the horses. A grizzled shepherd barely cast a glance their way as he idly herded about a dozen sheep down the rutted street to their right.

They left their mounts with the blacksmith and Sine eagerly began to look over every item offered for sale or barter. She noticed that it was not long before the men began to lose interest in watching over her. Although they did not completely cease keeping an eye on her, they began to respond more fulsomely to the smiles of the young maids. Glancing up from a particularly lovely gourd bowl, she glimpsed Farthing slipping away with a buxom lass. Soon only Gamel would remain at her side and she wondered how long he could endure it as she examined some cloth and yarns. It was not a chore a proud knight could stomach for long, especially when there was no hint of an enemy amongst the hardworking common folk crowding the market square.

"I think ye would be much happier if ye went and had an ale with your brothers," Sine finally suggested to Gamel after nearly an hour of idle shopping. "Ye begin to look more like a martyr than a guard."

"I shouldnae leave ye alone," he murmured, casting a covetous look toward his brothers, who stood near the alewife's table drinking deeply of her brew and laughing heartily.

"Gamel, ye have studied everyone here and found naught which worries you. Go. I shall cry out if there is any danger. E'en if an enemy of mine is here and I doubt it, he, or she, wouldnae do verra much. This village teems with witnesses and the Brodies dinnae like witnesses."

"Nay, that is true enough. Stay with the crowd, dinnae go off anywhere alone. I shall be right o'er there at the alewife's table." He kissed her cheek and walked away.

For one brief moment after Gamel left her side, Sine felt panic stir within her. She began to look suspiciously at everyone, wondering if she saw the glint of a knife in a certain man's hand or a sly, traitorous look in a woman's eyes. It took an exerted effort to rally her strength and calm herself. Sine forced her attention back to the cloth she was fingering and firmly told herself that Arabel and Malise would never linger in such a poor, tiny village.

"Cousin Thomas," Margot cried as she raced into the great hall, straight toward the head table where Thomas and William were sitting.

Lord Magnusson looked up from the map of Dorch-abeinn he and William had been diligently drawing and gaped slightly. "Margot, my child, where have your manners fled?"

Margot performed a hasty curtsy. "I humbly beg your pardon, m'lords, but I felt that haste was needed. I have received a message from Martin."

"Another? So soon? Weel, let us read it then if ye feel it is so verra important."

"Nay, 'twasnae a written message. Martin sent a wee lad to tell me to come and meet him."

"When and where?" asked Lord William.

"Within the hour in the wood about a mile north of here," replied Margot.

"The Brodies are already traveling from Stirling to Dorchabeinn?"

"Aye, but I fear 'tis far worse than that. The Brodies have halted not far from here in the small village of Kilbeg—the verra one Sir Gamel and Lady Sine have traveled to."

Sir William cursed. "Weel, the lass has six guards with her and all of them are weel skilled in the use of their swords."

"There is nothing we can do?" asked Margot. "They could come face-to-face with the Brodies."

"They could," agreed Sir William. "I will send someone to the village to warn them. 'Tis the best I can do. I truly believe that the secrecy we have enjoyed up until now is over. We had best begin to change our plans accordingly."

"What am I to do about Martin? Should I refuse to meet him?"

Lord Thomas shook his head. "Nay, lass. Ye will meet him. Two of my men will go with ye."

"Do ye think Martin means to harm me?"

"Nay, but ye should ne'er tryst with a mon alone and we already have some doubts about this particular mon.

My men willnae intrude, but they will linger near enough
to come to your aid if ye have need of them."

"And should I continue to hold silent about Lady Sine
and her brothers? This news, that their enemies are so
close, has upset me. I am not sure I shall be able to hide
that."

"Dinnae try, lass. In truth, I would be surprised if
Martin doesnae at least ask ye why the Logans are spying
upon the Brodies. Even if he doesnae intend to use ye to
betray us, his own curiosity must be aroused."

"Aye," agreed Lord William. "And Martin has proven
himself to be a mon who labors hard to protect himself.
Such a mon would be eager to ken why we try to gather so
much information. So, tell him why we spy upon his
masters—because we have allied ourselves with the children Lady Arabel tried to murder six years ago. Only that.
No more. His response could prove verra interesting."

"It seems a great deal to reveal to him," Margot said,
and frowned.

"Not now. In a village as small as Kilbeg, the Brodies
are sure to espy Sine Catriona. There is no longer any
need to be so secretive. And, I think 'tis time we gave our
enemies a wee jab to see how they jump."

A half hour later, as Margot stood in a copse a mile
from Duncoille and watched Martin approach, she was
not sure she wanted to be enlightened concerning
Martin's true character. Martin's reaction to the news
that Sine and the twins were still alive could put a painful
end to what few hopes she had nurtured about her relationship with him. He could easily reveal that he equaled
his masters in venality and then he would have to be cast
aside, as dead to her as the lover she had lost to the
plague. She gave Martin a weak, tremulous smile of wel-

come as he took her hand in his and kissed it. His dark
eyes were soft with concern. She desperately wanted to
trust him.

"I wasnae sure ye would come," he said as he led her
toward the lush grass beneath an aspen, sat, and lightly
tugged her down beside him.

"I havenae come alone."

He tensed a little but smiled crookedly. "Nay, ye
wouldnae have been allowed to do that, especially not
with all that now stands between the Logans and the
Brodies."

Margot stared off toward the trees where her cousin
Thomas's two burly men-at-arms lurked unseen. "What
do ye mean, Martin? What could stand between them?
They are barely more than acquaintances."

Martin took her small chin in his thin hand, turned
her face toward his, and smiled when she hesitated to
meet his gaze. "Ye are a poor deceiver, lass. 'Tis your
utter lack of that skill which draws me to ye e'en though
it can bring naught but trouble. The Logans spy upon
the Brodies. I ken it and so do ye. They gather a prodi-
gious amount of information on my notorious masters.
I but seek to ken the why of it. Howbeit, I will understand if ye cannae tell me. I would ne'er force a lass as
sweet and innocent as ye are to taste the bitter draught
of betrayal. Keep your secrets if ye must."

"Nay, there is no more need to keep this particular
secret. Your masters will have the answer themselves ere
the day is done. They will surely discover it in the village
they have stopped in."

"What do ye mean?"

"Sine Catriona Brodie and her young half brothers are
alive. As Lord Logan says—the Logans and the Magnussons have allied themselves with the children your masters sought to murder six years ago."

She watched, nervously twisting her hands together in her lap, as Martin sought to understand what she had just told him. All the color seeped from his face as he gaped at her, his eyes wide with shock. A moment later, to her utter confusion, he began to laugh, the color swiftly returning to his thin face.

"Alive?" he asked, still laughing. "Wee Sine and the bastards are alive?"

"Aye. Ye find this funny? What could possibly be funny about it?"

"Naught. Weel, naught that ye could e'er understand." He draped his arm about her shoulders and kissed her cheek, his mood a jovial one. "I could almost wish to be there when Arabel discovers it. After six years with no sight or word of the brats, she had begun to believe that her daughter and her husband's sons were indeed dead."

"Why would she wish them dead? Sine is her own flesh and blood."

"Aye, and Arabel hated that child from the moment she was conceived. Arabel's vanity is a madness. So is her greed. Not only did wee Sine have the impudence to mar Arabel's form while she was still within her mother's womb, but she also left a tiny blemish or two after she was born. Young Sine also looks just like Arabel. Arabel ages and sees each day that is added to her years as a curse. Every time she looked at Sine, Arabel could see how the child would grow to be more beautiful while her own beauty faded. I think Arabel began to believe that Sine was stealing that beauty from her, draining it away with each passing hour as a leech drains a mon's blood. 'Twas as if Arabel thought that she could halt her own aging if she killed Sine."

"That *is* madness," Margot whispered, and shivered.

Martin nodded. "The greed is a wee bit more understandable. Sine and her brothers were left much wealth by their father. Arabel and Malise want to hold fast to it. Their greed is a never satisfied hunger. They always crave more."

"Why do ye stay with them? 'Tis clear that ye can see all that is wrong in them, yet ye dinnae turn from it."

"And where shall I turn to, lass? I am but a poor kinsmon of Malise's. I have neither land nor coin. I was tied to Malise's service at a verra young age. 'Tis all I ken of the world. I am so sunk in their filth now that, e'en if I walked away from them, I would always carry that stink with me. I will be with them until the end. And I believe that end will come soon now. Wee Sine will deliver the punishment Arabel and Malise have so far eluded."

"Do ye really believe that?"

"Aye, I do. Mayhaps Arabel could see it years ago and it added to her need to end Sine's life. Arabel saw not only her fading youth in her child's face but her own dark fate, her own defeat, and it terrified her."

"So, do ye now hie to the Brodies' side?"

"Nay." He cupped her face in his hands again. "I am here with ye and here I shall stay until the day wanes and darkness puts an end to our tryst. I have ached to look upon ye again, ever since I left Duncoille. That need is strengthened by the knowledge that this may be our last time together."

Even though Margot knew he was right, she clung to him. "Nay. Ye must not speak so."

"Nay, not today. Today is for pretty words and sweet kisses. Soon I will return to those who hold my life in their hands and ye shall return to your own home—far away from here."

"Leave? Nay, I am staying at Duncoille. Farthing and Thomas are all the kinsmen I have left. How can ye ask me to leave them now, to flee to safety while they face danger?"

Martin sighed. "I was sure ye would answer so, but I had hoped that ye wouldnae. Ah, my sweet, wee Margot, we face a dark time. Once Arabel discovers that Sine and her brothers are still alive, the madness will truly begin. I but pray that the righteous are victorious."

Sine frowned as she held up two lengths of lace and tried to determine which was of the better quality. She had enough coin to be choosy now, but was finding it difficult. The woman trying to sell her some lace had realized that Sine could afford a finer quality than was on display in front of her tiny cottage. Sine had found herself gently but firmly urged inside a small room that was cluttered with samples of the woman's best work, work reserved for show to the wellborn.

As Sine picked up a third piece of lace she heard the woman usher in another lady. Sine paid no heed, despite the lacemaker's unusually excited tone of voice, until there was a strange cry very near to her, a noise much like someone choking. A chill rippled through Sine's body and, even as she puzzled over it, she turned toward the sound. The lace fell from her hands as she found herself staring into her mother's eyes. A still-calm part of her mind wondered if she looked as horrified as Arabel did.

"I told ye there was a lass who resembled ye, m'lady," the lacemaker said, her cheerful voice gaining an edge of nervousness. "I didnae think ye would take it so hard."

"Ye are alive," whispered Arabel, her voice hoarse.

"Aye—Mother." Sine spat out the word as if it were some foul curse. "Your only failure, was it?"

"Curse ye to hell, how did ye survive? Ye were but a child; those bastards were no more than bairns."

Sine ignored the snarled reference to the twins, hoping

that she could continue to hide them from Arabel. "Not everyone views a child with the hate that ye do."

Sine felt the sting of pain as she saw the fury and hate twisting her mother's features. That angered her. She wanted to feel nothing. She had spent six long years convincing herself to feel nothing. It was infuriating to know that she had not been fully successful in that aim. Within her heart still lurked that little girl who had so often longed for the love of her beautiful mother.

Not so beautiful now, she mused as she closely studied Arabel. Her mother's mouth was gnarled into a tight-lipped grimace of anger. Arabel's eyes were cold, glittering, and narrowed into a fierce glare which revealed that all of Arabel's care had not fully banished the wrinkles. It was a hard, dangerous face Sine now looked into, the face of a stranger, a murderer, and an enemy. What truly chilled Sine was how much it still resembled her own in shape and coloring.

Her close study of her mother allowed her to see Arabel's subtle, threatening reach for her knife. Sine leapt out of the way just as Arabel lunged for her. She heard the lacemaker cry out in panic and flee her own house. Sine caught the brief glint of a blade in Arabel's hand. She prayed that the lacemaker would raise an alarm, for, unarmed and caught within the cluttered, dim interior of the cottage, Sine did not feel sure that she could successfully fend off Arabel's attack.

"Isnae that Blane o'er there?" asked Ligulf, frowning toward a crowd of men watching a cockfight.

Gamel abruptly stopped laughing at Sir Lesley's somewhat crude dissertation on the attributes of the alewife's two daughters and looked in the direction Ligulf pointed. He tensed when he recognized his squire pushing his way

through the boisterous crowd, clearly looking for someone. The moment Blane glanced his way, Gamel waved to
the man. When Blane immediately started to run toward
them, Gamel felt the first tickle of alarm.

"Is something wrong at Duncoille?" he demanded
when Blane finally reached their side.

"Nay, although there soon shall be. The Brodies are
here, right here in this village."

"Here? Why in God's name would they be here? They
cannae have learned about Sine yet and, e'en if they
had, how could they ken that we would be here today?
Where did ye hear this?"

"From their own mon—Martin Robertson. He sent
word to Mistress Margot, for he wished to meet with her.
The Brodies *are* here, sir. The why of it doesnae matter.
I was sent to warn ye."

After glancing around the market square and seeing
no immediate sign of Sine, Gamel turned to his three
brothers and Sir Lesley. "Where is Sine?"

"I last saw her talking with the lacemaker in front of
that cottage o'er there," replied Ligulf.

There was no sign of Sine anywhere near the cottage,
and Gamel was about to go over there when Farthing
strolled up to them. Gamel was briefly distracted by the
sight of Farthing and a buxom young maid with their
arms wrapped around each other's waists. The pair
looked very much like well-satisfied lovers, but Gamel
knew that was impossible.

"We have to find Sine," Gamel told Farthing. "The
Brodies are here."

Farthing swore, kissed the maid he had just spent a satisfying hour with, and shooed her away. "Then we had
best find her, and quickly."

"Ye cannae believe they would try to murder the lass

here?" Sir Lesley shook his head. "The place is crowded with witnesses. They could ne'er escape hanging."

"True, but they shall be sorely offset, mayhaps e'en flung into a panic," Farthing replied. "There can be no guessing how they might act. Sine shouldnae be left alone."

"She shouldnae e'en be here," Gamel muttered as he started toward the lacemaker's cottage. "We shall get her away with as much haste as we can," he added, and his six companions agreed without hesitation.

Gamel came to an abrupt halt when the lacemaker came hurrying out of her house. The woman was so clearly agitated that he felt the icy grip of fear tighten around his heart. He stood, held in place by a disturbing reluctance to see what had upset the woman. Gamel watched her run toward them with a growing sense of dread.

"Oh, sirs, 'tis glad I am to see ye," the lacemaker cried, grasping Gamel by the arm and tugging him toward her house. "The lass who came with ye may be in sore need of ye."

"Is someone in there with her?" demanded Gamel, shaking free of his fear-induced stupor.

"Aye, m'lord. I thought 'twould be such a fine surprise. That other woman looked so much like your wee lady. Yet, when they espied each other 'twasnae surprise upon their faces. I think I may have unwittingly committed a grave wrong."

"The young lass isnae hurt?" he asked.

"Nay, but I fear she soon may be. Ye didnae see the look upon the other woman's face, m'lord. 'Twas the look of murder, I am certain of it."

He set the woman aside and ran toward her house, drawing his sword as he went.

* * *

Sine neatly avoided yet another deadly lunge by Arabel. She moved so that the work-worn table was between her and her enraged mother. Her only plan was to reach the door and flee the cottage, but Arabel had so far successfully blocked her every attempt to do so.

"Ye must be mad," Sine said as she kept a close watch upon Arabel and held herself tensed and ready to elude the next attack. "Ye willnae be able to deceive anyone into thinking ye are innocent this time. There are too many eyes here to see ye commit your crime."

"Only that fat lacemaker saw me come in here with ye. I can shut her mouth easily enough. I had the hood of my cloak o'er my head most of the time I was outside. Those village fools can only say that they saw a woman wrapped in a rich blue cloak. 'Tisnae enough to hang me. I doubt they saw even that much, for the cockfight held most everyone's attention. Ye will die here as ye should have died at Dorchabeinn six years ago."

"Others now ken what ye had planned for me and why I ran away. They will speak out against ye. Aye, and many of your enemies and allies are now eager to relate your crimes."

"Mere talk cannae hang me either. Nay, Sine Catriona, ye have seen your last sunrise. Ye will die here and then I shall have those bastards of your father's gutted."

Gamel stepped inside the cottage in time to hear Lady Arabel's cold words. It took all of his strength of will not to strike the woman dead on the spot. As his companions crowded in around him, he struggled to control himself. He found it impossible to believe that the woman could really be Sine's mother.

"If ye spill but one drop of her blood," he said, causing both women to look his way, "I shall cut your heart out here and now, and toss it to the gamecocks to feed upon."

"Gamel," Sine whispered, nearly weak with relief as she hurried to his side.

He nudged her behind him so that he shielded her front while Sir Lesley shielded her back. She peered around Gamel in time to see her mother slyly tuck her dagger back into a pocket hidden in her full skirts. Sine felt a bit of a coward but firmly told herself she was acting out of common sense. Arabel had a weapon and she did not. Wisdom demanded that she try her best to escape such an unequal confrontation.

"I wasnae intending to hurt the lass," Arabel said in her smoothest voice. "I was but overcome with emotion. Aye, and anger, for she has left me to suffer for six years believing she was dead." Arabel held out her hands in a gesture of pleading, a soft smile curving her mouth. "Ye cannae believe that I would hurt my verra own flesh and blood."

"Save your lies, m'lady," Gamel snapped. "We ken all too weel what ye are."

"Ye speak of lies but 'tis Sine Catriona who has lied, and ye have believed her without question."

"Why persist, Arabel?" Sine shook her head. "Ye cannae believe that we are all so lack-witted."

"Not lack-witted, simply misled. Your freedom has made ye even more disrespectful than ye were as a child. I should leave ye to your fate, but ye are my only child. So come with me. We shall return to Dorchabeinn immediately. Mayhaps there we can heal this breech between us."

"Go with ye? Ye *must* be mad." Sine harshly subdued that small child within her who so desperately wanted to believe in her pretty mother.

"I am your mother."

"Ye were ne'er a mother to me."

"Your opinion of how I performed my duties matters verra little. Ye are my child and the law says that ye are mine to do with as I please. My pleasure is to return ye to Dorchabeinn. 'Twill save us all a great deal of trouble if ye cease arguing with me." Arabel glared at Gamel. "Ye, sir, shall release my daughter to me at once. I suggest ye dinnae try to impede me in taking possession of what is mine. To do otherwise could be called abduction."

"Nay." Gamel smiled coldly. "'Tis just a husband holding his wife firmly at his side, as is his right by law."

"Husband?" Arabel nearly screeched the word, her hands clenched into fists at her sides. "Ye are wed?"

"Aye. Sine and I were married nearly a fortnight ago."

"Handfast, was it? That willnae hold."

"Not handfast. We were married by a priest. She is my wife, m'lady, and I shall ne'er hand her over to ye."

"Ye shall regret this. Her kinsmen ne'er approved this marriage. It willnae stand. I shall fight it and ye."

"Fight away," said Farthing. "There are many of us ready to parry any thrust ye make."

Arabel turned her glare upon Farthing. "And now I see the purpose of your seduction of me."

"*My* seduction of ye? I but answered your invitation, an invitation cast out far and wide whilst ye were at Duncoille. While your skill at betrayal and deceit is unmatched, ye arenae the only one who can play those games."

A hiss of rage escaped Arabel and she strode toward the door. Sine and the others quickly stepped out of the woman's way, more to avoid her touch than out of fear. Once outside, Arabel turned and gave them all a twisted smile.

"Ye will ne'er get out of this village alive." She hiked up her skirts and raced toward the inn at the far edge of town.

"M'lord," the lacemaker cried as she stepped over to

Gamel. "I heard what she said. She has twenty or more armed men here with her. Ye had best flee if ye can."

"Wise words," muttered Farthing. "The battlefield isnae a good one and the odds not on our side. I choose to retreat and fight another day."

"Aye," agreed Gamel. "We dinnae wish to lose the fight ere it has begun."

"Farthing," Sine called as, lifting her skirts, she ran toward their horses, Gamel and the other men following. "I wish to speak with ye about something Arabel said."

"We can talk later, dearling. Save your breath for the business at hand."

Sine decided that was good advice as they raced into the blacksmith's stables, Gamel bellowing for their mounts and saddles. She did not think she had ever seen horses readied so swiftly. The moment their mounts were prepared, Gamel tossed her into her saddle and lightly slapped her mare's rump.

She spurred her mount into a faster pace once she was completely clear of the stables, then glanced over her shoulder. A crowd of armed men and horses stood outside the small inn at the far end of the village. They appeared confused, their mounts restive and unbiddable, and there was a great deal of shouting going on. Sine knew she would be foolish to take what she saw at face value. Well-executed haste could look like pure confusion to anyone watching from a distance. She concentrated on keeping pace with her companions and getting back to Duncoille safely.

They were barely a mile or two outside the village when she heard the dull pounding of horses in pursuit. She gritted her teeth and concentrated on riding. It was hard, but she resisted the urge to keep looking behind her, for she knew that would only slow her down. When Duncoille's thick walls loomed into sight, she heard

Blane give a gruff, short shout. One swift peek showed her why he was so pleased. Arabel's hired rogues were giving up, reining in and halting just out of arrow range.

When they finally reached Duncoille, Gamel shouted for the gates to be shut even as he rode through them. They all dismounted inside the bailey and the stablehands hurriedly led the horses away. Sine struggled to calm her fears and catch her breath as Gamel told the guards on the wall exactly what to watch for. She was not surprised when Lords William and Thomas hurried over, but she did wonder about the identities of the two dour-faced gentlemen with them.

"Sine, ye had best get inside," Gamel ordered.

"Why? We are back inside Duncoille and I wish to speak with Farthing."

"Ye can speak with Farthing later. We may yet find ourselves with a battle to fight."

She was about to argue further when she saw Farthing nod at her. She inwardly sighed and headed to the keep. It was irritating to be ordered around, but she decided this was one of those times when it was wisest to bow to the wishes of those with greater experience. Gamel and the others in the bailey were fighting men and she was not. She would wait until the immediate danger had passed before she questioned Farthing about Arabel's talk of seduction.

"There has been some trouble?" asked Lord Magnusson as he stood by his son. "Blane didnae arrive in time with our warning?"

"The warning wasnae wasted, Father, but the Brodies now ken that Sine is alive and just where she is. Sine had to face her mother." Farthing shook his head. "The woman was enraged to discover that her daughter is still alive. It only added to her fury when she learned about the marriage. Arabel intended to take Sine right there."

"And the woman's dogs chased ye back here?"

"They were chasing us, but when Duncoille came into view, they fell back."

Gamel nodded. "I think they hoped to run us to ground, but when that failed, they drew back to make new plans. I believe we will be safe enough for a while."

"Ye may be safe, but he isnae," growled one of the men who had followed Lords Thomas and William into the bailey, and he stepped forward to glare at Farthing. "I am Sir Peter MacDougal, and ye, Farthing Magnusson, owe me an accounting. Ye stole my honor whilst ye were in Perth."

"And mine," said the second man. "I am his cousin, David MacDougal."

"Have I insulted ye in some manner?" Farthing asked, frowning as he struggled to recall the men.

"I dinnae consider it a compliment when a mon mounts my wife," snapped Peter, drawing his sword.

"Or my daughter," muttered David, also unsheathing his weapon.

Gamel hastily stepped between the two men and Farthing. "Nay, sirs, that isnae possible."

"Nay?" Sir Peter turned his glare on Gamel. "He was sniffing 'round my wife the whole time he was in Perth."

"Aye," agreed David. "And he slipped away for a tryst with my lass."

"I willnae deny that he may have done that much, sirs, but he didnae mount them." Gamel leaned closer toward the men so that he could speak softly and keep Farthing's tragic secret as private as possible. "He cannae mount any lass. Some mon made him pay a verra dear price for his licentiousness years ago."

"Ye lie to protect him," muttered Sir Peter.

"I shall let that insult pass because I ken weel that ye feel ye have been gravely wronged. Howbeit, I swear to ye that Farthing Magnusson may act the rogue, but he is no longer able to be one. If ye have truly been cuckolded, 'twas by another mon, not Farthing."

As Gamel continued to argue with the men, he noticed that his father, Lord Thomas, and even Farthing all had amused looks on their faces. He wondered what could possibly be funny. He also wondered why he was laboring so hard to save Farthing's hide, then answered his own question in one word—Sine. She would never forgive him if he did not at least try.

Chapter 11

"That was a verra clever lie," Farthing complimented Gamel as they strode toward the great hall, leaving their fathers to tend to Sir Peter and his cousin. "I ne'er would have thought ye could be so deceitful."

"Farthing, ye need not play that game with me. Sine told me about your grievous wound on the first night she shared my bed." Gamel pushed open the heavy door to the great hall and smiled when he saw Sine pacing there.

"My grievous wound?" Farthing muttered as he followed Gamel into the hall. "What are ye talking about?"

Before Gamel could reply, Sine stopped pacing and looked their way. He frowned a little when he saw that her attention was on Farthing. Despite his best efforts to conquer the emotion, Gamel had to admit that he was still jealous of the closeness between the two of them. It did not help to know that Farthing undoubtedly knew Sine far better than he did. Gamel was startled out of his dark musings when Sine marched over to Farthing and pointed at the man with a mixture of fury and accusation.

"Ye bedded Arabel, didnae ye?" she snapped, sure of it yet praying that Farthing would deny it.

"Now, lass, why would ye think such a thing?" Farthing responded.

"Because of what she said."

"The woman said a great deal."

Sine clenched her hands into tight fists but resisted the urge to hit Farthing. "She said that she now saw the purpose of your seduction of her."

"And I said I ne'er seduced the woman and that is the truth."

"The truth is something ye seem verra reluctant to tell me. The truth I want to hear is—did ye or did ye not bed Arabel?"

Farthing grimaced, ran a hand through his hair, and smiled at Sine a little sheepishly. "Aye, I did."

Sine felt as if she had been soundly slapped. "Why? Why would ye bed down with that woman, a woman who wishes me and the twins dead? Ye have slept with my deadliest enemy."

"I wish ye would cease to look at me as if I am the lowest of traitors," Farthing grumbled. "I accepted Arabel's flagrant invitation to sample her favors for the verra reasons ye think I shouldnae have—*because* she is your enemy."

"Wait a moment!" Gamel realized that he had yelled the words, causing both Sine and Farthing to stare at him in surprise, and he struggled to calm himself. He was completely confused and did not like how it felt. While he could easily understand why Farthing might talk as if he could still bed a woman, Gamel could not comprehend why Sine was now playing along with the ruse. He began to get the uncomfortable feeling that something was not quite right.

"Is something wrong, Gamel?" Sine asked, eager to continue her discussion with Farthing, yet concerned about the odd look upon her husband's face.

"Why are ye beleaguering the mon when ye ken that he couldnae do what ye are accusing him of? His grievous injury—remember?"

A soft curse escaped Farthing and he glared at Gamel. "Yet again ye babble about this 'grievous injury.' What in God's sweet name are ye talking about?"

"The injury ye got which makes it so that ye cannae mate with any woman," Gamel snapped. Then he frowned, for the stunned look upon Farthing's dark face told him that something was definitely amiss.

"Ye mean ye think I have been unmonned? Do ye actually believe the deceits ye told those two cuckolded fools outside?"

"I told the truth as I kenned it."

"The truth? Where did ye learn such utter nonsense?"

"Sine told me." Gamel pointed at Sine and joined Farthing in glowering at her.

Sine gave them a wavering smile as she frantically tried to think of something to say. She heartily wished she had used the diversion of their brief squabble to flee the hall. In her upset over Farthing and her mother she had forgotten about the lie she had told Gamel weeks ago. In truth, since telling it she had hardly thought of it at all. She was now facing the consequences of that omission.

"Ye told him that I had lost my monhood?" Farthing demanded.

"We—ell, not exactly that." She shrugged. "I can explain."

"Ye lied to me," Gamel said, his voice very soft.

The way Gamel was looking at her made Sine feel oddly afraid. Farthing was furious, but although she did not particularly like that, she knew it would pass. She was not at all sure what Gamel was feeling, though his expression made her think it was something very complicated and not easily mended. With growing distress, Sine realized that she did not know Gamel well enough to judge his reaction. The man was her lover and husband, yet she could not even begin to guess what he was thinking or what he would do. Before she could try to defend herself, however, Ligulf marched into the great hall.

"Ye had best come back outside, Gamel," he said. "Ye too, Farthing."

After giving Sine one last piercing look, Gamel turned to Ligulf. "They have come to our gates, have they?"

"Aye. There arenae enough of them to wage a successful battle, but Lady Arabel and Lord Malise have ridden close to our walls. They wish to speak with ye, Gamel. In truth, they demand to speak with 'the mon who claims to be our daughter's husband.'"

"Demand it, do they? Weel, let us see what they want." Without another glance toward Sine, Gamel strode out of the hall, nudging Ligulf ahead of him.

"I will speak with ye later, Sine Catriona," Farthing snapped before following Ligulf and Gamel out of the hall.

Sine stared at the shut door for a moment, then cursed. She gave a startled cry when someone touched her arm. It was Lady Edina. Sine stared at the woman in open-mouthed surprise.

"Have ye been here the whole time, m'lady?" she asked, a blush of embarrassment rapidly heating her face.

"Aye. 'Tis a habit of mine. I have a verra comfortable seat near the fireplace at the far end of the hall, but 'tis in the shadows most of the time. People often miss my presence. 'Tisnae really eavesdropping, though my husband claims otherwise. I prefer to say that I dinnae wish to intrude. Howbeit, I will confess that it may weel be a bit of both."

"So, ye heard about my lie."

"M'dear, I kenned all about that weeks ago."

"I dinnae usually lie to people," she mumbled.

"I ken that too. Once I learned of the lie, of when it was told and to whom, I was sure of the reason for it. Ye had to have an explanation for your innocence."

"Aye, I did, but I should have told Gamel the truth before now. I shouldnae have left him to find out in this abrupt manner. 'Tis just that, weel, it eased some of his anger toward Farthing so I took the coward's way out and kept letting him think that Farthing had been un-monned." She bit her bottom lip lightly and took a hesitant step toward the door. "I really should hear what is being said."

"So ye should." Lady Edina linked her arm through Sine's and, opening the door with her free hand, led her out of the hall. "I shouldnae fret too much about your lie, m'dear."

"I think Gamel is verra upset."

"He is, but I shouldnae feel guilty about that. Ye and Gamel didnae meet under the most auspicious of circumstances. I fear that Gamel was neither honorable nor considerate when he first saw ye. Ye were forced into a verra strange and awkward situation. Gamel has the wit to see that for himself once his anger cools. Howbeit, if he remains sullen and willnae heed what ye have to say, I shall have a strong word with him. No matter what ye mean to do in the end concerning this marriage, we must all be closely united until your foes have been overcome. So we cannae have Gamel sulking about over some imagined slight."

"Thank ye for that, m'lady. I pray I willnae need to impose upon ye." When they paused in the bailey, Sine asked, "Do ye think there is a place where I can listen yet not be seen? They are talking now, but I cannae hear each word clearly."

"They are most likely just exchanging a few belligerencies. William will demand an explanation for the presence of armed men approaching Duncoille and the Brodies will try to explain and remain uncowed yet not throw out any direct challenge. Come along." Lady Edina led Sine toward the front gates. "There is a small spy portal nearby where ye can both listen and watch."

It was a minute or two before Sine could make use of the spy hole, for the guard stationed near at hand had to fetch her a block of wood to stand upon. Her first glimpse of her mother caused her to shiver. She began to believe that she would never be able to think about the woman without experiencing a slight chill. As she observed her mother's arrogant pose, the elegant and powerful image she presented upon her white mare, Sine felt her confidence in her own chance of victory begin to waver. She gritted her teeth and fought Arabel's dangerous effect upon her.

"Sine Catriona is now a Logan," Gamel called out loudly so that his strong voice could easily be heard by Arabel and Malise at the foot of Duncoille's thick wall. "Ye waste our time and your own in coming here. When Sine exchanged vows with me before a priest, all bonds with ye were severed. Ye have no claim upon her."

"Lord Logan," Malise called, ignoring Gamel and turning his attention to the master of Duncoille. "Ye are said to be an honorable mon, one with great respect for the law and customs of our land. Surely ye can see the wrong done here? We, the lass's only kinsmen, were ne'er consulted on this marriage."

"M'lord Brodie, let us cease this game. We have learned a great deal about ye—"

"Rumors and hearsay," Malise interrupted. "Accusations with no proof. They are naught but the malicious mutterings of jealous fools."

"I might consider that if 'twas but a trickle, a few ill

words from malcontents. Howbeit, 'tis a veritable flood, m'lord, and told by good and honorable men. Ye challenge me with my love and obedience of law and custom yet ye have ne'er shown either. E'en if the lass wasnae wed to my son, I would still deny your claim to her. I have no stomach for turning such a wee, sweet lass o'er to murderers and rogues."

"So now ye respond to my rightful demands with slurs and insults."

"They deserve no less."

"I will fight this injustice."

"Aye, I pray that ye do, for if ye lift a sword against me, ye give me the right to cut down ye and yours without troubling myself with explanations. Ye are a curse upon this land and I should welcome the freedom to put an end to ye."

"I can see that there is no reasoning with ye. The lass has bewitched ye, clouded your wits with her lies. We can argue in the courts about which of us has the strongest claim to her. Howbeit, ye have no claim to the lads."

"What lads?"

"Her brothers, twins of nine years of age. If ye hold the lass, ye hold the lads too. I willnae heed any denial. Ye must give them o'er to me. Or have ye wed the boys to some kinswomen?"

"Nay, but ye have no claim to them either."

"They are our kinsmen," Malise shouted, revealing his anger and frustration for the first time. "They are Brodies and should be returned to Dorchabeinn."

"They are the bastard offspring of your wife's late husband. 'Tis a verra thin claim ye have. Lady Sine Logan has a stronger claim than ye do. She is their half sister, their blood kin, and she wishes to keep them with her. Begone and take your hired dogs with ye. If those armed men linger before my gates much longer, I shall view it as an attack and act accordingly."

"I am not finished with ye yet, m'lord Logan," Malise bellowed, then he turned his mount sharply around and galloped back to his small army, Arabel following at his heels.

Sine turned to face the bailey and slumped against the cool stone wall. She moved only a little to allow Lady Edina a chance to look through the spy hole. Matters were moving at a furious pace now. Bloodshed was the only possible consequence of today's confrontation and she dreaded being even partly responsible for it. She told herself yet again that the Brodies would allow no other resolution and then concentrated her attention on a rapidly approaching Lord Magnusson. The man looked deeply concerned and she felt a tickle of unease.

"Have either of ye seen Margot?" he asked as he stopped before Sine and Lady Edina.

"Nay," replied Lady Edina, looking briefly at Sine, who shook her head. "She isnae within the keep?"

"She hadnae returned from her tryst with Martin Robertson when Farthing and the others rode back."

"Bringing the Brodies with us," mumbled Sine, and grimaced. "Do ye think she has been caught out on the enemy's side?"

"I fear so. I sent two of my men-at-arms with her."

"But they would prove little impediment to the Brodies' twenty." Sine peeked out of the spy hole. "And the Brodies are being verra slow to leave so we cannae begin a search just yet."

"Do ye think Martin would turn the lass o'er to the Brodies to use against us?"

A sigh escaped Sine as she shook her head. "If he has any feelings for her, I would be inclined to say nay.

Howbeit, are we yet sure that he truly courts the girl and isnae merely trying to spy upon us through her?"

"Nay." Lord Thomas ran a hand through his hair and scowled at the sturdy, securely barred gates of Duncoille. "So there is naught we can do but wait and pray that, when the cursed Brodies leave, they dinnae carry off poor Margot with them."

Martin cursed softly and tried to shift his prone body into a more comfortable position, but with Margot pressed close on his left and one of her guards on his right, he had little room to maneuver. He glared through the gnarled thorn bushes the four of them hid behind and tried to will the Brodies to leave. A sigh escaped him as he glanced at Margot's sweet pale face then at the stern faces of the Magnusson men flanking them. He doubted he would ever see Margot again and this was not the way he would have chosen to spend his last moments with her.

"Why dinnae they leave?" whispered Margot, blushing a little when Martin put his arm around her. She did not protest the familiarity despite the frowns of her guards.

"I suspect they will soon. They are probably arguing amongst themselves as they try to decide upon some action besides ignominious retreat."

"There is none," muttered Angus, the guard on Martin's right.

"Nay, there is none," agreed Martin. "But 'twill take those fools time to concede."

"And what will ye do when they leave?" Margot asked.

"I shall find my horse and follow them," Martin replied, his voice flat and weighted with despair.

"Will they not ask where ye have been?"

"Oh, aye, but I can answer that satisfactorily. This con-

frontation between the Logans and the Brodies was un-
planned. 'Tis no fault of mine that I wasnae present. Also,
I am no soldier. I am a steward. They had no need of my
services for this. I wouldnae be surprised to learn that
they havenae e'en noticed I am missing yet. Dinnae fret
o'er me, dearling. I feel certain I face no real danger."

"Martin, why must ye follow them at all? Why not just
join us here at Duncoille?"

"I cannae."

"Why?"

"'Tis too difficult to explain. I am not sure I understand
it myself." He smiled at her, sadness tainting his expression. "I am a Brodie mon, lass. I have ne'er been anything
else. 'Tis probably far too late for me to change."

He touched her lips with his finger to silence her
when she began to speak. "Nay, dinnae argue. I do what
I must do. And, consider this—if I do decide to betray
the Brodies and join with your side, would I not be of
far more use if I was still deep within the lair of your
enemy? Leave it be, lass. We must each meet our fate
in our own way."

"The Brodies are leaving," murmured Angus.

After one look to be sure the man was right, Martin
lightly kissed Margot on the lips. He slipped away to get
his horse and follow the Brodies, yet felt torn by indecision each step of the way. Although his life in Malise's
service had never been happy, he had never before
viewed it with such despair. He wondered if he was at
some great turning point in his life and if he would have
the wit and courage to choose the right path.

Sine continued to stare out of the spy hole long after
the Brodies had disappeared from sight. She was faintly
aware that Lord Magnusson was requesting a search for

Margot. The guard informed her finally that she would
have to move because they needed to open the gates. He
was just about to help her down from the block of wood
when she spotted three riders approaching. For a brief
moment she feared that her enemies were returning to
try some new ploy, then she recognized Margot's rich,
bright green dress.

"Lord Thomas," she cried, hurrying over to the man,
reaching his side just as he was about to mount his horse.
"Margot is coming back. I just saw her and your two men
riding this way." A call from a guard upon the walls confirmed her words.

There was hectic activity as Margot arrived. It was several moments before they could all gather in the hall to
actually speak with her. Sine sat near Lady Edina and
Lord William. Across from her was Gamel, flanked by his
three brothers and Sir Lesley. Sine finally had to turn
away from Gamel's steady, piercing gaze, only to catch
Farthing scowling at her from where he sat with his
father and Margot. She prayed that Margot had a great
deal to say, for she knew she would face two extremely
angry men just as soon as the meeting ended. She took
a long drink of wine and wished that she could be as
carefree as the twins, who were out in the practice yard
gleefully wielding their wooden swords. Life was so much
simpler for them, she mused with a twinge of envy.

"We feared Martin Robertson might hand ye o'er to
the Brodies," Lord Thomas said. "'Twould have brought
him high favor."

Margot patted the older man's hand. "Nay. I dinnae
believe he e'en considered it. In truth, I am sure of it.
We were on our way back here and Martin had already
started back to the village. He returned to warn us of the
Brodies' approach. If he hadnae done so, they would
have caught us in the open land surrounding Duncoille.

As it stood we barely had time to hide amongst the brambles at the edge of the wood."

"So, the lad does care for ye," Lord Thomas murmured.

A blush stained Margot's cheeks as she nodded. "Aye, but not enough to leave the Brodies."

"Lass, dinnae judge the mon too harshly because of that. He is nearly their bondsmon and there is also a blood tie. These arenae easy things to shake free of. Also he could feel himself such a part of their perfidy that he sees no other choice, simply cannae believe that he could find another place to go. Twice now he has risked his own life, even if in a small way—to save Sir Lesley and now ye. 'Tis a step forward."

"I ken it, Cousin Thomas. I but wish he could leave them ere he loses his life. He did speak on the matter. He said he is a Brodie mon and has ne'er kenned another way. Howbeit, he said that if he does decide to betray them, it would be better if he was still within their camp. He could be of far more use that way."

"'Twould be useful to have one of their own on our side," agreed Lord William. "We cannae count on that though. Howbeit, I swear this to ye, lass—we shall give the mon every chance to save his own neck."

"Thank ye, m'lord. 'Tis more than I have a right to expect."

"Did ye tell him about Sine and the twins?" asked Lord Thomas.

"Aye." Margot looked at Sine. "'Twas verra odd. He grew pale at first, but then he laughed."

"Laughed?" Sine could see by their faces that the others shared her confusion.

"He said there really wasnae anything funny about it but I believe his delight was in the fact that Arabel and Malise have been thwarted. Martin also believes that ye will be the one to make them pay the penance they have eluded for so long. He believes that Arabel read her own fate in your eyes when ye were but a child."

"Methinks the mon is a verra superstitious sort."

Margot smiled and nodded, then quickly grew serious again. "He believes that Arabel's vanity is a madness, that the woman sees ye as a witch who bleeds away her youth and beauty."

"'Tis glad that I am not the only one who has had such thoughts about her," Sine muttered.

More questions were asked which Margot did her best to answer, but Sine could see that the girl had little more information of any great consequence. In the hope of eluding a confrontation with either Gamel or Farthing, Sine waited until the men were deeply involved in discussing possible tactics to use against the Brodies before she slipped out of the great hall. She nearly made it to the safety of her chambers, but just as she reached out to grasp the door latch, someone grabbed her arm. When she was somewhat abruptly turned around, Sine was faintly relieved to find herself facing Farthing instead of Gamel.

"Ye forgot to explain to me why ye felt it was necessary to tell Gamel I was less than a mon." Farthing crossed his arms over his chest and frowned down at her.

With a grimace, Sine slumped against her chamber door and eyed Farthing a little warily. "'Twas all I could think of to explain why I was an innocent when I was supposed to be your wife."

"Could ye not have simply told him the truth?"

The anger was already fading from his face and Sine relaxed a little, offering him a weak smile as she shrugged. "'Twasnae the best time for thinking clearly. So too did I believe I would ne'er see him again, that all we would e'er share was that one night in the inn."

"Fair enough. But why have ye left the lie to stand? Did ye ne'er think that he would discover the truth?"

"I honestly ne'er gave the matter much thought, quite forgot about my lie at times. And, mayhaps, I suffered a touch of cowardice. I kenned it would only make him eye ye with even less favor if he learned that ye were the fully able and licentious rogue ye are. Do ye think that Gamel is verra angry?"

"'Tis clear that he doesnae like being lied to, especially by you. Howbeit, that has surely been made worse by the discovery that he was the only one left to believe it."

"Oh, sweet heaven, so now he feels the fool."

"I fear he might. Not that he isnae one. Weel, whatever ye choose to do in the future, if ye must tell some lie about me, I should prefer it if ye would keep my monhood intact." He smiled when she laughed softly. "I will leave ye now, for I can hear someone coming up the stairs and my guess is that it is your husband." He kissed her cheek and started off toward his own chamber. "Dinnae let him badger ye into feeling ye are all wrong and he is all right."

Sine nodded and quickly slipped inside her chamber. She had barely shut the door and moved away from it when it was thrust open so hard it slammed against the stone wall. Gamel stepped into their chambers then shut the door behind him with equal force. Sine was sure she heard the thick wood crack.

"Ye lied to me," Gamel said softly as he advanced on her.

"'Twas but a wee lie," Sine murmured as she backed up until she bumped into the bedpost.

"I dinnae think Farthing considered it was so wee. Why did ye lie to me?" He stopped just in front of her, the toes of his booted feet nudging the tips of her soft slippers.

"Weel, ye didnae really give me the time to prepare a reasonable explanation for why I was a virgin when Farthing and I were telling everyone that we were mon and wife. And when ye did press for an explanation, I wasnae really thinking verra clearly so uttered the first thing I could think of."

Gamel stared at her for a moment, then sighed. "Fair enough. Howbeit, did ye have to let the lie stand? I was the only one who believed that nonsense. I look the complete fool. Aye, and a liar, for I told those Mac-Dougals exactly what ye told me. Farthing probably did bed Sir Peter's wife and Master David's daughter."

"I suspect he did. I am sorry that I ne'er told ye the truth. Truly, I am. But I am not sure ye would have believed the truth anyway. Despite the fact that I was innocent when ye took me to your bed, and e'en when ye thought Farthing unable to possess me, ye still eyed him and me with suspicion."

"And why shouldnae I think it now?"

She shook her head. "Farthing and I have ne'er been lovers and ne'er will be. Aye, I love him and he loves me, but 'tis the love of close kin. How often must I tell ye that ere ye will believe me?"

He stared at her for a full minute before he sat down on the bed, put his head in his hands, and threaded his fingers through his hair. Some of the hurt he had felt when he discovered that she had lied to him was fading, but he still felt like an utter idiot. He also admitted to his own culpability. He had managed it all wrong from the beginning. He had once thought to woo her, but much to his annoyance, circumstances were making that difficult. Worse, he feared he could well be handling Sine all wrong now.

Sine cautiously sat down beside him. "I dinnae usually lie," she murmured.

"I ken it," he said, and sat up straighter, turning his head slightly to look at her. "And I ken that I havenae conducted myself weel in all of this."

"E'en so, I shouldnae have lied. But 'twas no time to go into lengthy explanations, and when I told the lie, I did so believing that I would ne'er see ye again."

Gamel suddenly turned, caught her up in his arms, and tumbled her back onto the bed. "'Tis done and forgotten. I should like to swear that I willnae watch ye and Farthing with suspicion, but I cannae. I find that I am a fiercely jealous mon." He kissed her and was pleased when her response was as swift and fiery as always. "So, Farthing's parts are still with him and working." He slid his hand beneath her skirts to stroke her thighs above her gartered hose.

"Aye." She gasped as she recalled what she and Farthing had been arguing about just before her lie had been revealed. "And he used those parts on Arabel— that traitor!" She tried to get up, but Gamel neatly pinned her to the bed with his body. "I have to go and speak with Farthing. He hasnae explained himself."

"Aye, he has." Gamel began to unlace her overtunic. "He told ye—he bedded Arabel because she is your enemy."

"That doesnae make any sense."

"It does. Ye just wish to be troublesome. Come, lass— think. Ye ken as weel as I do that many a secret has slipped from the lips of lovers. Farthing but hoped to seduce a few secrets from Arabel."

"And did he?"

"Weel, nay, not many. He discovered a few names of people she held in her thrall. He also learned a great deal about how she entices men into her web. The woman kens how to flatter a mon, how to act so sweet yet fulfill his every lustful dream. That was helpful, and worth taking the chance for."

"Aye." She sighed and shifted her body so that he could tug off her gown. "'Tis just that . . ."

"Ye are jealous?" He skillfully stripped her down to her thin lacy chemise and stockings.

"Nay. Weel, aye, a wee bit, but certainly not because I wish to bed with him. 'Tis hard to explain." She ran her hand down his broad back when he sat up to tug off his boots and remove her slippers. "I just dinnae like the thought of him with Arabel. Mayhaps I fear that she will entrap him as she has so many others."

"Not Farthing. He did confess that she is verra skilled in the art of seduction, but he is probably as sly as she is. Yet he doesnae use that cleverness to do harm. No need to look so surprised," he said as, having shed all his clothes save for his braies, he settled himself in her arms. "I may often have the urge to securely chain the mon in the pits of Duncoille, but I can still recognize his worth. I also ken that he would ne'er betray ye or the twins. He would cut his own throat first."

"I ken it also, which is why I didnae tell him of my fears. 'Twould have hurt him deeply. I must also cease this habit of seeing Arabel as some omnipotent demon. She *can* be beaten. And I am sure that her ability to be-witch men isnae nearly as strong as I fear it is."

"I wasnae bewitched by her." Gamel untied her garter and began to slowly unroll her stocking.

Sine murmured her pleasure as he followed the de-scent of her stocking with light, teasing, yet arousing kisses. "'Tis chilling to see how alike Arabel and I are. 'Tis as if I am staring into a looking glass."

"Ye arenae all that alike." He started to remove her other stocking. "She is your dark reflection, no more."

"My dark reflection," she whispered, and inwardly shuddered.

She knew that Gamel had meant to ease her concerns, but he had only increased them. What if Arabel was the cursed image of herself? They shared more than looks; they shared blood. Sine suddenly wished she knew exactly when the evil in Arabel had begun to show itself. If she knew that, she might be better able to judge whether or not she too carried that bad seed.

Gamel tossed aside her stockings and began to unlace her shift even as he hungrily kissed her. Sine clung to him, seeking the power of desire to drive the troubles from her mind. Yet, even as she began to succumb to her passion, she began to worry about its strength, about her insatiable hunger. A small voice in her mind kept whispering that Arabel was a whore, that Arabel had that same insatiable carnal hunger.

With a small cry, Sine clung to Gamel even more tightly, hoping to silence the voices in her head. She did not want those whispers to steal the beauty from what she shared with Gamel. Her time with him could prove to be very short. For now she would savor every moment she could grasp with him.

Chapter 12

"**A**nd what rock did ye climb out from under?" Martin looked at the strident Arabel in feigned surprise as he sat down at the head table in Dorchabeinn's great hall. He made no reply as he filled his bowl with steaming oatmeal and cut himself a thick slab of bread. Even though he had not dawdled he had still been far behind Arabel, Malise, and their men in returning from Duncoille. It had been sunset by the time Dorchabeinn had loomed up before him and, as was the rule at sunset, the gates had been securely shut, not to be opened until sunrise unless otherwise ordered by Arabel or Malise. Even he was left stranded if he did not get within Dorchabeinn's stout walls before the sun went down. For the first time, he had not even tried to get inside but had found a place to camp and spent most of the night staring up at the stars. He was not sure if he had reached any real decisions, but he did feel unusually content. Even Arabel's sharp angry tone did not disturb his sense of peace.

"Weel?" she snapped, glaring at him from across the table.

"Weel what?" He saw her eyes widen slightly and realized that he had been almost impertinent.

"Where were ye? Certainly not with us."

"I wasnae far behind ye. I arrived at sunset."

"Did ye? I didnae hear ye whining to get in as ye usually do."

"Nay, because, after all these years, I finally realized that that only served to entertain your sullen guards. I set up camp not far away and waited until the morning."

"Fine, but why were ye not in the village?" Malise asked. "Why were ye not with us at Duncoille?"

"I was trysting with a young maid and only learned about what had happened after it was all over."

"Ye were with that Magnusson wench?" demanded Arabel.

"Aye, and for a brief moment, I had thought that I could bring ye some startling news. Howbeit, I soon realized that the lass had only told me what the Logans felt sure ye were about to discover for yourselves."

"That—that little sorceress, Sine Catriona, is alive," Arabel hissed, and slammed her fist upon the table. "She and my first husband's brats by that Seaton whore. We demanded their return, which is our right as their kinsmen, but that ugly, arrogant Lord Logan refused us. If that isnae bad enough, Sine has wed herself to one of the Logans–some bastard git of the baron's. Now even our claim as her kinsmen is sadly weakened. We *must* come up with some plan."

"Ye could seek the aid of the law," suggested Martin, confident that the Brodies would never do so. "To wed a lass without her kinsmen's approval is verra nearly abduction. Ye would have no trouble finding witnesses to claim that Logan kidnapped the lass."

"We cannae go to the court. The mon has gathered together far too many who ache to speak out against us."

"We could silence them. We need only use the threats we used before, simply remind them of what they might lose if they betray us."

" 'Twill no longer work. Not on all of them. That cursed Lord William has promised them aid and protection. The traitors also gain strength as they realize that they arenae alone in turning against us."

"Then mayhaps ye should hide here for a while. If ye are verra quiet and little seen, the trouble will pass."

"How can ye be such a fool? We cannae do that. There is far too much at risk—including Dorchabeinn itself. This is all Sine Catriona's and the bastards'. Now that they are alive and protected, they can lay claim to nearly all that we own. We should ne'er have ceased the hunt for them, ne'er have assumed that they were dead. Now we must face the consequences of that failure to be diligent."

Martin successfully hid his concern for Arabel's offspring as he asked, "So what can ye do?"

"We must gain hold of something that will pull that wretched lass into our hold."

"Such as what?"

"Dinnae fret, Martin. I shall think of something."

That was exactly what Martin feared, and he felt a chill run down his spine, shattering his sense of peace for the moment. His first thought was to warn Margot, but he realized that even if he could successfully do that he had no idea what to warn her about. He prayed that Arabel did not plot something too despicable and that she failed in whatever scheme she did devise. Martin also prayed that he was right to believe that Sine Catriona would be the one to bring about the end to the Brodies. He knew his fate was tightly bound to theirs, but he no longer cared. All he wanted was for their reign of greed, bloodshed, and lechery to end.

* * *

Sine stretched slowly, all the while watching Gamel slip on his braies and begin to wash up. It was the first morning she had woken up unafraid. For one full week after the Brodies had fled Duncoille, she had been scared of every shadow and everyone she did not know well. She had woken up from nightmares soaked in sweat and shaking. The twins had become extremely annoyed with her, for she had refused to let them out of her sight. It had been much the same with Gamel and Farthing. Finally, after a week of such foolishness, she had managed to quiet her fears. She knew the danger was still present, but she no longer tortured herself, or others, about it.

A soft smile curved her lips as she continued to observe Gamel. He had been extremely patient with her, understanding her fears and soothing her when they tore apart her dreams. Passion had been his strongest weapon to combat her terror. She did not believe there was a private corner of Duncoille where they had not made love. And some not so private, she mused with an inner chuckle. When Gamel turned to look at her, she gave him a smile that brought that delightful spark of interest into his fine green eyes. He tossed aside the cloth he had been using to dry himself with, strode over to the bed, and bent down to kiss her. She murmured her delight in the greeting and twined her arms around his neck, returning his kiss with far more fervor than which he had begun it with.

"Do ye mean to idle the day away in bed?" he asked as he sat on the edge of the goose down mattress.

She turned on her side and smoothed her hand over his strong, lightly haired thigh. "'Tis a thought, but I should soon grow bored if I was here all alone."

"Ye shouldnae tempt me. I have a great deal of work to do."

Although she sighed and nodded her head, she began to brush lingering kisses over his thigh and stroke his lower back with her fingers. "I ken it. I have been distracting ye from your work far too often."

"Aye, and ye are verra distracting indeed." He buried his fingers in her hair. "I allow ye your way far too much."

"My way, eh? And here I was thinking that I was letting ye have your way with me."

"Mayhaps our ways are more alike than we realized."

Gamel closed his eyes. He savored the way her warm mouth felt against his skin, the soft erotic touch of her fingers at the base of his spine. When he felt her loosen his braies, he opened his eyes just enough to see what she was doing, then groaned, shuddering with pleasure when the warmth of her kisses reached his groin. His breath coming in short, swift gasps as he vainly sought to control his passion, he gave a hoarse cry and fell back onto the bed as the moist heat of her mouth engulfed him.

His enjoyment of that intimate pleasure was short-lived despite his efforts to rein in his desire. When he knew he could last no longer, he grasped her beneath her arms, dragged her body over his and neatly set her on top of him. She looked breathtakingly lovely as she rode him, her natural skill bringing them to a quick release. He caught her firmly in his arms when she collapsed on top of him.

As they lay quietly entwined, regaining their breath and their strength, he idly wondered if she knew the power she held over him. He just wished he knew how to gain a little power of his own. At times he felt as if she owned all the bread and he was the ragged beggar groveling for a few crumbs. Shaking free of that somewhat dark thought, he eased free of her body, sat up, and reached for his braies.

"Ye have become a terrible wanton," he teased as he stood up and moved to don the rest of his clothes.

"The blame for that can be laid squarely at your feet," she said as she wrapped the linen sheet around her and sat up on the bed.

"'Tis my fault, is it?" His voice was faintly muffled as he tugged on his jupon.

"Aye. Ye taught me the ways of the flesh. I believe I have simply caught your greed."

After tying the last of the points on his hose and yanking on his boots, he walked back to the bed and gave her a quick kiss. "I but pray that I can survive both yours and mine." He winked at her, then strode to the door. "I wouldnae linger in bed too long or the maids will begin to whisper about why ye are so weary each morn," he called over his shoulder as he went out the door.

She laughed and, after another long stretch, got out of bed. The maids had already been whispering about grass-stained clothes, hay caught in petticoats and hose, and bedclothes so badly tangled that the bed needed to be completely remade each morning. At first Sine had been embarrassed, but she had soon shrugged that emotion away. She doubted she could hide every sign of the passion she and Gamel shared from the keen eyes of the maids. None of the whispers were malicious and some were even envious, so she simply ceased to worry about it.

It would be nice if she could cast all her concerns aside with such ease, she mused. Although she could accept and not fight the fierce passion she and Gamel shared, his gentle attempts at romance were worrisome. The maids were not the only ones who noticed how often he gave her flowers or pretty ribbons that matched

her eyes or even the various treats cajoled out of the
cook especially for her. All of these things made Sine
soften to Gamel in a way that deeply concerned her. She
sighed and shook her head. There was nothing she
could do except pray that she retained the strength to
do what she must—let him go.

A moment later, her spirits rose again. To her delight,
a bath was brought in, ordered up by Gamel. He was
clearly learning what she liked. Troublesome though
that was, such a courtesy was impossible to scorn. The
door had barely shut behind the maids before Sine submerged herself in the hot, lavender-scented water.

Her pleasure lessened as she relaxed, her mind filling
with thoughts she continually tried to banish. After such
a happy, sensuous morning, she did not want to think
about how her marriage must end, but her mind refused
to allow her the comfort of ignorance. Each time she
grew too complacent in her role as Gamel's wife, her
stubborn common sense recalled her to some hard
truths.

"Wanton," Gamel had called her. He had been teasing
and his words had not stung her then, but now they
haunted her. There might come a day when he spoke
the word with bitterness, hurt, and hatred glittering in
his eyes. She grimaced as she recalled talking to Farthing
about lovemaking just before she met Gamel. She had
stoutly vowed that she would know the full richness of it,
would taste of the Land of Cockaigne—of paradise. It
had seemed like such a reasonable thing to hope for, but
now it was her curse.

She knew why her fierce passion for Gamel had
frightened her so at first and still worried her from
time to time. She feared that some day, like Arabel, one
man would no longer be enough to satisfy that hunger.

Sine certainly did not want to be with Gamel when and if that happened.

"Curse ye, Arabel," she whispered, and began to vigorously scrub herself. Even when her mother was finally defeated, Sine knew it would not be the end of her troubles. She would spend the rest of her life fighting the taint of her heritage.

It was late in the day before Sine braved the chamber where the women had gathered to do their needlework. Margot, Lady Edina's two eldest daughters, and their handmaidens were all there. They smiled in welcome and Sine returned their silent greeting. She had not yet gained the courage to ask for some instruction in the more complicated types of stitchery. As always, she had collected a few of the clothes that needed mending. Sine was confident of her skill in that regard and did not mind performing the chore before the other women. After exchanging another smile with Margot, she sat on the bench next to the girl and began to mend a large tear in one of Gamel's jupons.

"Has Lord Angus MacGregor arrived yet?" asked Margot as she carefully changed the yarn color in her tapestry.

"Aye, and all the men are secluded within the Logans' solar. Lady Edina is there as weel."

Margot smiled faintly. "But ye werenae invited. That must be highly irritating."

Sine laughed. "Highly." She grew serious. "'Tis my fight, 'tis a battle *I* began, and 'tis *I* who gains if we are victorious. Yet, most often, *I* am naught but the one who stands aside, waits to be told what must be done. That can become verra tiresome." She idly tucked a stray lock of hair back beneath her crisp linen headdress. "I do grow more understanding, however."

"I am not sure I would be."

"Weel, I am no soldier. I have no skill at plotting how to deal with an enemy. What I have done for six long years is hide. And now isnae the time for me to learn those other skills. That would be like allowing a beardless page to command the charge in some great battle. I also think they are trying to protect me."

"That is what a mon is trained to do—protect his lady, to keep safe the women and children in his care."

"Aye, and I can accept that. I am a wee lass and, e'en if I had been trained in the arts of fighting, I couldnae win against a full-grown mon. Weel, not all of the time. Nay, I speak of a different sort of protection. Lord Mac-Gregor is undoubtedly telling some verra dark tales about Arabel and Malise. I believe the reason I have been excluded from the meeting is because Gamel and the others dinnae want me to hear such things. They think they will only hurt, mayhaps frighten me."

"But dinnae ye *want* to learn these things?"

"Oh, aye, I do. Howbeit, I will confess that I like the way Gamel tells me what has been learned. He softens it, as much as such evil can be softened. Besides, I dinnae need to learn how dangerous Arabel is. I already ken that weel. While a part of me feels annoyed and insulted about being set aside, another part of me is glad not to hear the Brodies' victims relate their sordid tales. I carry enough shame."

Margot shook her head. "The shame isnae yours."

Sine set aside the mended jupon and picked up some hose, the knees sadly torn. "She is my mother."

"From all I have learned, ye were but born of her body, then ye became your father's child. When he was

so cruelly murdered, ye became Farthing's child. They
are the ones ye have learned from, not Arabel."

A flicker of hope rippled through Sine. "I pray ye are
right. 'Twould please me no end if Arabel's taint ne'er
touches me. Howbeit, she is of my blood. I can ne'er
ignore that." To her disappointment she noticed that
Margot had no more to say.

When Gamel's five-year-old tiny half sister, Lilith, arrived to tell Sine that Gamel wished to see her, Sine did
not hesitate to leave the other women. She was beginning to run out of mending to do and Margot was talking of helping her begin a tapestry. Trying not to look
too eager to answer Gamel's summons, she followed
Lilith out of the women's quarters and hurried away to
where Gamel waited for her in the outer bailey. He
stood by the open gates watching a small knot of riders
leaving Duncoille. Frowning a little, Sine walked over
to him.

"Is that Lord MacGregor leaving?" she asked as she
stopped by Gamel's side and he draped his arm about
her shoulders.

"Aye. The mon isnae in the best of health. He wished
to stay, but my father convinced him to return to his
wife. He left us a dozen good, strong men, however."

"Do ye think we shall have need of them?"

"There is a good chance. The Brodies dinnae want to
lose all they have gathered up over the years. They need
their lands and coin to support their sumptuous life. If
they surrender, they ken that they will lose most of it.
Land and money will be returned to those they have
tricked to gain it. I suspect they will be willing to fight
to keep every sheep or tuft of moss they now hold."

Sine nodded. "Aye. They will and they shall use my

presence to make it appear justified. Do ye think anyone will believe them?"

"Nay. My father sent word to the king and has already received a reply. The king says that he will not make a judgment on this. He considers it a family squabble." Gamel looked down at her and smiled.

"A family squabble?" She laughed, but knew that it was more sad than funny. "The king has closed his eyes, turned his back, and decided to leave it to the fates, hasnae he? I ken that 'tis rare for a king to interfere in such things, but I had thought he would take a wee bit more interest in this particular one. He must ken that this family squabble could become a verra bloody one."

"Aye, but one mustnae judge the king too harshly. We are two wealthy, if small, clans, each with some power, declaring that we have a claim to ye. Since he doesnae want to take any chance that the Brodies might use him to try and hurt us, to pull him to their side through the courts or their allies, and thus win, he has chosen to retreat from the matter. It may seem as if he treats the Brodies a wee bit too kindly by allowing them a free rein here, but dinnae forget, he has given us free rein to do what we feel we must as weel. 'Tis no small thing."

"I ken it. Weel, what did Lord MacGregor have to say? Anything helpful?"

"Nay. We had hoped that he would recall more of Dorchabeinn than he proved able to. It seems he was soaked in wine for most of his stay there. Still and all, Father and Lord Thomas added a wee bit to their map."

"I dearly wish that I could recall more. 'Twas my home. Ye would think that my memories of it would be stronger than they are."

"Ye were but a wee lass when ye fled and ye havenae seen the place for six long years. Also, ye werenae yet of an age to notice what could be useful to us. Then, too, the place has undoubtedly been altered some since then."

She nodded, then peeked up at him. "Ye didnae really tell me what Lord MacGregor had to say."

"I swear to ye, he didnae add much to what I have already told ye. In truth, we now but reaffirm what we have already learned elsewhere. Ye shall have to work verra hard to restore honor to Dorchabeinn and the Brodie name. Arabel and Malise have soaked both of them in treachery and dishonor."

"Mayhaps I will ne'er be able to scrub it away."

He kissed her cheek, took her by the hand, and started toward the keep. "Aye, ye will. The tale of your quest to regain your birthright has already traveled far and wide. Your father is also weel remembered. I but wished ye to understand that removing Arabel and Malise willnae completely remove the harm they have done, not considering everyone they have wronged. Ye will have to deal with the mistrust and hate they have left in their wake. There will be those who will demand that ye make atonement for your mother's crimes—especially those who have lost land or money to her."

"I believe I have understood that from the verra beginning," she murmured, and prayed that her heritage did not doom her to add to that harm.

Sine watched young Lilith skip down the hall toward the nursery and frowned. The little girl had not been very helpful. She had seen the twins but was not sure where they were at the moment. No one seemed to know. Sine began to feel concerned. Even reminding herself that Duncoille was a very large keep with many places for two small boys to hide did not calm her growing apprehension. Arabel's cold threat whispered through her mind, the fury and hatred behind her words giving them force.

Sine softly cursed her fears and the Brodies for causing them as she hurried toward the great hall. It was time to cease depending upon the youngest Logans and the other children of Duncoille to keep an eye on her half brothers. They could not really understand why it was so important to maintain a watch on Dane and Ree. In their short lifetimes the safety of Duncoille had never truly been breached. Children also needed to see a danger to fully comprehend the threat, and there was no hostile army clamoring outside Duncoille's thick walls. There was only talk—threats and whispers of wrongdoing.

In the great hall the servants were preparing for the evening meal. Sine nevertheless asked if any of them had seen her brothers. She got the answer that was beginning to chill her—no one had seen the twins for several hours. Although she tried not to give in to panic, she knew there was a frantic air to her actions as she retraced her earlier, calmer route through Duncoille. The blacksmith, the stable master, and even the dairymaids all gave her the same reply.

Her heart was pounding with fear as she left the falconer having heard yet another reply of "I dinnae ken." She hiked up her skirts and raced back inside the keep. Sine entered the great hall with an abruptness that drew the immediate attention of the four men now gathered near the fireplace at the far end of the hall. Slowing her pace only a little, Sine moved toward Gamel, Farthing, and their fathers, pleased that she would not have to search for them as well.

"What is wrong, dearling?" Gamel asked, taking her hand when she reached his side.

"Have any of ye seen Dane and Ree?" she asked, including Sir Lesley, Ligulf, Nigel, and Norman in her question as, just then, those four joined them.

"I was tossing the dice with them this morning, but that was hours ago." Gamel frowned.

"I saw the boys in the armorer's shed," replied Sir Lesley. "'Twas not so long ago."

"Nearly three hours ago, or so the armorer says," Sine corrected. "He appears to be the last one to have seen them. Although I can find a score or more who saw them at some time today, I can find no one who has seen them since they left the armorer's shed."

Gamel gently urged her to sit down on a stool near the massive fireplace. "Calm yourself, Sine. Dinnae forget that Dane and Ree are but lads and there is many a place in Duncoille where they could hide or play unseen. The people ye have spoken to could easily be mistaken as to when they last saw them. They could be recalling only when they last spoke to the boys or had to shoo them out of the way."

"None of the other children can recall having seen them in the last few hours either."

"Come, Sine, ye ken as weel as I that a child oftimes has a poor sense of time."

Out of the corner of her eye, Sine could see the other residents of Duncoille entering the great hall, including Lady Edina and Margot, who made their way toward them. "They both have a good sense of when it is time to eat, yet I still dinnae see them," Sine added, and it did not help her regain any sense of calm when the men just frowned.

"Is something amiss?" asked Lady Edina, stopping next to her husband.

"Young Dane and Ree cannae be found," replied Lord William.

"Mayhaps they have just become entangled in some

mischief and have forgotten how much time has passed,"
Lady Edina said, reaching over to give Sine a comforting
pat on the shoulder.

"Weel, when I find them, they will sorely regret the
lapse," muttered Farthing. "Sit here, lass." He kissed
Sine's cheek. "Calm your fears. We will ferret them out."

The other men murmured agreement and all of them
followed Farthing out of the great hall. Gamel paused
only to give her a quick kiss. Sine tried to smile as Lady
Edina called for a goblet of mulled cider, then urged Sine
to drink it. A few sips of the hot, spiced drink did ease her
fears a little, but she could not stop herself from constantly looking toward the heavy doors of the great hall.

"Lass, I am certain we have no traitors here," said Lady
Edina, tugging a stool closer to Sine and sitting down.
"Not one of our people would aid the Brodies."

"I ken it." Sine sighed and shook her head. "That was
ne'er one of my fears."

"Then the laddies must be about somewhere."

"Must they? M'lady, ye ken weel how children are. If
the knife's blade isnae tickling their throats, they can
forget that they are in danger. My fear is that the twins
have become infected with the sense of safety all the
other children of Duncoille feel. What if they forgot the
need to stay close at hand?"

"Ye think that they might have ventured outside of the
walls?" asked Margot.

"'Tis possible." Sine shook her head. "There would be
no need for the Brodies to try and get someone within
the gates of Duncoille then, would there? Nay, they
could but stand aside and wait for my brothers to come
to them."

"But the Brodies would have to sit outside of the gates
and wait for what might ne'er happen," murmured
Margot. "Ye dinnae think they would do that, do ye?"

"Aye. I believe that they have spies set all about us even now, waiting for commands from their masters, ever watchful for some chance to curry favor with Arabel and Malise."

Lady Edina nodded and grimaced. "Aye, Margot. Sine is right, I fear. Our men-at-arms have been trying to keep the land cleared of Brodie spies, but 'tisnae easily done. The curs just slink back when darkness falls or our men leave the area. The enemy *is* out there." She looked at Sine. "Howbeit, Dane and Ree have spent most of their young lives aware of the need to hide. It must be a lesson weel learned by now."

"I pray that ye are right, Lady Edina. I shudder to think of what could happen if the Brodies got hold of them."

When Lady Edina reached out to pat her hand in a gesture of silent comfort, Sine tried to smile but knew that she failed miserably. If her brothers had fallen into the hands of their enemies, then all she and her allies had done would be for naught. The Brodies would have a weapon to wield against her that she could never turn aside.

Gamel cursed and stood before the keep, wondering where he should look next. Even as he acknowledged that there was nowhere within Duncoille that had not been searched, he saw Farthing and the others coming toward him. None of them wore an expression which raised his hopes. The servants and soldiers were also returning to their work or their evening meal. Only a few glanced his way, and he knew that their searches had been as fruitless as his own. Gamel began to feel some of the panic he had seen in Sine's pale face.

"Nary a trace of the little fools," snapped Farthing as

he stopped before Gamel, concern making his tone sharp.

"Mayhaps there is someplace we have failed to search."

"I fear not, Gamel," replied Sir Lesley as he brushed grayed cobwebs from his fine blue jupon. "Ligulf and I peered into some places so small we nearly didnae get out of them."

"They cannae have just disappeared." Gamel looked around as he ran a hand through his hair.

"Nay." His hands on his hips, Farthing scowled toward the gates of Duncoille. "Howbeit, I could almost wish they had. 'Tis certain that they are no longer within these walls."

"I dinnae like to think that there is a traitor here," said Lord William.

Farthing shook his head. "I dinnae believe there is one, m'lord. 'Twould be nearly impossible to try and drag two unwilling lads away. Nay, I fear the wee pair of fools have put themselves in danger without any aid or guile. One thing is certain—they arenae within Duncoille."

"So they must be outside." Gamel cursed and looked up at the sky. "We have about an hour of daylight left to us. That doesnae seem verra much."

Lord William scowled and rubbed his chin. "'Twill be enough, mayhaps, to find some sign of them."

As he met Gamel's gaze, Farthing asked, "Should I tell Sine or shall ye?"

"I will tell her simply that we are still searching. 'Tis the truth."

"Ye should tell her the full truth as ye ken it. Ye willnae ease her fears by trying to be secretive."

Gamel nodded and started toward the keep. "Saddle my horse. I will join ye in a moment."

* * *

Sine tensed when Gamel returned to the great hall alone, his expression solemn. In her mind's eye she could see herself running over to him and demanding information, but her body refused to move. As he drew near, she even felt the urge to run and hide in her bed-chamber, as if she could avert the tragedy by refusing to hear what he had to say. She did neither. She sat stiffly on the stool, clutching her goblet so tightly that her hands ached, and staring up at Gamel beseechingly when he stood before her.

"Ye havenae found them," she whispered.

Gamel gently grasped her by the shoulders and brushed a kiss over her forehead. "Nay, but we will. Dinnae think the worst. We have no proof of it yet." He prayed that his voice held only comfort and confidence and none of the very real fear he felt for the boys' safety.

"The lads arenae at Duncoille. Isnae that proof enough that the worst has happened?"

"Nay, dearling, and if ye werenae so worried, ye would ken it. It but means that we havenae found them. It does-nae have to mean that the Brodies have."

"And just what else could it mean?" she snapped.

"That they have wandered away from Duncoille, may-haps gotten a wee bit lost. It could be as simple as that. We may e'en meet them as they return. Now, I had best leave so that we can begin the search."

"I will go with ye." Sine began to stand, only to feel Gamel's grip tighten upon her shoulders. He held her in her seat. "Ye mean to deny me the chance to search for my own brothers?" she asked.

"Aye, I do. If, and I say if, the worst has happened and the Brodies have caught the lads, 'twill be best if ye are here. We dinnae want to give them the chance to capture all of ye. Then we will have lost the battle ere we have struck the first blow."

"Ye dinnae think we have lost if they have taken the twins?"

"Nay. We might still have a chance, for they need ye far more than they need those two lads. They will try to use the boys to bring ye to them. If they get ye as weel, they will simply kill all three of ye as swiftly as they can. Then all we could do would be to try to make the Brodies pay for those murders. I prefer to stop the killing rather than have to avenge it. So, stay right here, and let us hunt for Dane and Ree. We will find them. Ye can spend your time here thinking of how ye will punish them for their carelessness." When Sine did not speak, he brushed a kiss over her lips. "We *will* find them, lass. Believe that."

"Aye, I shall try," she whispered.

After Gamel left, she looked at Margot and Lady Edina. Both women tried to smile encouragingly, but Sine could see the concern in their eyes. They feared the same thing she did.

"The Brodies have my brothers," she murmured.

"Lass, ye cannae be sure of it," Lady Edina said.

"Oh, aye, I can be. I ken it in my heart, my mind, and with every drop of blood in my veins."

"Ye didnae see the boys taken away by the Brodies." Margot spoke with a firmness that made Lady Edina and Sine look at her with a touch of surprise. "Weel, ye didnae. And ye dinnae possess the sight. So how can ye be sure?"

Margot was speaking perfect sense, but even her calm, firm logic did not make Sine's conviction waver. Instead of being able to dismiss her certainty as an unproven thing born of fear, she grew more sure with each passing moment. Arabel had Dane and Ree. Sine shuddered. She could almost hear Arabel's triumphant laughter.

Chapter 13

"I dinnae see why we must linger here," muttered Gamel, frowning at Farthing, who was crouched down and staring intently at the ground.

Gamel glanced up at the sky, which was already clouding over with the deep gray of night. His sense of urgency made him irritable. Once outside Duncoille, the searchers had spread out in all directions. But now the men had gathered a short distance inside the wood to the south of Duncoille to decide where to search next. Suddenly, Farthing dismounted and, leading his horse, walked a few yards away. The rest of them also dismounted and stood like silent fools, watching Farthing's strange actions.

"The boys were taken from here," Farthing abruptly announced, standing up and scowling down at the ground.

"Are ye sure?" asked Lord Thomas.

"Aye, Father. They were seized by three men." Farthing carefully took a few steps, his gaze still fixed upon the ground.

After moving to the spot where Farthing had crouched for so long, Gamel asked, "How can ye be certain of that?"

Farthing pointed at the ground by Gamel's feet. "The

signs are all there. The three men carried the lads off in this direction. Farther along I am sure we will find the signs of their mounts."

"And ye can read all that from this patch of disturbed ground?"

"Aye. The three men charged the lads from the south, east, and west. There was a brief struggle and then, carrying the boys, the men strode deeper into the wood."

"Ye have honed your skills at reading such signs, Farthing," Lord Thomas said quietly. "Ye have had a chance to do some hunting, have ye?"

"Ye need not be so careful in your choice of words, Father." Farthing grinned. "We both ken that 'twas poaching I was indulging in. My other skills werenae always adequate to feed all of us." He grew serious again. "I now wish I had taught the lads a wee bit more about protecting themselves."

Lord William patted Farthing on the back. "Accept my word on this, son. Ye couldnae have taught them enough to have avoided this. I fear that children can often be their own worst enemies. My brood has taught me the truth of that often enough."

Farthing nodded in silent, heartfelt agreement, and looked toward the south. "Shall we follow the trail a ways to be certain that it was truly the Brodies' curs who stole the lads?"

Everyone murmured agreement, and as they fell into step behind Farthing, Lord Thomas said, "Ye should have come to me for help, son. It wasnae right that ye should have been forced to break the law."

"If I had found myself in real difficulty, ye would have heard from me, Father. We were gifted with a great deal of luck—until a certain keen-eyed rogue caught up with us," he said with a pointed look at Gamel. Then he shook his head and looked down at the ground. A moment later, he continued, "Here is where they left their horses. They mounted and rode off to the south. There is no doubt that some Brodie swine grabbed Dane and Ree. The poor lads stumbled right into the hands of their enemies."

"Should we follow them?" asked Gamel.

"God's tears, but I ache to do so. Howbeit, they have several hours' lead on us. Dark will soon hinder us as weel. We would find the gates of Dorchabeinn secured against us and the lads inside, even if we managed to reach the castle without mishap. If we accomplished anything, 'twould probably be to put the lads in even more danger than they are now. Nay, I think we must return to Duncoille and wait for Arabel and Malise to tell us what demands they wish to make."

"Ye ken verra weel what their demands shall be—they will ask for Sine."

"We all ken that," said Lord William. "Sadly, we also ken that we can do nothing now. Farthing is right. The Brodie men are three hours or more away. We could ne'er catch them even if we had the light to do so, which we willnae in but a few moments. We must return to Duncoille."

Gamel found it painful to do so, but he nodded in agreement. As they all mounted, Blane blew three blasts of the hunting horn to call the rest of the men still searching for the twins back to Duncoille. Gamel fought his fear for the boys, who were now in the hands of their enemies, but, more than that, he tried to conquer his dread of telling Sine the news. She would be terrified for her brothers and he knew he would face a lengthy battle to convince her not to immediately sacrifice herself in an exchange. It would be what the Brodies would demand, but it would not save the boys. Gamel prayed that he could make Sine understand that.

"Do ye want to tell Sine or shall I?" asked Farthing as he rode beside Gamel.

"I dinnae think either of us will have to tell her anything."

Farthing cursed and nodded. "Aye, she will ken it the moment we return without Dane and Ree. She will read it in our faces. The lass has an annoying skill in that regard."

"I dinnae dread that as much as I do telling her that she willnae be able to save those boys by sacrificing herself. She has the wit to ken the truth of that, but I dinnae believe her wits will be what commands her this time." Gamel sighed with a mixture of resignation and disappointment when Farthing's only response was a look of sympathy.

Sine grew so tense with apprehension when she heard the men return that she feared she could shatter. Gamel and Farthing were the first to enter the great hall, which was now empty except for Margot, Lady Edina, and herself. She took one look at their solemn, wary expressions and knew the worst.

"Arabel has them," she whispered, and fought the urge to succumb to weeping, something she knew would be a waste of precious time.

"Aye. The boys must have stumbled upon some of the Brodie men, who quickly snatched them," replied Gamel even as he crouched before her and took her hands in his. "For reasons only the lads themselves can explain, they had wandered out into the wood. I suspect Arabel's hirelings were stunned by their good fortune."

"Ye are certain of this?" she asked, although she knew it was a foolish question because the men would have made sure of it before telling her such horrifying news.

"Verra sure, dearling," Farthing murmured as he stood beside her and lightly clasped her shoulder. "There was no denying the signs. We didnae immediately set out after them for they left hours ago and the night was but moments away. I am sorry for that, lass."

"Nay." She reached up to pat his hand where it rested on her shoulder before allowing Gamel to renew his gentle hold upon both of her hands. "Ye have naught to apologize for. The fault is all mine. My thirst for vengeance has brought them to this fate. I should have kept them hidden, not stepped forth to challenge Malise and Arabel. Dane and Ree were safe and I put them in danger."

"Dinnae talk like a fool," snapped Gamel, abruptly standing up to frown down at her. "Ye carry no guilt for this trouble. That rests fully at the feet of the Brodies."

"The Brodies didnae e'en ken that we were still alive until I dragged us all out of hiding. Dane and Ree were content. 'Twas *I* who felt the pinch of being denied all that our father had left to us."

"It wouldnae have been much longer before the lads felt that same pinch. As they grew to manhood they would have become more and more determined to wrest back from the Brodies all that is rightfully theirs."

"Aye," agreed Lord William, moving to stand beside his son. "I suspect they have felt it from time to time but simply didnae trouble ye with it. And, lass, hiding away doesnae necessarily mean that ye are safe."

"But we *were* safe." Sine knotted her fingers together in her lap.

"Nay." Farthing bent and kissed her cheek. "We were but undiscovered yet. We were ne'er completely safe, and if ye werenae so determined to flay yourself with a guilt ye dinnae deserve, ye would agree."

"The twins werenae prepared to fight and I dragged them into this battle. Weel, I must correct my own error."

"Oh, aye?" Gamel shook his head. "Do ye truly think that ye can mend matters by dying? Ye ken as weel as I do that Arabel will demand that ye return to Dorchabeinn and that only death awaits ye there. And, if ye would pause in your wallow in guilt, ye would also ken that the laddies will die right at your side."

Sine was stung by Gamel's and Farthing's criticism, but she did not want to hear the things they were saying. She did not want to hear that she could not save her young brothers by handing herself over to Arabel and Malise. The very last thing she wanted was to turn her back on even the slimmest of chances to save her brothers, but she knew that was exactly what she was being forced to do.

"They will ask that ye trade your life for your brothers'," Gamel continued. "Ye ken what deceivers the Brodies are and ye ken that they cannae allow any of ye to live if they are to survive. There can be no bargaining with them. Dinnae fool yourself into thinking otherwise."

"Do ye have some other idea? Some other plan? I should dearly like to hear that there is some choice."

"We need time to form a plan," Gamel replied, inwardly cursing the inadequacy of his answer.

"Mayhaps, there are no plans one can make in such a situation."

"We simply havenae been able to consider the problem," said Lord Thomas. "Keep in mind that none of us will gain if ye do as the Brodies will ask, child. The laddies will lose, ye will lose, and all those who have allied themselves with us will lose as weel."

"I ken it." She wrapped her arms about her waist, but it did little to ease the painful churning of her stomach.

"Do ye think that my brothers will be kept alive at all?" She felt Farthing's grip on her shoulder tighten and remembered that she was not the only one who was suffering.

Lord Thomas shrugged but hastily said, "There is no means of kenning what the Brodies will do. Howbeit, if they kill the boys, they will have no lure to draw ye into their trap. Nay, I think the boys will be safe enough for now. In truth, I think ye can do more to keep them alive by *not* surrendering."

Gamel placed his hand on her arm. "Come, dearling, have something to eat and—"

"I couldnae swallow a bite."

"Then let me take ye to our chamber so that ye can rest."

"Rest? Do ye think I should just go to bed and close my eyes until Arabel arrives to gloat?"

"Nay, but naught can be solved now. We must talk o'er all we can and cannae do. Ye are too upset to endure that. Ye need to try and calm yourself. Ye need to be ready, strong, and rested for whatever we must face next."

Sine knew that Gamel was right. She was far too afraid for Dane and Ree to be of any help to anyone, even herself. No one had said so, but she knew she was already causing some difficulty. They were all huddled around her, trying to soothe her, instead of planning what might be done to help her brothers. She hated the weakness she was showing. Sine glanced up at Farthing and could see by his pale, drawn features that he was suffering as much as she was, yet he had himself under control and could still think clearly.

"I shall go and rest then," she said, smiling her thanks to Lady Edina when the woman helped her to her feet. "I dinnae think I shall sleep though."

Gamel watched his mother and Margot lead Sine away. His mother briefly glanced his way and winked. He knew Sine would be given some potion to help her go to sleep and he was glad of it. As he, his family, Blane, Sir Lesley, and the Magnussons moved to sit at a table and try to salvage a meal from what the others had left behind, Gamel heartily wished that he could do more to ease Sine's pain.

"She will recover her strength," Farthing said as he helped himself to some bread and thick honey. He faintly smiled at Gamel from across the table. "She hates this weakness and will fight it. 'Tis just that she loves the twins as if they were her own children."

"As ye do," murmured Gamel, watching Farthing closely as a page filled their tankards with wine, and feeling that he was nearing a new understanding of the man.

"Aye, as I do. Howbeit, Sine needs time alone to subdue the urge, mayhaps the need, to succumb to tears whilst I but fight the aching need to ride like the furies for Dorchabeinn, screaming for Arabel's blood. Fortunately, I retain the wit to ken the futility of that. 'Twould get the twins killed and myself as weel."

"And anyone fool enough to ride with ye," Gamel agreed.

"Do ye think we have lost this battle already?" asked Ligulf from his seat on Farthing's right.

"The chances of winning a full, satisfying victory have certainly been diminished," replied Farthing. "Howbeit, I am not ready to set the laurel wreath upon Arabel's head just yet."

"Nay, nor am I," said Lord William, and a murmured ripple of agreement went through the others. "We must try to anticipate the Brodies' next move. Then, when they finally come, we will be able to act immediately."

Although Gamel participated in the planning and in the discussion of what they might face in the morning, his thoughts were fixed upon Sine. She was so afraid for her brothers, so quick to blame herself for their fate. He ached to banish both of those emotions from her heart and mind, but he was not sure he had the skill or the time. If his mother gave Sine a potion, it could mean that Sine would sleep deeply until the morning. Gamel was certain that the Brodies would be at their gates soon after sunrise. Arabel and Malise would be confident of victory and try to grasp it as quickly as possible.

It was late before Gamel was able to seek out his bed. When he first entered the bedchamber he shared with Sine, he felt the sting of panic. She was nowhere to be seen. Then he noticed the door of the large clothespress was open. He sighed with relief. Sine had used one of the many hidden passages in Duncoille to slip away unseen. Gamel got a lantern and set out after her.

He was not surprised when he found her on the southern wall, staring out over the parapets toward Dorchabeinn. As he walked over to her, he mused that she looked very lovely with her dark cape draped haphazardly over her white linen nightdress and her pale hair loose, the night air gently ruffling its thick waves. She also looked tiny, lost, and forlorn.

"Ye will catch a chill," he murmured as he reached her side and leaned against the damp stone wall.

"Nay, 'tis pleasing. The bite of the coming fall isnae in the air quite yet." She sighed and shook her head. "They will be so afraid, Gamel."

"Fear is a curable thing, dearling." He reached out to toy with a thick lock of her hair. "Ye must cease to torment yourself. Ye can do naught about this, not yet."

"But that is what is such a torture. Cannae ye see that? I am sure my brothers are afraid yet I must stand here, unable to soothe them or offer them hope. 'Tis much akin to a mother hearing her bairn cry from hunger yet having no milk or bread to give the poor child."

He put his arm around her shoulder and tugged her closer to his side. "Arabel willnae kill them, not as long as she thinks they can be used against ye."

"The twins were so young the last time they were at Dorchabeinn, too young to recall Arabel's cruelties. Aye, and I sheltered them from her as much as I was able. Since the day I took them away from there, they havenae really tasted the meanness she can so skillfully mete out. They willnae understand how to protect themselves from the sting of her cruelty."

"I havenae known the lads for verra long, but they may be a great deal stronger than ye think, lass." He pressed a kiss to the top of her head. "And, dinnae forget, they have each other. Try not to think so much on what they might be enduring, but on how we shall free them."

Sine slipped her arms about his trim waist and looked up at him. He brought her such comfort and helped her to regain her strength when it wavered. She feared she was growing too accustomed to it, yet knew she would not turn from it either. Before her stretched empty year after empty year of facing every trial alone. She would be a fool to turn aside his support while she was still able to have it.

"Do ye really believe we can free Dane and Ree?" she asked him.

"Weel, I willnae promise ye that we can, but it isnae impossible. If we can use our wits and are graced with a wee bit of luck—aye—there is a chance we can save them from that shewolf."

"Thank ye, Gamel. I cannae say I fully believe your hopeful words, but they are a comfort to me."

"Ah, so ye have found some use for a husband eh?" He

inwardly cursed, certain that it was a poor time to talk about their marriage.

Her cheek resting against his chest, Sine grimaced and pretended that she had not heard his remark. Little by little, he had begun to make such comments. She knew he was trying to get her to say something—anything—about how she felt about their marriage. It seemed cruel to leave him plagued with uncertainty, to never tell him anything about how she felt, yet she was sure that such cruelty would become a kindness when she was to end their marriage. There would be no soft words for him to remember.

There were times when she wanted to open her heart to him so badly that she ached. The most difficult moments were just after they had made love or, as now, when he held her close and offered comfort and hope. It was yet another thing she could curse her mother for. She knew she would spend the rest of her life regretting all the words left unsaid.

"Have ye gone to sleep, loving?" Gamel asked, his voice soft and teasing.

She shook her head and held him a little tighter. "Nay, I was but trying to pull some of your strength into me. I am verra sorry for my weakness earlier. 'Twas no help to ye or my brothers. Wits were needed, not weeping."

"Ye werenae weeping. Dinnae think so poorly of yourself."

"And why shouldnae I think poorly of myself? I needed to be sent to my chambers and given a potion to calm me like some swooning maiden. It shames me to recall it."

"Ye are too hard upon yourself. 'Twould have been strange if ye had not been upset. Ye recovered quickly and now ye can do what must be done. That is the truer test of your strength."

"I hope ye are right. I shall need a great deal of strength. Ye spoke of my doing what must be done. Do ye ken what that will be?"

He combed his fingers through her hair. "The Brodies will demand that ye come to them in trade for the twins."

"Aye, I feel certain they will ask for that too. I seek the strength to face that defeat and the courage to put myself into the hands of my foes."

"That is exactly what ye must *not* do. I had thought we had made that clear." He quickly covered her mouth with his hand when she started to protest. "If ye do exactly as they ask then we will all lose. 'Twill not save the twins. When they ask for a trade, ye will deny them."

"I cannae," she whispered when he removed his hand.

"Ye can and ye will. My father will instruct ye in what to say when the time comes. 'Twill most likely be in the morning. Ye have the wit, Sine, to see that we must play a delaying game." He sighed with relief when, after a brief hesitation, she nodded.

"Waiting can be such torture."

"Aye, it can," he whispered, thinking of his interminable wait for some sign or word of caring from her.

Sine bit her lip to stop from blurting out words of devotion and some wild vow to stay with him forever. She grew more certain every day that he would return those feelings, that he was only waiting for some hint of love from her. At times she selfishly considered nudging him into confessing what was in his heart so that, after she had to leave him, she would have his words of love to cherish. Then she would see the cruelty of that and be appalled. She would not steal his pride. Sine prayed that acting so considerately would someday help to ease any bitterness he might feel. The knowledge that he could easily end up hating her made her shiver.

"Here, ye grow chilled." He stepped back, tugged her

cape around her more securely, and took her hand in his. "We had best go back inside. The morrow isnae so verra far away now and ye should be weel rested, strong, and healthy."

"Ye think that Arabel will try and strike her bargain as early as tomorrow?" she asked as they walked back toward the keep.

"Aye. She willnae wait to act."

A child cried out and Martin was abruptly torn from his concentration upon the accounting ledgers. He frowned, wondering why he should imagine such a sound. There were never any children within the keep. Although there were a number of children in the area around Dorchabeinn, they were rarely seen and never within the walls of the castle itself. Arabel's hatred of children was well known. Malise's appalling carnal taste for very young girls and boys was also strongly suspected. Anyone under the rule of the Brodies who had a child did his best to keep the innocent out of sight.

Just as Martin had convinced himself that he had been mistaken about the noise, he heard it again. It was unquestionably the pained cry of a child echoing through the shadowy halls of Dorchabeinn. He got up from his stool and briefly paused to stretch out the aches and cramps caused by bending over the ledgers for hours, then left his tiny steward's chamber. Once outside of the room, he listened carefully for a moment before heading toward the studded doors of the great hall. As quietly as he could, he slipped inside, and nearly cried out in surprise.

Malise, grinning widely, poured wine into an ornate silver goblet held by an equally cheerful Arabel. They laughed, touched their goblets together, and drank. To the right of the table was the reason for their high spirits.

One slender boy was helping another to stand up. That second child wavered unsteadily for a moment as he wiped the blood from his mouth. Martin was certain they were the late Lord Brodie's sons. His conviction was affirmed when the boys briefly glanced his way. It had been six years, but he had never forgotten those wide, rich blue eyes. Nay, he thought, I cannae close my eyes to this.

"Ah, Cousin Martin," called Malise. "Come here and have a drink to celebrate our triumph."

Martin fought to hide his dismay as he walked over to their table and accepted a tankard of wine. As he drank, he covertly studied the boys. They were bruised and battered but struggled to stand tall and uncowed. Their efforts cut Martin to his soul. He cursed the fates which had seen fit to put the twins into the cruel hands of the Brodies, then cursed his own fate.

His moment of decision was being thrust upon him. He had kept silent when the children had fled six years ago, but this time he would have to do a great deal more if he did not want their blood on his hands. The two small boys had more strength than he did, he thought with a pang of self-disgust. Even now he wavered, but no more, he swore to himself. This time he would use his gifts of stealth and guile to save lives. This time he would choose the more dangerous path and do what was right.

"Ye dinnae seem verra pleased, Martin," said Arabel, her eyes narrowed as she looked at him.

"I was only wondering if we celebrate a wee bit too early. Ye dinnae have the lass yet."

"We have her brothers." Arabel grabbed one of the twins by his thick fair hair, shook him, and then flung him aside.

"Aye, so half the battle has now been won." Martin wondered what madness had seized him, for he was very nearly baiting Arabel and that was a highly dangerous game to play. "The less important half."

Arabel slammed her goblet down onto the tapestry-draped oak table. "Aye, 'tis only half, but 'tisnae *un*important. These bastards will bring Sine Catriona into our grasp. She will walk into our hands like the lamb goes to slaughter."

"A verra apt comparison, my sweet," murmured Malise.

After giving her husband an irritated glance, Arabel turned her tight-lipped glare back on Martin. "These little fools wandered beyond the protection of Duncoille and our men stumbled on them. By now my daughter will realize that the bastards are missing and she is sure to ken who has them. The moment I tell her that the price for their miserable lives is her own she will come."

"And then ye mean to let the lads go free?" Martin sincerely doubted that and was not surprised when Arabel laughed. He felt badly for the lads, who were forced to listen to her gloat.

"Of course I willnae set them free. Ye cannae be so great a fool, Martin. The bastards will die just as their sister will. In truth, I believe I shall allow wee Sine to watch them die. 'Twould add to her bitterness to hear that not only had she given up her life for naught, but she must also see her beloved brothers bleed."

"She willnae be duped by ye," snapped one of the boys. "She will spit in your eye."

"Which one are ye?" Arabel asked, staring at the child with cold distaste.

"Beldane." He softly grunted when she slapped him, causing him to stagger a little.

Martin was mildly surprised by his sudden urge to reach out to the boy. He hastily subdued it. The admiration he felt for the boy was a little harder to conceal as Beldane quickly steadied himself and glared at Arabel.

If Arabel lusted after the sight of the boys' fear and the loss of all their hope, she would be left hungry.

"The lass might not take your bait," Martin said.

"Why would ye think that?" asked Malise as he sprawled in his heavy oaken chair.

"I suspect that she is aware that your promises are often broken. She and the Logans have spent these last three weeks talking to your reluctant allies and those ye have betrayed. Lady Logan—"

"Dinnae call her that," yelled Arabel. "She is Sine Catriona Brodie. That marriage is no more than a ploy to hinder my rightful claim to the little slut. If I wished to take the time, I could have that marriage ended like that." She snapped her fingers.

"Mayhaps ye should end it before ye kill the lass."

"Before or after—what does it matter?"

"A husband not only has the right to hold his bride at his side, he also has a right to all that belongs to her. Ye wish Sine Catriona dead so that ye can gain her lands and fortune, but as long as Sir Gamel Logan claims her as his wife, he will gain all of that."

"He willnae, will he? Not whilst we are still alive. And 'twasnae an approved marriage," muttered Malise.

"She is the heir, fool," snapped Arabel. "None of those things really matter. He would own all that is hers. We would have to fight it in the courts and I wouldnae wager much on our winning against the Logans."

He frowned at Arabel. "Then, mayhaps, we should be careful not to act too hastily."

"Nay. That bastard son of the Red Logan willnae savor his wealth for verra long. I ne'er meant for him to survive his whore by many days. This but gives me one more reason to wish him dead. He will be the price the Logans pay for setting themselves against me. Ye two," she called to the pair of burly guards who stood a few feet behind the boys. "Take these whelps to the dungeons. And ye need not be gentle," she added when the guards started to pull the boys toward the doors.

As the doors shut behind the twins, Martin heard the sound of a fist striking flesh and inwardly winced. He forced his complete attention on Arabel and Malise. Arabel was furious over Beldane's defiance, but her expression also held a hint of gloating. Martin was a little dismayed that his reminder about Gamel Logan claiming Sine's fortune had not caused Arabel any qualms. He did not give up all hope, however. Malise had hesitated and the man still held some small power over his wife. As he finished his wine, Martin again vowed that he would not be a part of any more killings.

"They carry the stink of their father." Arabel took a deep drink of wine. "We shall send a messenger at first light. I am quite sure Sine will demand some proof that we hold the bastards." Arabel tossed a small silver medallion onto the table. "The messenger can give her this."

Martin reached for the medallion, which consisted of the Brodie crest and the name Beldane. He was startled when Arabel slapped her hand down on it, halting him from grasping it. It took some effort to hide his nervous alarm as he met her cold gaze.

"Not ye, Martin," she said. "I dinnae believe ye are suitable for this particular errand."

"I may be a poor soldier, but I can find Duncoille and deliver your demands," he murmured, silently cursing the loss of a chance to speak to the Logans.

"I am sure ye can find Duncoille. After all, ye have a lover there, dinnae ye—although I dinnae ken how e'en that plain, pale lass can find ye of any interest. Howbeit, 'tis enough to make ye the wrong mon for this chore. We cannae afford to have ye dawdle."

"As ye wish, m'lady. I have never been fond of rising early anyway."

He bowed and took his leave, his heart beating frantically as he strode out of the great hall and hurried to his tiny bedchamber. Once there, he poured himself a large tankard of the strong wine he hoarded for himself. Martin sat on his rope-slung cot and gulped down the heady brew, but it did not completely banish his fears.

For the very first time Arabel had openly displayed mistrust of him. As he had watched the twins and listened to Arabel's brutal plans for them and their sister, he had finally decided to betray her and Malise, to try to save Sine and her brothers' lives. Now he had to worry about his own. Now he could well be useless to the Logans and their allies.

Suddenly he sat up straighter. All was not lost. He might still be able to help. Since Arabel had made it clear that she already had some very strong doubts about his loyalty, he did not need to fear arousing her suspicions any longer. He was already as good as dead. With what time he might have left, he could still try to do some good. Martin was sure that the Logans would not allow Sine to just ride to her death, that they would at least try to outwit Arabel. He might be able to assist them in that effort.

"Aye," he muttered, and slowly smiled. "And, if 'tis my fate to die in this battle, at least I shall have the sweet pleasure of destroying all of Arabel's schemes ere I face my maker."

Chapter 14

Sine clenched her hands together tightly in her lap as the Brodie messenger was led into the great hall of Duncoille. She struggled to remain calm. The people seated with her at the head table gave her some help. She could depend upon the experience of Lords William and Thomas. Gamel, his three brothers, Blane, and Sir Lesley offered their strength. Lady Edina and Margot gave her sympathy. Farthing, she mused as she glanced at him, shared her deep love for the twins.

She had slept very little after Gamel had urged her from the parapets of Duncoille and back into their bedchamber. As he held her close throughout the night, she had concentrated on regaining her strength and will to fight. She had carefully considered every possibility, even the ones she dreaded, and prepared herself to meet them. When the morning had finally come, she had felt able to face anything. At breakfast Lord William had carefully instructed her on what to say when the messenger came.

Now Sine stared cooly at the Brodies' man as he bowed, cleared his throat, and began to speak. "I am Andrew Moore, a messenger in the service of Dorchabeinn. I have been sent to inform ye that Lord and Lady Brodie have taken possession of the late Lord Brodie's bastards, Beldane and Barre."

"Have they?" Farthing smiled coldly. "And we are to simply accept their word on that, are we?"

The short, heavy-muscled man stepped a little closer and held out a small silver medallion. "Lady Brodie believes that this will serve as adequate proof of her claim."

Farthing took the medallion and studied it. Sine could tell by his faint loss of color and the way his jawline tightened that the medallion was Beldane's. It had been given to the boy by their father to mark him as the first-born. When Farthing held it out toward her, she shook her head. She did not need to look at it. Neither did she want to unclasp her hands, for she feared they might tremble and she did not want to expose any weakness.

"Aye, 'tis proof enough," Farthing said. "What does Lady Brodie want?"

"Her other child. Although she loves all children and is hurt by her daughter's fears and accusations, she will agree to release the boys if Sine Catriona returns to her."

"And are we to believe in her word?" asked Sine.

"Lady Arabel Brodie's word is her bond," Andrew Moore said in a strong, firm voice. "As is Lord Malise's."

Sine shook her head. "I dearly hope ye dinnae really believe your fine words, Master Moore, or ye are a doomed mon. Half of Scotland has proof that the word of the Brodies is as empty as a beggar's belly. I certainly wouldnae ever accept the word of Arabel or Malise without great hesitation."

"Am I to tell my masters that ye willnae return to Dorchabeinn?"

"Ye are to tell your masters that I must consider the matter. I need some time ere I can make any decision."

She almost felt pity for the man; he looked frightened at the thought of returning to Dorchabeinn empty-handed.

"How much time?"

"Two days. If I dinnae appear at the gates of Dorchabeinn by sunset on the morrow 'twill mean that I have decided I dinnae like Lady Brodie's terms. She can then decide if she wishes to offer me some new ones."

The man bowed and left. As soon as the doors of the great hall closed behind Arabel's messenger, Sine slumped in her seat. She felt weak, as if all her strength had been drained out of her. When Gamel urged her to drink some wine, she smiled faintly and took a sip from the tankard he pressed into her hands.

"Ye did the only thing ye could do," he said, taking her hand in his and brushing a light kiss over her knuckles.

"Aye, but 'twas the hardest thing I have e'er done. 'Twas nearly impossible not to see my words as a cruel betrayal of my own brothers. And then I could all too easily imagine Arabel's reaction to my refusal. She will be incensed and my poor brothers could weel suffer dearly for it."

"What ye do or dinnae do will make verra little difference to how they suffer," Lady Edina said. "'Tis a harsh truth, but one it may help ye to remember."

"Aye, and I tell it to myself often. It does help to ease the guilt I feel. I but pray that my brothers will understand."

"They will, lass," Farthing said. "They will turn whatever anger or blame they may feel upon those who so richly deserve it—the Brodies. Dane and Ree have the wit to ken that naught will be gained if ye blindly walk into Arabel's trap. In fact, I wouldnae be surprised to learn that the woman has made her vile plans verra clear to the poor lads."

"Aye, she probably has. She would do so in the hope

that it would terrify them. Arabel has always enjoyed seeing fear in others." She frowned. "'Tis somewhat of a surprise that Martin Robertson didnae act as her messenger."

"And not a verra nice surprise either," muttered Margot.

Sine sent the girl a sympathetic look. "True. Martin always performed such errands for Arabel and Malise in the past. One has to ask oneself why it was different this time. I fear the answer to that question may not be good."

"Martin once told me that he believed that they had already begun to suspect him."

"That would certainly explain why he wasnae used on this errand."

"Ye dinnae think they have hurt him, do ye?" Margot asked in a small voice.

"I wish I could say nay without any doubt, but I fear that I cannae. I am sorry."

"There is no need for ye to apologize. Ye cannae take on the guilt of your kinsmen. Nay, nor of Martin. If he is in danger now, 'tis mostly his own fault. If he isnae already dead, then it is how he acts now which is most important. Will he let his fear direct him again and just flee Dorchabeinn, or will he stand firm and help us?" She shrugged. "I heartily pray that he chooses the latter."

"So do we, lass," said Gamel. "'Twould be an assistance we should be verra grateful to receive. Howbeit, we must continue to act as if we have no one to rely upon but ourselves."

"Now that we ken what Arabel's game is, what *is* your plan?" Sine asked Gamel.

"Farthing, Blane, Sir Lesley, and I shall leave for Dorchabeinn in just a few hours. That will allow us to arrive there by nightfall. We shall perform a little reconnaissance during the night. 'Tis always wise to ken the land of the enemy ere ye ride into it. If God so pleases, we may e'en discover a weakness which will aid us. Come the morning, lass, ye and a small force from Duncoille shall start on your own journey to Dorchabeinn. We will meet up together a few miles north of Dorchabeinn and that is where we shall make our final plans about the best way to confront the Brodies." He watched her warily as she considered all that he had said.

"'Tisnae really much of a plan, is it?" she murmured.

"There is more to it, dearling, but—again—there are some things that simply cannae be determined until we have had a chance to closely study Dorchabeinn."

"Are ye absolutely sure ye must do this study?" She did not like the thought that Gamel and Farthing would be drawing so close to the treacherous Brodies without a well-armed force of men right behind them.

"Weel, as I said, we cannae ride in there blind. Aye, we have some information on the strength and habits of the guards at Dorchabeinn, but we would all feel a great deal more at ease if some of our own people had a wee look at the place ere we ride up to the gates."

It still did not sound like much of a plan to Sine, but she said no more. The men had all had years of experience in battle. They all seemed very confident. She would do her part as well as she could and pray that their confidence was justified.

Sine clutched her cloak more tightly around herself as a chill breeze curled around the walls of Duncoille. She stared out over the parapets, south toward Dorchabeinn, and prayed. Everyone she cared about was now within Arabel's murderous grasp. Gamel and Farthing had left just a few hours ago, and the woman already held the twins as well. The mere thought of that made Sine feel nauseous with fear. A soft footfall drew her out of her dark thoughts and she turned to find Margot at her side.

"Have ye come to gaze uselessly toward Dorchabeinn as weel?" she asked.

Margot smiled briefly. "Aye. I also saw ye up here and thought ye may be in need of some companionship. If ye would rather be alone, I will not be offended."

"Nay. Stay. 'Tis a lovely night, if a wee bit cool when the wind stirs. Soon the cold will come. Fall draws near and winter isnae far behind and *why* am I babbling on and on about the cursed weather?"

"Ye are worried about what may happen at Dorchabeinn."

"Aye, mayhaps. Ye have your own fears about that, dinnae ye?"

"Some. I try not to let them prey upon my mind. 'Tisnae the same trouble as ye have. The one I worry about isnae an innocent victim of the Brodies' greed. I cannae help him either. He must choose his path himself. All I can do is pray that he chooses the right path this time and that the Brodies allow him to live long enough to do so. I have but one person I love in danger, although I care for all of the people caught o'er there. Ye have your brothers, Farthing, and your husband to think about. *Everyone* who is dearest to ye is at Dorchabeinn. I couldnae bear it."

"I keep telling myself that God couldnae allow Arabel and Malise to win."

"Nay, He couldnae." Margot placed her hand over Sine's where it gripped the rim of the wall tightly. "All those ye love will return to ye. Justice demands it. Do ye also think about what ye will do when all of this is finally over?"

"I shall have to try and clear the name of Brodie and

banish the darkness which has hung over Dorchabeinn for so many years."

"'Tisnae enough that the ones who caused such harm are gone?"

"Nay. I am their kinswomen."

"How can ye mend such damage?"

"There are many ways. I cannae bring back the dead, but I can undo other crimes. I can return what has been stolen and work to cleanse any names that have been sullied."

Margot nodded, then asked softly, "And what of Sir Gamel, your husband?"

"What do ye mean?" Sine asked, tensing slightly.

"I am not really sure." Margot's smile was a little crooked. "I but have the feeling that ye dinnae intend to remain his wife." She waved her hand. "No need to speak. 'Tis a strange thought and I cannae guess how it entered my head. 'Tis also none of my concern."

Sine stared at Margot for a moment, a little astounded by the girl's insightfulness. She had such an urge to talk to someone about all that she felt that it actually hurt. With a sigh, she turned around, leaning back up against the parapet and staring down into the bailey. Mayhaps, she thought wryly, it would be good to talk it all out with Margot. When she had to end her marriage to Gamel, he might well demand some explanation.

"Will ye swear not to speak to anyone about what I tell ye now?" she asked.

"Aye, of course I will swear, if ye are verra sure that ye want to tell me at all."

"I need to say it to someone." Sine ran a hand through her hair. "Nay, I dinnae intend to remain Gamel's wife."

"Ye dinnae love him?"

"Oh, aye, I love him. I am almost certain of it now. Weel, at least as certain as I can be, considering that the mon hasnae given me one wee moment to think clearly since I first set eyes on him. It doesnae matter—neither what I feel or what he may feel for me. I cannae allow it to matter."

"But why? Such feelings are verra important. They shouldnae be cast aside or ignored," Margot urged, gently grasping Sine by the arm. "What could possibly make ye wish to turn away from love when there are so many who are starved for it?"

"My heritage," Sine whispered. "I am my mother's child."

"Ye said that once before. She didnae have the raising of ye, Sine."

"Nay, but her tainted blood runs through my veins." She met Margot's wide-eyed stare. "I carry that evil seed within me."

"Mayhaps it will ne'er affect ye. Mayhaps it isnae e'en there. Ye carry your father's blood as weel and he was a good mon. His name is honored. That is also your heritage."

"True." Sine felt slightly comforted by Margot's words, but she knew that it was not good enough. "Howbeit, I cannae ignore the fact that part of me comes from Arabel." She gave a short, bitter laugh. "I see the truth of that every time I peek into a looking glass. 'Tis Arabel who stares out at me. 'Tis Arabel's hair, Arabel's eyes, Arabel's face."

"That doesnae mean that ye will become just like Arabel in nature."

"I pray that I am not and ne'er will be, but the chance is there. That is why I must leave Gamel and why, someday, I may have to send the twins far away from me. I couldnae bear to turn upon the ones I love. 'Twould kill me to see Gamel look at me with loathing or to see fear and hurt in my brothers' eyes. And, if I do carry that bad

seed, I could pass it along to whatever children Gamel
and I might have." Sine shuddered. "'Tis a thought too
dreadful to consider."

"Could ye not just wait until ye see it begin to
happen?"

"I dinnae think it is something ye can see. Nay, I must
leave Gamel ere I hurt him or those he cares about."

"I think ye will hurt Sir Gamel when ye end the marriage," Margot said as she slumped against the wall by
Sine's side. "But ye must ken that for yourself."

"Weel—aye and nay. I havenae allowed any talk between us about how we feel, not even of our marriage.
'Tis rather a surprise to me that Gamel hasnae pressed
the matter more vigorously. I just felt that it would be
much kinder to keep silent and thus leave him with his
pride intact. 'Tis sure that he *would* be deeply hurt if he
spoke of whate'er is in his heart and I repaid those sweet
words with an annulment."

Margot winced and nodded. "And if ye had spoke any
sweet words to him, after he left he would think they
were lies and be painfully confused. Being kind isnae
always easy, is it?"

Sine laughed softly and shook her head. "Nay, curse it.
I have ached to speak my heart so many times, only to
have to bite back the words. Sometimes I have even had
to pretend not to hear what he has said, for fear of revealing something of what I am feeling. So, we let our
passion rage and keep all else to ourselves."

"It sounds verra sad. Do ye mean to spend the rest of
your life alone?" Margot asked.

Sine shrugged. "I think I must. If I dinnae wish to do
the harm which my mother has done, then I must place
myself in seclusion."

Margot bit her bottom lip lightly, studying Sine intently for a moment before asking, "Will that be enough?

If ye do carry the same evil which taints Lady Arabel, will ye not break that vow of seclusion? Ye willnae care anymore, will ye?"

A chill went through Sine's body that had nothing to do with the slowly falling temperature. She felt as if she might drown in the hopelessness that washed over her. She could not bear to believe that she might give up everything that meant anything to her and still end up hurting people just as Arabel did.

"God couldnae be so cruel," she whispered. "Jesu, Margot, if I turn away from all that I want, from all that I love, then God *must* spare me from the torment of committing the sins my mother has."

Margot briefly clasped Sine's hand in hers. "I have often heard talk of bad seeds, of tainted blood. It troubles me, yet I cannae say that I believe it with all my heart. For each child who is born of a bad parent and grows up to be equally bad, there is another who grows up to be a good and honorable person. There are many of us who can point to some rogue amongst our kinsmen yet the whole family doesnae become tainted in the same way."

"Arabel Brodie is far more than a rogue."

"Ye dinnae plan to tell Gamel any of this, do ye?"

"Nay. He would undoubtedly try to dispute it all. He would try to convince me that there is no chance that I could become like Arabel. And he could convince me because I so want to stay with him. It makes my head ache just to think about it."

Margot shivered and held her cloak more tightly around herself. "I think we had best go back inside the keep." When Sine nodded, they linked arms and began to walk back toward the keep itself. "Ye must do what ye think is necessary, but I wish ye would speak with someone else about it. I ken so verra little . . ."

"Ye ken more than ye realize, Margot. I pray that Martin Robertson has the wit to recognize all that he would gain if he but chooses the right path."

"Thank ye. And I shall pray for ye, Sine. I shall pray verra hard that ye are wrong, that although ye look like Lady Arabel there is none of that woman's poison in ye."

Gamel turned his head to scowl through the dark at Farthing, who kept shifting around. They were at the edge of the woods bordering the cleared lands encircling Dorchabeinn. From the moment they had reached their hiding place to try to study the movements of the guards upon the walls, Farthing had not been still. Gamel began to wish he had paired himself with Blane or Sir Lesley, both of whom had wended their way around to the southern side of Dorchabeinn. Instead, he lay on an uncomfortable patch of ground next to a man who had contracted an irritating and continuous twitch.

"Cannae ye be still, curse your eyes?" he hissed.

"I think I am lying on top of a thistle," muttered Farthing.

"Weel, endure it. There is far more at stake here than your comfort."

Farthing edged a little to the right. "I believe I realize that more keenly than ye do. I raised those lads." He looked toward Gamel. "As I raised Sine."

A brief curse escaped Gamel and he glared through the dark at Farthing. They had been lurking around Dorchabeinn for several hours, but had accomplished very little. Gamel knew that frustration was feeding his irritation with Farthing, but he decided not to fight it. If nothing else, a squabble with Farthing would help to distract him from

his own fears and doubts about the chances of beating
Arabel and Malise.

"Ye need not keep reminding me of the place ye hold
in Sine's life. 'Twould be verra nice, howbeit, if ye would
keep your long nose out of our lives from time to time. I
might have a wee bit more luck in wooing her if ye werenae always lurking close at hand."

"Wooing her? What need do ye have to do that? She is
your wife."

"For now. I ken that ye were told of the promise I had
to make. Weel, Sine still hasnae agreed to remain my
wife when this trouble is at an end."

"I begin to question why she should. A lass like Sine
needs a husband with some sense."

"And just what do ye mean by that?"

"'Tis clear that ye have verra few wits rattling about in
your head. If ye had *any* ye would ken how she feels
about ye and about the marriage."

"If ye two raise your voices a wee bit higher, they can
enjoy this bickering in Dorchabeinn," drawled a voice
from behind Gamel and Farthing.

Gamel flipped onto his back and drew his sword. Out of
the corner of his eye he saw Farthing do the same. For a
moment, all he could see was that the man leaning against
a tree a foot or two away had his arms held out to the sides
and there were no weapons in his hands. It took Gamel a
little longer to recognize the man as Martin Robertson. He
relaxed somewhat, but did not yet resheath his sword.

"How long have ye been standing there?" asked
Gamel, sitting up slightly and idly brushing off his
clothes.

"Long enough to see that your spying has served only
to leave ye empty-handed and angry."

"We arenae here alone."

"I ken it. Your two companions are watching the

southern walls and have had as little luck." Martin sat down facing Farthing and Gamel. "They willnae discover verra much either. At sunset Dorchabeinn is shut up tight and no one, absolutely no one, is allowed in or out."

"Then how is it that ye are outside?" demanded Farthing as he sat up, put away his sword and began to pluck thistles off of his clothes. "Were ye locked out at sunset?"

"Nay. I slipped out. There is an escape route, which should come as no real surprise. Most places have one, and the Brodies are in need of one far more than most."

"So ye never get locked out, hmmm?" Farthing muttered a curse as he yanked a thistle out of his hair.

"Oh, aye, I do. Arriving late is often a difficult thing to plan for, and if one doesnae secure the door to the passage it cannae be opened from without—only within. If ye let it shut behind ye, ye *will* be locked out."

"And do ye mean to show us this passage?" asked Gamel, struggling to not let his hopes grow too high.

"Aye. All I need to ken is whether ye wish to slip inside now or wait until ye have a few more men with ye."

"Why should we trust ye? It could be a trap ye are trying to lure us into."

Martin smiled faintly. "It could be, but it isnae." He shrugged. "What else can I say? I offer ye a chance to get within the walls of Dorchabeinn and gain the advantage o'er your enemies. I offer ye a chance to save the twins. All I can do is give ye my solemn word that I plan no treachery. The decision of whether to trust me or not is all yours."

"Mayhaps if ye offer us a reason for your change in loyalty we can better decide whether we should put our lives into your hands."

"'Tisnae so simple to explain. There are many reasons—some good, some selfish, and some I dinnae much understand myself. I realized last evening when the lads were brought before Arabel and Malise that I have earned the mistrust and suspicion of the Brodies."

"We suspected as much when ye werenae sent to Duncoille as their messenger."

"'Twas that which told me that Arabel has ceased to consider the matter of my trustworthiness and decided against me. 'Twas that which told me that I am a dead mon. E'en if I decided to stand back and allow Arabel to win this battle, I wouldnae long survive the twins and Sine." He cocked his head slightly to one side as he studied Gamel. "Nor would ye, m'friend. I thought to buy ye some time by reminding Arabel and Malise that just as ye can claim Sine as wife, so can ye claim all that she owns."

"And did it buy any time?"

"Who can say? Malise grew deeply thoughtful, but Arabel just demanded that ye be killed as weel. There does seem to be more behind her wish for your death than whatever claims ye may be able to lay upon Dorchabeinn. Ye have inspired her hate by ignoring her invitations at Duncoille that day and then standing between her and Sine. Howbeit, Malise may yet convince Arabel to move with a wee bit more caution, although he has had less and less influence o'er the woman of late."

"Her madness probably grows too strong to be tempered, but all of that matters little right now." Gamel leaned forward, trying to read Martin's face more clearly despite the shadows. "So, ye have decided to aid us because your masters have turned upon ye. Ye mean to slight them first."

Martin grimaced. "Mayhaps. After all the years of service I have given them that they could so easily discard me breaks all bonds in my eyes. I have sold my verra soul for them and they repay me with the threat of death. To be loyal after such a slap is to be a fool. I also thought that, ere I died, I might be able to do some good. Aye, and I would have the pleasure of stealing a victory from that shewolf, Arabel."

"Not exemplary reasons, but believable ones," murmured Farthing. "And Margot is an understanding lass."

"Aye, almost to a fault," Martin agreed, and sighed. "I would be lying if I didnae confess that pleasing her, mayhaps bettering myself in her eyes, had something to do with my choice. There is also the matter of the lads."

"Have they been harmed?" demanded Farthing.

"Weel, they arenae dead. I fear they have been knocked about some. Arabel enjoys that sort of thing. The children of Dorchabeinn have always been kept out of her sight. Mayhaps wee Sine Catriona can find some comfort in the knowledge that she isnae the only child Arabel hates."

"She just hates Sine the most."

"Aye, and 'tis a chilling thing to see. She loathes the twins too. They are living proof that her grip upon Sine's father wasnae as tight as she had thought. Arabel has been in the brightest of humors since she got her hands on them. Even the return of Andrew Moore without Sine Catriona didnae really change that. Aye, Arabel was enraged, but not for long. She is verra, verra confident that she holds the perfect lure to attract Sine into her grasp."

"I fear she may have a reason for such confidence."

"Aye, I can recall Sine with the lads ere they disappeared from Dorchabeinn. She was only a child herself, but she was already a mother to them. I kenned that they were going to run away from Arabel, but I said naught. 'Twas for the same reason I am forced to act now. I cannae be part of the murder of children. With the others, I could always tell myself that they werenae so verra innocent themselves, that greed or lust had led them astray, and that they had the strength and skill to fight if they chose to. 'Twas mon against mon, adult against adult. But children? The boys are barely nine years of age. They cannae fight Arabel and Malise. Children are innocents. They are to be protected. It chills me to the bone to think of staining my hands with the blood of bairns."

Martin stared at the two men he faced, waiting for some sign that they believed him. In aiding the Logans and Sine he was casting aside all he had ever known. He was reaching out for another chance. Nothing could fully absolve him of the wrongs he had committed for Arabel and Malise, but he ached to at least try for some absolution. He also feared that, if they refused to believe and trust him, the twins could never be saved.

"Where does this secret passageway lead?" Farthing asked. He glanced quickly at Gamel, who nodded and finally resheathed his sword.

"It winds through the inner walls of Dorchabeinn and opens into the steward's chambers."

"Which is near the great hall?"

"Aye, mere steps away from it."

"Do Arabel and Malise ken where this passage is?"

"They do, but I believe they often forget about it. They worry more about keeping people out of Dorchabeinn than about escaping themselves. 'Tis why they secure the gates at sunset. Aye, 'tis true that most folk do the same, but Arabel wouldnae let her own mother in. Since the passageway cannae be opened from outside, without the aid of some traitor from within, they pay it little heed. There are no living traitors within Dorchabeinn." He gave a short, faintly bitter laugh. "Weel, until now. And who kens how long this one will live?"

"If ye can elude being killed until the morrow, ye will survive their mistrust," said Gamel. "Now, shall we make our plans so that we can *all* survive the confrontation to come?"

Farthing and Gamel looked at each other in silent agreement.

"I think ye had best try and slip back inside Dorchabeinn, Martin," Gamel said. He edged away from the shallow brush into the denser concealment of the trees, then he stood up, stretched, and brushed himself off. "'Twill be dawn before too long."

Martin stood and stretched along with Farthing. "Are ye certain it wouldnae be better to creep inside with me now? I cannae be certain what the next few hours may hold for me. I may lose the chance to fulfill my promise to aid ye."

"We must await the arrival of our full ranks. Once a few of us enter by way of the tunnel, we can throw open the gates to let the rest of our men in. Besides, I dinnae think ye need to fear for your life. Arabel thinks to gain all that she covets today. She will be far too busy to bother about ye. I wouldnae eat or drink anything, however."

Farthing laughed softly when Martin grimaced. "Just show us the way in, and make sure that we can open the door and slip inside."

"Aye. I will. But be careful, for I cannae leave it open too wide or the guards may spot it. 'Twill be barely unlatched. If ye arenae careful, ye could lock yourself outside. Then all will be lost. I may be able to slip away and correct the problem, but I cannae promise anything."

"Dinnae take any risks, Martin. If ye are seen now, we could indeed find ourselves walking into a trap after sunset."

"I understand." Martin took a step, hesitated, and then looked at Farthing. "I will also understand if ye feel ye must deny me the chance to woo Margot. As her kinsmon ye have the right to demand that she look higher.

Aye, she could do a great deal better than to choose me, a mon soaked in sin."

"She has chosen ye, Martin Robertson," Farthing said. "I havenae kenned my wee cousin for verra long, but I trust in her judgment already. Aye, and I can say verra little about what a mon has done in his past. I am not without sin myself."

"*There* is a truth that none can argue," muttered Gamel. "Go back inside, Martin, and try to stay alive. We will return an hour before sunset. Dinnae fear, we will be sure that all of our people ken just whose side ye are on now." As soon as Martin was gone, Gamel turned to Farthing. "Do ye think we are fools to trust him?"

"Nay. Although he may waver o'er Margot or e'en his need to strike at Arabel and Malise, there was one thing that he spoke of which will ne'er change. I believed him when he said it and I believe it now."

"And what is that?"

"He cannae stomach being part of the murder of children. Martin saved the twins and Sine six years ago with his silence and he will save them again."

Gamel nodded and started to walk through the thickly shadowed wood to the place where they had hidden their horses. "I too believed that. Aye, far more than I believed anything else he said."

"We had better hurry." Farthing took a quick look up at the sky. "We dinnae want to be late in meeting with Blane and Sir Lesley. They could easily think that something has gone awry and start to look for us."

"God's beard, and then we could waste hours just trying to find each other in these cursed woods."

"Aye, and I am far too weary to play that game."

"'Twas a long uncomfortable night," agreed Gamel. "'Twill be a verra long day ahead of us as weel."

"Howbeit, each cold, cramped hour we crouched outside of Dorchabeinn was weel spent."

"Aye, it was, for it allowed Martin to find us and reveal Dorchabeinn's weakness. 'Twill be a delight to have some good news to relay to Sine for a change."

Chapter 15

As covertly as she could, Sine shifted her position in her saddle. She discretely rubbed her increasingly sore backside. Just as she began to consider asking Lord William if she could rest for a moment, four riders approached. She was relieved to see that Gamel and Farthing were among them, as were Blane and Sir Lesley. They all dismounted so that they could confer before riding on to Dorchabeinn.

"Sine." Gamel briefly but firmly embraced her before recalling how many people were watching them and turning to face his father and Lord Thomas. "Martin Robertson has joined us."

After a moment of stunned surprise, Sine felt weak-kneed with relief and renewed hope. She slipped her arm about Gamel's trim waist and lightly used him to support herself as he told his father and the others all about the plan to save Beldane and Barre. Sine dared not believe in their good fortune. It seemed too good to be true. When Gamel said they still wanted her to go to the gates of Dorchabeinn and confront Arabel, she frowned.

"Ye dinnae think that we can just go inside secretively and defeat the Brodies that way?" she asked.

"It could be done," replied Gamel. "'Tis better to divide our strength, however. Arabel will be expecting us to come to her gates. If ye dinnae arrive, she may grow dangerously suspicious. Also, if ye are there, confronting her, it will make for a very good distraction. The Brodie guards will be easing their watch, for they shall scent victory."

"There is probably no way to keep the twins out of all this either. I dinnae believe we can just creep in and grab them." Sine sighed.

"I think not," said Farthing. "Martin is certain that Arabel shall want the twins close at hand as sunset nears and she begins to look for ye to arrive. 'Tis yet another good reason for ye to do as we originally planned and go to the gates of Dorchabeinn pretending to accept Arabel's offer of a trade. Ye dinnae want the woman to suspect that ye are refusing her. That would send her into a rage when the lads are still in her reach."

"Nay, nay, of course not." Sine grimaced. "I just hoped that I could avoid facing the woman again. I truly dread it," she whispered.

No one spoke. They all just looked at her with varying expressions of sympathy. Lord William suggested that they take a moment to rest and water the horses. Gamel took her by the hand and led her over to a gnarled pine tree. Sine shook her head when he indicated with a smooth sweep of his hand that they should sit down. She leaned against the stout, crooked tree trunk and prayed that the respite would ease the aches in her backside.

"Is something wrong?" Gamel asked as he stood in front of her.

"Nay, not truly. I but wish to stand up for a while." She made a disgusted face at him when he slowly grinned. "I am not accustomed to spending so much time bouncing about on the back of a horse."

"'Twill soon be over, dearling."

She studied his face for a moment, idly thinking how she would never be able to forget it. "Do ye truly believe that we shall win?"

"Aye, I do. It may weel be a verra closely won victory, but 'twill be ours. Martin has given us all we could have hoped for. We have now gained the advantage of surprise. And, aye, ere ye ask—I am certain that we can trust Martin."

"So Margot has reached the good in the mon," Sine murmured, and was pleased for her friend.

"I believe she has. But I think Martin would have aided us even if he had no Margot to consider. 'Tis the boys."

"The twins? Do ye think they have somehow convinced Martin to help us?"

"In a way, although I doubt that they realize it. Martin cannot stomach aiding in the murder of children."

"Ah, of course. 'Tis probably why he allowed us to run away six years ago. I am convinced that he was weel aware of my plans, yet he ne'er said a word to Malise and Arabel."

Gamel nodded. "Martin said as much himself. We spent a great deal of the night talking and I *do* think that he can be trusted. Aye, not only to aid us now but to give us his full loyalty afterward. He has been the steward of Dorchabeinn these past six years, ye ken. Ye may wish to allow him to continue in that position."

"I suspect Martin is verra good at it. Arabel would ne'er have let him hold such a place in Dorchabeinn for so long if he wasnae. 'Tis something to consider." Just then Lord William called for them to remount. She tensed.

"'Tis time to begin the game," Gamel said quietly.

Sine took his face in her hands and gently kissed him.

"Take care, Gamel. When this is all over I wish to celebrate a victory, not mourn a loss."

"When this is all over, I intend to be verra much alive and ready to talk about us for a change." He gave her a quick, hard kiss and walked away.

That was something she wished to avoid, Sine mused as she moved toward her mount. She watched Gamel leave with a small group of about twenty armed men that included Farthing, Gamel's three brothers, Blane, and Sir Lesley. She felt a quick, deep stab of fear. If Martin was laying a trap for them, she and her allies would be thoroughly devastated by the resultant loss.

Lord William helped her mount her horse and she forced a gracious smile for him despite the protesting twinge of pain she felt as her backside touched the saddle. Her mind was crowded with thoughts of Gamel as she rode toward Dorchabeinn, Lords William and Thomas flanking her. *Ready to talk*, he had said. She could almost hope that he was only planning to tell her that *he* wanted their marriage annulled, but she was sure that was not the case. He was tired of the gentle wooing he had been doing and now wanted to speak more forthrightly. Sine winced as she thought of how she was going to have to stop his words—forever.

She tried to fix her thoughts upon the twins and the coming confrontation with Arabel, but it was impossible. Gamel was about to risk his life for her. She would thank him for that heroic act by telling him to leave her alone. She heartily wished that there was some painless way to do that, but she knew she would probably hurt him and was going to be tearing her own heart into a thousand cutting pieces. Suddenly the strength to face Arabel did not seem so hard to grasp. It paled in comparison to what she would require to endure the final confrontation with Gamel.

* * *

Daylight was waning by the time Sine reached Dorch-abeinn. She was somewhat taken aback by her first sight of her home in six long years. It was not quite as she remembered it.

As a child she had never seen it as the cold, forbidding keep it looked to be now. The main tower was now L-shaped. Arabel had also erected a second wall with huge iron-studded gates. Dorchabeinn squatted in the middle of a flat, barren acre of land and Sine felt no kinship with the place as she stared at it.

"Ye look surprised, lass," murmured Lord William.

"'Tis much larger than I recalled, much more of a fortress than I remember."

"Ye were still verra young when ye left, and the Brodies have strengthened it."

"Which shouldnae surprise me, considering the enemies those two have made for themselves." She smiled faintly. "'Tis glad I am that I ne'er gave any serious thought to storming the place."

Lord William chuckled. "A charge can be a glorious sight, but 'tis rarely the way to bring down a strong keep. Those upon the walls have the advantage and can easily cut down many a mon. 'Tis often no more than slaughter. Nay, more often than not, and more often than any soldier cares to confess, the battle is won by siege or stealth."

She frowned as they slowly approached the huge gates. "Do ye think that the others are all right?"

"Dinnae think on them, lass. They can take care of themselves. Ye shall soon need all of your wits to fight your own battle."

Sine nodded and stared up at the well-armed men upon the walls as Lord William obeyed the call from one

of the Brodie men-at-arms and signaled his group to
stop. She wondered how her mother would play the
scene and prayed that she was right in thinking that
Arabel would not hurry, would in fact try every sort of
trick to delay the process of the trade so that she could
fully savor her daughter's defeat. Every moment that the
final meeting between her and Arabel was delayed, the
better the chances that Arabel would see her victory
turned into a rout.

"State your name and the reason ye are here," bellowed a guard from up on the walls.

"This is the Lady Sine Catriona Logan," Lord William
yelled back. "She is here to answer a summons from your
mistress."

"And what proof do ye have that the lass is truly Lady
Sine?"

"Take off your headdress, lass," Lord William commanded gently.

As slowly as she dared, Sine removed her headdress
and undid her loose braid. It surprised her when the
men upon the walls stared at her long and hard. They
clearly had not been told how strongly she resembled
their mistress. Sine had to smile as she thought of how
many of them were suffering from the sharp bite of superstition.

"I will inform Lord and Lady Brodie," the guard called
down, and then hurried away.

"How long do ye think she shall make us wait?" Sine
asked Lord William.

"At least until sunset, I hope," he muttered as he
glanced up at the sky.

Sine also glanced up and briefly prayed that night
could come with just a little more haste than it usually
did. "Mayhaps e'en long enough for our men to get
through the passage and inside of the keep itself."

* * *

"Lady Sine is at the gates," the burly guard announced after Arabel admitted him into the great hall.

"Alone?" demanded Arabel.

"There is only a small force of armed men with her."

"How small?"

"Twenty, mayhaps thirty."

Arabel laughed and clapped her hands. "I was right. She has indeed come like the lamb to the slaughter. Fetch those little bastards," she ordered the guard, and turned to Malise the moment the man had left. "We have won."

"I believe I shall wait to heft my tankard in a celebratory toast," said Malise, idly drumming his long, soft fingers on the table. "If ye recall, we thought she was dead once before, only to have her return to disrupt our lives."

"Weel, she cannae escape this trap." She gave Martin, who sat on Malise's right, a malevolent look. "And soon I mean to discover exactly how she managed to slip away six years ago."

Martin returned her glare with a look of bewildered innocence. "Do ye think that *I* ken something about that?"

"I think ye ken a great deal about it. Ever since the first day ye arrived here ye have been aware of each and every thing that happens within these walls, yet somehow ye failed to learn of Sine's plans to flee with the bastards."

"I can only profess my complete innocence and pray that ye will believe me."

"We shall see just how long ye continue to profess your innocence. Howbeit, our talk must wait." She frowned at her husband. "I still dinnae understand why ye hesitate to celebrate our victory."

"Because we havenae succeeded yet. We have not won

until your daughter and those bastard brothers of hers are dead and buried. Aye, and Sir Gamel Logan interred at their side."

"And most of that shall be accomplished in but a few moments."

"Dinnae ye think ye ought to wait a wee while ere ye kill Sine and the twins? It might not be wise to murder them whilst the Logans and the Magnussons are just beyond our gates. They might not see ye when ye wield the knife, but their tale of what happened here will leave few people with any doubts about our guilt."

"Nay. In truth, I have begun to see the presence of Sine's allies as a good chance for us to do as we please and not be seen as the guilty ones. When the twins arenae sent out immediately, I am sure that her little army—"

"'Tisnae that little," muttered Malise.

Arabel ignored that sullen interruption. "Her little army will surely attempt something. We only need a wee fight to claim that Sine and her brothers died in that fray. If ye dinnae like that explanation, then we may say that the army's presence inspired Sine to try and flee with the boys. When we tried to hold them, as is our right, they turned on us. In the ensuing struggle, they were all killed. Do ye have an idea ye think is more clever?" she snapped when Malise continued to frown.

"Aye—just wait. Wait until we can do what we want with a wee bit more privacy."

"I have waited six years. I willnae wait another day!" Arabel yelled. "I willnae allow Sine the chance to get away from me again. Do ye ken how close she came to stealing all that we have?"

Martin watched Arabel as the woman screamed at Malise. Her husband was gazing into her enraged face with near fascination. Arabel was swiftly losing whatever tenuous grip she had had upon her sanity. As she sank into the black depths of her madness, Malise acted as if he were no more than a spectator at some grand tournament. Martin did not think that Malise was particularly sane either. No sane man could watch Arabel with the calm interest and slowly growing lust that Malise did. While Martin found Arabel's madness chilling, Malise clearly found it arousing.

The appearance of the guard dragging in the twins put an abrupt halt to Arabel's tirade, if not to her fury, which she turned on the boys. Martin felt a little sick when he looked at Beldane and Barre. They were even more battered than they had been when they had first been brought into Dorchabeinn. He doubted Beldane could see very well, for the child's eyes were nearly swollen shut.

"Your sister is here to watch ye die," Arabel said, walking around the children and studying them with a cold-eyed detachment. "She has come to Dorchabeinn to accept the trade I offered her."

"Sine doesnae believe ye," said Barre, helping his brother stand straight with a supporting arm about his waist. "She kens what a liar ye are. She will ne'er fall into your trap."

"So arrogant," she murmured, and casually slapped the boy. "Ye carry the stink of your father."

"At least we were spared the taint of your foul blood." Barre staggered a little from the force of yet another blow to the side of his head.

"Ye ne'er should have survived this long." She looked at Malise. "Are ye coming up onto the walls with me?"

"Nay, love. Ye will enjoy it far more than I shall." He lifted his goblet in a brief, silent toast. "Go and play your game."

After glaring at the twins one last time, Arabel walked out of the great hall. Martin heard her order the guard who had brought the twins in to be prepared to bring them to the walls if it was necessary. He looked at his cousin Malise the moment Arabel was gone and wondered how Malise could look so unconcerned.

"'Tisnae a verra wise time for Arabel to commit murder," he said, watching his cousin closely and realizing that he did not really know or understand the man he had served for so many years.

"Nay, but dinnae expect me to stop her from doing it. E'en if I took a firm stand, she would find a way to kill Sine and the bastards. I could probably chain the woman in the depths of the castle and she would still find some way to kill them." He shrugged. "I cannae see the sense of working so hard when I ken verra weel that I will accomplish naught."

"Those men outside your walls willnae meekly allow ye to kill Sine and the twins. They will raise an outcry."

"I am not verra concerned about that, cousin. Arabel's tales are a wee bit weak and simple, but I believe I can think of a better one. Aye, there may be some trouble, but 'twill pass. The matter of Sir Gamel Logan does trouble me a bit. The Logans have power. Ending all chance of Sir Gamel being a threat will be difficult, but I will soon think of a reasonable plan."

Martin took a long drink of his wine. In his way, Malise was just as mad as Arabel. And he began to fear that no plan could be successful against the Brodies. How could it when the people he was dealing with possessed so little reason? They had to know the danger they courted, yet they seemed confident that everything would go as they wished. Such blind assurance made Martin suffer a brief chill of superstitious dread. He prayed that Gamel and Farthing were fully aware of what they were about to confront.

* * *

Gamel grit his teeth and forced himself to stop pacing. It did no good. The minutes did not pass any more swiftly because he was wearing a rut in the moist ground. They were waiting in the wood just beyond sight of Dorchabeinn for the sun to set and give them the shadows they required for their stealthy work. He was sure that Sine was already at the castle gates and would soon be entering the keep. The longer they had to wait before making their way to the secret entrance Martin had revealed to them, the longer Sine would have to be with Arabel.

"It willnae be much longer now," murmured Sir Lesley.

"'Tis far too long already." Gamel glared up at the sky, watching the gray clouds seep across the sky with an irritating slowness. "Sine is probably standing before Arabel right now."

"There is still time," Farthing said. "Arabel will want to savor her victory. She willnae cut Sine down the moment the lass enters Dorchabeinn. Nay, Arabel will want to taunt Sine, and gloat."

"Aye, ye are right." Gamel grimaced and ran a hand through his hair. "'Tis just that we have a chance to win this fight and I want to have at it."

"Ye cannae want that any more than I."

"Nay, of course not." Gamel sat down next to Farthing, who was propped up against the rough trunk of a tree. "I think I also wish to get to that cursed passage to be sure that Martin has left it open for us."

Farthing nodded. "I have been having a doubt or two myself. Not only about our being able to get inside, but about what might await us there once we do. 'Twas easy enough to trust him last night. 'Tis not so easy now."

"Weel, there is no altering the plan."

"Nay, of course not."

Gamel laughed shortly. "I am also eager to be finished with this so that I can have a talk with the lass."

"Talk to her? About what?"

"Ye are looking at me rather suspiciously."

"I just wonder if ye are about to confess that your passion for the lass has faded. I cannae think of what else ye would need to say to her."

"Ye wish to discuss this *now*?"

"We arenae going anywhere for a wee while and I certainly dinnae wish to stand here and mull o'er all that could go wrong."

"Nor do I. Weel, my passion hasnae wavered," Gamel snapped. "I mean to speak to Sine about our marriage, about that fool promise she made me make ere she would kneel before the priest. 'Tis a discussion she has neatly avoided. Aye, and I havenae pressed her on it, for she had more than enough to worry about. Weel, once her enemies are gone, she will have no more distractions." He picked up a leaf and began to meticulously shred it into tiny pieces.

Farthing shook his head. "I begin to think that the pair of ye are mad. All this time that ye have been locked up in Duncoille together and ye havenae talked to each other? I thought ye were going to woo the lass."

"I was wooing her—gently, carefully. Howbeit, rare was the time that I got any chance for wooing."

"It sounds as if ye were so gentle and careful when ye did have the chance that she probably doesnae ken that she was being wooed."

"And just when did a lecher like ye become such an expert on courtship and love?" Gamel was beginning to feel highly insulted, an emotion fed by the irritating suspicion that Farthing was right.

"I ne'er claimed to be an expert, but it doesnae take much to see that ye and Sine Catriona are managing this business verra poorly indeed. I will tell ye something else ye willnae like to hear—ye pick a poor time to talk about your marriage."

"What do ye mean? Sine will be safe. Her enemies will be defeated. She will finally have the time to think on other matters." Gamel leapt to his feet and scowled toward Dorchabeinn.

"Aye—like the burying of her mother." Farthing nodded when Gamel whirled to stare at him, then cursed. "I wondered if ye had forgotten what the price of our victory may be."

"Nay, not truly. I but forgot who Arabel is. I find it verra difficult to think of that shewolf as Sine's mother, despite how chillingly alike they are in appearance. So, I must wait some more. I grow verra weary of waiting."

"I have begun to notice that ye dinnae do it weel," drawled Farthing, watching Gamel pace back and forth over a tiny square of ground.

Before Gamel could respond, Sir Lesley said, "I think the shadows are deep enough to hide us now."

After a quick look around, Gamel nodded, surprised at how engrossed he had become in his bickering with Farthing. He absently checked his sword and, keeping within the shadows he had so impatiently waited for, he made his way toward the secret entrance into Dorchabeinn. With each step he took he became more tense, more afraid that he was about to discover that Martin had betrayed them. He sagged faintly with relief when they reached the entrance. The door was neatly hidden at the base of a large boulder a few yards away from the walls of Dorchabeinn. Martin had kept his promise and left it propped ajar just enough for Gamel to get a grip on it and heft it open.

Blane was the first to slip inside. He lit a torch and the others crept in one by one. Gamel was the last to enter, carefully easing the door shut behind him. The passage was tall enough for them to stand in, but so narrow that they were forced into single file. In the dim light from Blane's torch, Gamel could see everyone looking back at him, waiting for his command.

"'Tis no place to be faced with a fight," whispered Farthing, who stood in front of Gamel.

"Nay," muttered Gamel. "'Twould be easy to cut us down as we step out."

"Dinnae worry on that, sir," said Blane. "If I step out and find a trap, ye will be warned of it loudly."

"Weel, so far Martin Robertson has kept his word." Gamel waved Blane onward. "Lead us out of here, Blane."

As they walked along the slowly rising passage, Gamel was a little dismayed at the noise they made. They wore their lightest armor, but there was still the occasional sound of the metal clinking as they walked, as well as the occasional scrape of a scabbard against the stone wall. The sound of their booted feet seemed deafening as it echoed through the narrow tunnel. Gamel prayed that it was merely his imagination which caused each noise they made to sound so dangerously loud. If it was as thunderous as it seemed, they had lost all chance of surprising their enemy within minutes after entering the passage.

"She is here, lass," said Lord William, lightly touching Sine on the arm to draw her attention back to the walls of Dorchabeinn.

Sine looked up and grimaced. Arabel's very posture conveyed the woman's triumph. A small part of Sine had hoped that Arabel would not play the game out, that her mother would realize she had gone too far and retreat. It was all too clear that that small hope had been in vain.

"There was no need to bring an army," Arabel called down.

"The journey here can be verra treacherous," Sine replied. "So many cutthroats and thieves roam about. One must protect oneself against a dagger in the back."

"How wise of ye. Have ye decided to come home then? Where is your fine husband? I dinnae see him."

"Did ye really expect him to escort me when I am leaving him?"

"Verra weel said, lass," murmured Lord William.

"Thank ye, m'lord," she replied in an equally soft voice.

"I ne'er asked ye to leave the mon," Arabel said.

"Nay? Ye said that ye could have the marriage set aside. Ye made your displeasure clear. When I chose to come here to Dorchabeinn, Gamel saw it as desertion. And, may I say, your kind invitation didnae include him."

"A landless bastard is a poor choice for my daughter."

Arabel was clearly trying to goad Lord William, but when Sine glanced at the man, he winked and said, "She is wrong—Gamel isnae landless. Tell her ye wish to see the twins."

"Ere I accept your generous hospitality, I wish to see the twins."

"Ye can see them when ye come inside Dorchabeinn. They are here," Arabel said.

"Nay, I believe I should see them first. If they are truly there, then it shouldnae be any trouble to show them to us."

"If ye insist."

"I believe I must."

As Arabel sent a man to get the twins, Sine turned to Lord William. "'Tis hard to keep talking as if all were cordial between us."

"Ye are doing verra weel, lass. We are wasting a fine piece of time here. That can only help us."

"Aye, I ken it. 'Tis all that keeps me from screaming accusations and making some demands of my own. I but pray that Martin has done as he promised." She did not care to think about how much depended upon it.

"I think he has or we should have heard something from Gamel and the others by now. True, 'tis barely nightfall, but they have the shadows they need and we are holding everyone's attention."

She nodded, then grew tense as her brothers were dragged to the parapets, their movements stiff and awkward and their clothes shabby. "Sweet Mary!" she exclaimed.

Lord William frowned. "They dinnae look weel, poor laddies. They probably had to endure a night in the dungeon."

"Aye, and they have been beaten." Sine needed to take several deep breaths to control her anger, for even from a distance she could see the swelling and bruising on the boys' faces. "There was no need to beat them so. Arabel did that for her own pleasure."

"Here are the boys," called Arabel. "Now, I believe 'tis time ye came inside."

"Release the boys first. This was to be a trade. I return to Dorchabeinn and ye set the twins free."

"Nay, I think not. If I free them ere ye are inside, I cannae be sure that ye will honor your part in the trade. Ye could easily just take the children and run back to Duncoille."

"If I do as ye suggest, Arabel, then ye could hold me and the children, breaking your part of the bargain. Mayhaps the trade should be made partway between."

"Nay. Ye will enter Dorchabeinn. Inside these walls is where the exchange must be made. To meet halfway between would require that my gates be held open for longer than I can allow." Arabel gave an abrupt signal and the twins were led away. "Come along, Sine Catriona, and dismiss your army."

"We will wait for the twins, m'lady," Lord William yelled.

"There is no need to do that. I can provide the lads with an escort to Duncoille."

"Dinnae trouble yourself, m'lady. We will camp here for the night and ye can send the lads out to us at dawn."

"Please yourself. Now get in here, Sine Catriona. I grow verra weary of this game."

Sine sighed. Clearly, they had bought as much time as they could. And if Sine's warriors lost the day, it mattered little whether Arabel kept the twins. They would all be massacred anyway. Lord William gave her an encouraging pat on the back and she started to ride toward the gates of Dorchabeinn. It did not surprise her to see Arabel leave her place on the walls. The woman did not like to expose herself to her enemies. She suspected Arabel also wished to be ensconced in the great hall to greet her long-lost daughter appropriately—like some queen condescending to heed a serf's petition for justice.

As she neared the walls, the gates were eased open just enough to allow one rider through. For a brief moment, Sine fought the urge to bolt, to get as far away from Arabel as she could. The only thing that gave her the courage to ride into the keep was the recollection of how her brothers had looked upon the walls—bruised and unsteady. She prayed that Gamel and his men had enough time.

Chapter 16

With a guard on either side of her, Sine marched into the great hall of Dorchabeinn. Her steps faltered a little when she got her first good look at the twins since they had been taken from Duncoille. Although she had guessed that they had been beaten, she had not been near enough to tell how badly. Now that she could, she was appalled. Her stomach knotted up with fury. Ignoring the hesitant attempts of her guards to stop her, she marched over to the twins and crouched down in front of them. The boys hugged her, but the embrace was stiff due to their injuries and she wanted to weep for the fear and the pain they had been forced to suffer.

"Dinnae fret o'er us," whispered Barre.

"Aye," agreed Beldane. "It looks worse than it is."

"Ye are both verra brave. Ye are also verra foolish, for ye left the safety of Duncoille."

"We ken it. 'Twas a doltish thing to do." Beldane gave her a look of embarrassment. "We went to find some flowers for ye."

"Flowers for me?"

"Aye. We decided ye must like them a lot, for Gamel is

always giving ye some and that makes ye smile. Instead we get taken prisoner and ye get called here. Ye should-nae have come, Sine."

"Nay," agreed Barre. "Ye shouldnae."

"Come, dinnae worry o'er me." She kissed each boy's cheek. "All is not as it appears," she whispered. "Take heart."

"How touching," Arabel drawled from her seat at Malise's side. "I am quite moved to tears."

Sine leapt to her feet and glared at Arabel. "Such brutality was unnecessary. Howbeit, now that ye have had your fun let the boys go. I am here, trading my life for theirs."

"Are ye really so naive that ye thought I would keep that promise?"

"Nay. I but prayed that, for once, I could place some trust in the word of a whore."

Arabel moved so fast that Sine had no time to elude the slap the woman swung at her face. The force of the blow caused Sine to stagger a little, but she quickly recovered. She stood straight and watched Arabel return to the table as if her outburst of rage had never happened.

"So, tell me how it is that ye have survived for all these years," Arabel ordered.

"I was fortunate," Sine answered with a calm she did not feel, wary of Arabel's sudden curiosity about her past. "Soon after I fled from here I met up with a mon. I believe ye ken the fellow verra weel—Farthing Magnusson?" Sine found a small touch of satisfaction in the fury and surprise which contorted her mother's face.

"That bastard!" hissed Arabel. "I cannae believe I allowed myself to be soiled by one of your discarded lovers."

"'Tis my belief that Farthing was the one who was soiled."

Malise grasped Arabel by the wrist to stop her from attacking Sine again. "Wait," he ordered his wife. Then he looked at Sine. "Were you married to Gamel Logan by a priest?"

"Aye, sanctified by the Church and thoroughly consummated. Ye havenae won yet. Gamel will legally inherit all that is mine."

"Mayhaps, my sweet, we should keep her alive a wee bit longer than planned," Malise suggested to Arabel. "She could aid us in entrapping Sir Gamel."

With a sharp, obscene exclamation, Arabel yanked free of his hold. "I have waited eighteen years to kill her. She was always watched over. Then she escaped me. Weel, that willnae happen again."

"If we arenae careful, Arabel, we could find that, in death, she finally defeats us."

"And why are ye so eager to keep her alive? Do ye lust after her?"

Although Sine knew that the man lied—for she had seen the lecherous way he had watched her—Malise vehemently denied his wife's accusation. As the pair bickered, Sine looked around in the vain hope of seeing some means of escape. She felt her heart skip with hope when she realized that Martin was gone. He had been there when she had entered the great hall, but had somehow managed to sneak away. She prayed that it was to aid Gamel, that rescue was close at hand.

"Dinnae waste your strength and my time with your foolish denials. It isnae important anyway," Arabel replied.

"Weel, 'tis certainly important that we play this game warily. We are close to winning. There is no need to be careless and hasty."

"We *have* won. I have her and the bastards. And those fools out there cannae reach them. I see no need to concern ourselves with those impotent champions. Do ye grow lily-livered in your old age, my husband? Afraid of the Red Logan, are ye?"

"Do as ye will then," bellowed Malise, throwing up his hands in a gesture of utter surrender and then helping himself to a large tankard of wine. "If this all sours and your impatience ruins everything we have achieved, I shallnae sink with ye."

"I ne'er expected ye to do anything so noble and useless," Arabel said, her tone a cool sneer. Then she looked at Sine. "Nay, Sine will survive the night, but I shall make it a night that will have her still screaming when she is deep in her tomb."

Sine could not fully suppress a shudder and took a more protective stance in front of her brothers. She had no doubt that Arabel could do exactly as she promised. As she met her mother's hate-filled look, Sine prayed that, if her rescue was not forthcoming, she would be able to endure with courage whatever Arabel dealt her. She did not want to give the woman the pleasure of scenting her fear or of hearing her beg.

"I dinnae suppose that 'twill do any good to remind ye that ye are my mother and that what ye plan to do is one of the darkest sins ye could commit."

"Dinnae claim me as your mother." Arabel slowly got to her feet as she spoke. "I loathed ye from the moment your father seeded ye in my belly. I hated the mon who made ye. I cursed what ye did to my body whilst I carried ye. I tried to rid myself of ye, but that fool wisewoman's potions didnae work. She died for her failure, but not before I had gleaned from her the way to stir up a number of other useful potions."

"Your poisons."

"Aye, my poisons. Gentle ones and cruel ones. Howbeit, even the worst of poisons, the slowest and the most painful, is too good for ye. Do ye ken how many times I tried to kill ye? The first time was when ye were still slick from birth, but the cursed midwife protected ye."

"I suppose she died for that moment of mercy."

"Aye, as did anyone who helped ye or protected ye. Weel, except one—Martin."

"Martin? Your faithful cur? Why, in God's sweet name, would he help me?" As she listened to the hatred her mother spat out, Sine was torn between nausea and pain, sickened by the woman she feared she could one day become just like, and deeply hurt by the proof of how much her own mother loathed her. "Martin has e'er been loyal to ye at the cost of his own soul," Sine said.

"Martin has e'er been loyal to but one person—himself. I cannae prove it, but I am now certain that he aided ye to escape from me, if only through his silence. He will pay for that, but first I mean to see to your death."

Arabel gave a signal to the two guards standing behind the twins. Sine turned in time to see the thickset men pin the two thin boys in their arms. She lunged toward them, but her own guards quickly grabbed her, each man holding her painfully by an arm and standing too far away for her to give them a sharp kick. They yanked her back a little when Arabel stepped closer and studied the twins before looking at Sine.

"Ere ye die, I decided, 'twould suit me to make ye watch your brothers die first."

"Their deaths will gain ye little. Let them go. Ye risk more by killing two bairns than ye e'er would by releasing them. As bastards, whatever claim they tried to make on my father's land and fortunes would be easily cast aside."

"I wonder—will ye plea so eloquently for your own life?" Arabel withdrew an ornate dagger from a hidden pocket in the seam of her skirt and laid it against Beldane's throat.

Sine suspected that she did little to actually help the twins by pleading for their lives, but she could not keep silent when they were in such danger. "Leave them be, Arabel. Ye can gain no honor by killing wee boys." Her stomach was knotted with fear for her brothers, but Sine struggled to hide it from Arabel, to deny her the pleasure of seeing it.

"True, but I can hurt ye badly by doing it, cannae I, Sine Catriona?"

"And what inspires your hate for them? That some other woman was able to give my father sons?"

It was hard not to cry out when Arabel suddenly slapped her, but Sine bit back the sound. Arabel's eyes were ablaze with fury and Sine realized that she had briefly distracted the woman. Sine braced herself for another vicious verbal assault from Arabel. It was a small sacrifice if it bought some time for Gamel to rescue them.

Gamel cursed as he stumbled against Farthing and jabbed the man in the backside with his sheathed sword. He grimaced with a touch of embarrassment when Farthing also cursed. If the danger was not so great, the way they were forced to creep along would be laughable. It felt as if they had been entombed in the passageway for hours, somewhat clumsily groping their way along by the dim light of Blane's torch.

"Why have ye stopped?" he asked Farthing.

"Not so that I can learn the joys of intimacy with your cursed sword." Farthing rubbed his backside.

"My apologies." Gamel scowled down the passageway. "God's tears, I think we have come to the end at last."

"Aye, but there does appear to be some difficulty in opening whatever door is down there."

"He almost has it, sir," whispered one of the men halfway along the tunnel. "'Tis just stuck, I think."

"Where in God's name is Martin?" Gamel muttered, and slumped against the wall.

Martin slipped into the steward's alcove and tensed. One of Arabel's large personal guards was in the room. The man had pushed aside the chest which hid the sunken entrance to the tunnel and was crouched in the small hole, his ear pressed against the door. Since Martin could hear the subtle scrape of armor, the soft rhythm of footsteps, and an occasional whisper from behind the walls, he was not sure why the man had not yet raised an alarm.

With a brief prayer of thanks for his good fortune, Martin eased the door shut behind him. He silently crept over to the table that held his ledgers and picked up one of the heavy candlesticks. Just as he got close enough to strike, the man looked his way. Martin cursed and swung. He shivered when he felt the candlestick hit flesh and heard the guard grunt.

It took Martin a moment before he understood precisely what he had done. He felt a little ill when he saw that he had caught the man squarely on the temple and crushed his skull. Although he was no stranger to death, Martin realized that he had never actually ended another man's life with such violence. His job had always been to prepare the way for someone else to do the killing.

The sound of the small tunnel door being nudged open from the other side brought Martin out of his distraction. He grabbed the guard by the arm and tried to drag him out of the way of the door, but failed to move the man more than a few inches. As he cursed Arabel for insisting upon having such huge guards, Martin grasped the man under the arms and, with a great deal of effort, pulled the body out of the way of the door. He was on his knees, gasping for breath, when Blane cautiously opened the door and, bending over to clear the low opening, stepped into the room. Blane cursed, hopped up the two steps and crouched by the guard.

"Dead," he announced, and sat down.

"He was blocking the door," Martin explained as he watched man after well-armed man slip from the passageway to crowd into the small room.

"Did he have a chance to raise an alarm?" Blane asked.

"Nay." Martin managed a tired smile for Farthing and Gamel as they stepped into the room.

Farthing looked down at the dead guard, then at the heavy candlestick Martin had dropped onto the floor. "Ye shall have to learn how to wield a sword as weel as ye do a quill. Although, a good cudgel often takes the mon down with less noise."

"There was barely a grunt. And this has proven to me that I had best stay with my inkpots and ledgers .The only reason I was able to fell the mon was because I caught him completely by surprise." Martin stood up and brushed himself off. "Lady Logan is already in the great hall."

"Is she still unharmed?" demanded Gamel.

"Aye, although one cannae tell what injuries are inflicted by the type of poison Arabel is spitting at her."

"And the lads?" asked Farthing.

"Still alive," replied Martin.

"How many are there inside the great hall itself?" asked Gamel.

"Arabel, Malise, the twins, Lady Logan, and six guards."

"Are they skilled fighters?"

"I fear I am not a good judge of such things, but they are hired swords and they didnae ask much coin for their work, if that helps ye at all."

"Some. And how ready are they for an attack?"

"There is an odd thing. They act as if they have already won. 'Tis a chilling blind confidence that makes one wonder if they possess some knowledge I dinnae or have the gift of foresight and already ken that they will win. Howbeit, when I think straight, I realize that they have neither."

Gamel nodded. "Their foolish arrogance can only help us." He pointed to Blane and half of the men in the room. "Take these men and see if ye cannae get the outer gates open as we planned. The rest of our men are watching for just such a chance so they will be quick to respond. I will give ten counts of one hundred, then the rest of us shall go into the great hall."

"I still think we can manage the gate," said Martin as he went to peer out into the corridor. "A wee bit of guile is all that is needed and I have a proven skill in that. 'Tis still somewhat unknown that I am no longer trusted." He glanced at the group of men standing with a scowling Blane. "If I give an order, will it be heeded?"

"Aye," grumbled Blane. "I will obey it if I am sure it willnae get my throat cut."

Martin slowly smiled. "Fair enough. Follow me then."

"Count for me, Ligulf," Gamel ordered the moment Martin led the other men away. "I would ne'er be able to keep the count straight." He ran a hand through his hair as Ligulf began to count. "Even the time I have allowed Martin feels too long," he muttered and moved to stand against the wall near the door.

"'Tis the wisest way to play this game," said Farthing, his gaze fixed upon the door.

"Wisest mayhaps, but not easy. Sine is but a few yards

away with a woman who aches to see her dead and I stand here listening to Ligulf counting."

"'Twould be certain to get us all killed if we start a row in the great hall ere Martin gets the gates open—"

"I ken it—we will all be slaughtered or captured and our help still locked outside the walls. 'Tis just that my innards are knotted with the fear that I shall get in there to find that Sine is already dead."

"These boys are proof that your father betrayed me," Arabel yelled as she paced the floor in front of Sine.

"Betrayed *ye*?" Although Arabel's rage was an unsettling thing to see, Sine tried to keep it stirred up, for it was distracting the woman from her plans for the twins. "'Tis ye who first betrayed him, and he tolerated it for years ere he turned to another. Your portrayal of the wronged wife is truly laughable."

"He betrayed me. No mon betrays me. No mon. Weel, he paid for it, he and his whore."

"I should be careful whom I called a whore."

Arabel whirled and struck out. Sine tried to duck the blow, but only partially succeeded. The way Arabel's guards held her with her arms spread so tautly, she could not dodge very far and every movement was painful. Arabel's closed fist scraped over her mouth and Sine tasted the salty warmth of her own blood.

"God's teeth, the little bastards even look like your father," Arabel muttered as she abruptly turned her attention back to the twins. "This one has the same prideful look in his cursed eyes." She grabbed a handful of Beldane's fair hair and tilted his head back a little, placing her dagger against his throat. "Weel, there is one sure way to dim that cursed defiance."

"And now ye mean to murder them as ye did my

father." Despite how it hurt her to do so, Sine began to struggle in her captors' hold, desperate to break free and get her brothers out of Arabel's reach. Even though she knew she was doing exactly what Arabel wanted she could not stop herself.

"Your father's death was far swifter and cleaner than the one I plan for his bastards."

Sine nearly cried out when Arabel lightly drew her dagger over Beldane's vulnerable throat. Blood slowly welled up from the shallow cut. Beldane's eyes were wide and he grew pale, but he made no sound, simply stared at his persecutor. Sine was so proud, the emotion briefly pierced through her grief and terror.

"Ye will rot in hell for your crimes, Arabel," Sine hissed.

"Do ye think to afright me with that poor threat? I have no fear of hell. I was destined for that ere ye were even conceived. I have grown quite accustomed to the thought of it."

Arabel suddenly tensed and frowned. Sine felt her guards grow still. She forced herself to listen as they were doing and felt a surge of hope. Although the sounds were dulled by the thick walls of the keep, she was sure she heard the distinct clatter of swords. She looked at Malise, who ran to a small window, flung open the shutters, and looked out into the bailey.

"They have taken the bailey! Some traitor has opened the gates. The Logans and their men are inside the walls," he cried, and drawing his sword, he started toward the doors of the great hall.

A scream of fury escaped Arabel. At the same moment Sine was so abruptly released that she lost her balance and ended up sprawled on the floor. The same thing happened to her brothers. Their guards were following

Malise, and Sine wondered fleetingly if they planned to join the fight or run.

"Malise," yelled Arabel. "Where do ye think ye are going? We arenae finished here."

Malise halted a step or two from the door and looked back at his wife. "Oh, aye, I am finished here. I fear we may all be finished here. The Logans are already within the inner wall. Most of our men will surrender or flee. Weel, ye wanted this. 'Tis yours, all yours. Save yourself or die. I dinnae much care, wife. I have my own neck to protect now."

Her dagger still clutched in her hand, Arabel looked at the twins, who were struggling to help each other sit up. Sine read the intent in Arabel's tight features. The woman did not mean to die alone. Although her muscles were so strained that they ached with every movement, Sine leapt to her feet. Arabel raised her dagger and smiled coldly at Beldane, who was trying to shield Barre. With a cry of fury, Sine lunged for her mother and grabbed Arabel by the wrist of her upraised arm.

The force of Sine's attack sent her and Arabel to the floor. She sought to disarm her mother, but she quickly understood that Arabel had other plans. Even now, with defeat staring Arabel in the face, the woman was determined to kill her. There was such hatred in the woman's eyes that Sine knew Arabel simply did not care that she could be caught with the bloodied dagger in her hand, proof that would send Arabel straight to the gallows.

A crash intruded upon their silent deadly struggle, followed by the sounds of battle. Sine forced herself not to be distracted by the clang of swords or the grunts and curses of men fighting. She watched Arabel closely as they wrestled, Sine trying to yank the dagger from Arabel's hand even as Arabel tried to bury it in her heart.

A scream echoed in the hall and Sine saw her chance as Arabel, distracted, looked to see what had happened.

Sine pinned her mother more securely beneath her and slammed the hand clutching the dagger against the rush-covered stone floor again and again. Arabel finally screamed with a mixture of frustration and pain. The dagger slid from her limp and bloodied hand. Sine sat up a little and punched Arabel as hard as she could. She grimaced as her fist slammed into Arabel's jaw, sickened by what she had done.

Arabel went limp beneath her. Sine straddled her mother's unconscious body for a few moments as she fought to calm her breathing and regain her strength. She was still trembling faintly from weakness as she hobbled to her feet and stumbled over to the twins.

"Are ye all right?" she asked the boys, her voice hoarse and uneven. "Ye look terrible, but do ye think ye suffer from anything more than the bruises I can see?"

"Nay. We were beaten a wee bit, but naught is broken or e'en bleeding anymore," Beldane answered. "How are ye? Ye were knocked about some as weel."

"Not verra much. The weapon they used upon me was words. 'Twill be over soon," she whispered, and turned to look at the men although there was little fighting left to be done.

Gamel faced a wounded Malise. Sine suspected it had been Malise's scream which had briefly distracted Arabel. The man was bleeding profusely from a wound in his side, but he still stood firm before Gamel, clearly determined to fight to the death. Sine prayed that Malise would not prove strong or clever enough to defeat Gamel. She sat tensely watching the final confrontation.

"Give up, Malise," ordered Gamel. "Ye cannae fight me now."

"Nay?" Malise thrust his sword at Gamel, but Gamel

blocked the lunge. "I willnae meekly succumb to the king's justice. Far better a swift death now than a slow hanging later."

Despite his wound, Malise attacked, furiously swinging his sword. Gamel was forced back a few steps as he skillfully deflected each blow. Malise quickly weakened, his attack growing awkward. Gamel found an opening a moment later and ended the uneven battle with one clean thrust, burying his blade in Malise's heart. When he yanked his sword free of Malise's flesh, the man fell to the ground, dying with barely a whisper. Gamel stood over Malise's limp body, using the man's jupon to clean off his sword. The last of the guards surrendered even as Sine watched. Gamel turned to look at her and she tried to smile.

"Where is Farthing?" asked Barre.

"He saw that he wasnae needed here," replied Gamel, forcing his gaze away from Sine's pale face. "He stepped out into the bailey to lend a hand there."

"Is it safe now to go and see him?" Beldane asked even as he stood up.

"Aye, I believe so. Even though I caught only a brief glimpse of the bailey as he left, it looked as if most of the fighting was done. He will be quick to tell ye if it isnae. Go on if ye think ye are able."

"We can walk across the hall if naught else," Barre said as, holding Beldane's hand, he led his brother toward the door of the great hall.

Sine sat where she was. She needed to regain her composure before she faced Gamel. The battle against Arabel and Malise had been settled in her favor. There was just one more terrible thing to face—the painful but necessary ending of her marriage. She knew he would be at her side in a moment or two and she struggled to make some plan on how to take that last step. Now did not seem a very good time to announce that she wanted the annulment, but to delay would allow Gamel to change her mind. She would make the cut swiftly.

A soft rustle briefly tugged her from her thoughts. Cautiously, she turned to look at Arabel. The woman was still, her eyes closed. Sine relaxed and realized that she had been nearly frozen with fear, her whole body stiff. She cursed that weakness, wondering if she would ever be truly free of Arabel. Then she saw Gamel starting toward her.

Sine did not look too badly bruised to him, but her paleness and obvious shakiness worried him. He took a few strides toward her and froze.

Arabel was slowly rising to her feet, her dagger in her hand. Sine, lost in her own thoughts, did not see the woman. He cursed the fates and Arabel as he drew his own dagger. He moved toward Sine with more caution, needing to get closer so that he could at least hurl his dagger with some accuracy, and he could not afford to startle or alert Arabel, as the woman was close enough to Sine to really hurt her before he could do anything to help. Even some attempt to warn Sine could cause Arabel to act before he was able to halt her.

He kept his gaze fixed upon Arabel as he edged nearer. The woman crept behind the unsuspecting Sine. Gamel shivered at the look on the woman's face—a mixture of insane hatred and pure glee over the chance to kill her own child. When Arabel suddenly lunged for Sine, Gamel could not withhold a cry of warning, but it did little good. Arabel grabbed a hank of Sine's hair, yanked her daughter's head back, and placed her knife at Sine's exposed throat.

A cry of pain and fear caught in Sine's throat when the cold steel of Arabel's dagger touched her neck. She instinctively reached up to pull Arabel's hand aside, only to feel the sting of the blade scoring her skin. The way Arabel held her head pulled back made it impossible for Sine to see if anyone was ready to help her. All she was aware of was a sudden silence all around her.

"Ye thought ye had won, didnae ye?" Arabel's voice was a soft sneer, heavy with a chilling bitterness.

"Dinnae do this, Arabel. Ye survived the battle. Ye will ne'er survive my murder."

"Survived? Should I feel pleased that I have been spared the sword so that I can taste the rope about my neck? Nay, let them kill me here. But they will have a verra sour victory, for I will take your life ere I die."

Sine tensed, bracing herself for the death stroke, but it did not come. Instead, she heard a soft thud and felt Arabel jerk. The dagger dropped from Arabel's hand, but she did not release her grip on Sine's hair. Sine cried out as she was first pulled backwards and then to the side. Her mother landed half on top of her after their clumsy fall and finally loosed her grip on her hair.

A dagger she recognized as Gamel's protruded from Arabel's back. Her whole body shaking, Sine carefully sat up and held her mother in her arms. She was swamped by a sudden sense of loss, but she knew it was not really for Arabel. It was for the mother she had never had. Even the lingering look of hatred in Arabel's clouding eyes did not dim that grief.

"I always kenned that it would end this way," Arabel whispered, her voice hoarse with pain. "I always kenned that ye would bleed me of my beauty and then of my life. I could see it in your wee face the day ye slid free of my body. I saw it in your wide eyes as I put my hands around your tiny throat."

Arabel shuddered, then went limp in Sine's hold, her sightless eyes fixed upon the ceiling and a malevolent look frozen upon her face. Sine hesitated to look at

Gamel when he approached. She shivered as he eased
the dagger from Arabel's back. It horrified her to think
that her mother had forced Gamel to kill a woman,
something she knew he would find difficult to accept.
He was a true knight and, as a knight, his duty was to
protect women. When she finally turned to him he was
pale and it appeared as if his feelings had been suddenly
and deeply hurt, but she was too weary and distraught to
wonder why.

"I am sorry ye had to kill her," she forced herself to
say, and wondered why that should make him look even
worse.

"Dearling," Farthing said as he reached her side. "Let
her go and come with me."

Sine dutifully relinquished her hold on Arabel and let
Farthing help her to her feet. "Where are ye taking me?"
she asked as he gently led her from the great hall.

"To someplace where ye can rest. The battle is over.
Martin and Blane opened the gates of Dorchabeinn to
Lord William and my father, who quickly led their men
into the outer bailey. There wasnae much resistance."

"She said such vile, wicked things, Farthing," she murmured, leaning into his hold when he put his arm
around her shoulders as they climbed the narrow steps
to the upper floors.

"Forget them, lass. I ken it willnae be easy, but put
them out of your mind. They were words with no purpose other than to hurt ye."

He was right and Sine prayed that she would be able to
do as he advised. She meekly allowed him to lead her
into a small bedchamber, settle her on the bed and tug
off her clothes. Once she was stripped to only her chemise, he tucked her beneath the lavender-scented sheets.

"I feel as if the life has been drained out of me, Farthing."

"'Tis but a weariness of heart and body, and some grief, lass. Ye have been through a great deal this night. 'Twill pass."

"I should be with the twins. They have endured a great deal since they were stolen from Duncoille."

"I will care for the boys. Aye, they have been frightened and hurt, but it wasnae *their* mother doing it to them. It wasnae their own flesh and blood who struck them and threatened them. Ye may not have as many bruises as the boys do, sweet Sine, but the pain is greater, the hurt deeper."

"Should I not speak to the people of Dorchabeinn? I should tell them that I will now be mistress of these lands."

"Martin is doing that. Ye can address them yourself at another time."

"Ye must tell Martin that he is still the steward if he wishes to be."

"I believe he will eagerly and gratefully accept the post." He bent and touched a kiss to her cheek. "Rest and regain your strength. Do ye wish me to send Gamel to ye?"

"Nay. I need to be alone for a while."

When Farthing left she closed her eyes and was surprised when the urge to fall asleep quickly gripped her. Her emotions were in such turmoil, she had not expected sleep to come for hours. She regretted her refusal to see Gamel, but forced that regret aside. In her weak and distraught condition she would cling to him. It was the worst possible time to have him near. Not only could it weaken her resolve to do what was right to set him free, but it would be unkind to use him to give her comfort and then push him away. She reached instead for the oblivion of sleep and prayed that she would wake with the strength she needed to deal with Gamel.

"She needs time to think," Farthing told Gamel, feeling some sympathy for the pale, stone-faced man.

Gamel felt such pain that he was unable to speak. He nodded. He could still see Sine's face as she had looked at him over her mother's body the night before. The look of horror in her beautiful eyes still haunted him. He had hoped that she would have recovered after a night's rest, but when morning came she had refused to see him again. As he walked to his horse he knew that it was over, that he had won the battle, but at a cost far higher than he had been prepared to pay. He had agreed to allow her to set aside their marriage once her battle was won and now he must honor that promise.

Farthing stood at his father's side and watched the Logans and their men ride away, back to Duncoille. Although he could understand Sine's need to be alone, to think without Gamel dogging her every step, he did not like to see the man in such pain. Leaving his father to direct the Magnusson men-at-arms in repairing the damage caused by the brief battle, Farthing went to the bedchamber where Sine was hiding. She had come out only once to thank her allies, then disappeared again.

He frowned when he entered the room and found her at the window watching Gamel ride away. "Weel, I told him that ye needed some time alone. He didnae take it verra weel."

"What did he say?"

"Nothing. He grew verra pale but only nodded and then he left. What could he say? He promised that ye could end the marriage when ye chose to and he is an honorable mon. Are ye sure about this, lass?" He moved to stand beside her and studied her wan, melancholy face. "Ye dinnae look like ye want him to leave."

"Sometimes what we want isnae always what is best for us. I see that Martin is riding with them."

"I gave him permission to go and visit Margot. He will bring her back here in a few days. And dinnae try and change the subject."

"I dinnae feel like talking about my decision. Not yet. 'Tis too new. My thoughts arenae clear."

"All right, but I shouldnae take too long in thinking." He started back toward the door. "Dinnae make it all too complicated either. Do ye want him or dinnae ye want him is the only question that needs answering."

When the door shut behind Farthing, Sine sighed and felt guilty over her evasive replies. She also felt guilty about not facing Gamel, about hiding away and letting him leave with no real decision made. It was the coward's way out, but she needed to be a coward for a little while.

Do ye want him or dinnae ye? Farthing had said. She heartily wished that it was that simple. Aye, I want him, she thought as her tear-washed gaze remained fixed on Gamel's straight, proud figure and she watched him ride away. That had never been in doubt. What she had to ask herself was—could she take what she wanted so desperately, knowing that she could easily destroy it? The only right answer to such a question was nay.

Chapter 17

Farthing smiled at everyone as he entered the great keep of Duncoille. It pleased him when they all returned the greeting, filling him with a sense of welcome. After a fortnight of aiding Sine Catriona in establishing herself and the twins at Dorchabeinn, he had spent a full six weeks with his father studying how to manage the lands he would one day inherit. Then he had ridden here for a brief visit with old friends before winter came. But now he could see that he had serious work to do.

"Weel met, cousin Margot," Farthing called as he strode into the great hall, idly noting that life at Dorchabeinn clearly suited her. He walked to the head table, bowed to Lord William and kissed Lady Edina's hand before sitting down next to his little cousin and her new husband, Martin Robertson. "My father sends his good wishes," he said as he accepted a large tankard of wine from a fair-haired page and took a deep, slow drink. He smiled amiably at his four companions. "That embues a body with a welcome warmth. If today is any proof, the winter could be a long and cold one."

"Do ye plan to visit us for verra long?" asked Lord William. "Ye are, of course, weelcome."

"Thank ye, m'lord. Nay, I dinnae intend to stay for long. I have come to talk to that fool son of yours. If he isnae here, then I will talk to ye and pray that ye can beat some sense into the empty-headed gosling."

"I believe your pretty cousin has come here direct from Dorchabeinn upon a similar errand."

Farthing smiled at the blushing Margot. "I had wondered about it from the moment Sine told me that ye and Martin had traveled to Duncoille. I was at Dorchabeinn but yesterday."

"Ye didnae make a verra long stay with Sine," murmured Lady Edina. "She may feel hurt by that."

"She willnae e'en notice that I have left. I have ne'er seen a more mournful lass. I had expected to find her and Gamel together and fondly planned to torment them for a fortnight or so." He winked when Lady Edina laughed. "I couldnae understand why Gamel wasnae there."

"To be fair, cousin, she sent him away after her mother was killed," said Margot.

"Aye, but after she had time to think, she should have called him back. That was *two long months* ago, yet she languishes alone at Dorchabeinn. And, considering how fiercely Gamel pursued her in the beginning, I am mightily surprised that he would wait for a summons from her. So since Sine did little more than sigh and mope, I told the twins to be patient, that I would come here and try and find some answers."

"I have but one," said Lord William. "Gamel feels that Sine blames him for her mother's death."

"Blames him for lancing that boil?" Farthing shook his head. "He cannae be that addle-witted."

"Mayhaps blame isnae the right word. No matter how

Sine felt about her mother, Gamel believes that she cannae see him without also seeing Arabel's blood upon his hands. He claims that he glimpsed horror in her eyes that day and willnae chance seeing it again."

"Idiots." Farthing groaned and shook his head. "My life is cursed with idiots. Weel, if that is all it is, it can be easily mended. I dinnae ken what Gamel thinks he saw, but Sine doesnae see Arabel's blood upon his hands. She has buried Arabel and put all of that trouble behind her. 'Tis past time that Gamel did the same."

"I fear there is more to it than that," Margot said softly. "Martin and I arrived here late yesterday, too late to speak to Gamel. We had hoped to see him today, but havenae caught sight of him. Since we cannae stay here for long, as I am only supposed to have come to collect a few belongings I left behind, we decided to speak to Lord and Lady Logan instead. 'Tisnae just Gamel who keeps them apart. Sine ne'er meant to send for him."

"She wants the fool. She always has."

Margot nodded. "She feels she has no right to claim him. The night before ye all rode to Dorchabeinn to save the twins, she spoke to me in confidence." She grimaced. "And I promised never to speak of what she said."

Martin took her hand in his. "Ye must. To hold to your promise now is to leave two people in misery."

"Aye," Farthing agreed. "I willnae trouble ye with a multitude of examples, but there truly are times when ye can harm a person more by keeping their confidence than by revealing it. 'Tisnae as if ye mean to ride about telling all and sundry either."

"Aye, I ken it." After taking a deep breath to restore her courage, Margot told them about Sine's fears of becoming like her mother. She began to frown when everyone stared at her without speaking for several moments. "Oh, sweet Mary, do ye think it might be true?"

"True?" Farthing bellowed. "'Tis the greatest pile of nonsense I have heard in my entire life!"

"Be fair," Margot said. "There are many who believe in the idea of bad seeds."

"Aye, there are many complete fools in the world too. God's tears, Gamel thinks himself cursed because he saved Sine's life and Sine believes she will wake up some morning wanting to bed her entire household guard and then go and poison a few people." He grinned when Martin laughed, only to be frowned into silence by his wife.

"Ye shouldnae jest about it, cousin," Margot scolded. "They truly believe these things and it hurts them."

"Then we had best get them to *un*believe these things."

"Ye make it sound so simple."

"'Tisnae so verra difficult. We simply have to lock the fools up together for a while. Eventually they will begin to talk to each other. Gamel will certainly demand a reason for why Sine pushed him aside, and when the lass explains he will soon show her how foolish that belief is. Then she will question why he so blithely accepted her refusal to see him, something he ne'er did before."

"And Sine will gladly dissuade him of his belief," Margot concluded, and started to smile.

"It could work," Lady Edina agreed. "I have believed from the verra beginning that they belong together."

"Aye." Farthing nodded. "They are certainly well matched in their idiocy."

"Shall we just drag them down to the dungeon and toss them in?" Lord William asked with a grin as he rubbed his hands together. "After enduring Gamel's surliness for two months, the thought appeals to me."

Farthing laughed and nodded. "They have earned a

few days in chains for this stupidity. Howbeit, they will undoubtedly protest it at first and I dinnae care to hear it. They need a place where they can be safe yet secluded and I believe I ken just the place. There is a wee peel tower on a small stream about half the distance twixt here and Dorchabeinn."

Lord William nodded. "Aye, I ken the place weel. Greyburn, I believe 'tis called. It has been empty for several years."

"But 'twill hold them comfortably for a few days. I stopped there to rest my mount and my backside on my way here. With a few supplies and the means to bar the door from the outside, all will be weel."

"There is the problem of how to get them to the place. We could just abduct them and toss them in, but 'twould sour their mood more than might be wise. There must be a gentler way."

"I may have an idea or two about that as weel, m'lord," Farthing said, and slowly grinned.

Sine inwardly grimaced when Martin strode into the solar at Dorchabeinn. She had retired to the small sunheated room with its large windows to be alone. In a small way she resented the intrusion. It was exhausting to constantly try to act as if she was happy—and she knew she did a poor job of it. Every now and then she had to go off alone to try to subdue her misery. Martin looked agitated, as if something was wrong, and Sine wearily prepared to sort out his problem. She sat up straighter on the cushioned window bench she had been resting on.

"Is something wrong?"

"M'lady." He gave her a brief bow. "'Tis my wife."

"Margot?" Sine suddenly realized that he was alone,

which was unusual, for he and Margot had been nearly inseparable since their marriage a month ago. "Where is she?"

"Several hours' ride north of here."

"What?" Sine stood up and grasped him by the arm. "Why didnae she return with ye?"

"There was a small mishap. She fainted and slid from her mount. Fortunately, she didnae injure herself in the fall, but she remained somewhat lightheaded e'en after she woke from her faint. There was a small peel tower near at hand so I made her comfortable and left two men to guard her. Then I rode back here. If naught else, I shall need a cart so that I can bring her home."

"Of course. I will come with ye. We shall need a few supplies as 'twill be nearly sunset ere we get there and we shall have to spend the night there. Ye go and ready the cart while I gather whatever else we may need. Dinnae worry, Martin. I am sure she is fine."

As Martin hurried off to the stables, Sine rushed to gather up some food, medicines, and clothing. A half hour later she was sitting in the back of a small cart leaving Dorchabeinn for the first time since Arabel's death. She and Martin drove onto the Stirling road and headed north. Sine found herself thinking of how she could follow this road to Duncoille and cursed. Somehow she had to free her heart and mind of Gamel Logan. She closed her eyes and tried to sleep, but the misery which had engulfed her from the moment Gamel had ridden out of the gates of Dorchabeinn persisted. If she did not cast it off soon, she feared that she would drown in it, or at the very least, make everyone heartily sick of her.

Gamel muttered a curse as the deer loped away and his arrow buried itself uselessly in the ground. "I hope ye didnae have a taste for venison tonight," he grumbled to Farthing as he spurred his horse forward to go and collect his arrow.

Farthing nudged his mount to keep abreast of Gamel. "Nay. I had but thought that an afternoon of hunting would offer your family a respite from your sullen company."

"I am *not* sullen company," Gamel snapped.

"Oh, aye, ye are. Ye are worse than any old lecher with the gout. But dinnae worry. Look there," he said as they reined in and Gamel bent to yank his arrow from the dirt. "Is that not your brother Ligulf's page?"

Once righted in the saddle, Gamel watched the boy galloping up to them and scowled. "Aye, 'tis wee Robbie." He steadied his mount when the boy abruptly reined in before them. "Careful, lad."

"I am verra sorry, sir, but I have important news. 'Tis my master, Ligulf. He is hurt."

"Hurt? How? Where?" Gamel demanded.

"He was tossed from his horse a few hours' ride from here near Greyburn, a small peel tower by a stream. We were escorting the Robertsons back to Dorchabeinn."

A sharp pain struck Gamel upon hearing that name, but he forced himself to concentrate upon the trouble Ligulf had gotten himself into. "Was Ligulf badly hurt?"

"He wasnae sure, but his leg is verra painful. He dares not risk riding again until he can be sure that he hasnae broken it. The Robertsons left a few of their men behind to guard him and continued on. I rode back here to get help."

Gamel nodded. "Fine work, laddie. Farthing and I will go there now. I ken the place ye speak of. Ye ride on to Duncoille and tell my parents. They will send out a cart. Ask for a few supplies as weel. 'Twill be nearly nightfall ere we get there and we shall have to camp."

The youth rode off and Gamel turned to Farthing. "I included ye without asking if ye cared to join me."

"Oh, aye, I will come along. I have naught else to do."

Farthing spurred his mount into a gallop and Gamel quickly followed. As they headed south, Gamel could not stop himself from recalling the last time he had ridden this road and with that memory came a renewal of his pain. He cursed himself, cursed fate, and cursed Sine. When his dagger had buried itself in Arabel Brodie, it had severed any chance he had had of staying with Sine, of being happy. Gamel knew he had to accept that. He had to conquer his pain or it would corrupt him. In fact, he decided, it was past time to get an annulment. He vowed that, as soon as Ligulf's trouble was corrected, he would go on to Dorchabeinn and confront Sine.

It was evening by the time Gamel and Farthing reached Greyburn. Gamel frowned as he dismounted. He was not sure what he had expected to find, but, as two men ambled over to take his and Farthing's horses, Gamel could not feel completely at ease.

"Where is Ligulf's mount?" Gamel asked the taller of the men-at-arms.

"In a field near the stream. The lad is inside the tower."

Gamel shook his head and strode into the peel tower. Just beyond the heavy iron-banded door, he stopped and looked around. For a place that had been empty for years, it looked very clean and well supplied. He took another step inside and stared up at the partial second floor. There was a large bed up there. There was also no Ligulf.

With a curse, Gamel turned back to Farthing, who stood in the doorway. "I think someone is playing a game with us."

"Do ye?"

"Aye." Gamel took a step toward Farthing, then gaped. It was all he had time to do before the fist he saw coming toward him struck his jaw and sent him plummeting into unconsciousness.

"I think ye enjoyed that."

Farthing grinned at Ligulf, who had stepped up beside him. "Aye, I did. Help me get the fool up on the bed. The mon sent to watch the road just signaled that Martin is in sight. We had better not be here when Sine arrives."

"We are here, Lady Sine," said Martin.

She rubbed her eyes and sat up, a little surprised that she had slept. She grabbed the basket of supplies and, with Martin's help, jumped down from the cart. A sense that something was not quite right washed over her, but she shook it aside, for she could see no reason to be suspicious.

"Margot is inside?" she asked, pointing to the peel tower.

"Aye. Go right in. I had best see to these horses."

She walked toward the tower nodding a greeting to the two guards who passed her on their way to help Martin. When she stepped inside the two-story edifice, she frowned. It looked as if someone was living there. She saw no sign of Margot either, and turned to step back outside and speak to Martin. Sine gaped when she came face-to-face with Farthing. He grinned, winked, and slammed the door shut. It was not until she heard the sound of the door being bolted from the outside that she shook free of the grip of surprise.

"Farthing!" She set her basket down, ran to the door, and pounded on it with her fists. "Farthing! Open this cursed door and let me out of here. What game are ye playing at?"

There was no answer, just a ripple of soft laughter. She cursed and looked up, espying a narrow arrow slit on the upper floor. Determined to get Farthing to speak to her, she scrambled up the ladder and rushed over to the opening. She gaped at what she saw below her. Farthing, Martin, Ligulf, and a very healthy Margot stood together talking and laughing.

"Farthing, ye arrogant, lecherous swine, let me out of here!"

When Farthing and the others just smiled and waved at her before walking away, she cursed some more. She was about to hurl a few very colorful epithets their way when she heard a groan from behind her. She told herself firmly that her friends would never knowingly place her in danger, but she still felt a touch of fear as she slowly turned around. It took her a moment to accept that she was looking at Gamel, a bare-chested Gamel, who was slowly sitting up in a large, simple bed. Then she noticed that he was gently touching his jaw, which was bruised. A thin streak of blood ran down his chin from his lip.

"The bastard hit me," Gamel muttered.

Her heart pounding in alarm, Sine hurried over to the bed. The fact that he had not yet commented on her presence confirmed her growing suspicion that he was hurt. A bowl of clean water and a rag were on the table next to the bed. Sine dampened the rag, nudged Gamel's hand out of the way, and gently bathed his lip and jaw.

She tried to keep her thoughts on the fact that he had been injured, but it was difficult. It had been so long since she had seen or touched him. It hurt to be near him now.

Sine realized that she had lingered too long over the

chore of tidying his little cut, but when she tried to
snatch her hand back, he grabbed her wrist. Her eyes
wide and her stomach knotted with conflicting emotions, she warily met Gamel's gaze. It was evident from
the look darkening his green eyes that the fact that they
had been deceived by their friends and locked together
in a peel tower was not what was foremost in his mind.
He was remembering the same things she was—the
heated kisses they had shared, the sweet touch of flesh
upon flesh. When he began to draw her closer to him,
she did not have the strength to resist.

"Nay," she whispered, yet did not stop him when he
slipped his arm about her waist and urged her down
onto the bed. "We cannae do this."

"We are wed." Gamel placed soft kisses over her throat
as he began to unlace her gown with unsteady hands.
"The Church sanctions it."

Sine had some doubts that the Church would sanction
everything she was feeling or thinking of doing to
Gamel. She was trying to form the words to remind
Gamel of all the trouble and unanswered questions that
still separated them when he kissed her. With each
stroke of his tongue within her mouth he stole another
thought from her mind. By the time the kiss ended she
was wearing only her shift and could no longer remember why she should vigorously protest his lovemaking.

"I should say nay," she muttered, and rubbed her
hands over his strong back, delighting in the feel of his
smooth, warm skin beneath her fingers.

"Ye should say, Oh, Gamel." He tugged off her shift,
tossed it aside, and pulled her beneath the linen sheet
which covered him.

"Oh, Gamel," she whispered when he pressed her
body against his and their flesh touched for the first time

in two long months. "Oh, Gamel," she repeated, thread-
ing her fingers in his thick hair and hungrily kissing him.

A carnal wildness seered through Sine Catriona. A desperate hunger drove her. She tried to touch Gamel every-
where at the same time. She touched her lips and tongue
to his skin at every chance she got, starved for the taste
of him. At times she clung to him so tightly that he
grunted in protest, but she only eased her grip a little. She
could not hold him close enough and, for a moment, savored the mad thought of pulling him inside of her so
that nothing and no one could ever part them again.

Gamel clearly shared her frantic need, and that knowledge fed hers, increasing it. She fought with him over
which of them would lead their passionate dance, yet was
equally as pleased when he won the silent struggle as
when she did. Even after they were one, the struggle
continued. They rolled from one side of the bed to the
other, first with him on top and then her. Release came
fast and fierce, and their cries blended as they shuddered from the strength of it.

But even as Gamel sank down into her arms, Sine
began to think again. His breathing was as ragged as her
own, the heavy, swift gasps heating the side of her neck.
She could feel his heartbeat and it echoed the rapid pace
of her own. They were united in so many ways—in body,
need, even the rhythm of their breathing—yet her first
clear thought was that the lovemaking had been a grave
error.

Nothing had changed. She was still Arabel Brodie's
daughter. She still had to remain alone. This time with
Gamel had been no more than a brief respite from her
loneliness and pain and she should have resisted the
temptation. All her memories would now be honed to a
more painful sharpness. When she felt him stir in her
arms she tensed, dreading the moment when she would

have to meet his gaze and tell him that they could never do this again.

Regret pinching at his heart, Gamel eased the intimacy of their embrace. When Sine tried to slip away, he held her in place gently but firmly. When she finally looked at him, he tensed, then felt the touch of confusion. Her expression held sadness, regret, and some wariness—but no horror, no loathing or accusation, none of the chilling emotions that had sent him fleeing Dorchabeinn after Arabel Brodie had died. He felt the first flicker of hope in two long months.

"Have ye forgiven me for the spilling of your mother's blood?"

Sine frowned at him, wondering why he should ask such a strange, foolish question. "What was there to forgive? We all kenned that it had to end with her death."

"Aye, but *I* killed her. 'Twas my dagger that pierced her heart." He sat up, though he still straddled her.

"Better that than her dagger resting in *my* heart, which was what she was trying to accomplish. Ye saved my life."

He moved off her to sit at her side and then ran his hand through his already badly tousled hair. "I dinnae understand."

"If ye find yourself confusing, then I dinnae feel so bad about finding ye so as weel." She sat up, tugged the linen sheet around her body and wondered where he had thrown her clothes. "I cannae think why ye should want forgiveness for anything ye did that night. Ye simply did what ye must. What wrong can ye see in that? I certainly see none."

"Nay? I saw the look upon your face. I saw the horror in your eyes."

"Did ye think that was for ye? For what ye had done?" she asked in soft surprise, an emotion which increased when he nodded. "Gamel, I had just spent what felt like hours struggling to survive, to endure her evil words and deeds. My brothers were bruised and bleeding. My own mother spat naught but hate and fury at me, then tried to kill me with her own hands. Of course I would have a look of horror on my face after enduring all of that. It took days for that horror to begin to leave me."

Gamel did not want to believe that he had erred, had left her when there had been no need. "Ye were weeping."

"Of course I was weeping," she replied, a hint of exasperation in her tone, then she sighed. "It wasnae for Arabel, not completely. 'Twas an odd grief. She was never a mother to me, and mayhaps I wept because her death meant that would ne'er change. She died speaking of her hate for me so now that hate is eternal.

"And weeping can be purging for a woman, Gamel. I had spent those two days while she held the twins torn by emotion and fear." She shrugged. "'Twas over, so I cried. None of it was aimed at ye or the fact that 'twas your dagger that killed her. I swear it. Ye did what ye had to do. 'Tis all. Now, I must get dressed and try to get that rogue Farthing to let me out of here." She gave a soft cry of surprise when Gamel suddenly pinned her back down on the bed. "Gamel, I must return to Dorchabeinn."

"I didnae hear ye ask me to journey there with ye."

She suddenly realized that relieving him of his guilt might have been the kind thing to do, but not the wisest. Now he wanted some answers as to why they remained apart. "Nay, I didnae ask ye to and I willnae."

That hurt, but Gamel fought his first reaction to it. Her words were cruel, but her eyes, her whole expression, held only regret and sadness. Nor did a woman make love to a man as she had just done if she did not want him.

"Why? If ye dinnae blame me for Arabel's death, then why do ye keep us apart?"

"Ye said I could end this marriage when my trouble was over."

"I ne'er said I wouldnae demand a reason. Ye are lying here naked, still prettily flushed from our lovemaking, yet ye speak of annulment and separation. I want to ken the reason."

"And ye willnae release me until I tell ye—aye?"

"Aye. I believe our friends willnae release either of us until this all makes sense."

Sine softly cursed, then sighed with resignation. He had a right to know her reasons for pushing him away. He had risked his life to help fight her enemies. He had been a friend, a protector, a lover. She prayed that he would not torment her with any long arguments, but would simply accept their fate.

"I am Arabel Brodie's daughter—her flesh and blood."

"I had noticed that." He eased his hold on her a little and frowned. "The woman is dead. She cannae hurt us."

"Nay? Her blood flows in my veins."

"Aye? Do ye fear I might hold that against ye?"

"Nay, but 'twould be wiser if ye did."

"What do ye mean?"

"The apple doesnae fall far from the tree."

"Oh, *that* is verra clarifying."

"I am Arabel's daughter. God's blood, I am her verra image."

"And I have told ye that it doesnae matter."

Sine took several breaths to calm herself. "Have ye ne'er heard of tainted blood?"

"Aye."

There was a tone to his voice and a look in his eye as he said that one word that made Sine wary, but she pressed on. "Weel, with a mother such as Arabel, I am certainly one who should deeply concern herself with such matters. I must surely carry a bad seed. Mayhaps it will ne'er blossom, but what if it does? I could become Arabel in spirit as weel as in appearance. I could turn on the ones I care about, even hurt them, as Arabel did. And, God help us, I could pass this curse on to any children I might bear."

Gamel had listened to her explanation with growing incredulity. He could not believe that she would throw away all they could share for the sake of a superstition. Despite recognizing her deep and sincere concern, her very real fears, he grew more and more annoyed. He knew he should speak calmly and should sympathize yet make her see reason but he ached to give her a shaking that would loosen her teeth.

"So, ye can see now that the only thing to do is for me to remain alone," Sine concluded, and eyed Gamel a little warily, for he looked inclined to throttle her. That was a reaction she had not anticipated.

"Were ye born this stupid or have years of listening to Farthing's prattle dulled your wits?" he finally demanded.

"I beg your pardon?" She had never expected such a reaction and was a little hurt by the hint of contempt in his voice.

Gamel hopped off the bed and began to pace the floor, pausing only to grab his braies up from the floor and put them on. "One of the things I appreciated about ye was that ye had some wit, that ye werenae some sheltered empty-headed lass who could talk about little more than tapestries and impudent handmaidens. Howbeit, now ye make me seriously doubt that there is anything behind those huge violet eyes."

"There is no need to insult me." She began to get angry, a feeling bred from his scorn over something that had tormented her for months. "We deal with madness here. 'Tis something to be concerned about. I carry Arabel's tainted blood."

He stood at the edge of the bed, his hands on his hips. "Let us summon the surgeon then and he can drain it out with his leeches. I now understand what our friends were about. They somehow learned of this nonsense ye have taken into your head and decided that we needed to be shut up together so that I could try and beat some sense into ye."

"Ye would ne'er beat me." She began to feel confused. His certainty that she was spouting nonsense began to make her doubt her own belief.

"'Tis sorely tempting. Sine, tainted blood is naught but superstition." He grasped her by the shoulders. "Aye, some verra important people believe it, but 'tis still nonsense. Ye can find as many people who prove bad seeds are not passed from parent to child as ye can ones who prove it. More of the former, I think. What tainted Arabel cannae be passed on to a child. Why do ye find that so hard to believe?"

"I *want* to believe it," she whispered. "That alone makes me hesitant to do so. Since I want to believe ye so badly, it could cloud my reason."

"Your reasoning cannae be any more clouded than it is." He sat down on the bed beside her. "I will concede that, at times, there does seem to be a madness passed from parent to child. 'Tis rare, but does happen. Howbeit, ye can see it in the child. The madness doesnae lay hidden for years, then suddenly leap out. What ailed your mother was not so much a madness as a lack of heart, of soul. What emotions she had were all the bad ones. Sine, how old was your mother when she bore ye?"

"Seventeen."

"And the evil was already there, already at work."

"Aye, it was. I ken it from all I was told, from what she herself spat at me." Sine began to feel the first glimmer of hope.

"Yet ye are a year or more older than that and there hasnae been a hint that ye are like her in any way except for how ye look. Arabel hated children, yet ye were willing to die for your brothers. Arabel hungered for any mon she saw, yet ye were with Farthing for six long years and ne'er slept with him. Arabel thought nothing of killing people for the pettiest of reasons. Ye are no murderer, lass. She was cruel and vain and ye are neither. There is none of that woman's blackness inside of ye.

"Ye need more proof? Why did ye turn away from me, plan to live your life alone, e'en though ye want me? Aye, the way we greeted each other today proves that ye want me as fiercely as I want ye. Yet ye were prepared to throw that all away. Why?"

"I couldnae stay with ye when I thought of what I could become," she answered in a slightly meek tone, color flooding into her cheeks as she began to understand how foolish she had been. "I feared that, if I became like my mother, it would hurt ye. *I* would have hurt ye. Aye, and mayhaps all the ones ye care about. I kenned that the kindest thing to do would be to leave ye."

"Ah, self-sacrifice. Arabel wasnae exactly brimming over with that characteristic either."

"Oh, Gamel," she murmured, running a hand through her hair and fleetingly wondering when he had taken it down. "I think I have made a verra great fool of myself."

He took her into his arms and held her close. "But for such noble reasons. I believe I can forgive ye."

"How kind." She laughed and realized it was the first time she had done so since leaving him. "What do we do now?"

"Live at Dorchabeinn. Or Duncoille, if ye would rather."

"Ye wish us to remain mon and wife?"

"Now, here I am thinking that your wits have returned and ye shatter my illusions with that stupid question. I have ye now, lass, and ye willnae slip away again. Ye put me through two long months of hell, loving. I cannae face that again," he whispered as he gently tumbled her down onto the bed, sprawled on top of her, and kissed her. "God's tears, how I have missed ye, woman." He nuzzled her neck. "If I had known how painful love can be, I would ne'er have let ye drag me into it."

Sine held him tightly, his words causing such a wealth of emotion to swell up within her that she was speechless for a moment. "Ye love me?"

Gamel lifted his head to look at her and cupped her face in his hands. "There ye go—being an idiot again. How could ye not ken it, lass? Ye are the other half of me, all that makes me complete. Without ye I am naught but an empty husk of a mon. Aye, and a surly one, according to Farthing."

Afraid that the tears stinging her eyes would be visible to him, she tugged him closer and pressed her face against his shoulder. "I love ye too, Gamel Logan." She laughed shakily when he hugged her tightly. "'Tis true that I was slow to guess at my own feelings, but the moment I found myself alone at Dorchabeinn I had no more doubts. I always felt that ye were pressing me so hard, I ne'er had time to ken my own mind. I had thought spending some time without ye would help to clear my thinking. Weel, five minutes, mayhaps less, was enough time alone."

"I apologize for pressing ye so, dearling. I was desperate to hold on to ye and each day that passed without some word of love from ye only made me more desperate." He lifted his head and brushed a kiss over her mouth as he tugged away the linen sheet between them. "I was so certain that ye were the mate I had searched for that I wanted ye to feel it too—immediately."

"I did, Gamel." She slid her foot up and down his leg. "I may not have recognized it immediately, but 'twas there in such strength it sometimes frightened me." She eased her hands down his sides until she grasped his hips and pressed his groin snugly against hers. "Weel, now that we have settled each other's fears and doubts, what can we do?" She laughed softly when he grinned with sweet lechery.

"I suspect our friends will think that it will take us a few days to untangle our troubles, not a mere hour. So, I think we shall be left alone for a while. I intend to love ye until ye havenae got a doubt left—not about yourself or me."

Sine opened her mouth to assure him that she had no doubts left already, then slowly smiled. "'Tis a fine plan. Ye ne'er can tell when a wee doubt might slip into a lass's mind."

Gamel laughed. "Do ye feel the nip of one now?"

"There is the wee shadow of one, I think."

"Then I shall smother it with loving." He grew serious as he traced the shape of her mouth with his finger. "Ah, lass, I do love ye."

"And I love ye, Gamel."

"Forever."

"Aye—e'en longer, if God allows." She grinned and winked at him. "And e'en when ye are a surly husk of a mon with the gout and not a strand of your bright hair left on your head." She laughed when he scowled, even though his fine eyes sparkled with humor.

"This is a most serious and tender moment, yet ye make jests," he said.

"'Tis because I am so verra happy. Ye love me and I can speak of my love for ye without fear now."

"And? I hear an 'and' in your tone."

"And I have finally won, truly won. I have finally beaten Arabel." She met his understanding smile with one of her own.

"We are both victorious, lass, and there has ne'er been a more glorious prize for winning," he said, and kissed her.

New York Times *bestselling author Hannah Howell delivers her most enthralling novel yet with the story of an innocent beauty and an unjustly accused laird who discover a rapturous passion as they embark upon a wondrous journey across the rugged Scottish Highlands . . .*

Swept overboard and stranded on the rocky shores of Scotland, Moira Robertson is left with only the tattered clothes on her back—and the mysterious stranger who came to her aid on the ship. Although their close surroundings unsettle her, she soon cannot resist his touch which awakens a burning ache deep within her. But can she trust her life—and her heart—to this darkly seductive man?

Tavig MacAlpin is a condemned man. Accused of murders he did not commit, his escape is thwarted by a flame-haired beauty. He must continue his search for justice, but fate has bound him to this Scottish lass—and to a slow, sensual desire that will not be denied . . .

Please turn the page for an exciting sneak peek of Hannah Howell's HIGHLAND FIRE, coming in June 2008!

Chapter 1

"Come, lass, surely my flattery deserves at least a wee smile."

Moira stole a glance at the man speaking to her. He had been watching her since she had boarded the ship three days before. Crooked Annie, her sharp-tongued watchdog, had grumbled about the man and sternly warned Moira to avoid him. That was not easy to do on such a small ship.

He made her feel uneasy. His black hair was heavily streaked with gray, and his middle was very thick, causing his doublet to fit oddly. His black beard was straggly, and he wore his hat so low she could not really see his eyes.

Everything about him indicated an aging, somewhat unclean man, yet she noticed a few things that sharply contradicted that image. The tight sleeves of his elegant black doublet revealed strong, slender arms. His equally black hose fit snugly over long, well-shaped legs. His voice was deep and rich, the voice of a vibrant young man. He moved with a lithe grace that belied his apparent age and overfed condition. Then he smiled at her, and Moira was convinced he was not what he appeared to be. The revelation made her even more nervous. Glancing around for Crooked Annie, she was a little annoyed to see the gnarled old woman cozening up to an equally gnarled old sailor.

"She will be over to scold ye and hurry ye away soon enough," the man said.

"I believe I will go and join her." She uttered a soft gasp of surprise when he caught her by the hand and held her in place.

"Now, lass, ye dinnae wish to ruin the old crone's chance for a wee bit of loving, do ye?"

Moira was shocked by his blunt words. The thought of Annie doing any loving at all was almost as unsettling as being touched by the strange man. He started to grin, then frowned. She realized he could read the fear she was unable to hide. Her guardian had taught her well to fear men. It was unfair, but the moment the man grabbed her by the hand, she tensed for a blow.

"Ah, my poor, sweet, timid bairn, ye have no need to fear old George Fraser."

It stung to hear this man call her a baby, and she quickly regained some of her lost courage, yanking free of his hold. "As I see it, Master Fraser, a 'bairn' ought to be verra concerned when a mon thrice her age cozens up to her."

"*Thrice* her age?" George gasped then fiddled with the front of his doublet for a moment before shrugging. "Age doesnae stop a mon from appreciating the sight of a bonnie wee lass."

"Then perhaps your wife ought to."

"She would have, save that she is no longer with us." He sighed, slumping against the railing. "My sainted

Margaret caught a fever and coughed her last but three years ago."

"Oh, I am so sorry, sir." She patted his arm, her sympathy waning a little when she felt how strong and slender that arm was. "I did not mean to stir any painful memories."

"Here now, ye keep your old eyes off this bairn," snapped Crooked Annie, snatching Moira's hand off his arm just as he was about to cover it with his own.

"We were just discussing his wife," Moira protested, trying to struggle free of Annie's iron grip, but the woman's weathered hand was wrapped around her wrist like a manacle.

"Weel, she ought to box the rogue's ears for being such a lecherous bastard."

"Annie," Moira said with a gasp, blushing a little over Annie's coarse language. "His wife died."

"Humph. He probably sent her to her deathbed with all his philandering about."

"I am sorry, sir." Moira's apology faltered a little, for she was sure the man was suppressing a grin.

"Come on, lass." Annie yanked her away from the man, continuing to pull her along as she headed for the ship's tiny cabins. "Ye dinnae want old Bearnard to catch ye talking to a mon, do ye?"

The mere thought of her guardian sent a chill coursing down Moira's spine, immediately ending her attempts to resist Crooked Annie's insistent tug upon her hand. "Nay, I shouldnae like that at all."

Tavig MacAlpin watched the scowling Crooked Annie drag Moira away and sighed. He leaned against the railing, checking to be sure no one was watching him as he carefully adjusted the thick padding around his middle. Ever since he had set eyes on Moira Robertson his disguise as the graying George Fraser had become a curse, even though he knew it was saving his life. The ransom offered for his capture was big enough to tempt even the most principled of men. There were none of those on the small ship.

It had taken him three long days to grab a chance to speak to Moira, but he wondered why he had been so intent on doing so. He had watched her avidly as she strolled the deck with her bent, gray-haired nurse. Moira's coppery hair was always braided tightly, but soft curls forever slipped free to frame her small oval face. Whenever he was fortunate enough to get a closer look at her, he marveled at how few freckles colored her soft white skin. He could clearly recall how startled he had been when he stole his first look into her eyes. Tavig had expected brown ones or even green ones, but never the rich, clear blue eyes she possessed. And such big eyes, too, he mused, smiling faintly. He admitted to himself with a soft laugh that he did whatever he could to get her to look his way so that he could see those huge eyes with their long, thick dark lashes.

A chuckle escaped him. It was possible he remembered her face so well because there was not much else of her to see. She was a tiny, too-thin lass. She had a woman's soft curves, but they were also tiny. She was certainly not his usual fare, yet Tavig had to concede that she had captured his full attention.

He cursed as he recalled the fear that had flashed in her beautiful eyes when he had touched her. That fear had returned in force when Crooked Annie had mentioned Moira's guardian's name. Even some of the color in Moira's high-boned cheeks had faded. Moira's guardian Sir Bearnard Robertson was a bully. Tavig had seen that from the start. Although Bearnard had not yet struck Moira, Tavig was certain that the possibility existed. He prayed Bearnard would not touch the girl, at least not until Tavig was within running distance of his cousin Mungan's keep and safety. He knew that if Bearnard Robertson raised a hand against Moira, he would rush to her rescue. A good tussle with a man the size of Robertson could easily ruin his disguise. Tavig knew that would mean being dragged back to his treacherous cousin Iver. And there awaited a hangman's noose for murders he had not committed.

A sudden chill wind swept over him. Tavig cursed again and shivered, pulling his heavy black cloak tighter around himself. He scowled up at the sky. Mixed in with the usual evening clouds that forecast the approaching night were some very ominous black clouds. Another chill wind blew over the deck with far more force than the first. Tavig cursed. A late summer storm was nearly upon them. He would soon have to return to the small cabin he shared with three other men and he dreaded it. Such close confinement with others only increased his chances of being discovered. The rain the storm would bring was far more threatening to his tenuous disguise, however, so he promised himself he would seek shelter at the first hint of rain.

A heavy weight across Moira's chest slowly pulled her out of her dreams. She opened her eyes and hastily swallowed a scream. By the dim light of a lantern dangerously left lit and swinging wildly on its ceiling hook, Moira saw that it was not Crooked Annie sprawled on top of her, but Connor, her guardian's man-at-arms. For one long moment she lay still, barely breathing, until she realized Connor was far too drunk to be a threat. Irritation quickly banished her panic.

Moira muttered a curse as she hastily untangled herself from the snoring man. Briefly she considered sleeping on the floor of the crowded cabin, but one look revealed that the wine-soaked people already sprawled there had left little room for her. Pressing against the wall in the hope of keeping away from Connor, who smelled strongly of drink and sweat, Moira cursed the ship. She wondered for the hundredth time why they had not allowed themselves enough time to travel by horse and cart. The ransom demand for her cousin Una had arrived weeks ago. Her guardian could easily have taken a longer, more comfortable route to rescue her. Even the poor roads would not have caused them to suffer such a rough journey. Nor, she thought crossly, would she have had to suffer sleeping in such close quarters with her kinsmen and as many retainers as they could stuff into the tiny cabin.

The ship tossed roughly from side to side again. Moira frowned, listening closely as she gripped the edge of the straw mattress to hold herself away from the loudly snoring Connor. Something was wrong. The tiny ship careened over some very rough seas. Her eyes widened as she heard the wind and rain battering the outer walls of their cabin. They had sailed into a storm and a very fierce one, too, if she was any judge of such things. The rain hit the outside of the ship so hard it sounded like drumbeats. The fierce wind howled as it slammed into the ship's wood, wailing as it tore around the ship.

Annie. Moira felt her heart skip with fear for her aging companion. The old woman was not in the cabin. She suspected Annie had crept off to see the sailor she had flirted with earlier and was now trapped out in the storm. She had to go see if Annie was safe.

Holding her breath, Moira carefully crept to the foot of the bed. She grabbed her cloak, which swung from a nail on the bedpost, and slipped it on. The moment she got out of bed she dropped to her hands and knees. The way the ship was beginning to rock it would be impossible to maneuver on foot through the people cluttering the cabin floor. Although everyone appeared to be deep in a drink-ladened sleep, Moira inched toward the door, tense with fear that someone would wake up and see her. Discovery would mean confronting her guardian Bearnard.

Once outside of the cabin she paused, bracing herself against the wall of the narrow passage. What should she do next? Annie could be safe and dry in some cabin. Moira shook her head. The man Annie had been cozening up to only hours ago was a mere deckhand, a poor lowly sailor of no rank. He would have no private place to take Annie except up on the deck. She simply had to look and assure herself that her old nursemaid was safe.

Her first attempt almost proved to be her last. Moira edged onto the first step leading up to the deck. The ship lurched, the violent motion knocking her off her feet. She slammed into the hard wall. For several moments she clung to the wall, gasping for breath. Her body still aching, she tried again.

When she first emerged onto the deck the wind and the pelting rain nearly drove her back. Moira gritted her teeth and, using anything at hand to hang on to and steady herself, started on her search for Annie. She could not believe Annie was still outside, yet the woman was not in her bed where she belonged, either. The storm had not completely dimmed the light of dawn, but it would still be difficult to find one thin old woman on the rain-washed deck. Moira heartily cursed Annie as she struggled over the pitching deck.

Tavig saw the small figure, bent against the wind and rain, edging her way along the deck, and cursed. He had spent the last hour trying to get back to his own cabin but, since the crew was a man short, the captain had forced him to help. Tavig knew that missing man was off with Annie. He also knew that his disguise was melting away with every drop of rain, but if he left he could easily be putting everyone's life in danger.

And now Moira was there. He had also spent the last hour praying that he was wrong, that she would not come searching for her randy old nursemaid. This was one time when he desperately wanted his accursed foresight to be proven wrong. The girl was stumbling her way toward a great deal of trouble, and he hated knowing that. He especially hated knowing that somehow he would be the cause. She fell to her knees, gripping the railing but a few feet away from him, and he sighed as he stumbled over to her. Now there was only one life he was concerned with.

"What are ye doing here, lass?" he shouted, fighting to be heard over the fury of the storm. "What few sailors are on deck are all lashed to their posts. The others will soon be wisely huddled below decks. 'Tis where ye should be."

"'Tis where ye should be as weel."

"I had to help batten down the hatches." He frowned, looking up at the sky as the wind suddenly eased and the rain grew almost gentle. "It seems the storm needs to catch its breath."

"Good. Now I can find Annie."

"Annie is off rutting with her sailor." He shook his head when she blushed so brightly even the dark could not hide it.

"That may be true, but she could be in trouble now. Once the storm started she should have returned to the cabin." A gust of wind slapped her, forcing her to cling more tightly to the ship's railing.

Tavig looked at Moira, trying to think of a way to convince her to go back inside, and froze. The cold familiar feeling that he was caught up in circumstances he could not control or change oozed over him. He tried to keep his frustration and fear out of his voice, but knew he was failing even as he spoke.

"Get away from that railing, lass."

Moira frowned. There was an odd, strained note to his voice. She tensed, wondering if Master Fraser was something more dangerous than the aging lecher she had thought him to be.

"I will as soon as the wind eases somemore," she replied, trying to decide if she should scurry out of his reach.

"It willnae ease anymore," he snapped. "'Tis a cursed gale. This lull willnae last much longer, and the storm will probably come back stronger than before. Now move away from that twice-cursed railing."

Even as she decided to do so in an effort to placate him, she suddenly noticed something that halted her. Master Fraser's hair was no longer the dull color it had been. The gray was seeping out of his shoulder-length hair to settle at the tips in sticky clumps. She stared at him, watching closely as another of the few remaining streaks of gray slithered down his hair. Master Fraser was definitely not what he appeared to be. Curiosity overwhelmed her, and she reached out to touch his hair.

"Your age is washing away in the rain," she murmured, her eyes widening at the curse he spat.

"I kenned that would happen. I have to get out of this rain." He grabbed her so forcefully she fell against him.

"So this is where ye disappeared to—out whoring!"

Moira cried out in surprise and fear as her guardian, Sir Bearnard Robertson, grabbed her by the arm, roughly yanking her to her feet. "Nay, sir, I swear I just came out to look for Crooked Annie."

"In this rogue's arms?" he bellowed, vigorously shaking her. "Dinnae add lying to your sins, ye little slut."

As Bearnard raised his meaty hand to strike her, Moira quickly turned to prepare for the blow. She fought to relax, to banish all tension and resistance from her body. Over the years she had learned that such limpness robbed his blows of some of their strength. She made no sound when he backhanded her across the face, sending her slamming onto the rough wooden deck. Landing on her hands and knees, Moira quickly bowed her head, all the while keeping a covert eye on her guardian. She wanted to be ready to avoid the worst of the pain if he decided to add a few kicks to his brutal reprimand.

An odd sound abruptly interrupted her concentration. She shook her head, but it was not a roar from inside her head, caused by the force of her guardian's blow. A soft, low roar of pure fury erupted from the man calling himself George Fraser. Moira spun around, sitting on the deck to stare at him. She gaped when he lunged at Bearnard, punching the bigger, heavier man and sending him sprawling onto the deck.

"Such a brave mon ye are, Robertson," he spat. "It takes such courage to strike down a wee, skinny lass."

"'Ware, sir," Bearnard yelled, scrambling to his feet. "A mon who scurries after a lass half his age has little right to speak so self-righteously of others. Ye are naught but an old lecher trying to seduce a foolish young lass."

"Even if that charge were true, 'twould still make me a better mon than some slinking cur who beats a wee lass."

A growl of pure rage escaped Bearnard as he charged Master Fraser. Both men fell to the deck with a crash. Moira cried out in dismay. Although she had no idea what she could do, she began moving toward the men. She had to stop the fight she had inadvertently caused.

"Dinnae be an idiot," said a deep voice as she was caught from behind.

"Nicol!" she cried, looking over her shoulder at her cousin. "Where did ye come from?"

"I followed Father when he came looking for you. I must have had a vision that ye were out to do something verra stupid. Sweet Lord, Moira, why would ye want to tryst with that old fool?"

"I wasnae trysting with him. I came looking for Crooked Annie, and Master Fraser was trying to get me to go back to my cabin."

"Ye should never have left it," Nicol muttered then cursed softly. "Your savior's belly has shifted."

Nicol's words made no sense, and Moira looked at the two combatants. They were on their feet again, warily circling as each sought a new opening to attack the other. She stared at Master Fraser and gasped. His soft belly was now an uneven lump protruding from his left side. His doublet was torn open, and she could see something sticking out. After staring hard for a moment she realized what it was. Master Fraser's soft belly was no more than rolled-up rags.

"His gray hair has washed away, too," she said.

"Aye," agreed Nicol. "The man isnae what he pretends to be. Curse me, but I think I ken who he is."

Before Moira could ask Nicol to explain, he left her side. Even as he drew near to his father, Bearnard charged Fraser, knocking the smaller man down. Fraser's hat spun off his head to be caught by the wind and flung out to sea. His now completely black hair whipped around his face as he fought to keep Bearnard from putting his meaty hands around his throat. There was no mistaking Fraser as anything other than a young, strong man.

Nicol took a step toward his father as Bearnard froze. The looks on their faces told Moira they now recognized the man and were stunned by his presence on the ship. The expression forming on Fraser's face told her that recognition was the very last thing he wanted. She tensed, suddenly afraid for the man who had so gallantly leapt to her defense.

"Tavig MacAlpin," Bearnard yelled, leaping to his feet and placing his hand on his sword.

"Aye, and what business is it of yours?" Tavig snapped as he cautiously stood up to face the Robertson men.

"'Tis the business of every righteous mon twixt here and London."

"Ye are no righteous mon, Robertson, but a brute who holds sway o'er others with his fists and an inexhaustible well of cruelty. Ye can command no respect or affection so ye instill fear in all those around ye." Tavig slowly put his hand on his sword, preparing for the attack he knew was to come. "'Tis a wonder ye have lived so long, that no one has yet cut your fat throat."

"And ye would be a good one to do it, wouldnae ye? Ye like naught better than to creep up from behind a mon and cut his throat. Or their bellies, as ye did to your two friends. Your cousin Iver MacAlpin is offering a handsome sum for ye, and I mean to collect it." Bearnard drew his sword, lunging at Tavig.

"Father," yelled Nicol. "Sir Iver doesnae want the mon dead."

"The bastard deserves killing," snarled Sir Bearnard.

"Come and try," taunted Tavig. "Aye, ye may yet get lucky, but I swear I will get ye ere I die, ye swine."

Bearnard roared with fury, and his attack became more vicious, but Tavig parried his every blow. He did not wish to die, but he did not want to be taken prisoner, either. If he was returned to his traitorous cousin Iver, he knew he faced a slow, painful death for murders he had not committed. If he could not win the battle against Robertson, then he would make sure the man cut him down.

"Nay, Cousin Bearnard," Moira cried as Tavig faltered and Bearnard raised his sword to strike the death blow.

As Tavig frantically scrambled out of the way of Bearnard's sword, he saw Moira rush toward her uncle. He cursed when Bearnard swatted the girl away, hurtling her back against the railing—the very railing Tavig had warned her to get away from. Bearnard's attention was briefly diverted, and Tavig took quick advantage of that. He charged the man, knocking Bearnard to the ground. With two swift, furious punches he knocked Bearnard out. He barely glanced at Bearnard's son Nicol as he leapt to his feet and ran to Moira.

"Moira, get away from that railing," he demanded, ignoring Nicol, who stood to his right, pointing a sword at him.

Still groggy from Bearnard's blow, Moira did not question him, but as she moved to obey his hoarse command, the renewed winds worked against her. They slammed into her, pushing her hard up against the railing. She tried to reach out for Tavig's outstretched hand, but the howling wind held her tightly in place, as securely as any chains. Moira felt as if the breath were being forced from her body. The rough wood of the railings dug into her as the gale pressed her harder and harder against them. She could see Tavig start to move toward her, determinedly fighting the winds, but she could not move or extend her hand toward him. Then she heard the ominous sound of wood cracking.

The railing Moira was pinned to gave way even as both Tavig and Nicol yelled a warning. She clung to it as the section swung out over the swirling waters. Moira looked back at the ship to see that the railing she clutched was attached by only one splintered piece of wood. Carefully inching her hands along, she tried to make her way back to the ship, to within reach of Nicol's and Tavig's outstretched hands. She was only a finger's length away from safety when the section of railing gave up its last tenuous connection to the ship. She screamed as she plummeted into the gale-tossed waters.

Tavig bellowed out Moira's name as he clung to the undamaged railing. He could barely see the white of her nightgown. She still held on to the piece of railing, but half her body was submerged beneath the cold, churning water. Tavig knew Moira could not hold on for long, nor would she be able to pull herself out of the water. Soon she would be dragged beneath the high waves. She needed help if she was to have any chance of survival.

"Get me that rope," he ordered Nicol, pointing to a length of rope knotted to a nearby bollard.

"What can ye do?" asked Nicol, resheathing his sword as he hurried to obey.

"Go after her." Tavig secured the ropes about his arm and moved to the gap in the railing.

Nicol grabbed his arm. "Are ye mad? Ye will be killed."

"Better to die trying to save some skinny red-haired lass than swinging from Iver's rope. And mayhaps I will-nae die."

As Nicol looked down into the churning waters, he cursed. "Aye, ye will."

"I prefer to think not. All I ken is that I *must* go in after Moira, or she willnae survive this. 'Tis cursed hard to trust that wee voice when it demands I hurl myself in after her, though. I just hope my intuition has the good grace to tell me how or why or even what will happen after I jump into these dark threatening waters."

"What are ye babbling about, MacAlpin?"

"Fate, laddie. Twice-cursed fate."

With a prayer that his intuitions continued to be correct, he took a deep breath and jumped. For a brief moment after he hit the cold water he panicked. He sank beneath the froth-tipped waves and feared that he would never get back to the surface. Tavig struggled upward, fighting the currents battering him. When he emerged, he took several hearty breaths, more out of relief than need. He looked for Moira and swam toward the white patch of nightgown he could still see.

Tavig cursed the waters as he struggled through the tumultuous waves toward Moira and the section of the ship's railing she clung to so desperately. He hoisted himself up onto her haphazard raft. Tying one piece of rope about his waist, he hastily lashed himself to the wood. As soon as he felt secure, he grabbed Moira by one of her slender wrists, hauling her out of the water, and she collapsed at his side. As the cold water washed over them, he secured one of her hands to the railing as well. He then took her free hand in his. When he pressed his body flat against the sodden wood he found himself nose to nose with Moira.

"Ye are mad," she yelled, coughing as a wave swirled over them, filling her mouth with salty water. "Now we shall both drown."

As another wave rushed over their bodies, Tavig could not help but think that she might be right.

Please turn the page for an exciting sneak peek of
Hannah Howell's newest historical romance,
HIGHLAND SINNER,
coming in December 2008!

Chapter 1

Scotland, early summer 1478

What was that smell?

Tormand Murray struggled to wake up at least enough to move away from the odor assaulting his nose. He groaned as he started to turn on his side and the ache in his head became a piercing agony. Flopping onto his side, he cautiously ran his hand over his head and found the source of that pain. There was a very tender swelling at the back of his head. The damp matted hair around the swelling told him that it had bled but he could feel no continued blood flow. That indicated that he had been unconscious for more than a few minutes, possibly for even more than a few hours.

As he lay there trying to will away the pain in his head, Tormand tried to open his eyes. A sharp pinch halted his attempt and he cursed. He had definitely been unconscious for quite a while and something beside a knock on the head had been done to him for his eyes were crusted shut. He had a fleeting, hazy memory of something being thrown into his eyes before all went black, but it was not enough to give him any firm idea of what had happened to him. Although he ruefully admitted to himself that it was as much vanity as a reluctance to inflict pain upon himself that caused him to fear he would tear out his eyelashes if he just forced his eyes open, Tormand proceeded very carefully. He gently brushed aside the crust on his eyes until he could open them, even if only enough to see if there was any water close at hand to wash his eyes with.

And, he hoped, enough water to wash himself if he proved to be the source of the stench. To his shame there had been a few times he had woken to find himself stinking, drunk, and a few stumbles into some foul muck upon the street being the cause. He had never been this foul before, he mused, as the smell began to turn his stomach.

Then his whole body tensed as he suddenly recognized the odor. It was death. Beneath the rank odor of an unclean garderobe was the scent of blood—a lot of blood. Far too much to have come from his own head wound.

The very next thing Tormand became aware of was that he was naked. For one brief moment panic seized him. Had he been thrown into some open grave with other bodies? He quickly shook aside that fear. It was not dirt or cold flesh he felt beneath him but the cool linen of a soft bed. Rousing from unconsciousness to that odor had obviously disordered his mind, he thought, disgusted with himself.

Easing his eyes open at last, he grunted in pain as the light stung his eyes and made his head throb even more. Everything was a little blurry, but he could make out enough to see that he was in a rather opulent bedchamber, one that looked vaguely familiar. His blood ran cold and he was suddenly even more reluctant to seek out the source of that smell. It certainly could not be from some battle if only because the part of the bedchamber he was looking at showed no signs of one.

If there is a dead body in this room, laddie, best ye learn about it quick. Ye might be needing to run, said a voice in his head that sounded remarkably like his squire, Walter, and Tormand had to agree with it. He forced down all the reluctance he felt and, since he could see no sign of the dead in the part of the room he studied, turned over to look in the other direction. The sight that greeted his watering eyes had him making a sound that all too closely resembled the one his niece Anna made whenever she saw a spider. Death shared his bed.

He scrambled away from the corpse so quickly he nearly fell out of the bed. Struggling for calm, he eased his way off the bed and then sought out some water to cleanse his eyes so that he could see more clearly. It took several awkward bathings of his eyes before the sting in them eased and the blurring faded. One of the first things he saw after he dried his face was his clothing folded neatly on a chair, as if he had come to this bedchamber as a guest, willingly. Tormand wasted no time in putting on his clothes and searching the room for any other signs of his presence, collecting up his weapons and his cloak.

Knowing he could not avoid looking at the body in the bed any longer, he stiffened his spine and walked back to the bed. Tormand felt the sting of bile in the back of his throat as he looked upon what had once been a beautiful woman. So mutilated was the body that it took him several moments to realize that he was looking at what was left of Lady Clara Sinclair. The ragged clumps of golden blond hair left upon her head and the wide, staring blue eyes told him that, as did the heart-shaped birthmark above the open wound where her left breast had been. The rest of the woman's face was so badly cut up it would have been difficult for her own mother to recognize her without those few clues.

The cold calm he had sought now filling his body and mind, Tormand was able to look more closely. Despite the mutilation there was an expression visible upon poor Clara's face, one that hinted she had been alive during at least some of the horrors inflicted upon her. A quick glance at her wrists and ankles revealed that she had once been bound and had fought those bindings, adding weight to Tormand's dark suspicion. Either poor Clara had had some information someone had tried to torture out of her or she had met up with someone who hated her with a cold, murderous fury.

And someone who hated him as well, he suddenly thought, and tensed. Tormand knew he would not have come to Clara's bedchamber for a night of sweaty bed play. Clara had once been his lover, but their affair had ended and he never returned to a woman once he had parted from her. He especially did not return to a woman who was now married and to a man as powerful and jealous as Sir Ranald Sinclair. That meant that someone had brought him here, someone who wanted him to see what had been done to a woman he had once bedded, and, mayhaps, take the blame for this butchery.

That thought shook him free of the shock and sorrow he felt. "Poor, foolish Clara," he murmured. "I pray ye didnae suffer this because of me. Ye may have been vain, a wee bit mean of spirit, witless, and lacking morals, but ye still didnae deserve this."

He crossed himself and said a prayer over her. A glance at the windows told him that dawn was fast approaching and he knew he had to leave quickly. "I wish I could tend to ye now, lass, but I believe I am meant to take the blame for your death and I cannae; I willnae.

But, I vow, I *will* find out who did this to ye and they will pay dearly for it."

After one last careful check to be certain no sign of his presence remained in the bedchamber, Tormand slipped away. He had to be grateful that whoever had committed this heinous crime had done so in this house for he knew all the secretive ways in and out of it. His affair with Clara might have been short but it had been lively and he had slipped in and out of this house many, many times. Tormand doubted even Sir Ranald, who had claimed the fine house when he had married Clara, knew all of the stealthy approaches to his bride's bedchamber.

Once outside, Tormand swiftly moved into the lingering shadows of early dawn. He leaned against the outside of the rough stone wall surrounding Clara's house and wondered where he should go. A small part of him wanted to just go home and forget about it all, but he knew he would never heed it. Even if he had no real affection for Clara, one reason their lively affair had so quickly died, he could not simply forget that the woman had been brutally murdered. If he was right in suspecting that someone had wanted him to be found next to the body and be accused of Clara's murder then he definitely could not simply forget the whole thing.

Despite that, Tormand decided the first place he would go was his house. He could still smell the stench of death on his clothing. It might be just his imagination, but he knew he needed a bath and clean clothes to help him forget that smell. As he began his stealthy way home Tormand thought it was a real shame that a bath could not also wash away the images of poor Clara's butchered body.

"Are ye certain ye ought to say anything to anybody?" Tormand nibbled on a thick piece of cheese as he studied his aging companion. Walter Burns had been his squire for twelve years and had no inclination to be anything more than a squire. His utter lack of ambition was why he had been handed over to Tormand by the man who had knighted him at the tender age of eighteen by the same. It had been a glorious battle and Walter had proven his worth. The man had simply refused to be knighted. Fed up with his squire's lack of interest in the glory, the honors, and the responsibility that went with knighthood Sir MacBain had sent the man to Tormand. Walter had continued to prove his worth, his courage, and his contentment in remaining a lowly squire. At the moment, however, the man was openly upset and his courage was a little weak-kneed.

"I need to find out who did this," Tormand said and then sipped at his ale, hungry and thirsty but partaking of both food and drink cautiously for his stomach was still unsteady.

"Why?" Walter sat down at Tormand's right and poured himself some ale. "Ye got away from it. 'Tis near the middle of the day and no one has come here crying for vengeance so I be thinking ye got away clean, aye? Why let anyone e'en ken ye were near the woman? Are ye trying to put a rope about your neck? And, if I recall rightly, ye didnae find much to like about the woman once your lust dimmed so why fret o'er justice for her?"

"'Tis sadly true that I didnae like her, but she didnae deserve to be butchered like that."

Walter grimaced and idly scratched the ragged scar on his pockmarked left cheek. "True, but I still say if ye let anyone ken ye were there ye are just asking for trouble."

"I would like to think that verra few people would e'er believe I could do that to a woman e'en if I was found lying in her blood, dagger in hand."

"Of course ye wouldnae do such as that, and most folk

ken it, but that doesnae always save a mon, does it? Ye dinnae ken everyone who has the power to cry ye a murderer and hang ye and they dinnae ken ye. Then there are the ones who are jealous of ye or your kinsmen and would like naught better than to strike out at one of ye. Aye, look at your brother James. Any fool who kenned the mon would have kenned he couldnae have killed his wife, but he still had to suffer years marked as an outlaw and a woman-killer, aye?"

"I kenned I kept ye about for a reason. Aye, 'twas to raise my spirits when they are low and to embolden me with hope and courage just when I need it the most."

"Wheesht, nay need to slap me with the sharp edge of your tongue. I but speak the truth and one ye would be wise to nay ignore."

Tormand nodded carefully, wary of moving his still-aching head too much. "I dinnae intend to ignore it. 'Tis why I have decided to speak only to Simon."

Walter cursed softly and took a deep drink of ale. "Aye, a king's mon nay less."

"Aye, and my friend. *And* a mon who worked hard to help James. He is a mon who has a true skill at solving such puzzles and hunting down the guilty. This isnae simply about justice for Clara. Someone wanted me to be blamed for her murder, Walter. I was put beside her body to be found and accused of the crime. And for such a crime I would be hanged so that means that someone wants me dead."

"Aye, true enough. Nay just dead, either, but your good name weel blackened."

"Exactly. So I have sent word to Simon asking him to come here, stressing an urgent need to speak with him."

Tormand was pleased that he sounded far more confident of his decision than he felt. It had taken him several hours to actually write and send the request for a meeting to Simon. The voice in his head that told him to just turn his back on the whole matter, the same opinion that Walter offered, had grown almost too loud to ignore. Only the certainty that this had far more to do with him than with Clara had given him the strength to silence that cowardly voice.

He had the feeling that part of his stomach's unsteadiness was due to a growing fear that he was about to suffer as James had. It had taken his foster brother three long years to prove his innocence and wash away the stain to his honor. Three long, lonely years of running and hiding. Tormand dreaded the thought that he might be pulled into the same ugly quagmire. If nothing else, he was deeply concerned about how it would affect his mother who had already suffered too much grief and worry over her children. First his sister Sorcha had been beaten and raped, then his sister Gillyanne had been kidnapped—twice—the second time leading to a forced marriage, and then there had been the trouble that had sent James running for the shelter of the hills. His mother did not need to suffer through yet another one of her children mired in danger.

"If ye could find something the killer touched we could solve this puzzle right quick," said Walter.

Pulling free of his dark thoughts about the possibility that his family was cursed, Tormand frowned at his squire. "What are ye talking about?"

"Weel, if ye had something the killer touched we could take it to the Ross witch."

Tormand had heard of the Ross witch. The woman lived in a tiny cottage several miles outside of town. Although the townspeople had driven the woman away ten years ago, many still journeyed to her cottage for help, mostly for the herbal concoctions the woman made. Some claimed the woman had visions that had aided them in solving some problem. Despite having grown up surrounded by people who had special gifts like that, he doubted the woman was the miracle worker some claimed her to be. Most of the time such *witches* were simply aging women skilled with herbs and an ability to convince people that they had some great mysterious power.

"And why do ye think she could help if I brought her something touched by the killer?" he asked.

"Because she gets a vision of the truth when she touches something." Walter absently crossed himself as if he feared he risked his soul by even speaking of the woman. "Old George, the steward for the Gillespie house, told me that Lady Gillespie had some of her jewelry stolen. He said her ladyship took the box the jewels had been taken from to the Ross witch and the moment the woman held the box she had a vision about what had happened."

When Walter said no more, Tormand asked, "What did the vision tell the woman?"

"That Lady Gillespie's eldest son had taken the jewels. Crept into her ladyship's bedchamber whilst she was at court and helped himself to all the best pieces."

"It doesnae take a witch to ken that. Lady Gillespie's eldest son is weel kenned to spend too much coin on fine clothes, women, and the toss of the dice. Near everyone— mon, woman, and bairn—in town kens that." Tormand took a drink of ale to help him resist the urge to grin at the look of annoyance on Walter's homely face. "Now I ken why the fool was banished to his grandfather's keep far from all the temptation here near the court."

"Weel, it wouldnae hurt to try. Seems a lad like ye ought to have more faith in such things."

"Oh, I have ample faith in such things, enough to wish that ye wouldnae call the woman a witch. That is a word that can give some woman blessed with a gift from God a lot of trouble, deadly trouble."

"Ah, aye, aye, true enough. A gift from God, is it?"

"Do ye really think the devil would give a woman the gift to heal or to see the truth or any other gift or skill that can be used to help people?"

"Nay, of course he wouldnae. So why do ye doubt the Ross woman?"

"Because there are too many women who are, at best, a wee bit skilled with herbs yet claim such things as visions or the healing touch in order to empty some fool's purse. They are frauds and ofttimes what they do makes life far more difficult for those women who have a true gift."

Walter frowned for a moment, obviously thinking that over, and then grunted his agreement. "So ye willnae be trying to get any help from Mistress Ross?"

"Nay, I am nay so desperate for such as that."

"Oh, I am nay sure I would refuse any help just now," came a cool, hard voice from the doorway of Tormand's hall.

Tormand looked toward the door and started to smile at Simon. The expression died a swift death. Sir Simon Innes looked every inch the king's man at the moment. His face was pale and cold fury tightened its predatory lines. Tormand got the sinking feeling that Simon already knew why he had sent for him. Worse, he feared his friend had some suspicions about his guilt. That stung, but Tormand decided to smother his sense of insult until he and Simon had at least talked. The man was his friend and a strong believer in justice. He would listen before he acted.

Nevertheless, Tormand tensed with a growing alarm when Simon strode up to him. Every line of the man's tall, lean body was tense with fury. Out of the corner of his eye, Tormand saw Walter tense and place his hand on his sword, revealing that Tormand was not the only one who sensed danger. It was as he looked back at

Simon that Tormand realized the man clutched something in his hand.

A heartbeat later, Simon tossed what he held onto the table in front of Tormand. Tormand stared down at a heavy gold ring embellished with blood-red garnets. Unable to believe what he was seeing, he looked at his hands, his unadorned hands, and then looked back at the ring. His first thought was to wonder how he could have left that room of death and not realized that he was no longer wearing his ring. His second thought was that the point of Simon's sword was dangerously sharp as it rested against his jugular.

"Nay! Dinnae kill him! He is innocent!"

Morainn Ross blinked in surprise as she looked around her. She was at home sitting up in her own bed, not in a great hall watching a man press a sword point against the throat of another man. Ignoring the grumbling of her cats that had been disturbed from their comfortable slumber by her outburst, she flopped back down and stared up at the ceiling. It had only been a dream.

"Nay, no dream," she said after a moment of thought. "A vision."

Thinking about that a little longer she then nodded her head. It had definitely been a vision. The man who had sat there with a sword at his throat was no stranger to her. She had been seeing him in dreams and visions for months now. He had smelled of death, was surrounded by it, yet there had never been any blood upon his hands.

"Morainn? Are ye weel?"

Morainn looked toward the door to her small bedchamber and smiled at the young boy standing there. Walin was only six but he was rapidly becoming very helpful. He also worried about her a lot, but she supposed that was to be expected. Since she had found him upon her threshold when he was the tender age of two she was really the only parent he had ever known, had given him the only home he had ever known. She just wished it were a better one. He was also old enough now to understand that she was often called a witch as well as the danger that appellation brought with it. Unfortunately, with his black hair and blue eyes, he looked enough like her to have many believe he was her bastard child and that caused its own problems for both of them.

"I am fine, Walin," she said and began to ease her way out of bed around all the sleeping cats. "It must be verra late in the day."

"'Tis the middle of the day, but ye needed to sleep. Ye were verra late returning from helping at that birthing."

"Weel, set something out on the table for us to eat then, I will join ye in a few minutes."

Dressed and just finishing the braiding of her hair, Morainn joined Walin at the small table set out in the main room of the cottage. Seeing the bread, cheese, and apples upon the table, she smiled at Walin, acknowledging a job well done. She poured them each a tankard of cider and then sat down on the little bench facing his across the scarred wooden table.

"Did ye have a bad dream?" Walin asked as he handed Morainn an apple to cut up for him.

"At first I thought it was a dream but now I am certain it was a vision, another one about that mon with the mismatched eyes." She carefully set the apple on a wooden plate and sliced it for Walin.

"Ye have a lot about him, dinnae ye?"

"It seems so. 'Tis verra odd. I dinnae ken who he is

and have ne'er seen such a mon. And, if this vision is true, I dinnae think I e'er will."

"Why?" Walin accepted the plate of sliced apple and immediately began to eat it.

"Because this time I saw a verra angry gray-eyed mon holding a sword to his throat."

"But didnae ye say that your visions are of things to come? Mayhaps he isnae dead yet. Mayhaps ye are supposed to find him and warn him."

Morainn considered that possibility for a moment and then shook her head. "Nay, I think not. Neither heart nor mind urges me to do that. If that were what I was meant to do, I would feel the urge to go out right now and hunt him down. And, I would have been given some clue as to where he is."

"Oh. So we will soon see the mon whose eyes dinnae match?"

"Aye, I do believe we will."

"Weel that will be interesting."

She smiled and turned her attention to the need to fill her very empty stomach. If the man with the mismatched eyes showed up at her door, it would indeed be interesting. It could also be dangerous. She could not allow herself to forget that death stalked him. Her visions told her he was innocent of those deaths but there was some connection between him and them. It was as if each thing he touched died in bleeding agony. She certainly did not wish to become a part of that swirling mass of blood she always saw around his feet. Unfortunately she did not believe that fate would give her any chance to avoid meeting the man. All she could do was pray that when he rapped upon her door he did not still have death seated upon his shoulder.

ABOUT THE AUTHOR

Hannah Howell is an award-winning author who lives with her family in Massachusetts. She is the author of twenty-eight Zebra historical romances and is currently working on a new Highland historical romance, HIGH-LAND SINNER, coming in December 2008! Hannah loves hearing from readers and you may visit her website: www.hannahhowell.com.